THE LAST
MAHARAJA

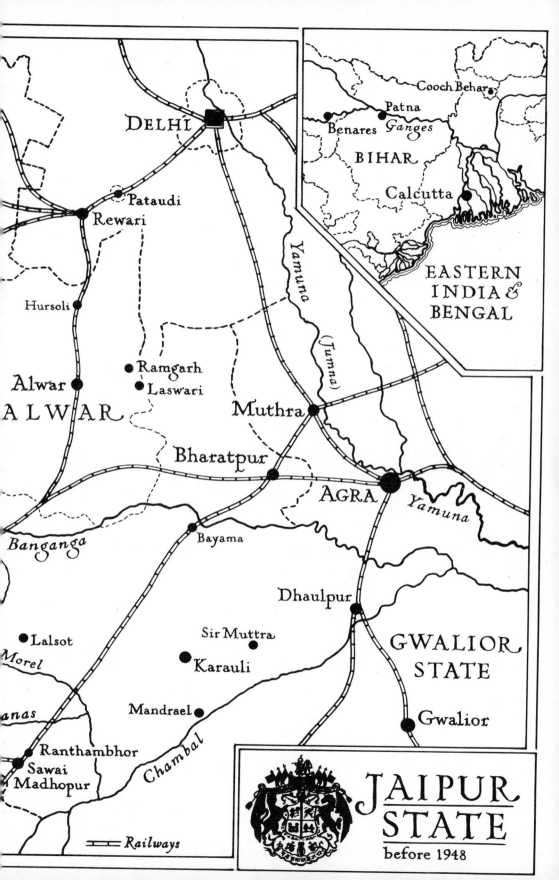

DELHI

Pataudi
Rewari

Hursoli

Ramgarh
Laswari

Alwar
ALWAR

Banganga

Muthra

Bharatpur

Bayama

AGRA

Yamuna

Yamuna (Jumna)

Lalsot
Morel

Sir Muttra

Karauli

Dhaulpur

GWALIOR
STATE

anas

Mandrael

Ranthambhor
Sawai
Madhopur

Chambal

Gwalior

— Railways

EASTERN
INDIA &
BENGAL

Cooch Behar
Patna
Benares *Ganges*
BIHAR
Calcutta

JAIPUR
STATE
before 1948

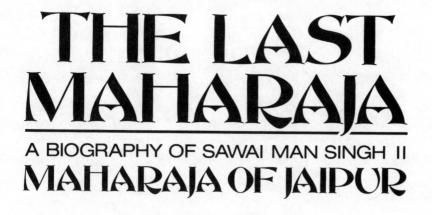

THE LAST MAHARAJA

A BIOGRAPHY OF SAWAI MAN SINGH II
MAHARAJA OF JAIPUR

QUENTIN CREWE

foreword by HRH The Duke of Edinburgh

MICHAEL JOSEPH
London

First published in Great Britain by Michael Joseph Ltd
44 Bedford Square, London WC1
1985

British Library Cataloguing in Publication Data

Crewe, Quentin

The last maharaja: a biography of Sawai Man Singh II,
Maharaja of Jaipur.
1. Sawai Man Singh, *Maharajah of Jaipur*
2. India——Kings and rulers——Biography
I. Title
954'.404'0924   DS481.S3/

ISBN 0 7181 2632 7

Typeset by Goodfellow & Egan (Phototypesetting) Ltd, Cambridge
Printed and bound in Great Britain by
Billings and Son Ltd, Worcester

CONTENTS

ACKNOWLEDGEMENTS

I owe many people profound thanks for giving me their time and help in the writing of this book. First of all, I want to thank H.H. The Rajmata Gayatri Devi of Jaipur for all the hours she spared to talk about her husband, all the trouble she took to find papers and photographs and all the entertaining occasions she asked me to in Jaipur. I am grateful to the Maharaja of Jaipur for allowing me to stay at his beautiful shooting lodge at Ramgarh, while I was researching, and his brothers the Maharaj Jai Singh and Maharaj Prithviraj Singh for their help. I am specially grateful to Mohan Singh, Thakur of Kanota, for his permission to use so many extracts from the diaries of his uncle, General Amer Singh.

For help and advice of all kinds, I would like to thank the Begum of Bhopal, the Maharaja of Bikaner, the Maharaja of Dranghadhra, the Maharaja of Dungapur, the Maharao of Kota, the Nawab of Pataudi, Raja and Rani Atal, the Rani of Barwara, Raja and Rani Jaswant Singh, the Thakur of Naila, Kanwar Ragunath Singh Kanota, Brigadier Harnath Singh, Colonel Govind Singh, Colonel Harnath Singh, Major Parbat Singh, Major Sumer Singh Naila, Professors Lloyd and Suzanne Rudolph, Dr Consul, Dr Asok Das, Dr Raghubir Singh, Mr Mathur, Mrs Gita Mehta, Mr Mohan Muckerji, Mr Yaduvendra Sahai.

The Duke of Wellington, Lord Roderick Pratt, Sir Robert Throckmorton, Colonel Alec Harper, Mrs Caroline Chapman.

Finally, I must thank Miss Nicola Fielden for her research, for her organisation, for her help in the preparation of the manuscript and for her advice and judgement in the selection of material.

ILLUSTRATIONS

FOREWORD

by HRH The Duke of Edinburgh

I remember watching the Maharaja of Jaipur play polo with his famous Jaipur team which he brought to this country shortly before the war, but I only got to know him as a friend several years after the war, when I had taken up polo myself and he was a regular visitor for the summer season.

I have met many people who could be described as charming, but few, if any, had quite Jai's special brand of kindly charm and gentleness of character. Together with his exceptionally beautiful and talented wife, Ayesha, they made the most delightful hosts. Always thoughtful and considerate, they had a genius for generating a light-hearted gaiety wherever they chose to entertain their friends.

Kipling may have written, 'East is East, and West is West, and never the twain shall meet', but anyone who ever had the pleasure of staying with Jai and Ayesha in India knows that they had a magic ability of making 'the twain meet' in the most delightful way. To experience the festival of Holi in Jaipur in the company of Jai and Ayesha was to gain a glimpse of the universality of mankind.

I am delighted that Quentin Crewe has written this biography. Jai's life spanned the most turbulent and radical changes that the sub-continent has experienced in many centuries and this book vividly describes their impact on the life of one of the last of India's ruling Princes.

xi

PREFACE

My purpose in writing this book was two-fold. In the first place, I wanted to redress, if possible, the unbalanced impression created by the quantities of books on the Indian Princes portraying them as glamorous, debauched autocrats, with few thoughts other than where the next diamond necklace was to come from or what new vice they might indulge in. Furthermore, so much attention has been given recently to the British Raj that it seemed a good idea to look at the other third of India during the same period.

Secondly, I wanted to help the Rajmata of Jaipur, who had made more than one attempt at having a biography of her late husband written, without success.

The Maharaja of Jaipur seemed to me to suit my first purpose more perfectly than other possible candidates, such as the canal-building Maharaja of Bikaner or the two most progressive Maharajas – Baroda and Mysore. Jaipur's life and reign spanned almost exactly the most interesting period, from the peak of wealth and the appearance of the first cracks in the feudalism of the Maharajas and their states, through the gradual diminution of their powers, to the day when Mrs Gandhi stripped them of every privilege and even of their names.

As a person, the Maharaja of Jaipur was charming, handsome and wholly lacking in any of the disagreeable characteristics that have been attributed to the Princes of India. He was not an intellectual, nor a great political reformer; by inclination, he was primarily a sportsman and a soldier. The circumstances

xiii

of his reign, however, brought out in him unexpected qualities and it intrigued me to trace the development of a rather innocent and simple character into a man of wisdom and stature.

I soon became aware of one of the reasons why the Rajmata had had such difficulty in enthusing writers with the project I had undertaken. It is not the business of writers to worry readers with the problems of their work, but gathering material in India has its very particular hazards.

In the first place, the keeping of papers is not thought so important as it is in Europe and, even if they are kept, there are other perils. I came to hear of some very special papers, stored in the present Maharaja's private treasury, to which only he has the key. I asked if I might see them. Of course, I was told. Some three weeks later, all the formalities having been observed, a tin box was brought to the office of a Palace official. Three witnesses watched while it was opened. There lay the papers. As each file was brought out, a shower of dust fell. Three quarters of them had been eaten by ants. They were useless.

Where were the Maharaja's files on his Governorship of Rajasthan? Last seen in the carpet store of a house which is now a hotel. Where were the administration's annual reports? Missing.

The people who had known the Maharaja were all delightful and anxious to help. One even wrote: 'Please do let me know if I can do any service for this Noble cause. (A book on my beloved master.)' On the other hand, they seemed never to have considered the Maharaja in a dispassionate light – neither the good which he did, nor any ill which he might have done. They surrounded him with a kind of mythical aura, telling what were obviously legendary anecdotes about him. They remembered the royalty, not the man.

On one occasion, I drove nearly two hundred bumpy miles to see a neighbouring Maharaja, who had agreed to help. He received me with exquisite courtesy and then said nothing. 'I believe Your Highness consulted closely with late His Highness Jaipur over the question of the privy purses?' 'Not particularly.' He had, of course, but for some reason was unwilling to talk about it – or, indeed, anything else. But he was too polite to refuse to see me.

The most difficult part was to try to distinguish between fact and fiction. The Rajputs, being not much given to reading, have a style of conversational reporting which resembles bardic narration. What might have happened and what the speaker might wish had happened are given as much weight as what did happen – people drop dead on hearing bad news, they acquire untold riches as a reward for good deeds, their dreams come true, their horoscopes are neatly fulfilled.

The Rajmata feels that I have relied too much on the diaries of General Amer Singh, but there is no other source of information about everyday life in the first twenty years of the Maharaja's reign.

Amer Singh was a remarkable man. His family came originally from Jodhpur, but they had entered the service of the Maharaja Ram Singh of Jaipur in 1849. Amer Singh was born in 1878 and was brought up partly in Jaipur and partly in Jodhpur. His diaries, which he started to write when he was twenty, cover his extraordinary career in great detail. He served first with the Jodhpur Lancers and then with the British Indian Army. He was in China for the Boxer Rebellion and in England and France during the First World War.

He became the Colonel of the Jaipur Lancers and eventually commander of all the Jaipur State Forces. He was, by his own account, one of the few people prepared to argue with the Maharaja. He was, by nature, a slightly cantankerous person, so that some of his views are somewhat prejudiced. Against that, he was remarkably well educated and widely read. (His lists of the books he had read each year make one blush for one's ignorance.) In consequence, he was more interested in accuracy than many of his fellow Rajputs. He died in 1942.

I am especially grateful to his nephew, Mohan Singh, the owner of the diaries, who has given me permission to quote from them. It was Professors Lloyd and Suzanne Hoeber Rudolph who introduced me to Mohan Singh. This was an act of great generosity as they are themselves preparing an abridged version of the diaries, although I must say that my raiding of the years I was interested in won't affect their work, considering that their heavily-edited version of the first twenty years covers 1,600 pages.

I should add here that for the section on the Sikar revolt in 1938 I am heavily indebted to Barnett R. Rubin of the Department of Political Science at Yale University. His account of that important turning point in the history of Jaipur state, and also in the career of its ruler, is lucid and invaluable.

Finally, a note about the Maharaja's spelling. This was so erratic that it is probable he was mildly dyslexic. I have therefore corrected it throughout.

CHAPTER 1

The village of Isarda lies about forty miles south-east of Jaipur city. Even today it is difficult enough to get there. The rough track, usable only by ox-waggons or vehicles with four-wheel drive, wanders across a partly-cultivated plain which is ready to revert to sandy, scrubby desert at the first moment of neglect.

The road passes through two villages, one ragged and untidy, the next inexplicably clean. To the north there are sudden, red and white hills, the first topped by the large fort of Shivad, the next by the smaller fort of Barwara.

Isarda does not stand out. From a distance it is merely a slightly raised patch of green in the dusty landscape. It is not until one is very close that one sees that it is a compact walled village, with a population of about 10,000 people.

There are few signs of prosperity. The streets climb gently within the walls. There is a fine tank of water, a few very modest little shops and a crowd of wide-eyed children, who have never before seen a European. At the top is a huge gateway leading into the fort. Through that is a courtyard, then another gate, then an open space in front of the main house. All is decay.

The elephant houses are falling down. Junk lies in the courtyards, which are gradually surrendering to grass and weeds. Parrots screech in the trees which encroach upon the buildings. Peacocks parade on the crumbling walls. Balconies

1

are leaning at steep angles, stairways are unsafe. The four servants who guard the place touch a visitor's feet with respect and talk of the grandeur they once knew.

Yet the place can never have been particularly elegant or beautiful. The rooms, now mostly locked-up owing to a dispute between the two widows of the last Thakur of Isarda, are ill-proportioned. The few vestiges of furniture are sadly ugly. But what it could well have been was a happy family home; and it was here that Mor Mukut Singh, the second son of Sawai Singh, the Thakur of Isarda, was born on 21 August 1911.

In Rajput princely terms, the boy was well-connected. His father, as chief of Isarda, came from one of the six branches of the Kachhawa ruling family of Jaipur, known as Rajawats, from which a Maharaja can be adopted, if the Maharaja has no legitimate male heir. The Maharaja at the time of his birth, Sawai Madho Singh, had been adopted from Isarda and so was the boy's great uncle. His father's sister was married to the ruling Maharaja of Kota, a bordering state.

At the same time, he was a second son with no particular prospects, primogeniture being of great importance in the Rajput culture. So for the first eleven years Mor Mukut was brought up quite simply. With his brother and three sisters, he would sit on a carpet for four hours a day doing lessons.

The boys played with the sons of the large staff or with, as his sister puts it, 'the village boys of better family'. There was not much to do. They would ride out in bullock carts and swim in the river, or they would play football – in fact live the life of country boys all over the world. They differed, however, in having instilled in them, very early, the almost Spartan principles of bravery which form an important part of the Rajput ethic.

Mor Mukut was one day teasing an elephant in the elephant houses and it cornered him. He did not shout for help, partly from fear of getting into trouble, but also because it would have revealed that he was afraid. Fortunately, one of the mahouts happened to pass by in time to save him.

One of the great excitements which the children looked forward to was the payment of rent to their father. The farmers brought money in bullock carts, guarded by men with swords and guns. The whole system at that time, and for a long time to come, was a feudal one. Land was granted by the Maharaja to nobles in return for loyalty, service and tribute. The service required took the form of armed men, horses, elephants and camels.

In Moghul times, these grants, known as jagirs, were technically held for the lifetime of the grantees, or Jagirdars. In Rajputana, it became usual for nobles of the ruler's clan to pass their jagir on to their sons. Outsiders from other states or clans were less certain of the heritability of their tenure.

The Thakur of Isarda's jagir, or thikana, consisted of about sixty-five to seventy villages. He was obliged to provide men, horses and elephants for the Maharaja's use. It was a serious obligation and if, for instance, one of the elephants died, he would have to pay a fine of five rupees a day until it was replaced. In addition, the Thakur had to pay an annual tribute of 14,000 rupees. On the other hand, he could keep the revenue of the land.

Mor Mukut's father was a man of little education, but he was shrewd. He had a great reputation for meanness; to such an extent that, even today, it is considered unlucky to say 'Isarda' before lunch, as superstition has it that, if you do, you will not eat that day. His grandchildren still prefer to refer to Isarda as 'the home town', rather than name it.

His shrewdness built up the income of his thikana from 300,000 to 600,000 rupees. Nonetheless, life at Isarda was not elaborate, being comparable perhaps to that of a prosperous eighteenth-century squire – much concerned with sport and with agriculture. The Thakur was said to have shot a total of 475 tigers in his lifetime. He was also fond of wrestling. Furthermore, he enjoyed, if not rights, then customs which had not been so easily available to English squires since the middle ages. There are still several old people in Isarda, one of the four guards for example, who are known to be the sons or daughters of the Thakur.

Certainly his wife's days, apart from the fact that she was in purdah, followed much the same pattern as those of a rich squire's wife. Mor Mukut's mother had, by way of an allowance, a small separate jagir of four or five villages. The income was not great and it was customary for her to pay for

3

the wedding clothes and the funerals of her villagers.

She would also make soup for them in times of famine, of necessity a simple soup because at that time the agriculture was limited. There were no vegetables and no fruit in the area. She was a simple, pious lady, rather fat and cosy, and a very loving mother.

In the summer, all the cousins and uncles and aunts who make up the extended Rajput family would come to stay at Isarda and, both in the men's quarters and in the zenana, or women's quarters, it was often difficult to find a corner to sleep.

Side by side with this bucolic, squirearchical life, ran the formal life of the court in Jaipur. The senior Thakurs, known as Tazimi Sardars, were obliged to attend the Maharaja on important festival days, on his birthday, or at any other time that they were summoned.

The Sardars and most of the Thakurs had houses in Jaipur City. For the great ceremonies in the City Palace they would set out dressed in great finery, the colour of their clothes depending on which festival it was. The Thakur of Isarda, although preferring to collect gold and silver on the grounds that their value was more stable, would on occasions appear wearing jewels worth 25,000 rupees, in addition to the gold anklet which was the privilege of the Tazimi Sardars.

At each of the ceremonies it was obligatory for the nobles to reaffirm their loyalty to the Maharaja by presenting their nazars. One by one they would come up to the throne, kneel down and hold out in their cupped hands a gold coin resting on a folded cloth. The Maharaja would take the coin.

Until Mor Mukut was seven or eight, he knew nothing of this other side of Rajput life. His father, perhaps regretting his own lack of education, decided to send his children to Kota, where his brother-in-law, the Maharao, had greater opportunities for the upbringing of children than could exist in the remote village of Isarda. So Mor Mukut and his elder brother Bahadur went to live with their cousins. Kota, being the capital of a state, was far grander than anything the boys had known; but even so, enjoyment was not much restricted and the children continued to be wild and mischievous enough, crashing the first motor car ever to be seen in the state.

This happy carefree childhood was soon to come to an abrupt end.

In 1920, Sawai Madho Singh II, the Maharaja of Jaipur, was fifty-eight years old. He had reigned for forty years. His predecessor, Ram Singh II, had, in the last hours of his life, adopted him from the Isarda branch of the Kachhawa ruling family.

In India, and particularly in Rajput custom, adoption forms a very important part of the system of inheritance. If there is a break in the direct male line, it is normal for a Maharaja or a Jagirdar to adopt a son. The boy or young man adopted must be a member of the same clan or branch of a clan as the adopter himself. So commonplace is this that it has been estimated that more than half of the accessions of Jagirdars, and even Maharajas, are by adoption. The state of Udaipur, for example, had five successive adopted Maharanas from 1895 onwards. As a system it ensured a certain continuity; but against that, in the times we are speaking of, the arbitrary nature of the selection of an heir led to bitter jealousies, feuds and frequent murders.

The failure of the male line in the case of Madho Singh had nothing to do with any physical inadequacy or shyness on his part. He was a man of considerable sexual appetite. He had two official wives and a prodigious number of concubines. The latter bore him some fifty or sixty children. (There were eighteen of his sons living in 1935 and one is still alive.) Only his senior wife had a daughter. The reason for this was abstinence, for fear, it is said, of a prophecy or curse. Because of a dispute between his mother and the Nawab of Tonk, a curse had been put on him which foretold that, if he had a son, Madho Singh would die within six months. There may have been more down-to-earth political reasons for his wishing not to have children by either of his wives, but, whatever the case may have been, from a certain time he treated his wives, according to his great niece, 'like his mother and sisters'.

Therefore, when Madho Singh's health began to fail, both the people of Jaipur and the British became anxious about the question of a successor.

5

In 1916, the Maharaja had given the Viceroy, Lord Hardinge, a sealed envelope containing the name of his chosen successor, the wishes of the ruler being always of great weight in the selection of an heir. His choice is unknown, but the British believed that he had named his favourite morganatic son, Raja Gopal Singh. It seems unlikely that so pious and old-fashioned a Maharaja as Madho Singh would have flouted Rajput custom by insisting on such an irregular course. Nonetheless, it was after Gopal Singh died that the Maharaja told Colonel Benn, the Agent to the Governor-General, that he intended to withdraw the sealed envelope because the person named in it had died, and to substitute a new name. Opinions as to whom he had named before were mere conjecture, prompted possibly by the fact that Gopal Singh's death depressed the Maharaja so profoundly as to be a major cause of his fainting fits and giddiness.

The choice of a new heir led to a dangerous dispute, which really came down to a question of Rajput custom which has never been satisfactorily resolved: is the express wish of the dying ruler more or less significant than genealogical proximity to the throne?

Shortly after Gopal Singh's death, early in 1920, the Maharaja had sent for photographs of the two sons of the Thakur of Isarda – Bahadur and Mor Mukut. It seems that Roop Rai, the Maharaja's favourite concubine, had done the same thing, unknown to the Maharaja. Gossip being the lifeblood of small, autocratic courts, it became common knowledge that the Maharaja was choosing an heir.

By May 1920, Colonel Benn had heard that the Maharaja intended to choose one of the boys from Isarda. His informant, a senior Thakur, went on to warn of trouble, partly because the Thakur of Isarda was himself adopted from some minor thikana, belonging to a distant branch of the family, to the exclusion of a nearer branch with a prior claim.

The problems were many and varied. The senior branch of the ruling family was always recognised to be that of the Thakurs of Jhalai. The present incumbent of that position was Goverdhan Singh, who was thirty-six at the time. Madho Singh's family had been on bad terms with his family for forty years and the Maharaja was afraid that Goverdhan

6

Singh would not 'look after his mothers, widows and family after his death'. Goverdhan Singh held a jagir in Bikaner, from which state he had been adopted. His late wife was a niece of the Maharaja of Bikaner; Madho Singh felt that this close connection with another state might be prejudicial to the interests of Jaipur state. Madho Singh also believed it was wrong to adopt the sole representative of the Jhalai family, leaving no heir to the jagir.

The legal arguments were intricate and obscure. The ruling family of Jhalai had been passed over at the time of Madho Singh's own adoption from Isarda, but the Thakur at that time was paralysed and a drunkard. There was talk, though no concrete evidence, of a pledge given at the time of Madho Singh's adoption that the by-passing of Jhalai would not be repeated.

Much weight was given to a phrase in *Annals and Antiquities of Rajasthan*, written by Colonel James Tod in 1839, who was still regarded as the leading authority on Rajput customs. He had written:

> The Rajawats constitute a numerous frerage, of which the Jhalai house takes the lead; and in which, provided there are no mental or physical disabilities, the right of furnishing heirs to the gaddi (throne) of Jaipur is a long-established, incontrovertible and inalienable privilege.

The sentence is ambiguous. Does the second 'which' refer to the frerage or to the Jhalai house? All this and much more was debated endlessly by the nobles of Jaipur and by the British Government.

On 3 July, Colonel Benn reported that:

> Up to quite recently only two names were popularly mentioned as possible claimants to the succession . . . the Thakur of Jhalai and . . . the Thakur of Isarda, or one of the latter's two minor sons. To these, however, must be added . . . the Thakur of Balir whom, report says, His Highness has practically decided to nominate as his heir. Each of the above has his respective supporters and

7

intrigue and bribery are said to be playing a very
prominent part in the Palace at the present moment.

In the event, Colonel Benn's earlier prediction was the more
accurate. Balir, a heavy drinker, was never a serious contender.
In the course of the summer, Madho Singh sent for the two
sons of the Thakur of Isarda, Bahadur and Mor Mukut.

There are several versions of what took place when the
two boys met the Maharaja. Their sister says that Madho
Singh asked them in turn: 'Who is your father?' Bahadur
replied that the Thakur was his father. Mor Mukut answered,
'You are.' And when the Maharaja asked Mor Mukut where
he wanted to sit he said, 'In your lap.'

Another more attractive account, written by his widow,
says that the nine-year-old boy got bored while the ailing
Maharaja dithered and fumbled over the ceremony of accepting the nazar which Bahadur presented, so he just pocketed
the coin which he had ready and wandered away.

Whether it was the obsequiousness or the cheekiness of
the boy which appealed to the Maharaja, we cannot know.
More probably, he was influenced by quite other factors –
first, his belief that an eldest son of a Jagirdar should not be
adopted; second, the reports he must have had on the boys'
characters. While both were endowed with great charm,
Bahadur revealed early the considerable weakness of character
which was later to turn him into an ineffectual, if agreeable,
drunkard.

Madho Singh had made up his mind. In August, he sent a
new sealed envelope to the Viceroy, Lord Chelmsford, explaining that he had made his choice. Chelmsford, in reply,
said that the action he had taken 'should go a long way
towards preventing a possible dispute'.

Nothing in Jaipur could be kept a secret. Those opposed
to Isarda were soon mounting an agitation and intriguing
against the Maharaja. In October, he wrote to the Viceroy for
reassurance. He explained that he had made the document
in the envelope more formal than the previous one, more
'regular' also, he suggested, than the hasty arrangements
made for his own adoption by Maharaja Ram Singh.

His reluctance actually to perform the adoption ceremony,

which was probably due to his fear of the prophecy, he explained thus:

> But I may be pardoned if I point out that if any further measures are taken the nomination will leak out and, situated as we are, such publicity is sure to give rise to intrigues which may endanger my life.

He went on to say that, when the law of the land respects the last will and testament of ordinary people, he hoped that:

> My nomination, which, I may assure you, is fully in conformity with the traditions and established usage of my House, will not be differently treated but will be regarded as final.

Chelmsford replied that, in view of his assurances that the nomination was, 'fully in conformity with the traditions . . . you may safely rely on effect being given to your wishes.'

It was not to be as easy as that. The Thakur of Jhalai made a formal representation to the British Government. He claimed that the Maharaja had no right to adopt a son or to nominate a successor from any other branch of the family but Jhalai.

This representation was backed by a long and forceful letter from the Maharaja of Bikaner, quoting instances where the British had backed claims of the nearest relation over the expressed wishes of a dying Maharaja. He said that it could cause feuds if Hindu law and Rajput custom were overthrown. Such a course would unnerve all rightful claimants to princely thrones.

The British evaded the issue by replying that they had no knowledge of whom the Maharaja might have selected and that, therefore, they could not discuss a contingency which had not yet arisen.

In January 1921, Bikaner returned to the attack. He wrote another immensely long letter to Chelmsford. He said he was relieved that no decision was imminent. He painted a picture of the court of Jaipur as being a hotbed of rumour and intrigue; and referred to the cunning of certain people who work on the minds of some rulers. There was a report, he said, of '. . . a very recent draining out from the treasury of very large sums for the *marriage in Heaven* [!] of the two morganatic sons of His Highness the Maharaja of Jaipur, one of whom died recently.'

The Maharaja was well aware of all the machinations of Jhalai and Bikaner and wrote again to Chelmsford for confirmation that, whatever happened, his wishes would be carried out. Chelmsford argued that he could not bind his successors to any certain course and pressed the Maharaja to adopt the person of his choice immediately, 'and to announce the adoption publicly in the state'.

This he was still reluctant to do. He did, however, instruct the Maharani as to his wishes, although the Viceroy had warned him that if there were objections after his death to whomsoever he had nominated, the Government of India would have to examine them.

Jhalai next produced two documents. One was signed by twenty-five Jagirdars, some of them leading Sardars. It stated that, in their opinion, Jhalai was the rightful heir. The other, saying the same thing, was signed by fifty of the fifty-five people who could be considered in line, however distantly, to the throne. The five exceptions, not surprisingly, included Isarda and Balir. Amer Singh, the diarist, refers to a document signed by two hundred Sardars, encouraged by Bikaner, but there is no record of its being presented to the British.

Things appeared to be coming to a head; there were even some opportunistic people who presented nazars to the Thakur of Jhalai.

Alarmed and infuriated, the Maharaja convened a darbar on 12 March 1921. Everyone could come, 'even such people who were forbidden to enter the Palace', wrote Amer Singh. Madho Singh was too ill to stand, but he made a speech explaining that he had chosen his successor according to proper custom. He did not wish to give out the name of his choice at once. Instead, he invited everyone present to sign a document acknowledging that he had full power to adopt whomsoever he pleased from the traditional families. He made it plain that he was not ordering anyone to sign. If anyone did not sign, he would not consider it an act of disobedience or be angry on that count.

10

According to Amer Singh, this darbar lasted for three days. Thousands of people came and signed the document. There were only two important abstentions among the nobles – the Thakurs of Chomu and Diggi, who asserted that the document gave the Maharaja too much discretion.

Evidently forgetful of his undertaking not to be angry, Madho Singh sent for Chomu, who was the premier noble of Jaipur, and accused him of faithlessness. Chomu went home and, with Diggi, composed a letter complaining that the Maharaja had used abusive language to him. The Maharaja's reply to that was to dismiss Chomu from his council and to bar him and Diggi from the Palace.

It became clear that even this darbar would not be enough. To be quite certain of the succession, the Maharaja would have formally to adopt Mor Mukut in his lifetime. On 24 March, he did so. Some months before, Mor Mukut had been brought secretly, by night, from Kota and installed in the women's section of the Palace to be looked after by the Maharani and other ladies of the zenana. They took great care of him, tasting all his food before he ate it, lest he be poisoned.

The actual ceremony went off well. Everyone presented nazars to the Maharaja and the new Maharaj Kumar. Guns fired long salutes. The boy looked a little pale and nervous, but conducted himself faultlessly. Crowds flocked to the Palace. The city was illuminated and Amer Singh talked of two or three parties a night for many nights. Even Chomu and Diggi now wanted to sign the document which they had refused to sign two weeks earlier. It only remained for the British to confirm the adoption and thus the succession.

Bikaner, however, had not finished. Another of his inordinately long letters arrived, begging that a final decision be deferred until after Madho Singh's death. No one could give a free opinion, he maintained, while the Maharaja lived. He wrote:

> For the prestige of the British Government and also in
> the interest of strict and impartial justice – for which
> the British Government stands – it is most desirable
> that another case should not be added to the long list of

11

notoriously wrong cases where former Viceroys have, on advice tendered to them, been let down.

The Viceroy took advice from many sources and the Maharaja set up a committee under the chairmanship of Sir Charles Cleveland, who had been Director of Central Intelligence, with three members from Jaipur. All the advice the Viceroy received suggested that the wishes of the Maharaja should prevail over any question of closeness of relationship. The Maharaja's committee, which was largely set up to counteract a report by Jhalai's lawyer, came to the same conclusion, speaking of 'the utter falsity and injustice' of Jhalai's claim. This seems a little harsh, but the argument was plainly more bitter than any surviving papers reveal.

Bikaner had threatened to go to England to see the Secretary of State. Madho Singh had been distributing many of the secret papers in the case to other Princes, in order to turn everyone against Bikaner. Sir Charles Cleveland maintained that, although it could not be proved, Chomu and Diggi were guilty of more than recalcitrance and had plotted to murder Madho Singh.

All the recommendations to the British having been in support of the Maharaja's choice, it was surprising that there was any further delay in confirming the validity of the adoption, particularly as the outcome was one which the British, for all their professions of disinterest, most ardently desired. Madho Singh was bound to die soon and there would inevitably follow a long minority before the child Maharaja would be given full control of his state. The British liked rulers who were minors. It allowed them, with no expense, to run a state according to their ideas. It also made it possible for them to mould the character of the future ruler. Jaipur was a plum – an extremely important state with a young boy to educate.

The delay was mostly due to a change of Viceroys. Chelmsford, who had muddied the issue somewhat by giving contradictory half-promises to Madho Singh and Bikaner, went home and was replaced by Lord Reading.

Reading finally gave his verdict in favour of Madho Singh on 21 April 1921 and, on 10 June, he came to Jaipur for the

12

official darbar, when nazars were presented to the Maharaj Kumar – Man Singh, as we must now learn to call him. 'Long confinement in the zenana has told on his health and he is no longer the cheery light-hearted boy whom I saw at Kota a few months ago,' wrote one English observer.

Madho Singh had triumphed. He made a list of people who were to be punished for opposing his wishes. He only had to reprove the Naib of Karkhanas for his intrigues and the poor man was so ashamed that he dropped dead of shock. Pandit Deo was accused of having performed a sacrifice to invoke spirits to plague the Maharaja. Everyone else was pleased that the Maharaja had a son. The Maharaja lived nearly eighteen months after the adoption date, confounding the prophecy.

CHAPTER 2

Jaipur, at the moment when its young future Maharaja was smuggled by night into the City Palace, was a state virtually in abeyance. The Maharaja Madho Singh's forty-two-year reign was what we might nowadays call a 'non-event'. His predecessor, Ram Singh II, had been a man of energy and vision. He had begun the modernisation of his capital and of his administration. Madho Singh was content merely to let things rumble along. He did not stop any project which Ram Singh had started, but he initiated very little, although he did reorganise the postal system, enlarge the railways and begin some building work.

The Maharaja was not an educated man and seemingly had few interests. He was an extremely orthodox Hindu and a highly-sexed person, which two characteristics are by no means mutually exclusive.

Every morning, at what ever time he got up, Madho Singh would cover his eyes and grope his way to the room where there was an image of his special household deity, Gopalji, so that this would be the first object he saw every day.

His traditional sense of loyalty to the paramount power made him want to go to England in 1902, to attend the coronation of the King-Emperor Edward VII. This desire conflicted with his religion. For a member of the high, 'twice-born' Kshatriya caste, crossing the 'black waters', or sea, could mean loss of caste. Madho Singh placated the 'black waters' by throwing gold, silver and silks into Bombay harbour before embarking on the *Olympia*, a brand new liner of the Anchor Line which he had chartered for his sole use. The image of Gopalji, of course, went with him, housed in a temple which he had built in the ship. The ship was first thoroughly washed and purified. The Maharaja also took with him vast, solid silver jars, taller than a man, filled with enough Ganges water to last him for his four-month journey, as well as a large quantity of Indian soil for his ablutions.

In London, he rented Moray Lodge on Campden Hill, where he dug a well in the garden to supplement his Ganges water, for less important purposes. His arrival in London on 3 June, with his turbanned and armed officers and retainers forming a procession headed by Gopalji, caused quite a stir.

Madho Singh must have had a measure of engaging charm. His portraits and photographs show him as a large, round-faced, bearded man of imposing presence. The British liked him very well, possibly because he gave no trouble and contributed with great generosity to their campaigns on the North-West Frontier and gave one and a half million rupees out of his own money to help in the First World War, also raising an equal sum from his nobles and officials. The British showered him with honours, including four separate knighthoods. He was even made an honorary LL.D. by Edinburgh University.

He may well have been cleverer than one thinks for, as Amer Singh pointed out, no one had a bad word for him; he spent money wildly, drank excessively and yet left three million rupees. The state revenue increased by four million rupees a year during his reign. When faced with awkward questions from the Viceroy, he would talk flat out in a kind of filibuster until the Viceroy gave up.

At the same time he was something of a degenerate. His superstition made him vulnerable to manipulation. Towards the end of his life, he fell pathetically under the influence of a man of the tailor caste, Bala Bux Khwas. This man, who, Amer Singh said, was not someone to be trusted in any way, came to be the fount of all favours. No one could get to see the Maharaja except through the offices of Bala Bux. What his hold over Madho Singh was is not known. Certainly it included providing him with women from the town to supplement the services of his three secondary wives and eighteen official concubines; but this would not seem enough to make him the dispenser of all royal favour, or to excuse his excesses. There was a story that Madho Singh asked Bala Bux what he had done with some gold he had entrusted to him. Bala Bux explained that it had got wet and he had put it into the sun to dry and, alas, it had all evaporated. Madho Singh was not an idiot, so he must, for some reason, have been prepared to ignore almost any impertinence on this man's part.

It may have been mere indolence. The Maharaja very rarely left the City Palace. According to Amer Singh, he used to take about a week to be shaved. It would be done in small bits according to his whims. The interval between shaves varied from three to six months. Here, Amer Singh may have been indulging in some fancy, for later portraits of Madho Singh show him very fully bearded.

He did not keep up any high standards of entertaining. Amer Singh complained that the formal dinners were disgracefully bad. The meat was often stinking. The food was served on leaves and the curries in cups made of leaves. Then there was no wine, usually only water, and anything else to drink was served in cheap, earthenware vessels. Bala Bux would wander round among the guests, shouting at them to eat up.

During the last months of Madho Singh's life, Bala Bux and his female colleague, Roop Rai, the Maharaja's concubine, perhaps realising that their intrigues and embezzlements would shortly have to end, indulged in even greater excesses.

Bala Bux, despite his humble caste, was descended from Rodaram Khwas, who had been Maharaja Jagat Singh's personal attendant a hundred years before. Jagat Singh was more interested in the women in his harem than in matters of administration, so that Rodaram Khwas virtually ruled Jaipur for a while. Bala Bux was a man of such intelligence and he gathered so much power into his hands that, even after Madho Singh's death, the British felt that, 'no administration can afford to disregard him', and even suggested putting him on the Minority Council – something which the

16

Rajput nobles, however toady they had been to him during the Maharaja's lifetime, could not countenance. One noble who had worked with Bala Bux on some of his nefarious arrangements voted against him in a curious twist of Rajput honour.

Madho Singh had promoted Bala Bux to noble rank, making him a Tazimi Sardar. He was in charge of five important forts; he was the head of the Kapadwara or private treasury; he ruled the household.

One of his main sources of income was bribes, from nobles who had recently inherited a jagir, to get the Maharaja to confirm their inheritance. Mr R.E. Holland, the Agent to the Governor General, reported that, according to an informant:

> ... during the past six months the administration has been a by-word and a mockery and wholesale bribery and corruption has been rampant. Offices have been bought and sold and impartial justice has been rarely obtainable.

Roop Rai, the concubine, is of necessity a more shadowy figure, living as she did in the zenana. The British hated her, referring to her as 'that pestilential woman' and 'that female Rasputin'. She was said to have possessed hypnotic powers and alleged to have had three girls beaten to death by the eunuchs and their bodies burnt. She also had some power over Bala Bux, so that he revealed the Maharaja's secrets to her, which gave her an even greater hold over the old man. The British, of course, were terrified about what effect this woman might have on the young Maharaj Kumar, Man Singh.

Once the adoption was settled, Madho Singh reverted more and more to Hindu customs. He would discuss at length the young Prince's education with Sir James Roberts, his medical adviser, and Sir Charles Cleveland, but it was learnt, in April 1922, that he was ignoring Roberts' advice and was employing 'a woman Hakim'.

In June 1922, Madho Singh went on a pilgrimage to Indargargh, taking with him Roop Rai and Man Singh. There they lived in tents, in pouring rain.

17

In July, two of the nobles came to Cleveland and explained that it would be an affront to state honour if the Maharaja were to die away from his capital. If his body had to be taken through the streets of the city before the usual funeral rites had been performed in the Palace, 'Jaipur would be a standing mark of shame and disgrace throughout Rajputana'. They said he must be brought in 'alive', even if he were dead – rather in the same way that no one is allowed to die in the Palace of Westminster.

Sir Charles said it would be impossible to conceal his death, because all the women would be wailing and tearing their hair. The Thakurs assured him that the women would have more sense. But it was decided to send Mr Patterson, the new Resident in Jaipur, off to Indargargh to persuade Mando Singh to come back. If the Maharaja were to die, then Patterson agreed, 'I would inform the Govt. by cypher telegram and . . . to treat HH as alive until he died officially in the Palace.'

Patterson wrote to Holland on returning from Indargargh:

> We arrived at Sawai Madhopur at 10 A.M. and as there was no passenger train till 4 o'clock we took our places in a goods train and arrived at Indargarh at 3 P.M. . . . We found that tea was ready for us and a dali of mangoes from His Highness. His Highness was in camp five miles away. I asked Gopi Nath to inform His Highness that I had come, had a letter from you to deliver to him and would be glad to go to him to deliver it at any time convenient . . . We waited for over two hours for a message when to our surprise at 5.15 two motor cars came up. In the first were the gentlemen I have mentioned and in the second His Highness himself. Dr Daljang Singh drove the car and His Highness had with him two Palace eunuchs. I at once went out to meet him. His Highness remained in the car, also the eunuchs, the latter standing. The State officials and others gathered round. His Highness looked very ill. He was very angry and excited. I enquired after his health. He replied by asking why I

18

had given him all this trouble and made him come to the Railway Station. I replied that my visit was with a view to ascertain his state of health and to deliver a letter from you; that I had hoped to do this in his camp and was most astonished at his arrival at the Railway Station. He replied that I must know that he adhered rigidly to old customs and that by these he was bound to meet me at the Railway Station. I replied that I knew of no custom under which the Maharaja of Jaipur met the Resident at the Railway Station and I reminded His Highness that during the five and a half months I had been Resident at Jaipur he had not once either personally or by deputy returned one of my visits. I made no complaint as I knew he was in ill health, that old custom had in these cases not been adhered to but I said that he must surely see that if I did not expect a usual courtesy in Jaipur where the Palace was half a mile from the Residency I could not reasonably have been expected to demand an unusual courtesy at a roadside station 5 miles from His Highness' camp. His Highness remained silent. I did not add that it was not an old established custom for His Highness to call on the Resident accompanied by two eunuchs. I was sorry for His Highness he looked so ill. He is dominated by the female Rasputin, whose creatures the eunuchs are, and he knew he was in the wrong. I then handed him your letter.

He gave it to Gopi Nath and said it would be read to him in the quiet in camp. He then flared up again and said I ought to have told him I was coming, that he only knew at 4 that afternoon. I replied that an urgent telegram had been sent the evening before. I refrained from adding that if he only knew for the first time at 4 P.M. it was surprising that all preparations had been made for my arrival, including mangoes from himself by 3 P.M. . . . . His Highness then asked me why I had come down to ask about his health. I replied saying that he came first to Indargargh for three days about three weeks ago, that he had remained there ever since,

19

living in a tent in rain and heat in great discomfort, that
Sir James Roberts was absent, that very disquieting
reports had circulated about his health, that the Agent
to the Governor General was most concerned and the
Government of India anxious . . . and that it was my
duty to come down, enquire and report. I added that he
was not a private individual but a Ruling Prince, a
friend and ally of Government and as such he could not
expect the Government to remain indifferent while he
disappeared into the jungle for an indefinite period in
ill health with his heir-apparent. All his subjects too, I
said, were most perturbed. He replied that he did not
think it was my duty . . . During this His Highness'
temper was improving. He then said he would fix his
departure for Thursday 27th . . . I said I was very glad
and enquired after the Maharaj Kumar. He said he was
in the best of health and would return with him. I asked
him if he would let Colonel Watson see him. He said
certainly not but added that he would after his return to
Jaipur . . .

After His Highness' departure I sent my vakil to his
camp to ask when it would be convenient for him to
receive my return call. The vakil returned saying that
His Highness had said very politely that he was too
exhausted for any further talk and would excuse my
return visit. He would send the Agent to the Governor
General a reply when better. The vakil told me that the
camp was in a deplorably filthy and insanitary
condition. Twelve hundred people and 150 animals are
in it and no attempt at sanitation. There was open
rejoicing at my visit (except in one quarter) as it put an
end to their agony which looked as if it would be
indefinitely prolonged. Khwas Bala Baksh sent me a
message thanking me warmly. I think and sincerely
trust that His Highness will leave Indargargh on the
27th. At any rate my visit shows that Government is
fully interested and partly alive to what is going on and
I feel pretty sure the woman will refrain from taking
any action at this stage . . .

Holland wrote to Delhi:

I recently heard from Patterson that the retreat of His
Highness the Maharaja from Indargargh was a very
difficult business and was carried out only just in time.
The motors had to traverse five miles of country road
from His Highness' camp to Indargargh station and
they were up to the axles in mud. Immediately after His
Highness reached Sawai Madhopur, very heavy rain
fell and he might have been imprisoned in his camp for
some time, if he had not escaped at the opportune
moment. There is a strong belief in Jaipur that the
concubine never intended him to return alive. She had
a large amount of jewellery with her and hoped to
escape with it. I was informed on arriving in Jaipur this
morning that two women servants had disappeared
from the Indargargh camp and the theory is that the
lady sent them off with a good deal of jewellery in the
hope that its disappearance would not be noticed.

The public are said to be greatly relieved by His
Highness' safe return as they dreaded the disgrace in
which Jaipur would have been involved, if His
Highness had died in a foreign jungle . . .

The Maharaja did not die until 7 September 1922, by which
time he was back in Jaipur. Holland reported after his death
that the 'infamous Pardayat woman' (Roop Rai) had deliberately neglected the old man at Indargargh, with the result
that he had caught pneumonia which led to his death. She
had, he believed, taken at least ten million rupees from the
private treasury, in addition to accepting bribes to use her
influence with Madho Singh. The jewels she had taken were
said to be of far greater value. It was thought that she would
soon escape from the Palace, taking her loot with her to
enjoy elsewhere.

Both Roop Rai and Bala Bux were still in the Palace in
December. Money and jewels were still disappearing. They
had even made eighty thousand rupees out of some swindle
to do with the Maharaja's funeral. Cleveland seemed power-
less. Although he said he felt 'like a dictator,' because no one

21

ever disagreed with him as President of the Minority Council, he also said he had 'met his Moscow' in the Jaipur Palace, especially the inner Palace 'with its swarms of ladies, women and eunuchs. He felt he could never tackle it, and that no Englishman could or should.' To help, they brought in the Raj Rana of Dhrangadhra to be a member of the Cabinet.

The Cabinet conducted a kind of treasure hunt in all the Palace storehouses. They found odd hoards of rupees in strange places. In one cell of the Treasury there was a 'tub full of sovereigns and a bundle of Govt Promissory Notes with dividends unclaimed for years'.

The British were very anxious to move Man Singh out of the Palace, away from the influence of Bala Bux and Roop Rai. There were suggestions that 'attempts have already been made in the zenana to debauch the young Maharaja by means of girls'. Sir James Roberts, who was now the boy's guardian, wanted him removed on medical grounds as the Palace, he said, was 'congested and unsanitary'. There were believed to be five thousand women and eunuchs living in the zenana.

Perhaps it was the plight of the elephants and horses in the royal stables which spurred the British on to action. There were liberal funds provided for the keep of these animals, but most of these funds were 'directed into the pockets of those in control'.

Late in December, a new will of Madho Singh's turned up in the zenana. Everyone agreed that it was a clumsy forgery perpetrated by 'the woman who makes herself a beneficiary under the alleged Will'. The situation was becoming farcical.

Finally, on 6 January 1923, Patterson wrote to Holland.

> RR has been tackled at last. On Saturday afternoon she was told she must vacate the Sr. Maharani's quarters which she occupied and move to one more suitable for her position. She absolutely declined and swore she had no money or jewellery with her. The Eunuchs were sent to remove her but she and her women drew swords and defied them. Eventually at night two of the Lalljis went to her and after some talk persuaded her to vacate . . . Her quarters were then searched and found to contain 3 lakhs in cash, 35 swords, many bottles of

poison, a great quantity of spirits and liquors and about 100 packs of cards. She had 100 women with her . . . Exit Rup Rai and a good thing too. A really terrible woman.

Three lakhs is three hundred thousand rupees, but the figure was later amended to between seven and eight hundred thousand, along with jewellery worth a further three or four thousand.

Two months later, Holland reported that Roop Rai had made a long statement. She claimed that Bala Bux was the leader of their group which included, incidentally, the noble who had voted against the idea of Bala Bux's joining the Cabinet. For the previous five years, quite apart from the substantial bribes paid in succession cases, not one appointment, even of the most humble clerk, had been made without Bala Bux herself, and sometimes the noble, receiving bribes. They had also squeezed large amounts of money out of the Maharaja by playing on his superstitious nature. They would tell him that they needed money to procure messages from Heaven for him.

Bala Bux himself eventually admitted that for years past he had sold appointments, taken bribes, substituted false jewels for real ones and manipulated the exchange between the local and government rupee to his own advantage. He also admitted having lent money from the Treasury at high rates of interest to people in the city, the profits going into his own pocket.

Despite his confession, the British thought that he had been so clever that it would be difficult to prove any charges brought against him. Furthermore, they wished to avoid a scandal and the inevitable 'painful exposures concerning his late Highness' which would result from a prosecution. The Cabinet estimated that Bala Bux had, in one way or another, acquired anything up to twenty or thirty million rupees. He agreed to give back to the Crown half a million, in the guise of a nazar. For a time, the authorities did nothing.

Amer Singh, the diarist, recorded that Bala Bux was prosecuted and describes the half million as a fine. He said, however, that his jagir and his honour of being allowed to wear a gold anklet were not touched. The following year, in June, he noted that Bala Bux was in prison.

Such, then, was the atmosphere of the court to which the young, future Maharaja was brought. Those months which he spent in the zenana, he was later to say, were the unhappiest of his whole life. This country-minded boy found himself boxed up with a lot of women, whose only interests were gossip and intrigue. They were kind to him by their lights, filling him with sweets and sickly cakes, so that he became fat and liverish.

None of his family came with him. They were allowed to pay him visits, but the visits were more like stilted interviews, conducted in formal circumstances. Awareness of the aura of royalty is a very strong part of the Rajput character, so that even close relations are inhibited in their dealings with Princes.

An unusual exception to this was Man Singh's younger, favourite sister. On the first occasion she saw him after his adoption, she had with her a coin ready to present to him as nazar. He told her to give it to him. She said she could see no reason for giving him a coin. He had lots and she had only this one. Man Singh said she had to give it to him as it was the custom. She said she was going to hide it up her skirt and buy toys with it. And she did.

According to Madho Singh's surviving morganatic son, Raja Jaswant Singh, there were about fifty children living in the zenana. Their lives were comparatively restricted in as much as they hardly ever left the Palace grounds, although it is true that these covered about one seventh of the total area of the walled city. The boys played Ganjifa, a card game using ninety-six cards; Chaupar, a game somewhat like ludo crossed with dominoes; and Daskana, which is not unlike chess. Man Singh was apparently a good loser, but he could also be selfish. Madho Singh gave him a pony and trap which he refused to share with the other boys, threatening them with his whip if they tried to get in. Naturally, in the general spirit of rivalry and intrigue, this was at once reported to the Maharaja. He said that he had given the boy the trap and he was quite entitled to exclude others if he wished.

Madho Singh was fond of children, but it seems that he

took no very great notice of his adopted son, perhaps because, by that time, his health was very poor. The boy would visit the Maharaja after his devotions in the morning and sometimes the old man would play with him before lunch, but he gave Man Singh no instruction. Life in the zenana was so crowded that there was little chance of any intimacy growing up between the two of them. So the boy's days were spent in loneliness and sadness at his confinement. He did get the Maharaja's permission to go outside the Palace but he always had to take with him four nobles and doubtless several servants to protect and look after him. Such expeditions were not much of an outing for a boy accustomed to wandering off in the forest with a couple of companions of his own choosing.

Madho Singh did, however, plan for the boy's future. He consulted very carefully with the British and his council about the kind of education he should have. More important still, in Rajput princely thinking, he set about finding Man Singh a wife.

In August 1921, Mr R.E. Holland, the Agent to the Governor General, discovered that Madho Singh had sent an emissary to Sir Pratap Singh, the Regent of Jodhpur, with the idea of negotiating a whole series of marriages. Holland reported that the marriages to be arranged were that of Man Singh to two Princesses and of one of his sisters to a Prince. The Maharaja also planned to marry off numbers of his morganatic children to corresponding children of the late Maharaja of Jodhpur and of Sir Pratap.

Arrangements of this kind were perfectly normal, but they were always anathema to the British. This particular case had aspects which especially aroused their horror. The two princesses that Man Singh was to marry were aunt and niece. The older one was twenty-two, that is to say twelve years older than Man Singh. She was the sister of the Maharaja Umaid of Jodhpur, who had succeeded their brother the Maharaja Summair. Holland reported that she was said to have had a drinking problem at one time. The only eligible man of suitable age and grand enough status for her to have married earlier was the Maharaja of Rewa. He was already married to her younger sister, to whom she could hardly be expected to take second place.

The second of Man Singh's brides was to be the daughter of the late Maharaja Summair. She was five. A younger brother of the ruling Maharaja of Jodhpur was to marry one of Man Singh's sisters.

By the time that Holland had heard what was afoot, much negotiating had taken place. Sir Pratap's attitude had been that he had two princesses of appropriate standing, but that Jaipur must take both or only the elder. Madho Singh had also heard about the elder one's drinking and, anyhow, thought her too old. He suggested to his emissary, Narain Singh, that he, Madho, should marry the elder one. Narain said bluntly, 'You are now making preparations to meet the funeral pyre – how can you think of marriage?'

The matter automatically became one for public discussion. The Jaipur nobles thoroughly enjoyed pointing out how discreditable it was for a Jodhpur Princess to be unmarried at such an advanced age. There was no more than a mild feeling that the betrothal of the elder Princess would be a pity.

The Maharaja of Nawanagar, better known as the cricketer Ranjit Singh, felt more indignant on behalf of the younger Princess, whose mother was his sister. He complained to Holland on her behalf and he reported that:

> Her Highness apparently objects to the marriage on the ground that her daughter will rival her own aunt for the affections of their joint husband, but I imagine that her real objection is that her daughter, being the younger of the two, will naturally be the second wife. On the other hand being nearer in age to Kumar [Man Singh], it seems probable that the younger girl will have the best chance of gaining a stronghold upon his affections.

British disapproval made no difference. Sir Pratap was put out because, when he came to Jaipur, Madho Singh was extremely rude to him on two occasions and, as one of Queen Victoria's favourites, he was not used to such things. But Sir Pratap was in the stronger position, being able to accommodate so many of the Maharaja's lalljis, as the children of morganatic alliances were called.

On 31 December 1921, Man Singh, aged ten, was formally betrothed to both aunt and niece.

The matter, like so many other problems which appeared to be settled, was to keep raising its head, always in the end being settled in the same way. Neither the Indians nor the British ever seemed able to let anything alone.

By the end of 1923, Holland was telling Delhi that the Jaipur Cabinet, with one un-named exception, was unanimously opposed to the proposed marriage to the older girl. They must all have known that it was impossible to do anything about it. In the first place, it had been arranged by the Maharaja. Secondly, to back out of a betrothal is unthinkable for any Rajput.

The Jodhpur court was by now pressing for, at any rate, the first marriage to take place. Man Singh was twelve, the same age at which Jai Singh III had impregnated Ram Singh II's mother, some ninety years before. That sort of reasoning was deeply repugnant to the British.

Everybody ultimately agreed that it was out of the question to repudiate the betrothal. Apart from anything else, if the older girl were rejected, Jodhpur would presumably withdraw the younger one. A feud which could last interminably would result.

Holland, in a Cabinet meeting at Jaipur, mouthed platitudes about, 'the marriage of a ruler educated on modern lines is a different thing from an old-fashioned marriage. Kumar might later turn round and complain that the Minority Administration had ruined his life.' The kind of ruler they hoped to create might well object. But the process of change had not begun. Jaipur was still the Jaipur of Madho Singh. His will was still prevailing.

It was probably the British who came up with a compromise that catered for that area of alarm which could have concerned them alone. They proposed to hold the wedding as soon as was convenient, but they would leave out of the ceremony the part known as muklawa, without which consummation may not take place. The bride would then return to Jodhpur to wait until her husband reached the age of eighteen.

Meeting after meeting took place. The majis, or ladies of

27

the Palace, were consulted. The plan was explained to Man Singh who, after giving the question what Holland thought was surprisingly mature consideration, agreed quite calmly.

Mr J.W.C. Mayne, who was to become Man Singh's guardian in February of that year, put up a vigorous protest. He said he thought of the boy as a son and he felt very unhappy that he would be unable to choose a wife for himself. 'Are we to jeopardise His Highness' chances of future happiness out of deference to an antiquated custom?', he asked. Perhaps it was Mayne who managed to unsettle Man Singh. On 6 December, a message to Delhi said that the boy had suddenly announced his strong opposition to the marriage.

It was the British boast that they did not interfere in private family matters of this sort. Nothing more appears in the British records on this subject. The boy's objections were presumably ignored.

On 30 January 1924, Man Singh was married to Marudhar Kanwar of Jodhpur. Amer Singh, the diarist, who was at the time commanding the Jaipur Lancers, tells us that he needed chain-armour for twenty-five sowars, or troopers, for the occasion. The repairs for this cost one thousand rupees. The young Maharaja, as is always the case with an important marriage as opposed to a ceremony with a girl whose children will not be in the line of succession, went to Jodhpur for his wedding. Besides the twenty-five cavalrymen, there was a need for fifty camel riders, a large number of other horses and several elephants.

Amer Singh describes the arrival of Man Singh's train at eight-thirty in the morning. A nineteen-gun salute was fired from the fort. The two Maharajas exchanged a formal sum of money known as Nachrawal, each giving the other 101 rupees. The Maharaja of Jodhpur took Man Singh to the Mediwala Palace, where they performed the ceremony of Atar and Paan.

The bridegroom's procession to the fort started at three-thirty. At the Murtia Gate, he mounted an elephant. As he had to stop six times to watch dancing, it took two hours to reach the fort. There, another nineteen guns were fired. The wedding ceremony, followed by sundry other ceremonies (whether or not including the muklawa, which so concerned

28

the British, Amer Singh does not say), lasted until nine o'clock, when yet another nineteen guns, plus an extra one, were fired.

The celebrations went on in Jodhpur for a week. On 31 January, there was a ball at the Residency, though it is not clear who would have danced, all the women being in purdah. The following day, Man Singh and his wife left for Jaipur. The arrangement that she should remain at Jodhpur until he was eighteen must have been abandoned. Certainly she was living in Jaipur early in 1925.

CHAPTER 3

When Madho Singh of Jaipur died on 7 September 1922, Man Singh became the thirty-ninth ruler, not of Jaipur, but of the Kachhawa Rajput clan and their lands in Rajputana. It is important for any understanding of the life and character of the new Maharaja to know something of what he was heir to.

The word Rajput means son of kings. The real origin of the Rajputs is obscure, but the Kachhawa branch claim to be descended from Kush, the twin son of the demi-God Rama, and thus directly from the sun. Whatever we may decide about that, the Rajputs belong to the Kshatriya or warrior caste of Hindus. They came southward into what became known as Rajputana in the twelfth and thirteenth centuries, the Kachhawa clan settling at Amer or Amber, there dispossessing and subjugating the Minas, who had ruled the area before. This was achieved, according to one legend, by getting the Mina leaders drunk and then butchering them. (The latest, rather sycophantic history of Jaipur maintains that the Minas got themselves drunk.)

Until the coming of the Moghuls at the turn of the four-teenth century, the history of the area is one of local squabbles and struggles for ascendancy, as often as not between the different Rajput clans. The establishment by the Moghuls of a highly organised Muslim power in Delhi in the early sixteenth century had a lasting effect on what was to be the state of Jaipur. In 1236, there had been built at Ajmer the most important Muslim shrine in Hindustan. For

30

the Moghuls, it was a religious duty to keep safe the pilgrims' route to this shrine, which ran through the land ruled by the Kachhawas. Accommodation with the Moghuls on this score coincided with the Kachhawas' desire to be relieved of their fear of the rulers of Jodhpur, who were a constant threat to their borders. With these two objects in mind, Bihar Mal, the ruler of Amber, married his daughter to the Moghul Emperor Akbar in 1562. At the same time, Bihar Mal's grandson, Man Singh, entered the service of Akbar, the Moghul Emperor.

This, and many subsequent marriages between the Kachhawas and the Moghuls, was to be the ground for much sneering and derision by other Rajput clans, in particular by the Sisodias of Mewar (later to be known as Udaipur), and the Rathors of Jodhpur. Even at the time, it was considered a matter of shame. One morning, Rai Singh, the Maharaj Kumar of Toda, came to court wearing a coat with a stain on it. Man Singh reproved him. The young man said, 'My stain is nothing, it will be washed clean by the dhobi, but how can you ever get rid of your stain?'

Man Singh's revenge for this insult was to persuade Akbar to marry Rai Singh's daughter. When ordered by Akbar to bring his sister to Delhi, the boy said she was already betrothed to Man Singh. Man Singh said he was prepared to give her up – a disgraceful act, as a Rajput should rather die than give up a girl to whom he is betrothed. Akbar did marry her, but at least the spirited Rai Singh managed to persuade the Emperor to go to Toda to do so and to lend him 300,000 rupees to pay for the privilege of entertaining him.

It was also to set a pattern of allegiance by the Kachhawas to the paramount power in Delhi, whether Moghul or British, which was not seriously questioned for four centuries. There had previously been some Hindu–Muslim marriages, but Akbar, with his unusually liberal attitude, was the first to make a Hindu wife virtually equal with his other wives; so that, while the Hindu men in his service might not eat or pray with the Emperor nor marry Muslim girls, they were respected as never before. The men could and did, according to Judanath Sarkar, 'drink with him and join his Sufi seances'.

By 1563, all the states of Rajputana, except Mewar, were paying tribute to Delhi. The capital of Mewar at that time was Chitor, which was famous in Rajput history for two dramatic sieges. The Rajputs, somewhat like the British, perhaps even more like the Spartans, have always glorified their most crippling defeats, that is if they did not deny that they had happened, or alternatively claim them as victories.

The first siege of Chitor took place in 1303, well before Moghul times, when Ala-ud-Din Khilji, the Pathan King of Delhi, surrounded the fort in order to capture the beautiful Princess Padmini, who was married to Bhim Singh, the uncle of the Rana of Mewar. Chitor is the most beautiful fort situated on an isolated, flat-topped hill. Like most such places, it can withstand siege for a time while provisions last, but it is easy to starve out. The result was the traditional Rajput reply to certain defeat, surrender being out of the question. Bhim Singh and his warrior nobles put on saffron robes, which are a symbol of martyrdom, and marched out of the fort to die. The womenfolk, led by Padmini, threw themselves on a huge fire built in a cave not far from the Palace.

The second siege was in 1535, when the Sultan of Gujarat arrived at the gates with an overwhelming force. This time, tradition has it, 32,000 warriors marched out in their saffron robes and 13,000 women leapt onto the flames.

The figures are doubtless exaggerated, but it might have been thought that after this the people of Mewar would have reconsidered their defensive arrangements. Not so. Thirty-three years later, Akbar advanced upon Chitor and besieged it for four months. Once more, 8,000 saffron-robed men marched out and once again the women died by fire.

This is the Rajput ideal and it colours the whole history of the Rajputana states, always reinforcing, as we shall see, their inability to compromise, always inspiring their contempt for those who do so.

Man Singh, the first Kachhawa to enter the Moghul's service, rose to be one of Akbar's greatest generals. He was a short man of stocky appearance, endowed with courage in the true Rajput style, which appealed to Akbar. Indeed, the Emperor, at a rather drunken party, tried to emulate the demonstrations of bravado that the Rajputs indulged in. As the Emperor's chronicler wrote, 'Rajputs would hold a double-headed spear and two men would run from opposite sides against the points, so that the latter would transfix them and come out at their backs.' Akbar had a sword fixed to the wall and proposed to throw himself against it, as a proof of his courage, but Man Singh restrained him. This exemplified the other more practical side of Man Singh.

It was he who set the pattern of obedience to the central power, shoring it up in times of its troubles, using its protection in times of his own difficulties. Thus we find him fighting on behalf of the Emperor, in 1576, against the Mewar Rajputs. Udai Singh, the Rana of Mewar, had himself avoided the last siege of Chitor and had set up a new capital which he called Udaipur. His successor, Pratap Singh, kept promising submission to the Emperor, but he never actually gave it. Akbar sent Man Singh to exact the promised surrender and tribute.

The Kachhawa leader and the Sisodia leader met at Haldighat. It was one of those battles in which old-fashioned heroics lose hopelessly to modern tactics. The Rana fought with prodigious valour. He was wounded twice, once by an arrow, once by a spear. Man Singh won. The Rana lost. In Rajput eyes, Pratap Singh was the hero prince; Man Singh was a servant. The fact that his actions were possibly more statesmanlike was of no interest to the romantic Rajputs.

The whole of Man Singh's life was devoted to a series of campaigns on behalf of the Emperor. He fought in Afghanistan, Bihar, Orissa and Bengal. It was when he was Viceroy there that he went to the help of Lakshmi Narayan, Raja of the kingdom of Cooch Behar. In 1596, he married Lakshmi Narayan's sister, an act which was to be of great significance for his namesake, Man Singh II, in 1940.

His last campaign was in the Deccan, fought on behalf of Jehangir, the new Emperor, who, although married to Man Singh's granddaughter, never treated him well. The Deccan campaign was unsuccessful and the Mirza Raja, as Man Singh was now known, died there an unhappy man. All his sons had died and by 1621, his throne had descended to his great-grandson, Jai Singh, who was the finest of all the Kachhawa generals.

Jai Singh was eleven at the time of his accession. By the age of thirteen, he was commander of 3,000, leading the Kachhawas in the Deccan against Malik Ambar, the Abyssinian slave who had revived the moribund kingdom of Ahmadnagar and whom the Moghuls were never able to defeat.

The young Jai Singh had the regular qualities of the Rajputs, but he was also unusually circumspect and tactful. He was as capable as the rest of them of pursuing self-interest, but he had a much clearer idea than most of them as to where that self-interest lay. Like his great-grandfather, he fought all over India, from Afghanistan to the Deccan, for his Emperor, Shah Jehan. When the Emperor became senile and a struggle for power broke out between his three sons, Jai Singh led an army nominally under the command of Sulamain, son of the heir apparent, Dara. When he saw that Dara was going to lose the struggle to his brother Aurangzeb, Jai Singh blithely abandoned Sulaiman and paid his homage to Aurangzeb. Soon he was sent off to hunt down Dara, his recent ally. Dara was captured, paraded through the streets of Delhi and then murdered by his brother Aurangzeb.

Aurangzeb gave Jai Singh a robe of honour from his own wardrobe, a jewelled fishtail ornament known as a punchhi, an elephant with a silver howdah and a gold-embroidered cover, another elephant and two hundred horses. Jai Singh exceeded even Man Singh's eminence by becoming a commander of 7,000 troops, which was the maximum permitted to anyone not of the Imperial family. His revenue from lands granted to him by Aurangzeb was half a million rupees.

His son, Ram Singh, was sent in pursuit of Prince Sulaiman who, once captured, spent the rest of his life in prison.

Jai Singh's finest exploit, in Imperial eyes, was the capture of the Maratha hero Shivaji, who had plagued Delhi from the south for a long time. After ingenious diplomatic manoeuverings to seduce away Shivaji's allies, Jai Singh cornered him in the fort of Purandar in April 1664. Jai Singh's siege tactics were excellent and Shivaji came out unarmed from the fort, early in June, and asked for a parley. In the chivalrous spirit of the times, the two men embraced. Shivaji was obliged to surrender the larger part of his kingdom to the Emperor and agreed thereafter to be a vassal of the Moghuls, although he begged to be excused attendance at court.

Aurangzeb was very eager to see Shivaji. After two years, during which Shivaji had stuck by every clause of their agreement, Jai Singh persuaded Shivaji to visit the Emperor. He guaranteed him a safe visit and the certainty of returning home. When he arrived, Aurangzeb treated Shivaji with so little respect that he stormed out of the court, refusing ever to see Aurangzeb again. The Emperor at first planned to kill him, but Jai Singh's son, Ram, with characteristic Rajput honour, offered his life instead, on the grounds that Jai Singh had given his oath to Shivaji that he would be safe. Shivaji was kept prisoner in his quarters. After three months, Shivaji and his son escaped in two baskets of sweetmeats, which he had taken to sending out each day to the Brahmin poor.

It is hard to say whether Jai Singh, through his son Ram, was in any way responsible for helping with this escape, but the Emperor showed his displeasure by reducing Ram's rank and banishing him from court.

Jai Singh's last campaign, like Man Singh's, was a failure. His object had been to crush the Kingdom of Bijapur. Twice he advanced; twice he was forced to retreat. He had spent not only the Emperor's money, but millions of his own. He was relieved of his command, despite paying a bribe of 30,000 rupees to the Prime Minister.

In 1667, three months after his dismissal, he died. He fell while climbing up a ladder onto his elephant and lived only two days. There were rumours of poisoning by his son, Kirat of Kama, for which reason that branch of the ruling family is still excluded from the succession.

The next two Rajas of Amber, Ram Singh and his grandson Bishan Singh, worked for the Emperor somewhat apprehensively, for Aurangzeb was thought to have ordered the killing of Ram's son Kishan, father of Bishan.

Bishan's elder son was eleven years old when he succeeded to the throne of Amber as Jai Singh II. (He had previously been called Bijai, but this name was now given to his younger half-brother.) By the age of fourteen, he was leading

35

the Kachhawas against the Marathas on behalf of Aurangzeb. Such was his courage at the siege of Khelna in 1702, that the Emperor called him 'Sawai', that is, 'one and a quarter' – a word which was confirmed as an official title in 1713. Aurangzeb, however, had neither the liberality nor the generosity of his predecessors. From religious bigotry, he kept all Hindus down and seemed to single out Jai Singh for contumely, though the Raja maintained his allegiance to Delhi throughout his reign.

When Aurangzeb died in 1707, his sons inevitably fought for the succession. Jai Singh joined Azam Shah at the battle of Jajau, but, with characteristic pragmatism, changed sides during the fight when he saw that Muazzam would win. Rather reasonably, Muazzam, on becoming Emperor as Bahadur Shah, did not much trust Jai Singh. Passing through Amber, he arbitrarily deposed Jai Singh and proposed to install his younger half-brother Bijai on the throne of Amber.

This action had the effect of uniting the three leading states of Rajputana against the Imperial power. Jai Singh and the Maharaja of Jodhpur met with the Maharana of Udaipur and formed a triple Rajput alliance, according to James Tod, renouncing, 'all connection, domestic or political, with the empire'. There followed a flurry of engagements and marriages between the clans. Jai Singh married one daughter of the Maharana. Ajit Singh of Jodhpur was betrothed to another (although there is no record of the marriage taking place). The agreement between Jai Singh and the Maharana clearly stated that the Udaipur princess would be his senior wife. He would sleep with her on all festival nights; he would rest in her palace on coming back from a battle; her palanquin would be foremost in a procession. The implication was that any son by her would automatically be his heir. It was an agreement which was to cause much trouble.

The Rajput armies went first to Jodhpur, driving out the Moghuls. It was the last time that the Moghuls held Jodhpur. Jai Singh, in honour of this success, was betrothed to one of Ajit Singh's daughters. Then they marched to Amber, where the Sardars pushed out the Moghuls and acclaimed Jai Singh as their Raja in October 1708. Bijai was thrown into prison.

In four years time, despite the Udaipur agreement, Jai

Singh was made a commander of 7,000 by the new Emperor, and was, soon after, serving the first of his three terms as Viceroy of Malwa. Over the next few years, he fought the Marathas and the Afghans and suppressed the Jats. Gradually, Jai Singh built up his power and his riches. Whatever the agreement at Udaipur, the Moghul Empire, albeit well on the way to crumbling, was still a power. It was, in Jai Singh's view, pointless to fight against it. It was better to unite Rajputana within the general embrace of the Empire and thereby acquire greater autonomy, in a climate of safety and reasonable peace. This proposition was briefly and not very enthusiastically accepted by most of the states of Rajputana. Udaipur was too far removed to care very much and Jai Singh left that state undisturbed. Jodhpur and Bundi were also bound to him through marital ties. He was held in such respect that the rulers of most Rajput states, even on occasions Udaipur, would look to him as the natural intermediary between them and Delhi.

By 1723, Jai Singh, confirmed as Maharaja Sawai Bahadur of Amber, had no special imperial duties. He was able to stay at home and indulge the other sides of his nature – the scientific and the artistic.

In 1733, Jai Singh described his astronomical studies in a book called *Zij-i-Muhammad Shahi*. In it, he explained his motives for building observatories in Delhi, Jaipur, Ujjain, Mathura and Benares. He wrote of himself:

> This admiring spectator of the theatre of infinite wisdom . . . was, from the first dawning of reason in his mind and during his progress towards maturity, entirely devoted to the study of mathematical science, . . . He found that the calculation of the places of the stars, as obtained from the tables in common use (Sanskrit, Arabic and European) in many cases give them widely different positions from those determined by the observation . . .

Considering he was leading armies long before boys today start on the real 'progress to maturity', it was a remarkable achievement.

He attributed the discrepancies he discovered to the smallness of the brass instruments used by others. So he built huge instruments 'of stone and lime of perfect stability'. With these vast and, incidentally, beautiful instruments, Jai Singh made no astonishing astronomical discovery. What he did do was to provide, in an era of pillage and slaughter, the possibility of serious academic study.

Jai Singh also decided to move his capital from Amber some twelve miles to an entirely new site on the plain. There was no tradition of planned cities in north India, so the idea of building an entirely new city, according to a definite scheme, was presumably conceived by the mathematical Maharaja himself. He laid the city out on a grid pattern, originally planning to have four rectangular blocks, one of which was to be a palace. Even by 1725, which was two years before the official foundation ceremony, the number of blocks had grown to seven.

Everything was planned, down to the number of shops to be built in each bazaar. Rich merchants, invited to settle in the new city, were allowed to design their own houses, but they had to conform to certain standards and all plans had to be approved by Vidhyadhar – the chief architect employed by Jai Singh to carry out his scheme. Tod gives Vidhyadhar the whole credit for the actual design of the city, but he was probably responsible more for the detail than the concept.

It is plain that the building of Jaipur, as the city was soon known, was not just an architectural whim of a rich man. Jai Singh envisaged a city which might one day become the capital of a united Rajputana. He saw it as a centre of trade. He also wished it to be a religious focal-point.

In all these designs, the Maharaja was either rapidly or ultimately proved right. The Vaishnava Hindu sects, in particular the Gaudiya, the Ramanandi and the Balanandi, all have temples of major importance in Jaipur. The Digambar Jainas have, over the years, produced scholars and administrators there. The city rapidly attracted traders, in particular jewellers and bankers. The British Resident, in 1870, wrote that, 'Jeypore is as it were a sort of Lombard Street of Rajpootana.' Today there are 40,000 stonecutters working in Jaipur. Finally, after the creation of the Indian state of Rajasthan in 1949, Jaipur became the capital.

The building of Jaipur, surrounded by its high walls, was nearly finished in a matter of six or seven years. By that time, Jai Singh had been drawn back from artistic and scientific affairs into both local Rajputana and broader imperial problems, which called upon the more robust side of his Rajput nature.

Jai Singh's half-sister was married to Budh Singh, the ruler of Bundi, a protégé of the Jaipur Maharaja. Budh Singh had been a valiant fighter, distinguishing himself in Jai Singh's earlier campaigns against the Marathas. Later, he succumbed to the Rajput vices of drink and opium. It is perhaps not surprising that so many of them became addicted to opium as it was the Rajput custom, copied from the Afghans, to go into battle always well stoked-up with the drug. The Afghans, one year, abandoned all campaigning because of a failure of the poppy harvest.

Jai Singh's half-sister was something of a termagant, forever nagging her indolent, drink-sodden husband. He found consolation with a secondary wife, a princess from Begham. In 1720, the childless senior Rani smuggled into the zenana a baby boy which she pretended she had borne. When the child was eight, she proposed to marry him to the daughter of the Maharana of Udaipur. Budh Singh forbade this, on the grounds that the child was not his. Jai Singh declared that this was an insult to his half-sister. Why, he asked, had the child not been killed at birth if he was a bastard? Was he now repudiating the child so that a son of his second wife might succeed?

Budh Singh denied this and sent Jai Singh a cringing document in which he promised to kill the boy, to exclude any sons of his other two Ranis from the inheritance and to allow Jai Singh to choose a successor for him. This was too much for Jai Singh's half-sister, who tried to attack the Maharaja with a dagger. Budh Singh then handed over the boy to Jai Singh who had him killed. Jai Singh persuaded the Emperor, Mohammed Shah, to take Bundi state away from Budh Singh and give it to another member of the family. At this moment, Budh Singh's second wife had a son. Jai Singh demanded that this child, too, should be

39

handed over for him to kill. Budh Singh refused and plotted with Jai Singh's half-brother Bijai, who was lying in prison at Amber, to overthrow the Maharaja.

Jai Singh promptly killed Bijai and set off to do battle with Budh Singh, who was attempting to seize back his state. The resulting fight, which Budh Singh was too doped to join in, was a scene of hideous carnage, but the Maharaja's forces won. Jai Singh's half-sister then plotted with the Marathas, inviting them to capture Bundi, which, briefly, they did.

This was the first Maratha incursion into Rajputana. It was to give the Marathas ideas. Jai Singh was well aware of this and once more tried to unite the rulers of Rajputana, calling a congress at Hurda in Udaipur. The draft alliance came to nothing. As Tod put it, 'no public or general benefit ever resulted from these alliances, which were obstructed by the multitude of petty jealousies inseparable from clanship'.

It will be remembered that Jai Singh had, at the time when they were both deprived of their states by the Emperor, allied himself to Ajit Singh of Jodhpur. Later, when Jai Singh had been reconciled with the Moghuls, he arranged for the Emperor to pardon Ajit Singh for his impertinent seizure of Ajmer in 1723. All the same, Ajit Singh, at a greater distance from Delhi, remained defiant towards the Emperor. When, therefore, Ajit Singh's second son Bakht murdered his father in 1724, it was suggested, at any rate by Jodhpur chroniclers, that Jai Singh had encouraged the murder in order to install Ajit's elder son Abhai, a rather feeble and drunken man, on the Jodhpur throne, with the idea that he would be more obedient to the Emperor's and Jai Singh's wishes.

Abhai was to prove tiresome in a different manner from his father. In particular, he invaded Bikaner in 1739. Jai Singh, in alliance with Bakht (which lent credence to the theory that he was working on Jai Singh's behalf), went to the defence of Bikaner. Abhai was obliged to surrender and to submit to particularly humiliating terms exacted by Jai Singh.

The indignity of the settlement united the Jodhpur brothers. In 1741, Abhai and Bakht together advanced towards Jaipur. Jai Singh met them at Gangwana with a huge army. Bakht, at the head of 1,000 cavalrymen, charged. Jai Singh's army fell back two miles and his tents were fired and his baggage plundered.

Bakht's 1,000 men were reduced to seventy and he lost his tutelary god, Girdharji, in the charge. Bakht sent a message to Jai Singh saying that he could eat nothing cooked, without his holy image. Jai Singh, in true Rajput style, sent it back in the middle of the battle. The fight went on for two days, but the Jodhpur brothers were completely outnumbered and Jai Singh eventually won this last battle of his life.

He lived on peacefully in Jaipur until 1743. According to the Jaipur court poet, Krishna Batta, he passed his last years in devout studies of Vaishnavism. 'He spent his time gazing with adoration at the face of Govindadeva'. The Bundi court historian, Suraj Mal Mishran, writing a hundred years later, gives a very different account:

> Jai Singh gave himself up to sexual excess. He had always been a deep drinker and now the habitual use of aphrodisiacs to stimulate his failing powers entirely ruined his health till at last he died of a loathsome disease on 21st September 1743.

As we have seen, religion and sensuality are by no means mutually exclusive in India. Jai Singh had twenty-seven wives and four concubines. He had only five children who lived to maturity, three of them sons. The oldest son, Shiv, died in 1724, according to rumour poisoned by his father, but more probably of cholera. His second son, Ishwari, succeeded him. He was useless. There was perpetual civil war, due to Jai Singh's promise that he would be succeeded by any son of his Udaipur marriage. The Marathas renewed their harrassment of the Rajputs. They advanced upon Jaipur. When they were twenty miles from the city, Ishwari performed the only distinguished act of his life, committing suicide by swallowing poison and getting a cobra to bite him. Three Ranis and one concubine took poison with him and twenty-one more wives climbed on his funeral pyre as satis. For nearly a century after this, the history of Jaipur was one of muddle and often of degradation. The crumbling of the Moghul Empire meant that India was in the same kind of turmoil that Europe experienced during the Middle Ages, but by this time a new element had entered the field – the British.

After Ishwari's suicide, the Marathas installed his half-brother, Madho Singh I (Jai Singh's son by his Udaipur princess), and then started to exact tribute from Jaipur. Madho Singh was the last of the warrior Maharajas, but he lacked the force of his predecessors. He could not throw off the Marathas, but exhausted the state by his attempts to do so.

His reign was followed by a series of minorities. These were not conducive to any combining of interests among the Rajputs. The Marathas, under Mahadji Sindhia, were nearing the possibility of taking over the whole of north India. Mahadji, with the help of his remarkable French General de Boigne, so thoroughly defeated the forces of Jaipur and Jodhpur at the battle of Patan in 1790 that, had it not been for a parallel tendency for the Marathas to quarrel among themselves, Rajputana might have become lastingly subject to them. The other consideration was the British.

Jaipur's first contact with the British came about as a result of an approach made, in 1776, by the Maharaja Prithvi Singh, son and successor to Madho Singh I. He wrote to Calcutta: 'Having learnt a good deal about the uprightness and amiable qualities of the Governor-General and other English men, I am anxious to open friendly relations with them.' What he wanted was for the British to put in a good word for him at the Imperial court in Delhi. Warren Hastings replied very cordially, and advised him to patch up his quarrel with the council members in Delhi, adding that the English were well disposed to both parties.

While Warren Hastings remained, a pleasant exchange of messages of friendship with no particular object continued. After the battle of Patan, however, the Maharaja at the time, Pratap Singh, made a positive appeal to Lord Cornwallis for troops to help him against the Marathas. Cornwallis was under orders not to interfere in the affairs of Indian states. More importantly, he wanted the help of the Marathas in suppressing Tipu, Sultan of Mysore, so he allowed Mahadji Sindhia to do whatever he wanted in Rajputana.

After the death of Sindhia in 1794, Pratap Singh tried again with the British, getting Jean Pillet, a French captain in his service, to plead for a defensive and offensive treaty between the East India Company and Jaipur. He undertook to raise 50,000 cavalry which the English could call upon in return for firm protection. Sir John Shore replied that, 'a treaty offensive and defensive is out of the question'. Pratap Singh was, in any case, a poet rather than a warrior. Moreover, he inherited his grandfather's good taste, and was responsible for the building of the Hawa Mahal, the Palace of the Winds.

The coming of Marquess Wellesley altered the situation. His objective was to crush any French influence in India. To this end, he had to destroy the power of the Marathas and in order to do so, he sought the help of their enemies. He fought a vigorous campaign through the autumn of 1803, totally defeating the Sindhias. To ensure his position he made an offensive and defensive alliance with Jaipur, signed by General Lake on 12 December 1803.

Within a year, the English invoked the treaty in order to deal with the threats of Jaswant Rao Holkar. The new Maharja Jagat Singh, obligingly abandoned a little war of his own in order to assist the English.

The English at home had by this time had second thoughts. Wellesley had been recalled and Cornwallis sent out again, with orders to reverse the Marquess' aggressive policy. The English were overstretched. The promises of protection, which Wellesley had so freely made, would have needed at least twice as many British troops to fulfil if called upon. Moreover, they had war in Europe to contend with.

Cornwallis told Lake that he was not to assist Jaipur if the Marathas attacked. Lake protested. Cornwallis relented, but then died. Sir George Barlow, who took over as acting Governor-General, had no such decent scruples. In November 1805, he signed a new treaty with Sindhia giving the Marathas a free hand, and he arbitrarily and unilaterally cancelled the two-year-old treaty with the Rajput states. Lake protested again, with great anger because the supposed reason for cancelling the agreement was 'the non-performance of his part of the compact' by the Maharaja. Lake and another general both wrote to Barlow to point out that the Maharaja had suspended a march on Udaipur and joined the British forces immediately upon being asked. Sir John Malcolm, an agent in the original treaties, said this was, 'the first measure of the kind that the English have ever taken in India, and I trust in God it will be the last.' The Court of Directors in England were embarrassed, but not sufficiently so as to insist on the treaty being renewed. They feared another Maratha war. The result of the British betrayal was an influx of Pindari marauders, in loose alliance with the Marathas and Pathans.

Incidentally, the small war which Maharaja Jagat Singh was conducting in 1803 was one of the supreme examples of Rajput romantic folly.

The Udaipur princess, Krishna Kumari, was betrothed to Bhim Singh, the Maharaja of Jodhpur. In 1803, before the wedding could take place, he died. The Maharana of Udaipur then betrothed her to Maharaja Jagat Singh of Jaipur. The new Maharaja of Jodhpur decided that he should marry the princess, claiming her as part of his inheritance from Bhim Singh. 'Naturally,' as Jadunath Sarkar put it, 'war ensued between the two Rajput houses.' This 'natural' war went on for seven years. In 1810, Amir Khan, a Pathan leader who was allied to Jodhpur at the time and did not want to see his friend overpowered by Udaipur and Jaipur, proposed a solution to the Maharana. Apparently with the agreement of the girl, and certainly with the approval of her father, an aunt of the princess gave her poison. Her death ended the war to everybody's satisfaction.

By 1816, the British had come to realise that Jaipur was a necessary buffer against the possibility of a Pathan attack on Delhi. The new Governor-General, the Marquess of Hastings, also felt some sympathy with Rajputana, noting in his diary in January 1815 that:

> . . . the unfortunate Rajput states of Jaipur, Jodhpur, Udaipur, mercilessly wasted by Sindhia, Holkar, Amir Khan, Muhammad Shah Khan, and the Pindaris, have assailed me with repeated petitions to take them under protection as feudatories of the British Government.

Jagat Singh was particularly pressing in his pleas to be protected from the Pathan Amir Khan, who was massing his forces to attack Jaipur. Hastings decided to help. He posted troops to frighten Amir Khan away and enough also to warn Sindhia and Holkar. The British initially asked for an annual tribute from Jaipur of two and a half million rupees, although the full amount would be reduced for the first five years.

This demand, and the fact that Amir Khan had lifted the siege of Jaipur, caused the Maharaja to hesitate. His nobles were opposed to any surrender of sovereignty, particularly if it meant a more orderly administration of the state, which might curtail their custom of grabbing each other's land whenever an opportunity arose. But a new outbreak of Maratha intransigence sharpened Jaipur apprehensions. That, coupled with a reduction in the tribute payable to 800,000 rupees, encouraged agreement. A new treaty was signed on 2 April 1818.

Jagat Singh died the following year. He was succeeded by a posthumous son, Jai Singh III, who although he lived to be barely fifteen, left a son of sixteen months. This son became Ram Singh II. The two minorities which these events caused led to the usual chaos. Jagat Singh, amorous and feckless, had left the state pretty well insolvent; his nobles had grown too powerful, seizing crown lands and not paying their feudal dues. The British representative, Sir David Ochterlony, reduced two of the more refractory barons' forts, but the corruption and lawlessness were such that a few gestures were not enough. In June 1835, the British Resident's assistant was murdered. The British imposed firmer control, reinstating the Regent they respected and, on his death in 1838, taking over the whole administration of the state.

Ram Singh II, taken under British care so early, was to some extent a product of the new paramount power. In his own right, however, he was a ruler of distinction – cultivated, intelligent and innovative. He was, as a good Rajput must be if he is not a warrior, a fine sportsman. Especially, he enjoyed shooting and fencing.

It is true that many of the early reforms, introduced in Ram Singh's reign, must have been inspired by the British, but they worked closely with a council of local nobles. It was, for instance, the Thakur of Jhalai who in 1844 pressed strongly for the prohibition of sati. Jaipur was the first Hindu state to abolish the practice.

Slavery had been forbidden by enactment in 1839, but bondsmen and some form of household slavery continued. Again the council eradicated all forms of slavery.

The sums paid in dowries had become so outrageously high that the murder of female infants was quite common. Jai Singh II had tried to restrict dowries, but Rajput pride soon blurred the good intentions of his edicts. In 1847, strict limits were put on the amount that could be handed over as a dowry and on what might be spent on weddings.

When Ram Singh got his full powers, he set about modernising his state. The administration became broader. Ram Singh introduced departments of government, each department being given jointly to two or three councillors, so as to avoid corruption. He built schools, colleges and a hospital. He brought more water to the city and opened a gasworks.

In the last hours of his life, Ram Singh adopted Madho Singh from Isarda. The boy must have had a strange upbringing. His elder brother was another case of a boy smuggled into the zenana by a senior, barren wife, when she realised that a junior wife was pregnant. No one could prove the deception, so that the boy became the Thakur of Isarda. (He died without issue, having adopted Man Singh's father from a junior branch of the Isarda family.)

Whatever the case, Madho Singh turned out to be largely ineffectual. Although his intentions were benign and he did good work in the course of famine relief, for the most part his reign was a period of stagnation.

Ram Singh had, however, set an example which Man Singh could look upon as part of his inheritance, along with the long history of Rajput warlike ferocity, self-interest, intrigue, murder and drink; all mixed with courage, a rigid sense of caste, a devotion to religion, honour and in the case of Jaipur a sense of loyalty to their overlords.

CHAPTER 4

Jaipur had been too long sunk in a debilitating mixture of intrigue and lethargy for any sudden change. Sir Charles Cleveland, President of the Minority Council, might describe himself as a dictator, but it is plain from Amer Singh's diaries and from rather obscure references in official British documents that much went on as before. The adoption fight had left great bitterness. The betrothals had stirred up other disputes. The usual dealings about appointments went on, even without Bala Bux's taking a cut.

Madho Singh's real will had re-opened some wounds. It appointed Sir James Roberts as Man Singh's guardian. The Thakurs of Chomu and Diggi, who had opposed his adoption of Man Singh, and one or two others were not to be appointed to any post. The Cabinet should have only one Rajput in it – no more, no less. (The Rajputs themselves recognise their complete inability to agree on anything.) The Thakur of Jhalai was not to be allowed into Jaipur at all and his descendants, natural or adopted, were to be excluded from succession to the throne.

The Cabinet initially agreed to all of the late Maharaja's arrangements, except the provision about Jhalai. It is interesting, though, that the old guard still had great power. It took only a month for the cabinet to change its mind about Chomu and Diggi, who, Cleveland had said, were guilty of murder. The ban on their coming to the Palace was lifted and, by the time of Man Singh's wedding, they were both consulted.

It would seem also that the old guard managed to get rid of Cleveland very quickly. On 9 March 1923, Amer Singh wrote in his diary, 'Cleveland is finished, kicked out today'. He went on to suggest that the reason for this was that Cleveland had been accused by the Cabinet of taking bribes.

This cannot have been very probable. Patterson had written of Cleveland that he was, 'an officer of very great force of character. He has a thorough knowledge of administration, unbounded energy and great driving power. He is unquestionably, in my opinion, the mainstay of the present administration. The late Maharaja placed very great reliance on him.'

On the other hand, there are official references to lesser misdemeanours by Cleveland. One example was the allegation that he had speculated in Jaipur gold mohurs, a fair number of which had been minted on Man Singh's accession. (This was the last minting of gold coins by the Jaipur state, though silver and copper ones continued.) Cleveland apparently made a profit of 6,000 rupees out of this manoeuvre.

Madho Singh's reliance on Cleveland was questioned by one of the Maharanis, who said that Madho Singh, six months before he died, had told her that Sir Charles had been brought in for a specific purpose, now completed, and he was searching for a reason to get rid of him.

On 26 March, Amer Singh wrote that the Government had decided that Sir Charles Cleveland should work for two more months and then be sent away, 'so as not to hurt his honour'. This suspicion of a cover-up is confirmed by a letter from a Colonel Watson:

> . . . I must maintain that Cleveland's usefulness in Jaipur has been so gravely prejudiced by his indiscretions that his retention is no longer either necessary or desirable beyond whatever period is needed to demonstrate to the world Govt's belief in his personal honesty.

Cleveland must have been difficult, because the benign Raj Rana of Dhrangadhra as well as, more predictably, Bala Bux's friend and another all threatened to resign if Sir Charles came again to Cabinet meetings. He came and they resigned. In any event, Cleveland did leave in May and was replaced by Mr R.I. Glancy. The old guard, incidentally, also got rid of Dhrangadhra not long afterwards.

There was one area in which the British were determined not to be thwarted and that was in the matter of the young Maharaja's education. Within a week of Madho Singh's death, Sir James Roberts wrote a long memorandum, setting out his views as to what should be done. He and Cleveland had had lengthy discussions with Madho Singh on the subject and the memorandum wavers between a respect for the old man's views and his own contradictory notions about the matter.

In 1910, Madho Singh had contributed to a survey of princely views as to how minority administrations should be conducted. He had written two long paragraphs on the question of the education of a minor prince. 'I consider the deputation of a European officer as Guardian an undesirable thing.'

Sir James could very reasonably suggest that the Maharaja had obviously changed his mind about this, otherwise how could he have nominated Sir James in his will. Harder to overcome were the Maharaja's repeated statements to him and Cleveland that:

> . . . the constant companionship of a European officer . . .
> engenders in him [i.e. the young Prince] not only loss
> of faith in the religious practices of his ancestors, but
> makes him sceptical of the very doctrines of his religion
> – a result deplorable in the extreme.

Sir James proposed that the late Maharaja Ram Singh's brother-in-law, Thakur Bahadur Singh, should, 'instruct the young Maharaja in all the usages, customs and traditions of his house and State, and further foster a respect for the religion of his ancestors and instill a knowledge of its practices.' At the same time, a Colonel Watson was to supervise his education in other fields, particularly exercise.

Sir James did not like the idea of the boy living in the City Palace, but this, of course, was what the conservative element among the nobles wanted and what Madho Singh would have wished. So Sir James had a lot to say about the influences which needed to be counteracted if Man Singh was to stay in the zenana.

Physical education . . . meets with the approval of all . . .
by means of exercises, games, horsemanship, and sport
it is necessary to make a man of the young Maharaja . . .
With this question is to be considered that of his too
intimate association with the Zenana . . . we can
counteract it by occupying his time fully by plenty of
work, physical and mental, and by warning him
against the unmanly influence of being too much
associated with women. From his position and
surroundings the young Prince is destined for much
sexual experience, but it is important to remember it is
better to guide this after puberty rather than to repress
it, the latter means the introduction of intrigues and
depravities of the worst description, and opens the
door to the machinations of unscrupulous blackguards.
We must trust to counteract these by the healthy life of
exercise and sport he will lead, and to the guidance of
Thakur Bahadur Singh.

At this point, Sir James' medical training and progressive
common sense overcame his bluff conventionality, thereby
guaranteeing his memorandum a not very sympathetic
reception:

Further I have seen such terrible examples of young
Princes ruined by the early infection of venereal
diseases, that I would seriously recommend his
association when about 15 years of age with a healthy
young girl, and that in moderation; rather than that he
should contract venereal disease, and unnamable vices.

Despite Sir James' assertion that this was a customary arrangement for young chiefs, this was not well received by the
authorities, who, in view of this recommendation, felt, 'doubt
as to whether his [Sir James'] advice on the matter would be
worth having'.

Sir James thought the boy's companions should be selected
for him from noble boys not 'much older than His Highness,
lest the elder one should corrupt the younger'. Too great
familiarity with servants should be discouraged, for they

were inclined to debauch and vitiate the ideas of a young Prince. At the same time, Sir James agreed that Man Singh should not go to a Chiefs' College, as the late Maharaja had expressly opposed this possibility.

How all Sir James' ideas for the protection of the young Maharaja were to be implemented if he was to continue to live in the Palace was not clear. Sir James, it may be thought, was a typical example of the inherent contradiction in the British attitude to their relationship with the princely states. They told themselves and each other that their role was one of non-interference, unless there arose a positive threat to the security of British India, but they were unable to resist giving what they saw as helpful direction. Sir James wrote in another letter:

> It should not be forgotten that modern changes need not be forced, for they come along of themselves, and it is to be remembered that the rulers of Jaipur, while retaining the ancient traditions, have pushed themselves and their families along the path of modern education. The Jaipur of today is not the Jaipur of 40 years ago and it should be left to the Maharaja and his people to make their own advance, in their own way, and in their own fashion.

Of course, the nobles had done nothing of the sort. Ram Singh had pushed them along but, as soon as he was dead, they had relapsed into their traditional concerns of advancing their individual interests, which had nothing to do with education. This, to a certain extent, suited the British, who had no desire to see the princely states progress too rapidly in a direction which might cause them to challenge British ascendancy. Let them go at their own pace, while Delhi and London could pride themselves on their abstention from interference.

Curzon, in a description of Madho Singh, summed up the British attitude with precision:

> He is one of the old-fashioned class of Princes whom I do everything in my power to encourage –

conservative, reluctant to move away from their own States, liberal in the distribution of their funds, intensely loyal to the Queen and the British connection, averse to being too much bothered or fussed, but capable, if skilfully and sympathetically handled, of being guided where we will.

However, the education of a Prince was a serious business. Princes must be loyal, obedient and preferably of reasonably restrained character. In serious matters, it somehow happened that the non-interfering British got their own way. And so it was to be in the question of Man Singh's upbringing.

A month after the Maharaja's death, Sir James started a school at the Rambagh Palace, about two miles outside the city walls. There were twenty-three boys of good family; Sir James himself did most of the teaching. Holland reported that the young Maharaja was said to be keen on his lessons, but even keener on riding:

> Although far more bloated than a boy of his age ought to be and a sad contrast to his slim elder brother, he is already a different person to the pallid, sheepish youth whom I saw a month ago, and there is good hope of his regaining his normal shape under the present regime.

The few surviving members of the class remember little about it, but it must have been extremely English, the boys even played grandmother's steps under Sir James' direction. The physical side was quite tough. The children were allowed no saddles, but learned to ride bareback. The new regime did so much good to the sheepish youth and his colleagues that reports suggested that the boys were getting out of hand. It was at this moment that Mr Mayne, the tutor, was sent for from Rajkot College. He was given the title of Deputy Guardian, but soon took over from Roberts, who became adviser rather than guardian; he was, in any case, retiring to England. Mayne cut the numbers of the class from twenty-three to six and the school carried on in a more orderly fashion for some months.

During the crisis about Cleveland, which must have been

more disturbing than either official papers or Amer Singh's diaries reveal, the Cabinet decided to take Man Singh away to Mount Abu, the Rajputana hill-station, for his safety.

In March, five days after Amer Singh had written that Cleveland was finished, the Jaipur cabinet sent a memorandum to the British authorities seeking advice about the boy's education.

The Cabinet also consulted Sir James Roberts, who replied by memorandum in May. He reiterated the fact that Madho Singh had always wanted the boy to be educated in Jaipur. Sir James had planned to do this and to educate with Man Singh, 'a number of his contemporaries among the nobles, with a view of their becoming his supporters in State matters in after life'.

The recent crisis when the Maharaja was removed to Mount Abu, 'served to open one's eyes to the danger with which he is surrounded, and it is impossible for some years to expect the administration to become an efficient and smooth working machine not torn by factions, plots or dissensions, I come to the conclusion . . . that for the present the young Maharaja should reside out of Jaipur.' Mayo College seemed to be the answer.

Sir James went on to suggest the six boys of his class going as well:

> . . . and as many others as can be induced to go. I have a sufficient knowledge of His Highness' character to be able to say, that he is a boy particularly strong in his friendships and attachments, and is also of so open a nature, that he would not carry school-boy pique into future official relations.
>
> His late Highness knowing Jaipur well was very loath that the Maharaj Kumar should leave the Palace, and we now understand the wisdom of his instincts. With our task of education and training before us, we feel we cannot keep him a prisoner in the palace, as his safety might require, so we must perforce take the other course and send him outside the State to the Mayo College.

From the strength of that paragraph, it might be thought

that there had been some sort of attempt on the Prince's life or, at least, the discovery of some plot to kill him. There are no records of anything of the kind and such few people as might remember are too inhibited by a keen sense of discretion about the former ruling family to reveal it.

In any case, the view prevailed that Man Singh should be sent to Mayo. Even the ladies in the Palace were in agreement. The lady whose view was most important was Dadiji Sahib III Rathoreji, one of Ram Singh's widows, who corresponded with the British about the matter and whose opinions they always tried to respect. So, with his six companions, the boy went to boarding school.

Mayo College was an extraordinary institution, founded by Lord Elgin in the nineteenth century for the education of the Princes and nobles of all the twenty-one princely states of Rajputana. It was built a few miles outside the town of Ajmer. The main part of the school consists of two enormous blocks, built of marble in a florid Indo-Victorian style. The grounds of the College, surrounded by a wall, cover several hundred acres. Each state had a house for its boys to live in, but actual rulers lived in separate houses of their own. Thus Man Singh did not live in Jaipur House, a hideous striped construction of alternate red and white sandstones, but in what is now Bharatpur House, a smaller, but just as gloomy, grey stone building.

The school was run very much on the lines of a British public school, with the considerable differences that the boys were allowed to bring servants to look after them and syces to care for their horses. Only about twenty of the two hundred boys could afford horses, but the young Maharaja lived in luxurious style. Mr Mayne, the tutor, went with him, as well as plenty of servants and nine syces. There was also an Indian tutor to coach him in Indian subjects.

The spirit of the college, certainly in Man Singh's time, was informed by the Rajput love of splendour and ostentation. When Lady Willingdon, the wife of the Viceroy, came to give away the prizes one year, it was known that her favourite colour was mauve. Everything was accordingly decorated in mauve. Mauve carpets were laid and all the boys wore mauve turbans.

54

Mr Mayne appears to have grown extremely fond of the boy and it must have been his suggestion that Man Singh should be sent to England. Together they discussed the possibility with the Viceroy. Man Singh was himself disinclined to go, until it was explained to him that he could go as a day boy and live with Mayne and his family. It was agreed that, were he to go, Mayne must go with him, as Man Singh knew his family well and his homesickness would be less with their company.

More lay behind this proposal than just the question of education. At the end of 1926, Patterson wrote to the Political Secretary in Delhi, saying that he was very much against the sending of any young Princes to England, including Man Singh. He went on:

> A boy must be taught religion and a Prince must be taught and kept in touch with the religion of his State and his people. If therefore there were not peculiar circumstances in this case I would unhesitatingly most strongly oppose the present proposal. But there are unfortunately peculiar circumstances. I mean of course the marriage. I need not dilate on this. I merely say that I share Cater's apprehension that 'given the opportunity there will come the one fatal lapse which will undo all the good years of careful training and guardianship. Alcohol is a far greater curse in Rajputana than opium.'

What they were worried about was the influence of the Maharani, who they believed drank.

Evidence of this has not survived. Equally possible as a reason for the British desire to send the boy to England was their perpetual worry about his sex life. Amer Singh, in September 1925, had had a chat with Mrs Patterson. She had said she felt sorry for Man Singh's wife – 'the girl ought to have someone educated enough with whom she could read, talk and play badminton'. Amer Singh had suggested croquet as well. He went on to suggest that the Lallji's wives also came from Jodhpur and could amuse her. Mrs Patterson said they were not educated enough.

55

It hardly sounds as if they were talking about an alcoholic, though, if she were lonely, drink might well have been a consolation for a bored woman in the confines of the zenana.

Mrs Patterson must have revealed to Amer Singh that the Maharani was not allowed to see Man Singh alone. Whenever he was allowed to visit her, an Englishwoman had to go with him. Amer Singh thought this unfair. 'It is true,' he noted, 'that the Maharaja is a boy and should not be allowed to live with her. But it is wrong to send a European lady with him.' Man Singh was at this moment just fourteen.

Anyhow, Patterson, fifteen months later, recommended that the British wait another year and then send Man Singh to England for eighteen months, not to a school but for private tuition while living with a family. During that time, he could travel in England and possibly on the Continent. Meanwhile, Man Singh should spend as little as possible of his holidays in Jaipur.

With this letter to Delhi, Patterson forwarded a letter from the Maharani. He wisely observed that her views could not be ridden over 'roughshod'.

Man Singh's wife had heard of the plan to send him to England and she wrote a forceful protest based on several objections. First, the late Maharaja had stipulated that Jai should be educated in Jaipur. The British had already gone against this by sending him to Mayo. Secondly, she referred to the caste objection to foreign travel. She reminded the authorities of the elaborate and costly arrangements which Madho Singh had made, taking water and earth on his visit to England, in order to maintain the traditions and observances of the Jaipur royal family. Thirdly, the family and the public would not like his going. For good measure, she added that her brother, the Maharaja of Jodhpur, would not like it either.

The Maharani appeared to think that Man Singh was being forced to go, possibly by Mayne, very much against his inclinations. There may have been something in this. The British did not allow Man Singh to mix much with any locals other than the ones they selected. Amer Singh records only one informal meeting with him during this period. He had been to Man Singh's apartments in the Rambagh Palace.

Madho Singh II with his Council of Ministers and two of his favourite sons by concubines – Gangaji and Gopal Singh.

An artist's impression of the dream that prompted Madho Singh II to adopt Mor Mukut of Isarda as his heir. Isarda is on the right; the City Palace, with Madho Singh standing on an upper balcony, is on the left; and in the centre the deity, Shri Gangaji, carries Mor Mukut to his new father.

(*above*) Madho Singh II at Jaipur railway station. The railway was narrow gauge (*Popperfoto*).

(*left and right*) Jai, at the age of twelve, at Scouts Camp in Dharbanga.

Jai (seated on the desk) with Mr J.W.C. Mayne, his tutor, and Bahadur (right) his brother.

Jai with his first tiger.

There were only two pictures on the wall, one of Raja Man Singh, Akbar's general, the other of Sawai Jai Singh, the builder of Jaipur. Amer Singh asked Man Singh which he considered to be the better man. Jai said:

'Sawai Jai Singh.'
'Why, sir?'
'Because Man Singh followed the lead of the Rathors [the Jodhpur family] and gave his daughter to the Moghuls.'

Following this rather prim reply, Man Singh added that he was afraid that the lead of the Rathors would again be followed. By this he meant that the Maharaja had taken his Maharani to England. Obviously the Thakur Bahadur Singh had instilled into the boy the rigid precepts of the Rajputs. So it may well have been that he was reluctant to go abroad.

Reynolds, the Agent to the Governor-General, was also against Jai's going. 'Education in England among all classes of Indians tends to develop anti-British feelings,' he wrote. He, too, was nervous of public reaction. He feared that the local people would 'regard it as the final step in a deliberate design to anglicize the Maharaja.' He was also seriously worried that the Maharani might demand to go with him.

In the end, Man Singh stayed at Mayo College until April 1929.

Nevertheless, there were many upsets of one sort or another. The Maharani must have been sent back to Jodhpur at some time in 1927, or she may have gone for a long stay. The records speak of her two visits to Jaipur.

In May 1927, the Political Secretary in Delhi wrote to Reynolds, saying that he had heard disturbing rumours about the Maharaja and his wife. She was said to have 'got hold of him', given him wine to drink and slept with him. Now, she was expecting a baby. The rumours further had it that the baby will not be the Maharaja's but probably a kamdar's (land agent) of the Maharaja of Jodhpur, who had just been imprisoned for allegedly having had a liaison with Man Singh's wife.

How the rumour-mongers could be so confident of the

paternity is not clear. Mayne was sure there was no truth in the story, particularly as on the Maharani's two visits she and Jai had only been together for twenty minutes – although once inside the zenana, Reynolds gloomily observed, 'it is impossible to check'. Presumably, by this time, the watchdog English lady had been withdrawn.

The British, one might have thought, should have learnt by this time to distinguish between fact and Indian fantasy or plotting. Reynolds, indeed, did suggest in his reply to Delhi that the Political Secretary's informant might be tainted and implied that these tales emanated from the relations of Man Singh's now eleven-year-old fiancée. Their object would be to discredit the Maharani and thereby prevent her giving birth to an heir to the throne before the younger girl was of an age to produce one. Reynolds' view was reinforced by the fact that the kamdar in question had been in prison for fifteen months and so could not be the father of the baby; and, later, even more by there being no baby at all.

In July 1927, Mayne left, to be replaced as guardian by Colonel H. Twiss. Mayne wrote a letter to Man Singh from Bombay on 10 July, just before he sailed for England. It is one of the very few direct clues we have as to the tone adopted by the British in their upbringing of Jai and to the charm of the boy himself, so it is reproduced nearly in full:

My very dear Man Singh,
    You will get this letter after we have left you. Leaving you is just like leaving a son and we shall miss you terribly. But, please God, we shall meet again before very long.
    I am sure that no guardian ever had a nicer ward than I have had. You have never resented anything that I have done in my efforts to guide you and my wife and I are very proud of you. We shall be a long way apart now but distance is nothing to heart and mind and we shall often be together in spirit: for we shall often think and talk of you and Jaipur, and I feel you will do so of us.
    If you really understand 'Noblesse oblige' I have no

58

fears for you – this and 'Ich dien' ('I serve'), the Prince of Wales's motto.

I am glad to say that you are 'princely' in many ways already – e.g. in your kindness to others, especially those lower than yourself and those less fortunate than you – this quality will make you beloved. Be 'princely' also in giving, *for giving is far better than taking*. The lame man at Abu will always bless you. Be 'princely' towards your Riaza by protecting them and having no mercy on those Nazims and Tehsitrars who rob and oppress them. This will make you beloved, and a Maharaja who has not the love of his subjects is like an egg without a yolk or a ship without a rudder. Think well on this. (A ship without a rudder will soon be wrecked.)

You have been very kind to our children and they love you . . .

You are already ' princely' in your dignity and bearing: it is good for a prince to be a big man, I think. Think of your state a little daily & more & more as you get older. If you see anything you don't like speak to the President about it when you see him. He will think all the more of you if he sees you interested.

Don't forget your prayers. I fear we all do this sometimes. I have always told you that Parameshwar has made you Maharaja of Jaipur: it was not just chance that took you away from Isarda. I am sure of this. And it was not just chance that sent me to be your guardian. This is a very sublime thought and like 'Noblesse oblige' will help you greatly. Col. Twiss will look after you well, I know. Trust him & continue to trust other real friends . . . We shall never forget you. God bless you and may he make you just the Ruler that Jaipur wants.

Yours ever affectionately,

C. Mayne.

It was a simple approach to kingship and a simple faith that inspired Mayne. Colonel Twiss proved to be a more vigorous figure who was soon known to Man Singh as Uncle Horace.

British worries about the Maharani and Man Singh's sensual nature, which was beginning to become apparent, did not abate. Reynolds wrote to the Political Secretary again in August, agreeing that if Man Singh were to go to England it should not be until he was over sixteen. (He seems not to have realised that Man Singh had just had his sixteenth birthday.) He thought that the boy should be prevented from co-habiting with his wife until he was seventeen, which meant keeping him out of Jaipur. This, in one regard, he thought was a pity. Were it not for the Maharani's propensity to drink, it would be a good idea for them to live together, as the young Maharaja was showing a regrettable interest in boys.

At the end of Jai's time at Mayo, the Principal wrote:

> His development from a fat little boy to a big athletic young man is as much a testimony to his inherent good qualities as to the system under which he has been brought up. He was never brilliant at his school work, but at subjects in which he was interested he showed himself quick brained and intelligent.

The Principal praised his skill at games and his horsemanship. As a monitor he had lacked initiative, but was capable of exercising authority. The major criticism of Jai was that he was very susceptible to the influence of others, so that he predicted that his immediate companions would have a direct bearing on his behaviour and outlook on life. The Principal ended by saying that the whole college would miss him and, 'I myself will miss his cheery personality.'

By now, Man Singh was nearly eighteen. The British had calmed down about his marriage, Colonel Twiss had allowed him to stay with his wife for the last year once a fortnight. The Maharani gave birth to a daughter two months after he had left school. They had also managed to agree that he should go to England for a year's training at the Royal Military Academy at Woolwich.

Man Singh sailed from Bombay in July, with his elder brother, Bahadur, and Colonel Twiss. Bahadur must have made a great difference on this alarming journey; he was always mischievous, rather hopeless and completely un-resentful of his younger brother's elevation. He was fond of practical jokes and had on one occasion caused dreadful consternation at the Mount Abu Club. Some grand British official was put up for election. In the morning of the committee meeting, Bahadur slipped a black ball into the voting box. An immense scandal ensued, until Bahadur merrily confessed.

All the same Man Singh was apprehensive. It was at this time that he started to write to a young friend, Man Singh of Barwara, a correspondence which was to continue all his life. It is the only set of letters which anyone has been able to provide. The Raja of Barwara's widow says that Man Singh first met his namesake when the boy was about thirteen and he was seventeen. The Maharaja's train had stopped at a station near Barwara and the boy was on the platform with his family, waiting to present nazars to the young ruler. He was so taken with the young Man Singh that he insisted on his coming with him to Jaipur. It seems an extravagant story but certainly Man Singh became very fond of him. He nicknamed him Rabbit and his first letter to him was written from the SS *Maloja* on 24 July:

> My Dear Baby,
> It was sad saying good-bye to you in Jaipur. I do
> wish you could have come with me but never mind you
> will be able to do that in the future.
> We saw no land for four days which was rather
> awful. We reach Aden tomorrow . . .
> I hope you are working hard at your studies.
> With best wishes
> Yours ever
> Man Singh

Quite quickly Jai acclimatised to his new life. By the end of October he was writing from Woolwich:

> My dear Baby,
> . . . I am having quite good fun here Baby, I do lots of
> dancing. I will teach you that when I come back . . .

61

And a fortnight later:

> . . . I wish baby you were here with me to enjoy
> London life. You must see London one day. It is a
> simply charming place . . .

Released from the formalities and the intrigues of Jaipur, Man Singh was discovering 'fun'. It was to be a word which recurred again and again over the years. Life from now on was to be divided into two separate existences – responsibilities in India; 'fun' abroad.

It was in England that Man Singh came to be called Jai by his friends. For simplicity's sake, we will from now on use that name, which remained with him till he died.

Jaipur, in the seven years since Jai had become Maharaja, had not changed all that much. The flavour of the place was still medieval. There were many leftovers from Madho Singh's time when, as Roberts put it, 'his every word and wish was law'.

The Maharaja's water was drawn from a special well outside the walls of the city. Four men carried it and a troop of soldiers guarded it on its way to the Palace. Passers-by had to put down their umbrellas in case any shadow should fall on the water. All traffic stopped. This custom continued well into the 1930s.

From Amer Singh's diaries, it appears that court life, and that was the only life that counted, continued as before, with its eternal jockeying for favour and position, with the same jealousies over inheritance, with the perpetual wrangles over betrothals and adoptions.

There was much violence. Amer Singh refers quite often to the continuing practice of killing infant daughters, especially in the rural villages. Amer Singh came home one day to find his brother wrestling with a panther. Before doing so, his brother had drawn all the panther's claws and stitched its lips together. He then set the elephants to trample the creature to death, in order to teach them how to deal with a panther if attacked on a shoot. Amer Singh was mildly shocked. The Thakurs regarded themselves as being above the law, which was to some extent the case. The senior

Tazimi Sardars could not be forced to appear in court.

Devi Singh of Chitora was said to have killed a number of men in a hideous manner but no charges were brought against him. It must have been a grisly case, as even today Chitora is another name which old people, superstitiously inclined, do not like to pronounce. One may wonder why the British did nothing about cases of this sort. Amer Singh maintains that a Mr Coventry was bribed 10,000 rupees to suppress this one. The British were certainly not above suspicion, as we have seen, but there is a feeling, perhaps, that many officials, most particularly in the princely states, whether from snobbery or atavistic and romantic feudal leanings (many of them were younger sons of old British families), somehow adjusted to what one might have expected to be their attitudes to a more Indian and particularly Rajput point of view. It is often reflected in their flowery style of writing and choice of metaphor.

Mr Coventry, as it happens, may have had reasons other than bribery to keep quiet. His wife was a woman of generous affections, who was said to persuade good-looking Indian men to sleep with her by promising them advancement in their careers. Silence about murders might easily have been exchanged for silence about Mrs Coventry's affairs. Fortunately, Coventry got a job at the Turf Club in Bombay and they left Jaipur.

It must also be remembered that, at this time, the majority of Jagidars and even Sardars were illiterate. (In 1921, only 12.4 per cent of the population of Jaipur city were literate.) Reynolds, the President of the Council in 1924, said that there were only three noble families which had any serious agricultural programme on their jagirs; curiously enough, Chitora was one, Chomu another. The third was Amer Singh himself. Both of these points had their origin in the principles of the Rajput ethic. There is a proverb: 'The Rajput disdains the plough.' Another says: 'A Rajput who reads will never ride a horse.' Reynolds also commented on the number of people who were paid for doing nothing.

Theirs was still an unsophisticated society, where the ideals were military valour and honour. Since 1835, they had not had any wars to fight, but honour can take many forms.

63

The sort of point which would be discussed and argued about for literally weeks was the question as to who had the right to drive up to the front door of the Residency and who must alight at the gate and walk the last fifty yards.

While the Maharaja's every word and wish might not be law, the obedience to the royal family was, to European eyes, remarkable. Amer Singh recorded, while Jai was at Woolwich, that:

> Devi Singh's coachman had not stopped his carriage when told to, at a time when the Maharani Sahib was walking in the Transport gardens. The result was that he [Devi Singh] was sent to Rambagh and made to stand in the sun for two hours.

In a way, this all suited the British. Provided that nothing too outlandish happened, they were happy to let progress come slowly. As one Political Secretary told Amer Singh, they were against introducing too many reforms in the administration of a state that had been run on old lines for a long time.

The old Maharaja's will had made it virtually impossible to administer Jaipur on any lines, old or new. He had laid down that there should be both a Cabinet and a Council, the former could only deal with the heads of departments through the latter. As Patterson put it: 'The Council is in fact the fifth wheel of the coach.' Something had to be done and it goes without saying, despite Amer Singh's Political Secretary, that there were many conscientious British officials who were anxious to improve the state they worked for to the highest possible level.

The minority administration did have a record of moderate achievement. In 1925, the British abolished the Cabinet and left the Council of State, with a President and six members, each responsible for different departments, as the sole executive authority of the state.

So much in Jaipur city had declined, or at best stagnated, under Madho Singh's rule. Even the population of the city had dropped by 40,000 between 1901 and 1921. More people died every year than were born; immigration, which might have made up for this, dwindled steadily. There had been grievous famines. Pierre Loti, visiting Jaipur at the beginning of the century, wrote of 'horrible heaps of rags and bones lying on the pavements' which turned out to be peasants, who had dragged themselves into the city in the hope of finding food. Plague had come to Jaipur in 1903. Nearly 5,000 people died of plague in 1910 and it killed more than 1,000 in 1918. Cholera claimed six or seven hundred people a year. On average, 2,600 people a year died of 'fever'. This meant primarily malaria, but included typhoid and tuber-culosis.

Health did improve in the decade during which the state was under British control. The death rate dropped from more than forty-eight per thousand per annum to fewer than thirty-eight per thousand. No major hospital was opened or started in their time, though a separate, small hospital for women was opened in 1931, staffed at first by the Scottish Mission.

The most important undertaking of the Public Works Department was the improvement of the water supply. The British enlarged the irrigation dam at Ramgarh, about twenty miles from Jaipur, vastly increasing the size of the lake there. They built a filtration plant and a pipeline to the city. (This achievement was deemed important enough for the opening of the works to be coupled with the investiture of the Maharaja with his full powers.)

In 1923, the Council decided to replace Ram Singh's gas works by electricity. In 1927, the 'electric works' were officially opened. According to Amer Singh, 'nearly everyone who is anyone was present. The Maharaja pressed a button and the whole place was lighted up.' (Evidently it worked better then that it does sixty years later.)

Various other administrative reorganisations were insti-tuted. No systems of accounts or budgeting had existed in Jaipur. The Revenue Department initiated these. There was no codified system of legal procedure, either civil or crimi-nal. The Council, early on, appointed a special Law Officer to regularise all proceedings. The police force of the old state was originally divided into four separate quarrelsome divi-sions. They were known to be both corrupt and brutal. The force was reorganised into a single unit. The army, too, was reshaped. Certainly the British brought Jaipur out of the middle ages, symbolised by the opening of the city gates at night. The gates used to be shut irrevocably at eleven at night and would not open for anyone before daybreak. (It was remarkably inconvenient for anyone either arriving or leaving by train between those hours.) The second, more important step, in 1928, was the conversion of the Jagirdars' feudal duty to provide either horses or men for state service into a straightforward cash payment.

It is worth noting that by comparison with these sound administrative and economic arrangements, little was done for the advancement of the people. As a simple example, the percentage of literate people in Jaipur, which we noticed in 1921 was 12.4, rose in the ten years of British supervision to only 13.3. It was to rise in the following ten years to 20.2.

What the British liked to see in a princely state was a pliant Maharaja, a soundly-run government and a placid, old-fashioned peasantry with no great knowledge of any other kind of existence. This they achieved in Jaipur.

From Amer Singh we learn about the influence of the Maharani, who, being much older than her husband and a woman of strong opinion, used the traditional power of the women of the zenana to affect events. In 1927, the police were attempting to stop gambling in the city. In the course of this campaign, they had a fight with a tonga driver which sparked off riots and a strike. The shopkeepers refused to open their shops and the disturbances lasted for more than a week. Jai's wife went on a hunger strike in sympathy with the people. She summoned several of the officials and tried to insist that Jai be brought from Mayo College and be given the full powers of a Maharaja. Amer Singh was of the opinion that the Maharani's protest had as much to do with the fact that she was still, at that time, not allowed to live with her husband as with the plight of the citizens.

Amer Singh himself had difficulties with the Maharani. On one occasion, she summoned him to the Palace. The system for communicating with ladies in purdah in the zenana was for a man to go to an entrance, known as the deodhi, and either a eunuch or a veiled woman servant would come to him with messages. He would reply and the messenger would run up the stairs to report to the lady and run back with her answer, or her next question. On this occasion, Amer Singh noted:

> I had to wait for a few minutes when I was called up at the deodhi where a woman messenger told me that my respects had been paid to the Maharani Sahib and she wanted to know why I never came to her when all the other Sardars did. Was I ashamed to come . . .?

Amer Singh was by nature cautious in his dealings with royalty and was also unusually unpushing in comparison with most other Rajputs, so he had kept away. He described his reply:

> If I were ashamed to come here, where would I go then? She was the daughter of Maharaja Sardar Singhji [of Jodhpur] and consequently my master. Then she was the Maharani of Jaipur. Thus she had two rights on me. I could not in any way be ashamed of coming to her but I certainly was frightened. This fright was only for a short time until the Maharaja got his powers.

(The 'two rights' arose because Amer Singh's family came from Jodhpur and so belonged to the Rathor clan rather than the Kachhawas.)

It turned out that what the Maharani wanted was promotion for a protégé of hers in the Jaipur Lancers, which Amer Singh commanded. Such promotions were not entirely in his hands, having to be approved by the Military Member of the Council, with whom Amer Singh was often at odds.

He replied through the woman messenger that he had already recommended the young man for promotion but that, if Her Highness wanted to hurry things up, she could send word to the Military Member. After that, 'the usual plate of cardomoms and betel nuts' was sent down to him to signify the end of the interview. It was, of course, exactly the sort of situation that the straightforward Amer Singh most disliked. Everyone always knew everyone else's business.

The Military Member would certainly hear that Amer Singh had been to the Maharani. When he received word from her about the young man's promotion, he would naturally assume that Amer Singh was using the Maharani to get approval for his recommendation. It is no wonder that Amer Singh avoided the Palace and its constant intrigues.

The unfortunate Thakur of Jhalai, having been deprived, rightly or wrongly, of the possibility of the throne, applied to the Council to be allowed to nominate his brother as his successor to the jagir. He had no children of his own. In return, he offered to obtain from the Nawab of Tonk some villages which the Nawab had confiscated from the Thakur of Isarda's father – Tonk being near Isarda. On getting possession of the villages, he would give them to the Thakur. In view of the adoption battle, this seems to have been a singularly generous gesture.

Mr Glancy talked to Jhalai and told him that he, Chomu and Diggi had a large number of enemies 'lurking in the grass like snakes'. Glancy did not want, he said, these enemies to have the chance later of telling the Maharaja that Jhalai had rushed his nomination through during the minority in case Jai would not have agreed to it.

During this period, Jai had very little power. He was, however, able to arrange that his schoolfriend, Parbat Singh, who came from Jodhpur, should be taken into the newly-formed Jaipur Lancers, contrary to the rules of enlistment. Amer Singh talks of his being consulted about the siting of a new polo ground and complains of the long delays in hearing from the Maharaja about what colours he wanted the Lancers' polo team to wear.

When he was in Jaipur, his time, apart from formal functions, was largely taken up with sport. In January 1926, he was taken on his first tiger shoot. Four tigers escaped and Jai spared a young one that he could have shot. But, in May, he shot a big one and it is a measure of the importance attached to sport by Rajputs that Amer Singh and others that evening presented nazars to Jai in honour of the occasion.

The most important skill, of course, was riding. Amer Singh did not have a very great regard for Jai's proficiency:

I said that he would certainly be a very good player [of polo] but it was a great pity he was not a good horseman . . . he rides and gallops as hard as anyone, but what he misses is the fine art of horsemanship . . . he [Mr Glancy] said that he quite understood what I meant, but with a rich man like him it would not matter much as he could afford to buy the best-trained ponies.

And Mr Reynolds had said that, when Jai came to power, he would 'have so much money on hand that he could not get through it if he spent it reasonably'.

Jai stayed for exactly a year at Woolwich. Quite early on, Colonel Twiss wrote to say that the young Maharaja was doing very well, 'far better than he realises himself – and is a great credit to Rajputana'. Jai came to life as never before. While he may have been 'cheery' at Mayo, at Woolwich he was truly happy.

The military uniforms, parades, medals, everything to do with the army, fascinated Jai. He always maintained that, had he not been a Maharaja, he would have joined the army. In addition, he had the amusements of London.

He was an extremely good-looking young man, not particularly tall, but now thin and well-proportioned. Despite his athletic strength, he had a gentleness which certainly appealed to young English girls, who were more accustomed to young officers being rough and insensitive, red-faced and raucous. Furthermore, he was a Maharaja. Soon after his arrival in England, he got in touch with the remarkably beautiful and frolicsome widow of the Maharaja of Cooch Behar. She introduced him to the racier element of the British aristocracy. In no time, he was to be seen at the parties of those smart, international, sporting people whose names filled the gossip columns of the newspapers of London, Paris and New York. His taste in friends was always to be for the glossier rich. At the same time, he was wholly without real snobbery. Throughout his life, he would have the engaging habit of asking literally anybody he chanced to meet, on a train or in a shop or wherever, to come to his house, seemingly quite unconscious of how they would mix with his more glamorous friends.

So agreeable did Jai find life in England that he proposed being attached to a cavalry regiment for more training in the summer of 1931. This idea produced a sharp reaction from India. Reynolds, the Agent to the Governor-General, wrote to Delhi, making strong objections. In the first place, it would mean postponing Jai's being vested with his full powers, which was provisionally planned for the spring of 1931. In any case, he questioned the value of any further military training. 'The object is to produce a good ruler not a cavalry officer and it is more likely that association with a wealthy cavalry regiment in England will develop tastes not altogether consistent with the qualities required for the ruler of a state like Jaipur.' Reynolds, in his innocence, further reported that he had heard rumours that Jai was taking dancing lessons. He concluded that the Maharaja should return to India in September and devote himself to important administrative training until he received his powers.

That was what happened. The Commandant at Woolwich wrote to say that the Maharaja's time at the Academy had been very satisfactory. 'He has identified himself closely with the life of the place and has taken part in all the activities. He has been very popular . . .'

The British, as usual, dithered about what form his training should take. They thought of sending him for two months to a British Indian district and for a month to his uncle's state of Kota. In the end, they concluded that he should spend all six months before his investiture in Jaipur itself, learning the work of each of the six departments.

On his return, Jai settled down quite easily. He was pleased to see Rabbit again, although the boy, who was by now at Mayo College, had to return to school almost at once. Jai wrote to him from Rambagh Palace in October.

My dear Rabbit,
    Thank you ever so much for your letter and the College magazine. I miss you very much Rabbit.
    There is nobody now to take off my clothes and rest in the afternoons.
    I am sending you a horse called Nabak . . .

70

I hope you are working hard. You must do well in the Xmas exams otherwise I shall beat you.

All the family and Sahib and Miss Sahib send their salaams to you. Miss Sahib often asks about you!

With lots of love from Jai.

(Sahib and Miss Sahib were Colonel Twiss and his daughter.)

After England, with only one soldier servant, it was plain that Jai had slipped back easily into the way of being waited on and into that very Indian characteristic of accepting what Europeans would regard as rather intimate services from friends. It is interesting that he gave the boy a horse, because he already had something of a reputation for meanness, a characteristic he was supposed to have inherited from his father.

Amer Singh made a note in his diary about the Maharaja's being:

> . . . not over fond of spending money or rather giving things away. Bharon Singh had asked him by letter to bring him a pair of Holland and Holland guns hoping that if he brought them he would give them as a present and when he was taking them out Donkhal Singhji begged that he may be given these. He was told that they had cost 3000 [rupees] he would find them rather expensive. The Maharaja Sahib would not give the bill to Bharon Singhji, he said that as he had brought the guns with him they had got into India customs free. He did not see why Bharon Singhji should get this benefit . . . Whatever the customs came to Bharon Singh should pay half of it to him.

After London, Jaipur must have seemed very confusing. The gossips were busy assessing his character and jockeying for his favour. Amer Singh wrote that three people were hoping to be made Prime Minister when Jai was invested. Mr Alexander, the Revenue Member, was reputed to be taking bribes. Jai listened to all of this, but, as was to be his usual practice, paid no attention to anything that was said to him until he had checked both sides of the story. His time in the

71

zenana had given him a lasting dislike of intrigue. He got on with his study of the workings of his state, accepting, without much difficulty, the customs of his people.

He wrote to Rabbit: 'Are you cleaning your teeth with the things Miss Sahib and I left for you. You must have nice clean teeth next time you come and stay with me . . .'

Rabbit must by now have been married, because within days of his investiture Jai wrote to him: '. . . do you want your wife to come to Ooty or not? Let me know . . . Well work hard. Love Man Singh.'

By the time he was invested with the full powers of a Maharaja, he was more readily accepted and more settled at home. But, from this time on, his life was to be divided and to contain an element of conflict, which ten years of British dominance had inevitably implanted.

CHAPTER 5

On 14 March 1931, Lord Irwin, the Viceroy, invested Jai with his full powers as Maharaja of Jaipur. No record of the ceremony survives, but it must have been a colourful occasion, with all the nobles in their finest brocades, excited at the thought that the management of their affairs would once more be, at any rate nominally, in their own hands.

The Viceroy made a self-congratulatory speech, listing all the reforms of the Minority Council and the improvements which the British administration had wrought in Jaipur State during their years as caretakers. Jai replied, with proper deference, thanking the British for their good stewardship, listing again the reforms and improvements on which he hoped to build in the future. There followed a large banquet at the Rambagh Palace.

Two days after the Investiture, Mr B.J. Glancy, who had been President of the Minority Council since September 1929, wrote to Jai:

> My Dear Darbar
> My wife and I are both very grateful to you for the kind letter of appreciation that you have sent us. I hated saying goodbye to you last night, & I was almost base enough to wish that your team would be knocked out of the polo tournament, so that we might meet again at Bombay.
> I claim very little credit myself for the success of the Investiture functions, but everyone from the Viceroy

73

downwards seems to have been most favourably impressed, & I felt personally very proud of the splendid way you played your part from start to finish.

I suppose that every Government official relieves his feelings from time to time by cursing & abusing the Government of India, & I confess now that I said some hard things about them when I heard of their decision that your training from last October onwards was to be confined to the Jaipur State. I didn't know you at all well in those days, I'd never been responsible for anybody's training & I had grave doubts as to my own capacity & as to how we'd get on together. Well, I take back all those wicked words today. For my part I could have wished for nothing better than the last six months, & the happiest days that my wife & I have spent in Jaipur have been the time that we were out with you camping in the wilds. . .

One thing I hope is that, however far you may advance as time goes on, you'll always remain the same at heart – just the same as you are at present . . .

Yours very sincerely,

B.J. Glancy

However splendid the ceremony, the so-called full powers of a Maharaja had a rather hollow quality. British policy towards the Indian states had varied over the previous hundred years. Immediately after the Indian Mutiny of 1857 and the establishment of the Government of India in 1858, there was a keen sense of gratitude for the Princes' support during the mutiny and an awareness of the need to foster their loyalty against the possibility of a recurrence of such troubles. The new Government anxiously demonstrated its intention to honour its pledges to annex no more territory and to 'respect the rights, dignity, and honour of the native Princes as our own.'

Later in the nineteenth century, the British began to interfere more actively in the internal affairs of the princely states, partly from a genuine wish to improve the lot of the people and partly from the need to exercise indirect control over the whole of India. The principle of paramountcy was constantly asserted.

At the beginning of the twentieth century, the question became more complicated. It was realised that British India would have to be given a measure of autonomy. This would naturally conflict with the idea of exercising firmer control over the Indian States. In 1909, Lord Minto, the Viceroy, made a speech at Udaipur which suggested that Political Officers should interfere less in the running of the states to which they were appointed. Their primary duty was 'the conservation of the customs of the State'. Yet even while they paid lip-service, when convenient, to the new policy of laisser-faire, their very presence in a state was a constant reminder of the real impotence of the Princes. A leader in *Gujarat Punch*, written two years before Minto's speech, quoted by Ian Copland in his book on the Raj and the Princes, makes clear the Indian attitude:

> . . . our Native Princes have been let alone – or rather allowed to exist. There is the rub! . . . mere existence and no animate, independent *life*. Deprived of all power, isolated from national and imperial questions, interests and aspirations, the heart lacerated, the mind benumbed, the brain paralysed, cheated with a mock independence, and as the 'unkindest cut of all', those invidious leeches, the Political Agents, thrust upon them – what wonder that our Princes should have got disgusted with the whole 'show' and begun to tread tortuous paths?

The East India Company, by its offensive-defensive treaties with the states, had, as it were, frozen the map of India. Whereas before, as the power of the Moghuls crumbled, there was constant turmoil, with each state endeavouring to enlarge its territory, the British treaties guaranteed the security of whoever happened at a given moment to control a particular region. Relieved of the expenses of constant war, with agricultural production less disturbed, with the coming of the investment of riches as opposed to the hoarding of gold, the wealth of the states, which is to say the wealth of the Maharajas, grew to immense proportions. In terms of splendour, extravagance and self-indulgence, the first half of the twentieth century was a golden age for the Princes.

The other side of the coin had been foreseen as early as 1817 by Sir Thomas Munro, who pointed out that by supporting a Prince against every threat, whether foreign or domestic, the British virtually underwrote bad government in the states. 'It renders him indolent, by teaching him to trust strangers for his security; and cruel and avaricious, by showing him that he has nothing to fear from the hatred of his subjects.'

Unless the misrule became outrageous or the Prince were guilty of some really serious crime, the British were latterly very reluctant to dethrone a ruler. The result was that the Princes had what one might call unlimited petty authority (even in a few cases the power of life and death), but no real political power.

The response of the Maharajas to this situation naturally varied enormously. In some cases, they simply amused themselves by exploring every avenue of vice; in others, they took refuge in an Indian contemplative existence. The most common reaction was to adopt a quasi-British stance, behaving not like rulers, but more like imitation Whig aristocrats. For the Rajputs, with their warlike tradition, seemingly perpetual peace was additionally irksome. For those not given to lechery, sport was the usual substitute.

Jai was not yet twenty at the time of his investiture. While his nature was intensely sensual, he was quite devoid of any vicious inclinations. Girls were to be of great importance in his life, but they were essentially part of having 'fun'; he was highly sexed in a perfectly healthy way. Again, while he was very properly religious, even devout, he had no mystical leanings. Neither depravity nor a spiritual existence appealed to Jai.

In his case, the British had had ten years in which to inculcate in him those aristocratic precepts of noblesse oblige and ich dien, of which his tutor Mayne had written so glowingly. The very survival of that letter, as a solitary record of that time, reveals the importance which its message must have had for the young Maharaja. Jai accepted almost eagerly the standards of behaviour which the British set for him. Throughout his minority, his state had been administered almost entirely by British officials. Having been educated by the British and having a very real dislike of the plotting and intrigue which surrounds any Indian-run court, Jai saw no reason to change the pattern. For nearly a decade he was to rely almost entirely on British advisers. There were Indians in his Cabinet, but the Prime Minister was always British. During that decade, Jai left the running of his state very largely in the hands of his advisers, rather as a young English landowner might leave his affairs in the care of an estate agent. He performed his ceremonial functions scrupulously, but was little involved in the details of administration.

This is not to say that he took no interest in the affairs of the state, but he concerned himself more with things to do with Rajput custom than with, for example, public works or the question of health. This admirably suited the egregious Sir Beauchamp St John, who was Vice-President of the Council, or Prime Minister, from 1933 until 1939. He was a pompous fellow, given to lecturing the nobles on their habits, telling them that they did nothing but drink and womanise. He would preface these homilies by saying that he was an aristocrat himself and so could sympathise with the Sardars, but they must reform, or their way of life could not last long. His advice to Jai was to amuse himself and play polo – and let him run the State.

St John interfered very little in the eternal wrangles about adoptions by the Jagirdars and the manoeuvres about marriages. The unfortunate Jhalai, who, it will be remembered, wanted to adopt his brother as his heir, was never allowed to do so. Jhalai seems to have been extremely good-natured and remarkably unresentful of his exclusion from the throne. He conducted his thikana well. When there was a serious outbreak of plague in the state in 1934, he had all his subjects inoculated at his own expense – a gesture which cost him what was then the large sum of 3,000 rupees. His brother, in the event, could never have succeeded to the thikana, for he was murdered in 1937. Even before that, Jai had ordered him to adopt one of his own sons. Eventually, he did adopt Jai's second son, Jai Singh.

On the whole, Jai had very good relations with his Sardars and Jagirdars. It was always a tricky balancing act because, as with any form of feudal system, there is the awkward matter of feudal dues. The majority of Jagirdars were illiterate and careless. They set nothing aside and kept no accounts. In consequence, they were nearly always in arrears with their present dues and their old ones, known as bakaya. Madho Singh had always liked keeping them in debt as it gave him a hold over them. Jai was more inclined to think that they should pay up promptly, but to be too demanding would incur fierce hatred. In the case of Rabbit, Jai paid off all his arrears himself.

Sometimes St John went expressly against Jai's wishes, making appointments he did not approve of, but Jai quite often echoed St John's complaints about the attitude of the Jagirdars to their villagers and workers; but he did so more tactfully.

In many of his dealings with the nobles, Jai could be extremely firm. He would endeavour to persuade them to look after their tenants better, particularly in times of famine. The nobles would sulkily reply that their villagers were happier than those on khalsa, or Crown lands. Moreover, if they were to make remissions of rent to cultivators during difficult times, he should remit their tribute money. In any case, they claimed that under the new arrangements he was making to pacify unrest among villagers they were going to lose revenue. Therefore, their tributes should be permanently reduced. They ignored the fact that the dues they paid were based on unrealistically low valuations of their estates. Amer Singh's thikana, valued at 12,000 rupees per annum, actually brought in 25,000. The Thakur of Naila's, supposedly worth 18,000 a year, yielded 50,000.

Jai handled these problems with such evident fairness that, despite the protests of his nobles, he quite early on established the base on which his later immeasurable popularity among all classes was built.

His own private affairs he managed quite sensibly. There is a record of his arranging, in 1932, to have nearly two million silver rupees (£153,000) of his personal money, which was lying in the Treasury, packed up in specially made wooden boxes and sent to the mint in Bombay. There it was to be melted down and put in the bank. Almost incredibly, the instructions to the mint and the bank and their replies were all sent by ordinary Post Office telegram. The silver, however, was to be packed in the presence of three witnesses and escorted by two fully-armed police guards, each guard consisting of one NCO and five men.

Apart from these things, Jai did have two absorbing interests. The first was his army; the second was polo. For the first years of his reign these two enthusiasms took up the greater part of his time and energy.

The Jaipur army at the time of Jai's investiture was an insignificant affair, although its actual numbers were fairly large. The state army consisted of some 6,000 infantry, 1,000 cavalry and somewhere between 3,000 and 6,000 Nagas. The last were a peculiar body of semi-religious irregulars, the followers of a saint called Dadu Dayal. In 1868, Colonel J.C. Brooke wrote: 'The Nagas are a body of religious mendicants, who are trustworthy and true to the State. They receive the small pay of Rs.2 a month, and Re. one for each child, averaging Rs.3 per fighting man. In the roll, children are counted as well as adults. They are armed with matchlocks, and will not undergo any discipline.' The Nagas were a relic of Moghul times and were symbolic of the generally low military standard.

Originally, the Jagirdars had been obliged to provide 5,600 mounted men for the state army, but during Jai's minority this feudal service had been abolished and a tax imposed instead. By the end of the 1930s, there were only forty-six soldiers supplied in this manner.

Jaipur also provided, for imperial service, a transport corps, which was first raised in response to an appeal by the Viceroy, Lord Dufferin, in 1888 for troops from the states to fight side by side with imperial troops. Jaipur had been considered an unlikely source of fine, fighting, modern soldiers. It was called upon to supply muleteers and stretcher-bearers. The Transport Corps, in 1919, had 1,200 ponies, 560 carts, sixteen tongas and 792 men. In the First World War, it had served in Persia and Mesopotamia. The limitation of providing only this corps, but no infantry or cavalry, was

79

thought of as something of an insult to Rajput honour.

The Jaipur army certainly needed to be reorganised. Jai, filled with ideas from his year at Woolwich, set about a radical improvement of his forces. He reduced the numbers of his existing regiments, getting rid of the aged, untrainable soldiers and insisting on higher standards. The infantry he formed into two regiments. The First Jaipur Infantry was composed of nearly 800 men and was intended for imperial service. The Second Jaipur Infantry, about 330 strong, was for state defence and internal security. The Jaipur Lancers, under the command of our friend Amer Singh, was reduced to 530 strong and was also meant for imperial service. Amer Singh was, without question, the best officer available. He had served with the British in the Boxer Rebellion and also in the First World War.

Jai maintained the Transport Corps with only 280 men. The Nagas were gradually disbanded, although this did not start until 1936. There were still some 2,000 of them on the rolls in 1937 and about half that in 1938. Their pay, however, did not seem to have advanced that much. They were earning, towards the end, a little over five rupees a month. (Less than 1.25p a day.)

Quite early on in his reformation of the army, Jai created what was virtually a whole new regiment – the Sawai Man Guards – although it could be said to have been formed from the base of an old regiment called the Khasa Risala. This regiment, nearly 700 strong, was a straight copy of the British Foot Guards. Jai insisted that all recruits should be Rajputs and at least six-foot tall. Their uniform was based on that of the Foot Guards, though with a turban instead of a bearskin. The badges of rank were swastikas instead of stars. The lower ranks were called by the English names – for example, sergeant, corporal and private rather than hawaldar, naik and sepoy. The only toast drunk in the mess was the health of the goddess Mataji. Not even the King Emperor was toasted, which led to some criticism when the regiment was on active service during the Second World War. The regiment was formed in September 1932 and took seven years to build up. Jai brought out a Coldstream Guards sergeant called Wells to drill them.

Jai aged ten.

Jai aged twelve.

Jai aged fourteen.

Jai aged nineteen.

Jai aged twenty-one.

Jai (second from right) with the all-conquering Jaipur polo team he brought to England in 1933.

Jai's polo team, as caricatured in *Tatler*.

The only other force was an irregular group of 132 officers called the Artillery. They were equipped with thirty-five muzzle-loading guns, drawn by bullocks. Their only role was to fire salutes – a matter of supreme importance in princely India.

Jai joined in with all the activities of the army, going out to camp with them, taking parades, teaching the Sawai Man Guards how to slow march. Amer Singh's diaries are full of entries about Jai's interest in the Lancers' sports day. Each year, the Commanding Officer had to put on a different show, which, judging by his accounts, was almost as complicated as the Royal Tournament in London. The Maharaja was exaggeratedly severe in what he expected of his troops. On one occasion, he told Amer Singh to dismiss one of his troopers, whom Jai had chanced to see rising in his saddle, rather than bumping along when trotting. (Amer Singh refused to deprive a man of his livelihood for so trivial an offence).

One of his Guards officers describes a day when he was summoned by Jai who had seen him on parade trailing his sword instead of having it hooked up. 'He shouted and banged on the table, swearing at me. When he had finished I produced from my pocket His Highness' own order of a few days before, saying we must trail our swords. He had forgotten it.'

By the start of the Second World War, Jai had built up a reasonably modernised force of nearly 3,000 troops, who were to fight for the imperial power on all fronts. Even at this time, defence cost Jaipur state rather more than a tenth of its income. A hundred years before, even well after the British protection treaties, it had cost one third of the state revenue.

Jai's love of military affairs gave him a training in administration, and to some extent in economic understanding, which were to prove valuable when, in later years, he started to take a real interest in the running of his state.

His other great enthusiasm, polo, was to win him worldwide fame and great popularity, both at home and abroad.

No one in the world was in a better position than an Indian Prince to become a champion at polo. He could start young, as Jai did, playing polo at school. He could buy the best ponies. He could employ countless grooms, which gives a huge advantage because a polo pony has to be re-schooled after each match and if each pony has its own groom the ponies must be better trained. That said, Jai was one of the greatest polo players of all time.

As soon as he came back from Woolwich, he began to collect a team together, with the idea of going to England in 1933 to compete in the major British championships. The team which he gathered was a powerful one, although its members, apart from himself, had nothing to do with Jaipur, rather in the way that footballers today need have no connection with the place they play for. Two came from Jodhpur – the Rao Raja Hanut Singh and the Rao Raja Abhey Singh. Hanut Singh was the illegitimate son of Sir Pratap Singh, a favourite of Queen Victoria, who had been regent of Jodhpur. Hanut was a tough man with an overpowering desire to win. He was also an extremely good judge of horses. The fourth member of the team was Raj Kumar Prithi Singh, a nephew of the Maharaja of Baria.

Both Jai and Hanut Singh had handicaps of eight. Abhey Singh and Prithi Singh had handicaps of seven. Hanut did most of the buying of the horses, which were Australian thoroughbreds rather than the traditional Indian marwari horse, with its distinctive curly ears.

In April 1933, this team sailed for England, taking with them thirty-nine horses, fifty-one syces and a polo-stick maker. For a month they trained at Westonbirt, accustoming their ponies to the restricting boards round the edge of the polo field, which do not exist in India.

Their season started in May, when they beat the west of England team. They then lost at Hurlingham to a team called Osmaston. No one at that time expected very much of them. With such high handicaps, they were obviously good players, but they were all young and had, as far as the British knew, little experience.

In June, however, they astounded the polo world. First, they beat Osmaston in the final of the Ranelagh Open Cup.

After that, they won the Ranelagh Challenge Cup and ten days later beat Osmaston again in the Hurlingham Champion Cup. By now, the Jaipur team, in their green blazers with gold borders and gold crests, were heroes. The popular papers were carried away by the glamour of the young Maharaja and his friends. When they won the Roehampton Open at the beginning of July, even the sporting papers excelled themselves in eulogistic praise. This was the first time that the same team had won all three open championships in one year.

Their triumphs went on until the end of the season. They won the King's Coronation Cup at Ranelagh, the Prince of Wales Empire Cup at Hurlingham, the Rugby Challenge Cup, and the Open and Senior Cups at Dunster. It was a feat that was never repeated. In September, the team and their horses returned to India.

From now on, Jai's life was to be divided between India and Europe, where he would spend four months of every year. The two worlds in which he lived could hardly have provided greater contrasts.

With the accession of a young, attractive, energetic Prince in place of the unlettered, old-fashioned Madho Singh, the tone of life in Jaipur was obviously bound to change, but the habits and customs of the Rajputs were deeply entrenched. Moreover, it was not Jai's intention that anything should change, for, in superficial terms as we have seen, this was a golden period for the Maharajas. Rajputana was comparatively isolated from the political currents which were burgeoning in British India. The status quo suited both the Princes and the British. The people, in consequence, remained backward and generally placid. Court life continued to be a hotbed of rivalry and intrigue.

At the very beginning of Jai's reign, there were at least four people scheming to become his Prime Minister. Amarnath Atal, a Kashmiri, who was later to be Finance Minister, was one contender. He was trying to prove that Mr Alexander, the British Revenue member of the Council, was taking bribes. Bhairon Singh Tanwar, whom we shall meet as

Master of the Hunt, was another. The Thakur of Chomu, now forgiven for his role in the agitation over Jai's adoption, also had aspirations of this sort. Jai, however, continued to rely on British advisers and it was not until 1940 that he took on an Indian Prime Minister.

Despite this strong British influence, one gets from Amer Singh's diaries and other sources a picture of a very closed, almost archaic society with very little sophistication of any sort. The etiquette of any small court is always a demanding business, for a circumscribed power requires more props than a fuller one. At the great festivals, although it was known where each man should sit, an undignified scramble always took place, each Sardar hoping somehow to enhance his dignity by sitting in a better place than that to which his true status entitled him. It was always noticed and gossiped about if the Maharaja stood up or walked a few paces to greet one of his nobles. Technically, he would stand up only for Sardars of Tazimi rank. If he helped a man to rise who had, in full obeisance, clasped his knees, it was a sign of favour.

Jai was immensely punctilious in these little matters of custom and manners. Amer Singh wrote: '. . . when the Maharaja Sahib saw me, he asked me to lunch. Then he said I was not properly dressed and he had a party on. I pulled out my necktie and asked him whether this was what he objected to. He said that it was both this and the colour of my shirt.' The old man had to go home and change.

This exactness of behaviour was a general concern among the Rajputs. Relations with Kashmir, for example, were threatened by two incidents in 1932. A Jaipur official was visiting Jammu and was under orders not to show nazar to anyone, on the grounds that Jaipur Sardars should do so only to the Maharana of Udaipur and the Maharaja of Jodhpur. Sensing that this was a cause of considerable offence, the official wired to Jai, asking permission to show his nazar to the Maharaja. Jai agreed, but such a decision could only be made by the Maharaja himself.

A month later, the leader of a deputation from Kashmir complained that he was received at Jaipur in a very casual way. The Maharaja of Kashmir wrote furiously that he resented this very much and that when a deputation next came from Jaipur it would be treated with equal contempt. Jai wrote a grovelling apology, explaining that he had been exceptionally busy at the time. Kashmir agreed then to expunge the matter from his records and to forget the whole affair.

Respect for the Maharaja was, in a sense, absolute. No one was the least put out when a dirt road along which he was going to travel was closed an hour before his arrival so that there was no risk of dust in his path. Amer Singh, who was an enthusiastic gourmet, used to send a dish or two to the Maharaja every second or third day. 'If I don't I am asked why I haven't.' While the Sardars might complain of Jai's occasional habit of staying in bed until noon and not letting his courtiers go to bed until dawn, no one questioned the right of a Maharaja to do as he pleased. This respect was largely for the throne and the principle of monarchy. That an individual ruler might be vicious or cruel, selfish or greedy, spendthrift or debauched, was of little importance. It might be aggravating, but it was not the man who mattered. If, as in Jai's case, the Maharaja happened to have great charm, to yield only to fairly everyday temptations, to fulfil his ceremonial duties conscientiously, then this was an unlooked for bonus.

The reverse side of this chivalrous punctilio and so ancient a concept of kingship was an equally outmoded sense of privilege. We have seen how the Thakur of Chitora, having murdered several men who were supposedly disturbing the running of his thikana, was never brought to trial. One of the leading Sardars heard a man in the street swearing at a woman. The Sardar hit him, knocking him to the ground, and then forced a stick up the man's rectum and stirred it around in his entrails. The man died. The Sardar continued in his royal post. One of the nastiest cases involved one of Madho Singh's illegitimate sons, Lallji Moti Singh, who attacked a Benya boy and then chopped off his testicles. The boy died. Moti Singh was, at least, arrested by the British police chief, Freddie Young. The senior lady of the zenana pleaded for him. He was locked up in a fort called Moti Doongri, not far from the Rambagh Palace. British visitors in the thirties remember seeing his food being sent from the royal kitchens to the fort.

Warrior classes the world over, whether they be Crusaders or Samurai or Rajputs, may be admirable for their courage, but they are ruthless, often cruel and extraordinarily quarrelsome among themselves.

Respect for the throne by no means excluded plotting and intrigue of all kinds, though straight treason was a rarity in the earlier decades of this century. Anonymous letters and invented scandal were very much part of court life. Jai was particularly averse to this type of scheming. Again and again the author was told that, while he would listen to anything anyone wanted to tell him, Jai would always thoroughly investigate any tale before believing it. On the whole, he was inclined to think less well of any informant, questioning his motive for reporting whatever it might be, rather than bothering with the burden of his tale.

On one occasion, he was told by an informer that Mr Mackenzie, a British official, had written a long report about him saying that he had no administrative ability or brains, that he should be removed from the throne and that his small son, then about three, should be installed in his stead. This report was said to be accompanied by six foolscap pages of signatures of leading nobles. Furthermore, there were said to be some compromising photographs in the hands of the British. The informer offered to steal the report, claiming that Madho Singh had paid 100,000 rupees to have extracted the evidence of his adoptive father Ram Singh's pledge that any future adoption would be from Jhalai. The price would not be so high and there was a hope that the Birla family would contribute to the cost.

Although the incident took place early in his reign, Jai treated this fairly ridiculous attempt at blackmail with the contempt it deserved. He understood perfectly that, while there might be an unfavourable report on him, there was nothing he could do about it. If it were stolen, it could easily be rewritten by Mr Mackenzie. He ignored the whole thing. Certainly no such report survives, although it is true that nearly all the secret dossiers which the British kept on the Princes were destroyed at the time of Independence.

For the first years of his reign, since the affairs of his state occupied comparatively little of Jai's time, he enjoyed himself. When in Jaipur he would, unless he was going shooting or flying, often sleep late. At the same time, he would quite often carry on a party in one of the officer's messes until six in the morning and then take them all out on parade for a couple of hours.

Shooting was a serious affair in Rajputana and, in common with royalty throughout the ages, the young Jai was always eager to extend the boundaries of the royal hunt. Quite soon after his installation, he increased the limits of his private hunting ground to fifteen miles around Jaipur city. The main game were deer and wild pig, for Ram Singh had prohibited bear, tiger and sambha shooting, except at the two large and powerful thikanas of Sikar and Khetri. This prohibition obviously did not apply to the royal family, and their privileges were jealously guarded. One farmer driving some wild pigs out of his field hit and killed a young one. The master of the royal hunt had the man brought to his house and there had a quantity of ground chillies pushed up his bottom. He then subjected the farmer to further indignities which killed him. More mildly, when a trooper in the Jaipur Lancers killed a pig in self-defence, Jai tried to insist the man pay a ten-rupee fine. (Amer Singh paid it out of regimental funds.)

Jai's physical energy, once he was up, was tremendous. If there was no shooting, he might well play squash in the morning. In the afternoon, he would nearly always play two and a half hours of polo. After that, he might go on an all night exercise with one of his regiments.

In the evenings, there were always parties, either at the Rambagh Palace or in the officers' mess of one of the regiments. These were nearly always all male affairs, unless some European women were invited, and they involved much horseplay and rough humour. There are accounts of Jai's throwing people's swords into the Rambagh pool. At one mess dinner, he emptied a bowl of water into Amer Singh's lap and then shouted to everyone to look at how the old man had peed in his trousers.

There was also much social life at the Jaipur Club, where

Jai would go every evening after polo to play bridge. The jokes there, too, would be of a broad nature. Amer Singh, one evening, obliquely attacked Jai, saying that at Mayo College boys learned only two things – to pee standing up and to think their elders foolish. For good measure he added that in England they learned to use Bromo paper after shitting instead of water. Jai laughed and asked him how he knew.

Drink played a large part in Jaipur society. At the house which Jai built for Rabbit, there was a bar on the verandah and another, added by Rabbit, by the front door, known as the 'one-for-the-road-bar'. Jai himself drank comparatively little, nearly always champagne. According to one of his ADCs, he once suffered such an immense hangover when young that he virtually gave up spirits thereafter. He would take a half-bottle of Bollinger to any party at which the host was unlikely to provide champagne. He was well aware of the insidious effect which drink had always had on his family. So many of his ancestors had succumbed to drink. Ram Singh II had taken to drink as soon as he had been invested with his full powers. He was so drunk one day when the British Resident called that, when the Englishman had gone, the Maharaja's servant threw his decanter and cups into a tank and left. The next day, Ram Singh had him brought back to explain his behaviour. The man said he could not bear to see his master in such a state in front of the Resident. He was embarrassed and ashamed. Ram Singh gave the servant a village in jagir and never drank again.

When Rabbit had been married for some time to his second wife, Jai wrote to her: 'Darling if ever you see him going the wrong way try and stop him. I am only afraid of him taking to drink as you know that weakness is in all our family and we all at some time or other fall to it. Other things don't matter so much . . .' The last sentence referred to his infidelities.

Much of Jai's entertaining was for his English friends. Every winter they used to come in large numbers, mostly from the rather glossy milieu he used to frequent in Europe.

In 1936, Jai much enlarged the Rambagh Palace, building a new dining hall which he had had designed in London.

Staying at the Rambagh was a luxurious affair. Jai had four or more ADCs, one of whom was meant to devote himself entirely to looking after the guests. This beautifully-uniformed man would come to each guest's room at breakfast time and ask what he or she wanted to do – shooting, riding, sightseeing, swimming or whatever. The ADC would tell them what to wear and give them some information about everyone they were liable to meet.

There would be ponies saddled and waiting at six in the morning. Cars would be standing by for anyone who wanted to go shooting. The royal hunting grounds were so carefully guarded that black buck lived in large numbers only a quarter of a mile from the Rambagh Palace, where now the university stands. If the guests went after wild pig, they could expect to kill fifty or sixty in the morning or they might spend two hours before a picnic lunch shooting 250 duck.

Naturally, many of Jai's friends were polo players, so their afternoons would be spent on the polo fields. After that, they might play bridge at the club. Dinner was a rather formal affair at which everyone wore white tie and tails. Usually, Jai did not dine with his guests but went to eat in the zenana with his wives, while the Europeans dined alone. On grand occasions, when there was a big dinner, the men would be expected to wear medals. Sometimes these dinners would be at the City Palace. The servants would wear long white tunics and magenta turbans which trailed half way down their backs. The whole place would be hung with fairy lights, and five men were specially employed to prevent the innumerable monkeys which lived in the Palace from pulling out the wires or the bulbs.

Dinner was normally at ten-thirty, but if Jai had been out drinking with some friends, they might not be back till much later. Sir Robert Throckmorton, one of Jai's closest friends, remembers evenings when they would arrive back at the Rambagh at two-thirty for dinner, to find the servants asleep on the floor of the dining hall. On earlier nights they might go out after dinner to shoot rabbits in the headlights of the cars.

It was a roistering life made healthier by the prodigious

amount of exercise everyone took and interrupted from time to time by quite arduous country expeditions. Sir Robert recalls going camping in Jodhpur for two weeks at a time for pig-sticking. The greater excitement was tiger shooting.

Ranthambhor, near Sawai Madhopur, about a hundred miles from Jaipur is one of the most beautiful places in the state. The road from Sawai Madhopur climbs up into the hills through a steep gully, passing through the remains of a huge gateway. At the very top are the ruins of a vast fort, with its little temples and keeps and storehouses and chakris, which looks out over three lakes and a wonderful landscape of plains and sudden valleys. Today it is a nature reserve, covering some 150 square miles, from which all people have been removed. Before Independence, it was a lost place with a few clustered villages. There was no paved road and no cause for anyone to go there. It was here that Jai took his special guests for tiger shooting.

Beside one of the lakes, next to one of the largest banyan trees in India, Jai built a little pavilion where he would sleep. Everyone else was put up in luxurious tents. It was an idyllic situation. Moreover, as the shooting was so important – the killing of beautiful animals being one of those many areas where Indian and British tastes coincided – it was beautifully organised. Elephants were brought from Jaipur for riding over the rough, jungly country. It took them two weeks to walk there and two weeks to walk back. There was no unpleasant slaughter. They did not lure the tigers with a tethered goat or buffalo or even a child, as was said to be the habit of the Maharaja of Alwar. The tigers were driven towards the guns who waited on tall machans (raised platforms). Unlike the many Maharajas who did not let their guests carry guns, Jai was exceptionally generous, always giving his guests the best position and allowing them to shoot first.

Now that Ranthambhor is a nature reserve, the villagers have been cleared off the land and the road to it is paved. There are far fewer tigers than in the days of princely rule. The warden maintains that Jai was, in fact, a conservationist; moreover, fear of the Maharaja's keepers kept the poachers away.

CHAPTER 6

At the times when he was in Jaipur, Jai was much involved with his family life. His first child, Princess Prem Kumari, known as Mickey, was born at Simla in June 1929, when Jai was at Woolwich. His eldest son, Bhawani Singh, was born in October 1931. It is difficult to form much idea of Jai's relationship with his first wife, or to gain any real impression of her character. She was undoubtedly popular with the people. Her protests at Jai being sent to England and her hunger strike in the city in 1927 were well-known. Everyone held her in respect for her adherence to traditional values and her courage in opposing the British. She was also generous. Whenever her train stopped at a station, she would distribute largesse to the beggars who hang around all Indian stations. Her life was undoubtedly rather lonely, for, as we have seen, she was more intelligent than most of the women who surrounded her. She could speak a little English and understood it easily. Her closest friend was her sister, married to the Maharaja of Rewa. They used to wear identical clothes and to exchange jewellery. Jai's wife was so soft-hearted that she even gave away her sister's favourite bracelet to an importunate woman who pointedly admired it.

What, on the other hand, can the rapport have been between a relatively sophisticated young man who had travelled abroad and a little-educated, old-fashioned woman twelve years older than himself who had lived all her life in a cocoon of female tittle-tattle and gossip, much of it, by all accounts, lewd and banal?

Nonetheless, throughout her life, Jai was to treat her with unfailing courtesy and she was, in the face of increasing difficulties, to maintain an unflinching dignity.

In April 1932, Jai went off to Jodhpur to marry his second wife, Kishore Kanwar, the niece of First Her Highness (as the elder one was called). In accordance with Rajput custom, there were sent ahead to Jodhpur exact measurements of Jai's arms, legs and hands, details of the shape of his head, the colouring of his hair and eyes. These are required, not for the information of the bride, who will never have seen her future husband, but to avoid any risks of a substitution being made. But before leaving, Jai did commit a breach of Rajput etiquette, which may have owed something to his British upbringing. A young man going away to get married should always suck the breasts of the senior lady in the zenana, in this case someone called Tanwarji Sahiba. Instead, he sucked the breasts of his own mother, much to the chagrin of Tanwarji and her family.

The origin of this custom, which still continues today and can be the source of similar disappointments, is uncertain. Some maintain that it stems from the days when infants in arms were married and had a last feed before going. This seems unlikely, as a baby travelling from Jaipur to Jodhpur would hardly survive till it returned home. In any case, they mostly employed wet-nurses. More probably it is a vow, on the mother's milk, to return home after marriage.

The wedding in Jodhpur was as splendid and as protracted as only a princely wedding in India can be. The bride, who was only fifteen, revealed almost at once the rather demanding character she was to become. On the day after the marriage ceremony, she and Jai were meant to leave the Palace at nine in the morning to make their devotions at various shrines and temples. She insisted that either the Maharaja of Jodhpur, her uncle, or her brother should go with them, which was not part of the official plans. This caused some delay. Then she insisted that, now she was a Maharani, a gun salute should be fired when she left the Palace and another when she arrived at the fort. The result of all this was that they did not set off until two-thirty in the afternoon.

None of this boded too well for relations between Jaipur and Jodhpur. Another Amer Singh, a cousin of Her Highness and an ADC to Jai, tried to arrange that the new Maharani should not be regarded as the junior wife, but that she should have equal rights with First Her Highness. The Maharaja of Jodhpur was indignant at this suggestion, the first wife being his sister, and sent a vigorous message to expostulate. He further demanded that Amer Singh be sent back to Jodhpur. The ADC had, he protested, only been lent for eighteen months. This kind of argument was always conducted in such a way that it gave the other side some leeway. Jodhpur promised to lend Jaipur a better polo player if Amer Singh was returned, but at the same time he threatened to put Amer Singh's father in prison if the son did not return. In rather the same way, the bride's dowry had included twenty-eight rather shoddy horses. While denying that the twenty-eight were shoddy, Jodhpur, as if it were quite another matter, offered to give Jai two good horses from his stables.

First Her Highness received the young bride into the zenana on her arrival with great kindness. It was said, however, that the elder wife never touched the dishes which were sent to her by various people, eating only simple things cooked by her own servants for fear of poisoning. It may well be that much of the rivalry between the two wives was fabricated by others; if not, it was certainly fanned by gossip and intrigue. People assumed that Jai must prefer Second Her Highness to his first wife, because she was younger and reputed to be much prettier. Therefore, to please the second wife, they would do things to annoy the first wife, such as arrest one of her servants. It is probable, though, that the new wife was given to intrigue. The relationship between the first and second wives was bound to be a difficult one and people took advantage of it to foment trouble.

Jai was in many ways a family man. He had the Rajput sense of broad obligation to the whole Kachhawa clan. Rabbit, whom he virtually adopted as a brother, was the perfect example of how much Jai could give to a relation, of how forgiving he could be. We can follow the course of this friendship in some of the letters which survive.

93

Rambagh,
13 Nov '31

Rabbit my dearest,

Thank you ever so much for your letter . . . My dear
babe I have already taken steps towards excusing your
debt & that will be perfectly all right. I did not tell you
anything about it as I wanted to make it a surprise for
you. You are my dearest nephew and I would do
anything in the world to help you. You can always rely
on that.

Lots of love   Yours ever
Man Singh

Much of the time, Rabbit was in trouble over various misdemeanours concerning his wife, his drinking and his extravagance. The troubles were constantly recurring, but were
always forgiven. Rabbit's matrimonial problems seemed to
start as early as 1932. At about that time, Jai wrote:

My dear Babe
. . . look here as Deshra [a festival] is so near shall I
send your wife away or not. I am ready to do exactly as
you like.
Lots of love from Man Singh

Jai always needed Rabbit as a companion, seemingly almost
the only one he could really trust:

Rambagh
27 Feb '34

My dear Rabbit,
. . . It was very sad saying goodbye to you on the
station & honestly Rabbit I feel very lonely without
you. I have got nobody to go about with or talk
confidentially with. Well anyhow Rabbit I hope you
will be of still greater help to me when you return from
Meerut . . .
Yours ever Jai

94

Ooty
4 May '34

My dear Rabbit,

. . . well I am glad we have made up and there is no ill feeling about anything. I do love you so much baby . . .

Do you want more money if so send me a wire. Now I am enclosing a cheque for hundred rupees and if you want more let me know by wire. Have just paid your mess bills for March & April. . .

It seems likely that it was during that year that Rabbit's marriage went wrong, but the letters on the subject have incomplete dates.

Jodhpur
20th Nov.

My Dear Rabbit,

You are a silly little fool. Why do you think I am angry with you. My reason for not being able to write to you lately was that we are so busy playing polo . . . & pig-sticking . . . There are a few exciting people here too which makes it more interesting . . .

I am going to Jaipur for a couple of days on the 26th and will talk to Achrol [the Thakur of Achrol] about your marriage. Don't worry I will fix you up with somebody really nice but I do hope you have not misbehaved with your present wife otherwise it will be hopeless. Write what you have done with her, after all we don't keep secrets from one another.

With love from Jai

Rambagh [undated]

My Dear Rabbit,

. . . There is quite hopeful news about your marriage and will fix you this summer with some nice girl. They want all sorts of guarantees which I am accepting on your behalf so don't let me down. I have sent for your horoscope . . .

Yours Jai

In 1936 Rabbit remarried. Jai wrote to him in April of that year from Arranmore Palace in Ootacamund:

> My dear Rabbit,
>   After an awful journey we have at last arrived here. It is heavenly only in the sense of weather not girls . . . the night before I left you made me the happiest man. I did not realize till then how much you loved me. Really Rabbit I want nothing else from you except your true love & companionship & in return you know I will do anything in return for you. I don't think there is any need for me to tell you how much I love you . . . bless you old boy . . .
>
>   Love Jai

Rabbit's new wife, Bunty, was a girl of great beauty who came from a simple family. She was quite unaccustomed to court ways, but was often able to stand up to Jai. At one time, she would not go to anything to which he invited her, perhaps because, although he tried to discourage Rabbit from drinking, he did not in any way discourage infidelities. Jai managed to charm her back by going to see her and begging her to come to a party, promising to 'put out a red carpet' for her. She relented and, when she arrived at the party, she was taken to a different entrance from all the other guests, at which Jai had literally had a red carpet laid.

Fidelity was, indeed, of no importance. Jai wrote again from Upper Brook Street:

>   27 July '36
> My dear Rabbit,
>   . . . hope you will find my letters waiting for you there [Jaipur], unless some of these damn fellows have opened them. So glad you have realized now who are your wellwishers & otherwise. My advice is to be friendly with all of them but trust none of them . . . Well dear brother I am having marvellous time as you can imagine. The girls are heaven. I will bring Molly for you to marry only if you allow me to see her sometimes? Is that O.K. by you . . . I met your friend Betty today you naughty boy you never told me anything about her. Babes I want you always to talk to me

all your secrets & difficulties. You know I am very understanding & after all we are both young want amusement from girls. So don't be shy in future about it. I will always tell you what I want & want you to do the same to me. Will you promise to do this. Well so long.

With lots of love from Jai

The letters to Rabbit go on for many years, mainly dealing either with Rabbit's regular troubles or telling him about 'fun' and girls. Jai was always extremely generous to his younger friend. In 1940 he writes, sending now not one hundred rupees, but two thousand.

In Jaipur, Jai was surrounded by sycophants. Even today, when the power of the Maharajas has been abolished for nearly forty years and their titles supposedly removed for almost fifteen, respect for royalty is still deeply ingrained among the majority of people in the former princely states. It was hard for the young Maharaja to know whom he could rely on as a friend. It is plain from these letters that he was lonely, and also, from the advice that he gave Rabbit to be friendly to everyone but to trust no one, that he did not dare to venture down from the royal pedestal.

He used to say to his ADCs, 'When you are off duty, for God's sake don't call me Highness or I'll go mad. Who can I talk to?' Rabbit was, it seems, almost the only person with whom he felt wholly at ease. He was part of the extended family, but was not so close a relation as, say, Jai's brother Bahadur, to whom some of the aura of royalty was inevitably attached. In any case, although Jai was fond of his brother, Bahadur was even more of a problem than Rabbit and could at times prove an embarrassment. He was known in Jaipur for his habit of sending his car round very late to people's houses long after they had finished dinner asking for food. Unable to send any, they would be deeply embarrassed at refusing the Maharaja's brother. His matrimonial arrangements were also a trial. He married a second wife without his father's knowledge, apparently on the understanding that she would bring 25,000 rupees by way of a dowry. In the event, she brought 5,000. Bahadur gave his first wife no money, so she borrowed fairly large sums which she could not repay. Although Jai's English friends remember Bahadur as a fairly jovial drinking companion (he died of it in the end), these problems, and many others besides, made him a poor confidant for the Maharaja, although there is no doubt that Jai was always extremely fond of his brother and saw him often. Rabbit, despite his lapses, was a far more reliable person. He understood about 'fun' and could be looked upon as a straightforward friend, to whom all secrets could be told.

One might have expected Jai's wives to fill that role, but it was not possible. The elder one was, as we have seen, an extremely orthodox woman who shared few of Jai's modern views. The younger one did venture out of purdah to the extent of accompanying him to England on two occasions, indeed her first son was born in Staines in May 1933. But even she, though young and pretty and readily welcomed by Jai's English friends, never really felt at ease. The narrow upbringing that both aunt and niece had had in the zenana had not fitted either of them to be the companions of so emancipated a man as Jai.

Then there was the matter of his own attitude towards women. There was no question, at that stage of his life, of his ever being faithful to his wives. Even if he had fallen in love with either of them, it is doubtful whether this would have curtailed his extra-marital adventures. The rumours in the Jaipur bazaars told of his womanising in the zenana. An English friend recalls that on some evenings Jai would say, 'Let's go and see young Captain Singh.' They would go and after a while Jai would leave the Englishman with the young Captain while he disappeared with the Captain's wife. After half an hour or so Jai would come back asking breezily, 'Well, what have you two been up to?' They did not like to ask the same question of Jai; but as often as not the young Captain would shortly become a young Major.

He enjoyed the company of English and American girls more, and even appeared to fall in love with them. He wrote to Rabbit:

My dear Rabbit,

. . . My pretty girl sailed for England on the 10th. Oh Rabbit I am heartbroken she has gone. I do love her so much and she was so marvellous. Have you found any girl? . . .

Yours ever Jai

Four days later he wrote again:

Rambagh
20 March '34

My dear Rabbit

. . . You lucky devil finding a girl so soon. I have not been able to look at any since Joan. Anyhow I have got 2 American girls coming to stay with me today. Will let you know what they are like.

Yours ever Jai

Ten days was, it would appear, long enough for love to fade. It has not been possible to identify Joan with any certainty. She was a long-lasting friend, although Rabbit did not like her. In July 1936, Jai wrote to him: 'Why such a dislike for Joan or is she too hefty?'

At the same time Jai was very fond of the beautiful widow of the Maharaja of Cooch Behar. She was a most glamorous person. The daughter of the Maharaja of Baroda, she eloped at the age of twenty-one with a supposedly ineligible young man, who somewhat unexpectedly succeeded his brother, the latter having died early. Unfortunately he too died at the age of thirty-six, leaving his thirty-year-old widow with five children. In 1928, she took her children to England to be educated. She rapidly became a familiar figure among the racier elements of smart society in London.

As they had met in India, it was natural when Jai went to Woolwich that he should call on her and very soon they became close friends. The Maharani was a woman of quite outstanding beauty. The portraits of her by Laszlo, and by several other painters, show us a delicately-featured young

99

woman of great elegance, with short, immaculately-arranged hair. Yet there was always about her a slightly wild look for which abandoned would be too strong a word, yet carefree too weak a one.

Not surprisingly, Jai was much drawn to her and equally she found this handsome, gentle young man extremely attractive. Jai's friendship with her, and later with her children, was to be the most important thing in his private life. On her return to India, she became a frequent visitor to Jaipur and he, when he went to Calcutta for the polo season each year in December, would usually stay at Woodlands, the Cooch Behar mansion in Calcutta. Amer Singh disapproved of this friendship. Seeing Jai buying her 'expensive trinkets' at Babumall's shop in Delhi, he noted in his diary '. . . this lady is going to ruin him as I hear she has done a good many before . . .'

Jai was certainly not going to be ruined by any woman. He was, in the first place, far too sensible; furthermore, he was both too conscious of his position to make a fool of himself and too eclectic in his fondness for women for any one of them to engage his full affections – until he eventually married the only woman he really loved.

Naturally, it was impossible for the young Maharaja to form any serious relationship with an Indian girl. Any suitable girls were in purdah and jealously guarded. Anyhow, he was already married and by 1935 he had four children. In 1933 and in 1935, Second Her Highness produced two more sons, Jai Singh and Prithviraj Singh. Neither of his wives provided the kind of companionship which he had come to learn was possible during his first visit to England. Apart, then, from his frolics in the zenana, for many years Jai relied for female friendship on English and American girls.

It was not just a question of girls. Jai's visits to England became an essential part of his life. It is not hard to imagine the attraction which England must have had for him. While it was delightful to be a Maharaja in India, it had many disadvantages. The continuous squabbling, the unending intrigues, the fathomless depths of sycophancy, the ever-present threat of British interference, the steady stream of

100

favour-seekers and, once again, the ultimately hollow quality of power were exhausting and demanding.

A Maharaja visiting England, particularly if he were as young and handsome and rich as Jai, had nearly as many advantages as at home and practically no disadvantages. Jai went to England every year from 1933 until the Second World War. He would take a house or flat in Mayfair and set about enjoying himself. His ADCs, if asked what he did in England, say, 'Oh, parties, of course.'

The parties ranged from Court Balls, at which Jai would appear in full Indian brocades with a huge ruby in his turban and long spurs, to evenings at the Café de Paris and the 400 Club. Besides parties, there were weekends in the country with famous hostesses like Mrs Ronnie Greville or with Sir Harold and Lady Wernher, or with ex-Viceroys and old acquaintances from India. There were trips to Paris and the South of France, shooting parties in Austria and Romania; and, above all, polo.

It was the life of a rich, European aristocrat and there is little wonder that girls found him attractive and that in return he found them 'marvellous', with their free and easy ways, compared with the few Indian women he was ever likely to meet. Europe represented a freedom and a quality of friendship with both sexes that he could never know at home.

It was still a life of privilege and one in which he could indulge his high spirits. Lord Roderick Pratt remembers that, in 1937, Jai found he had little to do in the mornings, so he got himself attached to the Life Guards. He had been made an honorary captain in the Indian Army in 1934. He was living in the Dorchester Hotel and in the morning he would appear in Lord Roderick's room. The servant would bring black coffee or a Horse's Neck (brandy and ginger ale), depending on the nature of the previous evening.

Jai was popular with both the officers and the men, but he did not always endear himself to those in command. He had a habit of racing round Hyde Park in his Bentley at enormous speed until he had as many as three policemen on his tail. Then he would shoot into the barracks and, when the police arrived, he would claim diplomatic immunity, much to the embarrassment of the commanding officer.

Considering how important it seemed to him to be connected with the Life Guards, Jai treated his attachment to the regiment with unexpected insouciance. He used to practise sword-play in Lord Roderick's room until he speared a painting, after which he used an umbrella.

After some weeks, they were transferred to Combermere Barracks at Windsor where, according to Lord Roderick, they blundered about together on military exercises, which a General came from London to watch.

In the first one, Jai and Lord Roderick were supposed to cross Windsor Great Park with great circumspection watching for their 'enemies' coming from the other end of the park. Instead, anxious to win, they went at full gallop, arriving early at their objective. When Lord Roderick introduced Jai as the Maharaja of Jaipur, the waiting General looked amazed and asked whether he should salute him. Hastily, Jai saluted. The General thought they had done well and said that, as everything was over, he might as well be off for breakfast and then wander back to the War Office. 'By the way,' he asked as he left, 'do you think you're learning anything?' 'I'm not sure yet,' said Jai. Finding the General had gone, Colonel Wyndham was furious.

Thinking to repair the damage at the next exercise, they used a little ingenuity. This time they had to guess which way the 'enemy' would go and to ambush them. There were several exits and they could see no way of guessing which to guard. So they bribed a postman to tell them which way the 'enemy' were heading. On getting the news, they rushed to the right exit. There was the General, impressed. How had they deduced the 'enemy's' intentions? With shining honesty, they explained. 'It's all over then,' said the General, 'I might as well be off for breakfast.'

Once again, Colonel Wyndham was chagrined at finding no General. Later, having presumably seen the General, he suggested that Jai and Lord Roderick had cheated.

'I thought all was fair in love and war,' said Jai.

'The British Army,' said the Colonel portentously, 'will always play the game.'

'Well,' said Jai, 'in that case you might lose a war.'

At that time, there were three polo clubs in London –

Roehampton, Hurlingham and Ranelagh. There were, there-fore, nine or ten polo grounds, all full every day. During the four months Jai spent in Europe every year, he played polo at least four days a week. It was a passion which excluded almost every other sport. He, for instance, never took any interest in racing, except for his visits to Ascot, which were entirely social rather than sporting occasions.

All in all, his visits to England provided him with a rest from the tediums of the painfully enclosed society of Jaipur. They were also a great stimulus for ideas about the running of his state. He would come back full of schemes for the re-organisation of his army, with liberal notions for the welfare of his people, with various plans for the modernisation of Jaipur.

He would also bring back masses of things which he had bought. The Lalique fountains outside the Rambagh Palace were the result of a visit to an exhibition in Paris. He bought Cartier 'mystery' clocks, trick lighters, elaborate cigarette boxes, fancy cocktail shakers. His taste was a shade chromium, perhaps, but by no means as vulgar as that of the majority of his fellow Princes at the time.

Second Her Highness would complain, on his return, that he had become too English: she would insist on fewer Western dishes from the kitchens and grumble that dinner was much too early. Indians do not usually eat until at least ten or eleven at night. Jai would get hungry at eight.

Soon he would settle down to the business of being a ruler, although there were a few not very important ways in which he stuck to British habits. In particular, he nearly always spoke in English to his officers and nobles, but he was pleased when they replied in Hindi, Urdu or Jharshahi, the local dialect. Similarly, he shaved his moustache, which few Hindus do while their fathers are alive, but he did not like others to copy him. Gradually, over the decade between his accession and the war, his character developed. The charming, obedient boy whose tutors had loved him, whom Lord Irwin regarded almost as a son, but of whom no one had any great expectations became a person of strength and wisdom.

The early predictions about his character by less well-disposed people were nearly all proved wrong. One Maharaja of Amleta had said of him at Mayo, 'I am afraid he is very *ghoona*', which meant that he would remember grudges and harbour them until he got an opportunity for revenge.

The Principal of Mayo College, although fond of Jai's 'cheery personality', had said he had lacked initiative as a monitor 'but proved capable of exercising authority'. More alarmingly, he had said that he was very susceptible to outside influences so that 'his immediate companions will have a direct bearing on his behaviour and outlook on life'.

The Thakur of Jhalai, who had reason, it is true, to be prejudiced, said that he had come to the conclusion that Jai 'is a very deep man but not of firm character. His favourites will be constantly changing.'

Quite soon after Jai was invested with his powers, people began to change their opinions. Amer Singh noted, early in 1932, that Jai had been beautifully trained and was very popular. 'He mixes up with everyone but at the same time keeps people in their places. There is no taking liberties with him.'

At first, he had some difficulty in praising people. Abhey Singh, one of the members of his famous polo team, said that, even when he felt proud of his regiments in his heart, something prevented him from expressing his feelings to the commanders. He managed to overcome this inhibition, so that later, people would speak of his capacity to enthuse those who were working for him in such a way that they exceeded their own expectations of themselves.

There was no question of his bearing grudges, nor of his being unduly influenced by his companions. Indeed, as we have seen, he managed to remain remarkably aloof from the intrigues and machinations of the Rajputs. His detachment had about it a certain cynicism, which caused him to observe on more than one occasion, 'Never trust a Rajput, he will always let you down.'

His ability to exercise authority was never in doubt. One of his English friends described this quality:

He was a most relaxed person. All problems were
solved in an amicable manner. He never raised his

104

The Maharaja's private apartments in the City Palace (*The British Library*).

Marudhar Kanwar (First Her Highness), whom Jai married at the age of thirteen. Jai's second wife is in the background.

Kishore Kanwar (Second Her Highness), Jai's second wife, whom he married in 1932.

The Rambagh Palace (*The British Library*).

The Palace of the Winds (*The British Library*).

voice but had what one might call a built-in authority. He never swore coarsely, though he had no objection to a little ribald chat. He was absolutely natural. He never said anything stupid. He was not a clever man, but he was unusually wise.

This view is possibly a little too rosy. Among his papers are some undated notes headed 'Talk to the ADCs':

> Gentlemen, this is no pleasure for me to talk to you today as this is a repetition of the same things for the 100th time if not more . . . I am convinced that none of you have any consideration for me or my family but your main consideration is yourself and your houses and what you can get out of us . . . you have made failures of your career and today you exist because of my kindness of the softness of my heart but you instead of having any gratitude do nothing but take advantage of us for your own selfish purposes . . . I must in turn be hard which you have driven me into.

He went on to tell them that they would never be able to get any other job as they were so incapable. From now on, they must work efficiently or get out:

> This is my final talk with you all . . . before concluding . . . I would like to ask a favour of the ADCs that in future if any of them neglect their duty or make a blunder I hope they'll have the decency to put in their resignation on their own without being asked by me.

No doubt he had to address them for the hundred and first and many more times, for their inefficiency was real enough, as was his 'softness of heart'. Those surviving ADCs remember vividly the blasts of wrath, yet there is not one who does not speak of him but with tones of reverence and hero worship.

His anger with the ADCs was not always over minor infringements of court etiquette. On one occasion, he had given special orders that no one was to go near the card room in the main part of the Rambagh Palace. Jai came there

105

to find a group of officers gossiping outside the room. The reason for his orders was that he had persuaded several ladies in purdah to flout the conventions and come to his part of the Palace. He was afraid that the women would be put off by all the men hanging around and might not come again. Jai banned the officers from the Palace for a month. One of them was to have had a Silver Jubilee medal. He did not get it. (Jai gave it to Rabbit instead.)

The ADCs suffered to some extent because of Jai's almost obsessive concern with little details of ceremonial. He fussed about the question of titles, gun salutes, medals, precedence. He was quite happy to insist that all the nobles be in their places in the darbar hall two and half hours before a ceremony was due to start. When they grumbled, he airily pointed out that in Madho Singh's time they had often had to wait five or six hours. Again, he changed the flag of the state. Previously it had been an extended triangle, long and awkward. He made it rectangular and, when he was in residence in the City Palace, he had one of the new flags flown and under it another, one quarter the size, to represent the title Sawai, meaning one and a quarter, granted by the Moghul Emperor to his ancestor, Jai Singh.

He would discuss at great length whether to have the Lancers shout 'Jai!' at big parades when giving three cheers, instead of the usual 'Hoorah!' In the end, he thought the former would be more effective. Sometimes, he could be almost winningly naive in his innocence. For instance, he once asked one of his commanding officers how he could become the Colonel of the Sawai Man Guards, which, after all, he had created. The commander patiently wrote out the order, with effect from the following morning, for Jai to sign.

In one important sphere, Jai's upbringing by the British and his subsequent association with and admiration for them had no influence. This was in his religious attitudes. The Government and the political officers who supervised the princely states were always scrupulous in observing the British policy of religious toleration. They were often embarrassed and irritated by the activities of the missionaries, although their medical work was useful. From the beginning, the Minority Council had encouraged Jai's religious instruction. It may be remembered that the late Maharaja Ram Singh's brother-in-law, Thakur Bahadur Singh, was appointed 'to foster a respect for the religion of his ancestors and instil a knowledge of its practises'. The Thakur must have been a good instructor for, throughout his life, Jai retained a deep-seated religious sensibility without any tinge of spurious piety.

The Maharaja in any Hindu state was, without its being expressly laid down, the defender of the faith. It was the custom for the Maharaja to lead the people on any religious occasion or festival. For Jai this was an important part of his function and he performed all the ceremonies quite naturally in a genuinely devout manner. He would surprise his English guests by getting into his Bentley and driving to Amber Fort and there, with his own hand, sacrificing a goat before the temple of Shila Devi.

There were three temples of great importance for Jai. First, the Govind Devi temple within the City Palace precincts. This houses the image of the god otherwise known as Lord Krishna, brought originally from Vrindaban and put here when the temple was built by Jai Singh in 1735. Whenever Jai addressed the people of Jaipur, he would start his speech, 'Subjects of Govind Devji . . .' implying that he governed only as an instrument of the deity, who remained their real ruler.

The second temple was that of Shila Devi, which stands within the walls of the Amber Fort. The image housed here was brought by Man Singh I from Jessore. Man Singh built the temple in 1604. Jai restored it, installing solid silver doors at the entrance as a thanksgiving for his recovery from his plane crash in 1939. Today, although the Amber Fort has been given to the state, this temple remains the property of the family.

The third temple is the oldest. Built in 1007, it is dedicated to Jamma Mataji. It lies some twenty miles outside Jaipur City.

Before leaving Jaipur for any length of time, Jai would always visit each of these temples and go straight to them again immediately on his return. As in all things to do with his position as ruler, whether secular or spiritual, he was most punctilious in his ceremonial, conducting very minutely the complicated rituals connected with religious festivals and observing rigidly all the fasts of the goddess Kali. He accepted obediently the Pandits ruling that he should not be allowed a punkah to cool him during the long performances of his birthday puja, held in the heat of the summer. All princely regalia and privilege had to be left outside when the Maharaja entered a temple.

When Jai was abroad, he still prayed every day. Before any polo match, he would put flowers in front of the deities which he took everywhere with him and, during the war, he carried with him a photograph of his battle goddess, Durga, and prayed to her daily.

At the same time, Jai was quite free of the sillier superstitions which trouble many Indians. There was an occasion when someone sneezed at exactly the moment when he announced that he would leave at half past seven the next morning for Delhi. All his attendants begged him to change his time of departure in view of this sinister omen. He paid no attention.

One rather touching memory of his piety survives. Before he went, at the time of Independence, to sign the instrument of Jaipur's accession to the Indian Union, he visited the Shila Devi temple. The Pandit gave him his blessing and, as is customary, a flower. This flower Jai put in an envelope which he filed with the papers dealing with the Accession. (The keeper of the papers maintains that when white ants ate virtually all the papers in this file – a circumstance, incidentally, which proved a great frustration to this biographer – they left intact only the envelope with the flower.)

There was one aspect of Jai's character which we cannot ignore. He was, in small things, quite astonishingly mean. One of his English friends benevolently attributed this trait to 'a great respect for cash'. This 'respect' took the form of never having any on him. The stories of his stinginess are too many for it merely to have been a respect for cash.

As early as 1932, when he was asked to contribute 1,000 rupees to a Mayo College fund and become a patron of the Old Boys Association, he refused, on the grounds that he could not afford it. Our friend Amer Singh recorded two somewhat absurd instances of this parsimonious side of Jai's nature. One concerned a fountain pen which Amer Singh had bought for himself out of regimental funds. Jai made an inordinate fuss about the expenditure, though even he found it a bit silly after an hour's discussion. The other involved a small cow and two white peacocks, which were to be sent as a present to the Maharaja of Kishengarh. The question was, who would pay the wages of twenty-five rupees a month for the cowman who was to look after the cow?

One of the Coldstream Guards instructors whom Jai had hired to train his Sawai Man Guards had been promised wages of £20 a month. When he arrived, Jai wanted to reduce this by nearly £5. Another Maharaja remembers being in the South of France with Jai. They used to go out in the evenings together. The Maharaja realised that he was getting through an unexpected amount of money. He asked his ADC what was happening. The man explained that whenever the two Maharajas went out, Jai would always tell the other Maharaja's ADC that he had forgotten his money and ask him to settle the bill.

Oddly enough, although everyone who knew Jai always mentions his stinginess, they do so without any resentment. It may just have been the natural caution of a very rich man, anxious not to be put upon; or it may have been hereditary, his real father being known as the most close-fisted man in Jaipur. Whatever the cause, Jai's charm and warmth of character overcame all antagonism. He could, in any case, be extremely generous. We have seen what he did for Rabbit. Similarly, when Prithi Singh, one of the members of his polo team, died suddenly, Jai looked after his family.

Jai could be as high-spirited in India as he was in England. There is an account of his flying himself back from Calcutta with his ADC. Landing at Allahabad, they found the refreshment room shut. They were hungry, so they broke in to find some food. The police were called. Jai told them to send him the bill for damages.

This spirited behaviour was inclined to have graver consequences, so that in the end it came to seem that Jai was highly accident-prone. His first serious accident happened at the beginning of December 1936. During a polo match in Jaipur, a well-known English player, Gerald Balding, collided with Jai, who fell heavily. At first it was thought that he had merely hurt his leg. Eventually, it turned out that his back had been severely damaged. He was sent to Austria on 1 January 1937 for treatment.

For a while, he was in hospital, where according to his ADC, Major Parbat Singh, 'he turned pale and blue and his eyes bulged under the traction. At first, I thought they were killing him and I wanted to order them to stop. His Highness laughed at me and said that instead of interfering with the treatment, I would do him better service by somehow getting rid of his fat nurse, who he couldn't face looking at.'

After a couple of weeks, Jai moved to the Hotel Bristol, where he continued his treatment. From here he wrote to Rabbit on 14 January:

> Dearest Rabbit,
>   . . . I feel very homesick and long to get back. The
> treatment is getting on but is very slow . . . in plaster
> like the one in Calcutta but this one is not so bad . . . I
> hope you are being nice and helpful especially to
> Virginia as she will feel a bit lost without me . . .
>   with love from Jai

There were several people staying at the Rambagh without him, including Steve Donaghue, the jockey, Sir Alfred Chester Beatty and Sir Robert Throckmorton. Virginia was the actress Virginia Cherryl, who married Cary Grant and subsequently the Earl of Jersey. She was Jai's favourite girlfriend after Joan. It seems likely that she went to Vienna to cheer him up, as Major Parbat Singh distinctly remembers her there.

There were, as it happened, plenty of diversions in the Hotel Bristol. First, there arrived the recently abdicated Duke of Windsor, with his ADC Major 'Fruity' Metcalfe. Soon Jai was writing again to Rabbit more cheerfully: 'I am much better and no pains but still five more weeks. All my love Jai.'

Next, came the deposed Maharaja of Alwar, a neighbouring state to Jaipur, which had at one time belonged to

110

Jaipur. He took over one whole floor of the hotel in order to accommodate his entourage of thirty-three concubines, a number of singers and three cooks.

It is interesting to compare Jai with Alwar, because the response of each one to the role of Maharaja was almost directly opposite. Alwar was a clever, immoral and rebellious man. The hollow quality of a Maharaja's power irked him, indeed goaded him into outrageous behaviour. At its best, his humour was witty and informed by an immense sense of style. The legends about him are endless.

One summer, when the Rajput Maharajas were at Mount Abu, Bikaner, who disapproved of him, failed to invite Alwar to a large party. Three days before the party, Alwar sent out his men to buy up all the food that was to be had for nearly forty miles around. Bikaner had to cancel his party as he could find nothing for his guests to eat. Alwar then invited Bikaner to dine with him.

His jokes were often in insupportably bad taste. The brother of one of his lesser wives came to stay one night. This man got tediously drunk and kept asking Alwar for a girl for the night. Alwar agreed to provide one, but the man still went on and on about it. Alwar finally said that he would send to his room the most skilful girl in his zenana, but he made two conditions: the man must not speak to the girl and he must not put on the light. The girl arrived and the two made love. When they had finished, the lights came on. Alwar had sent the man's sister. It is said that they both committed suicide.

Alwar's relations with the British were a balancing act. He did everything he could to provoke them, short of compelling them to depose him. They tolerated his pederasty, but were driven to the edge by his oppressive taxation and his stimulation of communal unrest. Each time the Viceroy was on the verge of dethroning him, he would contrive to dine with the Secretary of State for India in London. Erudite and urbane, he would impress the Secretary of State with a brilliant summary of the political situation. When the Viceroy's recommendation to get rid of Alwar arrived, the Secretary of State, remembering his agreeable evening with the cultivated Maharaja, would advise waiting a while before acting too hastily.

111

Alwar's method of protest against British domination was to adopt an excessively Hindu posture. He affected to believe that he was a reincarnation of Rama. He would not allow any leather in his palaces and his Rolls Royces were upholstered in French needlepoint. He would refuse to shake hands with any European unless he were wearing gloves. At one point, when he was in danger of deposition, he was invited to Buckingham Palace. His advisers besought him to take off his gloves when he met King George V. He promised to do so. Before shaking hands, he drew off his gloves with great ostentation. He had on another pair underneath.

Eventually the British did depose him, in 1933, although it was suggested that it was neither his misgovernment nor his sexual aberrations which precipitated their action, but rather that at the end of an unsatisfactory chukka of polo, he poured petrol over his pony, which had performed badly, and set fire to it. Offences against animals were more reprehensible than against small boys.

Jai's attitude to the British was the complete reverse of this. Following the pattern set by his ancestors, he was obedient and loyal to the central power in Delhi.

At the beginning of March, he was well enough to return to Jaipur. After only one month, he was off once more to England, where he attended the Coronation, sending to the new King Emperor George VI a telegram assuring him of his 'respectful homage and unswerving loyalty'. He returned, after his weeks with the Life Guards, at the end of September 1937.

His life and those of his fellow Princes were now at a turning point. The Government of India Act had been passed in 1935. A Federation Committee had recently been set up. The wheels which were to draw India to Independence had started to turn in earnest. The last churnings of feudalism were about to erupt in Jaipur state. Jai's private life was shortly to alter dramatically. The young Maharaja's character was about to be put to the test.

CHAPTER 7

In 1938, a situation arose which had in some ways a surprisingly medieval flavour, but at the same time was a turning point in the history of modern Jaipur. It was also to be the spark which brought out the more serious side of the Maharaja's nature. Until this moment, his main concerns in Jaipur had been sport, the creation of his army and the maintenance of dignity and pageantry. From now on, he was to be deeply involved in the real business of ruling and in the politics of his state. He was not to abandon the more frivolous side of his life, but the emphasis was to change.

The event which produced this change was, in its simplest form, a baron's revolt. There is a large area of Jaipur state known as Shekhawati. This area has a different history from the rest of the state, having been captured, before the time of Akbar, by Shehhaji, a younger son of the rulers of Amber. He declared himself independent of Amber and defeated the Maharaja in battle in order to prove it.

Jai Singh II brought the Shekhawatis back into the domain of Jaipur, but after his death they again refused tribute and seized crown lands. The arrival of the British reversed the situation once more, as a part of their freezing of the map of India. The British treaties with the Princes guaranteed whoever happened, in the general turmoil, to be the nominal ruler of a particular region at that moment. Jaipur's hold over Shekhawati may have been never so feeble, but the principle existed and the British were, therefore, ready both to endorse and enforce the right of the Jaipur darbar over Shekhawati.

113

The largest thikana in Shekhawati was Sikar. This thikana covered 1,600 square miles, almost exactly one tenth of all Jaipur state. The income of the thikana was 1,200,000 rupees, again a tenth of the state's income. There were some 440 villages and the population was nearly a quarter of a million. It was run like a state, having its own council, police force, civil and criminal courts and even a small number of troops.

The ruler of Sikar was the Rao Raja Kalyan Singh. He had been born in 1922. He was illiterate, dotty almost to the point of paranoia, vacillating and given to drink. He was steeped in the traditional notions of Rajput honour and yet had about him a certain pathetic appeal. He also had a measure of simple cunning. He could never understand why, as ruler of his thikana, he should have to have a council at all, least of all why Jaipur should have any right to appoint councillors or interfere in his administration.

The British view was the exact opposite of the Rao Raja's. Their policy was one of centralisation, involving the diminution, if not the total abolition, of the traditional, somewhat autonomous powers of the Jagirdars and thikana-holders. Shekhawati being a special case, the Jaipur council commissioned a retired Indian Civil Service officer, Mr C.N. Willis, to prepare a *Report on the Land-Tenures and special Powers of Certain Thikanedars of the Jaipur State*.

The Wills report was a masterpiece of ingenuity. He explained that the Shekhawatis really held their lands under a Moghul system, which meant that the Maharaja could take them away at whim. The only trouble with the basis of his argument was that, in that case, the Maharaja also held his state under the same system – that is to say, his sovereignty and independence were in doubt. Wills wriggled out of that by referring to the treaty of 1818, by which the British gave the Maharaja sovereignty but, by an authorised supplementary treaty between the Maharaja and his Thikanedars, kept them and his Jagirdars subservient to him.

The Jaipur Council, on receiving this convenient report, ordered a Commission of Inquiry into its findings. The Shekhawatis were both angry and insulted. Their honour was at stake and their powers threatened. They commissioned a barrister from Lucknow to formulate a reply. His arguments

114

were pertinent and telling. Nonetheless, the Commission declared, in March 1935, in favour of Mr Wills – a decision which even the least suspicious of minds may have thought had something to do with the fact that the chairman of the Commission was none other than Mr Wills himself.

The scene was thus set for conflict. Even so, the Jaipur authorities had won their point, by outwardly proper means, and they should, perhaps, have proceeded more tactfully than they did.

It is plain that Jai never cared much for the Rao Raja. In 1933, the Rao Raja had shot a tiger. Under hunting rules laid down by the Maharaja Ram Singh, no one was allowed to shoot tigers, bears or sambhar deer, with the exceptions of the Rao Raja of Sikar and the Raja of Khetri. Jai, however, decided to exclude them as well, and so wanted to fine Sikar 500 rupees for having shot the tiger. Amer Singh told Jai not to 'behave like a child'. Besides, as he pointed out, it was essential to tell people beforehand if you plan to take away their privileges.

Jai mouldered on about this for two months. In the end, he gave in and let Sikar off the fine; but he insisted that he accept an Englishman as Senior Member of his Council. The Rao Raja was quite crafty about this imposition, as he considered it. He got rid of the first of the appointees by giving him enough money to retire on and the second merely by making his life intolerable.

In June 1934, Captain A.W.T. Webb was appointed Senior Member. Webb was a much tougher proposition for the Rao Raja, who in any case quite liked him to start with. Gradually Webb took over everything. He even excluded the Rao Raja from any share in the administration. He started factories, built dispensaries, opened a model farm, inaugurated a museum and increased the revenue of the thikana by 100,000 rupees.

The Rao Raja's resentment grew. He protested endlessly to Jaipur. The final result of his protests was that in April 1937, the Jaipur Prime Minister, Sir Beauchamp St John, took all power away from the Rao Raja for ten years. He was to be allowed to stay in Sikar and was to be given 100,000 rupees a year as a Privy Purse. The education of his son was to be in

115

the hands of the Senior Member of the Sikar council, who was to be appointed by Jaipur. Any argument about the boy's education would be settled by the Maharaja. The timing of this decree had to do partly with the matter of Webb's contract. It would expire in June and the Rao Raja planned not to renew it. Once they had taken away Sikar's powers, they were able to engage Webb on a new contract.

Naturally, the Rao Raja did not like any of this, but it was the question of his son's education which was to be the direct cause of the baron's revolt in the following year. Hardayal Singh, the Rao Raja's heir, was born in 1921. When he was twelve, he was betrothed to the daughter of the Maharaja of Dhrangadhra. The wedding was to take place in 1938. The father was immensely fond of his son and spoilt him outrageously. Seeing Hardayal being made to do physical training one day, the Rao Raja pressed ten rupees into the instructor's hand, begging him not to bother the boy.

Hardayal had been sent to Mayo College, but Webb judged that he was falling under 'sodomistic influences' and removed him early in 1938. The question was what to do with him next. Then Jai intervened. He decided that Hardayal should go to England, possibly to Cambridge. No one else was in favour of this idea. In the first place, it would mean postponing the marriage, which was planned for the summer. Jai was against an early marriage in any case, although, if Webb's fears had any foundation, it might have been a good idea. Sir Beauchamp St John evidently thought the interference in a family matter too provocative. Webb continued to have dark thoughts. Most bitterly opposed to the plan was the Rao Raja himself. He was an old-fashioned man, as we have seen, and was unlikely to favour a Western education. Furthermore, he did not wish to be separated from his son. Perhaps most hurtful of all, he had not even been consulted, but was just told that his son was to be sent abroad.

In February 1938, he appealed to Delhi; but he was told by them to sort it out with his Maharaja. Thinking that women might understand his feelings better, he had the Rani write pleading letters to the two Maharanis and to Mrs Lothian and Lady St John. Sikar also saw the Crown Secretary in Delhi and called on Jai and the British Resident in Jaipur. He got no satisfaction from any of them and retired to sulk at home.

By April, Jai decided that the question must be settled. He sent for the Rao Raja. He refused to come. The Maharaja sent Webb, Mr F.S. Young, the Jaipur police chief and two Sardars to Sikar, with orders to bring the Rao Raja back to Jaipur.

When they reached Sikar, they found the Rao Raja living in a house outside the town. He had with him a noticeably large number of Rajput attendants, inside and outside the house. The deputation asked the Rao Raja to come with them back to Jaipur. He refused and stood up to go, saying he had to visit the Rani, who was ill. At that, Mr Young put his hand on the old man's shoulder and besought him to come.

The onlookers took this gesture of Young's to mean that he was arresting the Rao Raja. They knocked Young aside, grabbed the old man and ran. They rushed him to the fort, closed the city gates and declared a hartal (strike).

Webb and Young were for using force, and telegraphed to Jaipur for a large detachment of troops. In Jaipur, the Prime Minister was less precipitate. The Council decided to try again with a different kind of deputation, headed by our friend Amer Singh. From his diary, we learn of the undertakings he was to give to the Rao Raja. He was not to be kept under any restraint.

> His son will not go to England by aeroplane as the
> Maharaja Sahib was going by boat and they will go
> together. The boy will not be left in England but will
> return with the Maharaja Sahib in four months time. The
> Rao Raja jee would be allowed to go to Sikar when the
> situation has calmed down . . . As regards Hardayal
> Singh jee's marriage, this will take place on the date
> which the Maharajas of Jaipur and Dhrangadhra decide.

The Rao Raja was also to be allowed to go to England, by a later boat, if he wished, and Jaipur would contribute to his expenses.

When Amer Singh arrived in Sikar, he noticed that there were some three or four thousand Rajputs in the fort. More were on their way. The Rao Raja was gathering his forces

117

round him. He received Amer Singh, who was an old friend, well enough. Rather contrary to expectations, after complaining of how he had nearly been arrested, he agreed to go to Jaipur with Amer Singh the next day, 17 April.

When the next day came, the Rao Raja dithered, but mostly because the hour at which they had arranged to leave was inauspicious. He delayed until noon, which was more propitious. At last, he was ready to leave, but the crowd of Rajputs would not let him. They demanded from Amer Singh conditions which were far beyond his brief.

'After about an hour, another attempt to leave was made and failed. I was now clear that the situation was out of the Rao Raja jee's hands.' Amer Singh went back to Jaipur.

By now, quite other interests were having a marked effect on the course of events. There were two main groups who saw the discomfiture of the Jaipur darbar as an oportunity to advance their causes.

The first of these were the Jats. The Jats are a caste of cultivators, spread over a large area of north-west India. There were two Rajputana States, Bharatpur and Dholpur, ruled by Jat Sikhs. More importantly, the Jats were the largest agricultural caste in the neighbouring areas of British India. In Shekhawati, Jats far outnumbered Rajputs, but they were kept in decidedly inferior circumstances. Their produce was subject to heavy tithes from which Rajput cultivators were exempt. They were not allowed to carry weapons of any sort; nor were they allowed to ride elephants or even, in some circumstances, horses.

The Jats in Shekhawati naturally became aware of the comparatively greater prosperity of their fellow caste members over the border in British India. This led to the forming of Jat organisations of protest and, in Sikar in 1933, the withholding of rent. The demonstrations grew over two years until, in 1935, a Jat Kisan Sabha (Peasant Association) was formed in the thikana. The Council had to appeal for help from the Jaipur police and, in the end, were forced to make concessions – remitting the taxes for 1934, arranging settlements on the land held by the Rao Raja and allowing Jats into government service.

An incident involving the right of a Jat bridegroom to ride

118

past a Rajput house on a horse ended in the police firing on the quarrelling crowd, killing at least four Jats. Another hundred were arrested. The Jat organisations were declared illegal and their leaders arrested. Jat leaders from other areas were forbidden to enter Jaipur State. This repression was continuing at the time of the revolt.

The other group eager to profit from the Sikar disturbances was the Praja Mandal (Peoples Conference) of Jaipur. The Praja Mandals were organisations of the educated, urban classes, usually mercantile, but including the professional classes and intellectuals. They were closely allied to the Indian National Congress, who were anxious for a foothold in the princely states, where they wished to see representative government.

As one of their leaders, Jamnalal Bajaj, put it, 'The Princes remain Princes, but they govern not only in name but also at the will, indeed by the sanction of the people.'

The line-up of these different interests was imprecise, not least because they all changed sides at various moments. The Praja Mandal group, for instance, supported the smaller Rajputs, whose concerns were slightly different from those of the big, sometimes educated, Jagirdars. But when the smaller Rajputs arrived in large numbers, waving weapons and spoiling for a fight in the true, blind tradition, Jamnalal Bajaj, a believer in non-violence, wanted nothing more to do with them.

On 21 April, Sir Beauchamp St John made another attempt to solve the crisis, going himself to Sikar, and taking Amer Singh as interpreter because the Rao Raja spoke only the local dialect. St John met two deputations. The first consisted of the Rao Raja and the big Thakurs. They were, on the whole, amenable, fearing more the rise of the peasantry and modern democracy than the traditional rule of a Maharaja, even if he wished to curtail some of their powers.

The second deputation consisted of a mixture of lesser Rajputs, the supporters of the Praja Mandal and a few Jats. They called themselves the Sikar Public Committee. Their main demand was for the restitution of power to the Rao Raja and the dismissal of Webb. Their reasons were different. The Rajputs wanted the Rao Raja restored because they

119

romantically believed in his independence from Jaipur. The Praja Mandal wanted it because the Rao Raja had led them to believe that he was prepared to set up representative government.

As Barnett Rubin, author of a thesis on the revolt, points out, it is unlikely that he had any idea of what representative government was. 'He could read neither English nor Hindi, and he had never left India. Hence he had neither read about nor seen democratic political systems.'

The Jats were hoping to throw off the powerful domination of Jaipur which prevented their realising any of their aspirations. By joining the Rajputs, they might please them and later be rewarded by the concession of some of their claims.

This jumbled assembly of interests rejected Sir Beauchamp's only mildly moderated conditions.

The story from that point onwards became even more complicated and the details are outside the scope of this book. No one, with the exception of Mr Arthur Lothian, the Agent to the Governor General, and possibly Jamnalal Bajaj, behaved with much sense. Both these, of course, had their particular interests to care for.

Lothian was determined to prevent the Praja Mandal having an opportunity, as he put it, to 'fish in troubled waters'. At the same time, it was the expressed policy of the British Government in India not to interfere in the internal affairs of a princely state. Accordingly, Lothian himself went to Sikar, nominally in a private capacity as an experienced person seeking to avert violence. There were by now some 30,000 sabre-rattling Rajputs in the fort at Sikar.

For his mission, Lothian took the precaution of having something more concrete to offer: he had persuaded Jai to renounce his intention of taking the Rao Raja's son to England. He also agreed to a complete amnesty for all the Rao Raja's followers. On these terms, the Rao Raja agreed to leave Sikar with Lothian to make his peace with the Maharaja, and he ordered the city gates to be opened and the Government offices to resume work. Some thousands of people tried half-heartedly to stop his train from leaving, but the Rao Raja got safely away to Ajmer.

Lothian, before going to Sikar, had persuaded Jai and

Beauchamp St John to set up a Commission of Inquiry into the whole question of the administration of Sikar. Until it reported, no punishments were to be inflicted on any of those who had joined the rebellion.

Once the Rao Raja had come to Jaipur, shown his nazar to the Maharaja and begged his forgiveness, Jai sailed away, on 7 May, to spend the summer in England, as he had always planned. Beauchamp St John, left in charge, behaved with crass insensitivity. As Lothian had granted an amnesty to all offenders, St John saw no reason to appoint a Commission of Inquiry. Instead, he issued, on 8 May, an order stating that the Rao Raja was unable to manage his thikana, owing to 'mental infirmity'. Henceforward, it would be administered by the Court of Wards. He ordered troops to Sikar to enforce the order.

This action alienated everyone. The gates of Sikar shut. The strike resumed. The British Government planted paragraphs in the newspapers dissociating themselves from the order. One of these quoted an unnamed source as having said:

> ... the administration of Jaipur was sadly unprogressive and was making itself unpopular by tactless actions. It was necessary for the Prime Minister to get into more intimate touch with the people of the State and also for the Maharaja to remain in the State, when critical problems arise.

The criticism of Jai was possibly not wholly fair, as it seems that Lothian had told him that it would be all right for him to leave. Against that, he had undoubtedly been very much on Sir Beauchamp's side and it would seem likely that he must have discussed with his Prime Minister an order issued only a day after he left India. Certainly, he had enjoyed discussions with Amer Singh about the ways in which they might besiege the fort at Sikar. He was, after all, a young Rajput and, by inheritance, likely to enjoy the idea of a fight.

All through May and June, the problem was tossed to and fro, each and every side taking more and more entrenched positions. The Rao Raja at Mount Abu intrigued with the Rani, who was still at Sikar, via a messenger. Beauchamp St John took Lothian's advice to withdraw his offensive order and to set up a Commission. This did not prevent a baton charge by the Jaipur police on a crowd in Sikar the day after the Commission started its deliberations. The Public Committee refused to co-operate with the Commission until its pre-emptive demands were met. The Jats, on the other hand, decided to back the Commission on the grounds that it was likely to recommend reforms favourable to them. Congress made great capital out of the situation.

Jamnalal Bajaj was constantly offering to mediate between the parties, thereby acquiring a statesmanlike aura. The Rajputs continued to threaten to resort to the sword.

The Rao Raja, having for so long played one side off against the other, eventually agreed to sign a paper saying the Commission was to his advantage. The Public Committee ignored this, which made a nonsense of their demands for the restoration of his powers. The Jaipur darbar imposed a blockade.

On 4 July, seventy armed Rajputs arrived by train in Sikar. Mr Young, the police chief, whose excessive zeal had already been the cause of some difficulties, ordered them either to go back or go on, on the train. The Rajputs opened fire, hitting a policeman and then, with their primitive weapons, charged the far more numerous police. At least five of them died. The remainder were arrested.

This incident drew even more attention to the situation in Sikar. Questions were asked in the House of Commons. Amer Singh later wrote that Lothian had said that:

> It was a thoroughly bad show all through from beginning to end. It was very badly managed by everyone who had anything at all to do with it. Jaipur had become the laughing stock of the whole world, and there were illustrated articles about it even in the American papers.

It was not to last much longer. Lothian and Sir Beauchamp sent for Jai. He arrived by air on 16 July, apparently not very pleased. Amer Singh wrote the next day:

I was standing a bit away from the others, and he [Jai]
came to me. He said to me he had to come a month
earlier, and that was what he objected. I told him he got
his food and his enjoyment from Jaipur and must
attend to its affairs.

There may have been something of a joke in this, as Jai was
always teasing Amer Singh. Indeed, he threatened to send
Amer Singh singlehanded to sort out Sikar's problems. In
the event, persuaded by Lothian, Jai went himself to Sikar.
Perhaps weary of the prolonged struggle and divided among
themselves, perhaps swayed by the traditional magic of
royalty, the opposition melted. The Public Committee agreed
to negotiate, through Bajaj and the senior Thakurs. When Jai
arrived in Sikar, all the gates were open and he was given
the key to the fort by one of the Rao Raja's relations.

It was over. The Rao Raja, after a few attempts to have his
affairs arbitrated by Delhi, withdrew all his demands and
made unqualified apologies to Jai. But nothing would ever
be the same again. The points had been made; they would
not now just disappear. At the height of the crisis, one
Congress leader had said:

The Maharaja of Jaipur is regarded as an intelligent
ruler, having the good of his subjects at heart, and his
timely response to public demand will justify this
regard and enhance his reputation as a popular ruler.
Besides, he must have recognised by now that his
administrators had not only tactlessly handled the
present and the last Jat agitation, but had also damaged
his prestige and reputation greatly.
   It is in his and his subjects' interest, therefore, that I
implore the Maharaja of Jaipur to rise to the occasion
and not only get defined the political rights of Sikar Rao
Raja, but also declare his intention to grant all political
and civic rights to his people.

That was, obviously, not going to happen and not even the
speaker expected it to happen. But the Sikar revolt must
have had a very profound effect on Jai's thinking. He had,

123

with a certain insouciance, entrusted the running of his state very much to British advisers, notably Beauchamp St John. This rather pompous baronet, who was given to telling the nobles of Jaipur that they were a lot of womanising, hard-drinking pleasure-seekers and that, while he as an aristocrat might sympathise with them, they should change their ways, had handled the Sikar affair in a singularly reactionary manner. Jai might well have decided that the British were not, perhaps, the people to run his state.

Then he had met Jamnalal Bajaj. This wily politician had put Jai into an awkward corner. When he was debating, and Bajaj knew he was debating, whether to go to Sikar himself or send a representative, Bajaj wired to Jai from Sikar suggesting that he come. This meant that his going could be represented as being at the instigation of the Praja Mandal.

It seems likely that Jai, who had always been shielded from any intercourse with Indian intellectuals, might well have recognised in Bajaj something which appealed to his Indianness, as well as to his innate sense of justice, for it was not to be long before immense changes came about in the administration of Jaipur.

The war did not greatly affect the day to day life of the city and state. Germany and Hitler were a long way off. Almost the only person with any connection with the enemy was a curious woman called Miss von Pott. She appeared in Jaipur early in 1939 and was happily received at the Rambagh Palace.

She was reputed to be Austrian, of good family, and was by way of being a painter. She was also bossy and interfering. We hear of her, in April 1939, complaining about Jai's treatment of the sad Thakur of Jhalai, who had apparently applied through Sir Beauchamp St John for a loan. Motivated by 'petty jealousy and selfishness', according to Miss von Pott, Jai had refused the loan, saying that Jhalai was a dirty dog and had no son. When he died, the thikana would revert to the state and he did not want it encumbered with debts.

124

Miss von Pott put it about that Jai was stingy and paid his servants very little, while 'his sexual pleasures were costing about fifty thousand rupees a year'.

Nonetheless, for a while, Miss von Pott continued to be received, until one night Jai's brother Bahadur, in his usual drunken condition, drove her home. Having prudently asked his servants to warn him if there was anything on the road ahead, he alarmed Miss von Pott even more by telling her that she was unlikely to be asked to many more parties as it was being spread about that she was a German spy.

This did not stop her grumbling that the royal family had not been sufficiently polite to a grand Bavarian priest who was travelling around India at the time, collecting examples of Christian art for an exhibition. He came, it was said, with a letter of introduction (later regretted) from the Vicereine, Lady Linlithgow.

Miss von Pott must have had another more charitable side to her nature, because she also spotted among the Rambagh guests a man she recognised as being a Swiss waiter. She forbore to expose him.

As the year wore on, Miss von Pott became apprehensive. On 6 September, she was abruptly given an hour to get out of Jaipur. Then, instead, she was arrested. It turned out that she really was a spy and that her friend the holy Father was merely posing as an art historian. Among her luggage was a rifle and a camera. Her letters home had been intercepted and she had reported in them that the Maharaja and the people of Jaipur were so displeased with the Indian Government that they would surely back Germany.

Poor, deluded Miss von Pott – she was not even much of a painter to judge by the portrait she did of our friend Amer Singh, who for some reason became somewhat amorously inclined towards her. Eventually, after four months, she was released but banished from Jaipur.

Jai had, of course, no such traitorous intentions as Miss von Pott imputed to him. He had, by this time, in response to the troubles at Sikar, become much more involved in state affairs, working four or five hours a day, which to the Rajput nobles was a source of marvel. He had been endeavouring to persuade his Sardars that they must change their ways.

125

In May 1939, he addressed a meeting of eighty-one senior Sardars speaking, rather to their surprise, in excellent Jhar-shahi. He appealed to them in terms which they could understand. Their honour, he said, was bound together with his honour; if one went, the other must follow. They must abandon old ideas and introduce new ones. They must give up the unfair taxes which they levied on their tenants and agree to various proposals for the reorganisation of their jagirs. Despite this appeal to reason, only thirty-five out of more than seven hundred Sardars agreed voluntarily to the settlement proposed.

He had to deal with the recalcitrant Rajputs, who did not wish to obey a law which the British insisted be passed all over India requiring anyone who owned a gun to register it. The Maharaja of Jodhpur, for instance, agreed to pass the Arms Act, but said that he would not implement it.

Until now, Jai had been reasonably content to allow the British to guide his administration. It was their policies which had in the end prevailed. The change in his attitude to government did not come about suddenly and there was no one incident which could be said to have caused it. There was no doubt that he had found their handling of the Sikar revolt inept and heavy-handed. More than that, not so easily pin-pointed, he seems at this time to have become more aware of his Indian heritage. He was also developing a certain political instinct. He could not guess what form the India of the future might take, but he was well aware that Indians of all kinds would soon have a greater say in their affairs, that India would become more Indian and less British. This change in no way affected his loyalty to the King Emperor, but it altered radically his dealings with officialdom.

In April 1939, Jai finally got rid of Sir Beauchamp St John. He appointed in his stead a Mr Todd. This unfortunate person soon fell victim to a series of fits and had to leave in August. He was the last English Prime Minister to serve in Jaipur. Jai then appointed Raja Gyan Nath, a man of no great distinction.

Something of Jai's new spirit may be seen in the battle over the treatment of the Praja Mandal, the local organisation of the Indian National Congress, and in particular of Jamnalal

126

Bajaj. In contrast to what was happening in neighbouring states, the Praja Mandal generally enjoyed unusually cordial relations with the Jaipur Government. This was due to the friendship between Jai and Hiralal Shastri, who had been the leader of the Jaipur Praja Mandal since its foundation in 1936. Shastri had been one of Jai's mentors at Mayo College and he agreed to limit the organisation's activities to conform with the laws of Jaipur.

Opening the First Annual Session of the Praja Mandal in 1938, the chairman of the Reception Committee said:

> We would preserve the Crown with all its magnificent glory, with all its historic association, with all its rights and privileges and with all our traditional loyalty. The elimination of the monarchy, or causing any disaffection or disloyalty to the person and throne of His Highness, does not and can never appeal to us.

Hiralal Shastri, in a letter to Freddie Young, the Inspector General of Police, early in 1939, after remarking how well they had 'pulled on' for about two years wrote:

> The position as between the Government and the Mandal in Jaipur is unique . . . Jaipur's name will go down in history for the world will see in due course of time, that there were officials and public workers in Jaipur who achieved the same object with mutual agreement, which elsewhere was almost invariably achieved after agony and heartburning on both sides.

It is arguable that he was writing this in dismay at a change of policy, brought about by the Sikar revolt, but it was none-theless true. The change of policy involved the passing of a Public Societies Regulation Act, requiring registration of all societies. Praja Mandal was refused registration and thus banned. Shortly before this came a ban on Jamnalal Bajaj from entry into Jaipur State.

Both these acts were laid at the door of the British in the shape of Beauchamp St John, because they were known to be terrified of Congress, in any form, anywhere. The British

127

said they had not even been consulted. The fact is that Beauchamp St John would have known what they wanted; and what they did want became plain enough as things developed.

The Private Secretary to the Viceroy wrote to the Political Agent in January saying that the Jaipur state authorities should have all support in these matters as the other 'Rajput States all regard this as the critical case in the present trial of strength with Congress'. Gandhi had indeed said that he intended to make the situation in Jaipur an all-India issue.

Throughout the winter, Jamnalal Bajaj made several attempts to get into Jaipur. Freddie Young's intelligence was good. He always knew where and how Jamnalal would arrive. Each time, he arrested him and deported him. On the third occasion, the Viceroy wanted him imprisoned. He was merely sent away, on Jai's own orders.

The affair mouldered on, accompanied by a certain amount of unrest in the state. Bajaj was eventually arrested at the end of February and detained. In February, the Viceroy wrote to the Secretary of State in London, saying that he had seen Jai in Delhi, where he was playing polo, and had criticised Jai for leaving his state. The Maharaja had said that he was in close touch with events. The Viceroy went on to say, evidently forgetful of the full support he had insisted upon only two weeks before, that Jai and his Government could not continue to prevent 'progressive' activities in their state altogether and must find a way to modify their attitude without climbing down or losing face.

Jai was, in fact, proceeding in his own way. He had two entirely private meetings with Jamnalal before he went to England towards the end of May. The Secretary of State must have made some rude comments about Jai because, on 2 June, the Viceroy wrote to London: 'I quite agree with you about Jaipur. I doubt if that young man has any interest in the running of his state or in its problems.' Four days later the Secretary of State wrote to say that he had seen Jai in London. '. . . he told me that he thought that the Princes would eventually come into a Federation, though he felt doubtful whether they would do so without an attempt to

An artist's impression of all the Maharajas of Jaipur standing before the shrine of Shri Govind Devji (Jai is immediately next to the shrine on the right hand side).

Jai descends from an elephant in Cooch Behar in 1940, for his wedding to Ayesha.

Jai and Ayesha at the wedding ceremony.

Jai and Ayesha.

Jai and Ayesha in 1941.

secure some modification of the offer which we have made them.' Evidently the Secretary of State, despite his views about Jai, thought it worthwhile to consult his opinions.

The Secretary of State also 'suggested as tactfully as I could that there might be some risk in absenting himself just now from his state' – when there were strained relations with Congress and when his Muslim subjects were aggrieved. The British had got it into their heads that Jai had a strong anti-Mohammedan bias, which was, as we shall see, manifest nonsense.

Jai had replied that he was not expecting serious trouble on either score, that it was only in England that he could find any relief from the burdens of government and that, 'in any case, it now took him no longer to fly from England to Jaipur than it would take him to travel to his capital from Ootacamurid'.

Jai was right. Soon after he got back in July, he initiated a new act, called the Jaipur Unlawful Associations Act, which was to repeal the Public Societies Act and remove the requirement of registration – thus once more legalising the Praja Mandal. The Jaipur Resident, J.H. Thompson, reported that this was not what was agreed in Council when he was present. Thompson also said that the Council believed that, 'His Highness has implicated himself with Bajaj more deeply then he has admitted'.

Another way of looking at it would be to say that the young Maharaja was establishing contact with those who he foresaw would one day be people of great consequence in his state. Jai continued to meet Jamnalal and 'despite all warnings, sees him alone'. Jamnalal was a skilful propagandist and may have taken some advantage of Jai's inexperience. Jai's instinct, on the other hand, was right.

At the end of the year, the new Resident, Conrad Corfield, was still trying to get the new policy reversed, but it was too late. Jai had had a serious plane crash over Bombay in October. His plane had hit a vulture and plummeted five hundred feet. Both the pilot and Jai were seriously hurt. Both Jai's ankles were badly broken and he was to suffer the effects of his injuries for several years.

During the time of his convalescence, nothing much could

happen. By the time he was better, the Praja Mandal was too well and, incidentally, peacefully established.

By his quiet defiance of the British Government, he had convinced the general populace that he had their interests at heart and had much strengthened his popularity. Over the next few years, the rewards of his policies were manifold.

CHAPTER 8

While Jai had been taking on full responsibility for the affairs of his state, he had not by any means been neglecting his personal life.

The upper echelons of Indian society, even today, are small considering the population of the country. Before Independence, it was still more limited. Only a very restricted group travelled much, even within India. Those who did all knew one another and were, as often as not, connected to a greater or lesser degree by the web of princely intermarriage. If they happened to have some further interest in common, it was almost inevitable that they should be friends.

The widowed Maharani of Cooch Behar, who had known Jai as a child and had befriended him in London, was an enthusiastic horsewoman. The state of Cooch Behar lies in the north-east of India in Bengal. The Cooch Behars had a large house in Calcutta called Woodlands. They had a great reputation for entertaining. So it was only natural for Jai, when he came to Calcutta for the 1931 winter polo season, to continue his acquaintance with her and to stay with her at Woodlands.

The Maharani, who was universally known as Ma, had been in England for nearly three years. She had gone there because she feared that her eldest son, Bhaiya, the young Maharaja, was in danger of being spoilt. She had returned to India in 1930, and at once set about entertaining in the grand style which had made her a famous hostess.

Jai, in the following year, had been invested with his full

powers and was now the 'independent' ruler of an extremely important princely state, one of only twelve rulers entitled to a seventeen-gun salute. (There were five senior ones entitled to nineteen guns and five more who had twenty-one). At the age of twenty, tall, good-looking, already a great sportsman, he appeared to the Cooch Behar family as a most glamorous figure. His arrival was preceded by sixty polo ponies; each had its own uniformed groom with flowing orange turban. Then he arrived, driving a large, green Rolls Royce. The Maharani's five children – and the little girl, the daughter of a Hyderabad noble, Nawab Khusru Jung, who was brought up with them – were much impressed.

Jai must have been equally impressed by them. He was, by nature, fond of children and had a way of treating them quite normally. He liked to encourage them and teach them, to tease them, as he teased everyone, and to make them laugh.

These children, though, were different from other Indian children he had known. They had spent a long time in Europe and were, in many ways, more sophisticated than a great many adults, especially the girls confined to the rigours of purdah. He took to the family and they to him. It was as if they became the family he had never had after his removal from Isarda. Bhaiya was only four years younger than Jai and he eventually became almost his best friend. The girls, of course, entertained romantic fantasies about Jai. Gayatri Devi, the second daughter, more commonly known as Ayesha, was then nearly twelve. Not needing to be turned into a princess, she fancied herself transformed into a groom who would catch the attention of her master.

These dreams continued even when, a few months after the visit, Jai married his second wife, and Ma reported to the children that she was 'pretty and petite' as well as 'bright and lively'.

The following year, Jai came again to Woodlands for the polo season and, without recourse to magic spells, Ayesha managed to catch Jai's attention. The previous year, he had played tennis with her and her younger sister, in a brotherly kind of way. This year, he took more particular notice of her. Having won, as usual, the India Polo Association Championship, he was in a mood to celebrate. He asked Ma if Ayesha could come to a victory dinner party. He also arranged, on another evening, for Ayesha and her sister to join him and his staff for dinner when everyone else was out.

To European readers, it may seem strange that a young man who would never lack female companionship should take an interest in a thirteen-year-old girl. It must be remembered that in India, over the centuries, it was perfectly normal to marry girls of that age. Moreover, Ayesha at any age was a person of outstanding beauty and, even at thirteen, was probably better able to converse with Jai than any Indian girl that he could have met. Ma was wholly unconventional and brought her children up with cosmopolitan tastes and interests. For Indian readers, the surprise may rather be that a girl of that age should have had so free a relationship with a man. The answer lies partly again with Ma's unconventionality, but also in Jai's character. His sense of fitness alone would have been enough to set Ma's mind at rest, but his kindness and loyalty left no room for doubt. He had become a member of the family and would never have betrayed that trust.

Ayesha's younger brother, Indrajit, went that year to Mayo College, which is only two hours' drive from Jaipur. Jai therefore invited the whole family to stay with him at the Rambagh Palace, so that they could visit Indrajit. In the event, only Ma went to the school, because the boy begged her not to bring his sisters, which would have horrified his schoolfellows – their sisters were all in purdah.

Jai took them all on sightseeing tours of Amber and the City Palace and introduced them to his wives in the zenana. Ayesha he took riding by herself.

It was at this point that he decided that he wanted to marry Ayesha when she grew up. He suggested this to Ma, who laughed at him and told him that she had never heard such sentimental rubbish.

It is impossible to know what his feelings really were at that time. Certainly, whatever they were, he did not let them interfere with his amorous arrangements, even with quite emotional affairs. It was two years later that he was writing to Rabbit about being heartbroken at Joan's departure: 'I do love her so much and she was so marvellous . . .' He was absolutely capable of separating one kind of love from another. If, as seems likely, he had chosen Ayesha because of both her beauty and her intelligence, and to some extent her unruly nature, and had recognised that she was the one Indian girl of his own class who would make the kind of wife he needed, he would have, mentally as it were, sealed her in a separate, almost sacred compartment. It would never have occurred to him that loving her should in any way have inhibited his broad enthusiasm for women.

He said nothing to her of his intentions and over the next few years saw little of her, except during his annual, triumphant visits to Calcutta for the polo season; but during those visits he always made sure they had fun. They shared a love of the outdoors. Whenever he was at Cooch Behar, they rode together and went on picnics.

Nevertheless, for her he remained an unattainable hero, or at the most what she calls 'a specially nice friend'. It was hardly surprising, because it was not just to Ayesha and her sisters that he seemed out of the ordinary. In her book, *A Princess Remembers*, Ayesha quotes the English journalist Rosita Forbes' description of Jai:

> Because of his appearance and his charm, his possessions and his feats on horseback, this exceedingly good-looking young man, famous as a sportsman in three continents, occupies in the imagination of the Indian general public much the same position as the Prince of Wales did in the minds of working men [in England]. In no other way can I suggest the universal popularity, combined with a rather breathless wonder as to what he will do next, which surrounds this best-known of India's young Rulers.

In 1936, Ma took the children back to England. Ayesha's two sisters had gone ahead with their grandmother. Ma discovered that the elder girl, Ila, had married secretly just before leaving. Ma decided, as soon as she and Ayesha had arrived in Europe, to take Ila back for a proper Hindu wedding.

134

Ayesha was sent to a finishing school called the Monkey Club in London. She lived nearby in Pont Street, watched over by her Baroda grandmother and a German baroness. One elopement was judged to be more than enough and the two ladies kept a close eye on Ayesha, whisking her away to Paris on one occasion when they heard that Jai was arriving in London.

Their vigilance, however, was ineffective against what soon became a real romance. Ayesha was now seventeen. Towards the end of the summer, Jai proposed. Ayesha accepted. For a few weeks, they had an idyllic period of clandestine meetings, then Ayesha was sent to a domestic science school in Switzerland.

When, in the end, they told Ma of their plan she, in the way of all parents, advised them to wait for two years. The following year, they were all in Europe again. The restrictions were relaxed, but their engagement was not announced and they were obliged to be reasonably discreet. In India, they had to be totally discreet and could not meet. Jai wrote or scribbled to her with great regularity. He had various nicknames for her; the most usual was Pat:

> The Palace, Jaipur
> 28 Nov '37
>
> My Beloved Pat,
>   You will make me so happy darling I wish you could see me also it was heaven talking to you only I wish you had not insisted on business rather I wanted to know more about you darling . . . What is the idea of going to Agra and seeing the Taj. Beloved let's keep plans like that for us to do together and if you only do it for motoring sake please be more intelligent come towards this side you know how I long to see you and be with you so please beloved use the brains (if any) in the right direction!!
>   All my love [to] you for ever Jai.

The two years were to stretch into three. In January 1938, he wrote to her in Cooch Behar:

Pat darling

I am feeling miserable and very unhappy as no news from you but I suppose such is life! . . . so drop me a line . . . if you can as you know just one word from you makes all the difference to me. I need not tell you how I feel about you hardly a moment pass when you are not in my thoughts and I just long to see you again. I hope you are having fun in C.B. . . . all my love darling,
Yours always Jai.

They were together again in Europe in the summer of 1938, when Ayesha had finished a secretarial course in London. Jai joined the Cooch Behars in Budapest. It was the last time that they were to be in Europe together before the war and it was because they were so happy there that Jai was put out at having to return early to Jaipur to settle the Sikar revolt.

Things did not seem to be going so well at the beginning of the next year:

Bombay
15 Jan 1939

Darling Pat

It was heavenly and most surprising getting your letter today . . . but I don't know if it makes me miserable or unhappy. I am really at a loss to understand it and all what you mean in it. Before I answer your questions will you be frank and tell me that you really do trust me and believe me to be sincere to you. To know the truth from you would set my mind at ease because when I am with you, you are totally different to when behind my back and away from me. What does really come over you and I wonder if you really mean what you put in the letter. Really darling I am feeling too miserable now to write anything but on hearing from you I promise I will write and tell you every thing not that I have ever hidden things from you . . . I wish to God you were here and I could talk to you.

Your miserable Jai.

What had happened was that Ayesha's family were putting pressure on her. What they had thought was a juvenile infatuation which would pass, they now realised, with some alarm, was an implacable determination on Ayesha's part to marry Jai. Their objections to the marriage were very reasonable. While polygamy was perfectly acceptable in Indian eyes, no family relishes the idea that a favourite daughter or sister should be the third wife of even a grand Maharaja. While the principle was all right, it was for other people to take third place. Then there was the matter of purdah. The Cooch Behars had entirely abandoned this kind of segregation and Ayesha had been brought up in a particularly free and easy atmosphere. How could she accept being shut up in the zenana, having all her movements restricted? In fact, Jai had arranged that she would not be. The family also pointed out to her that Jai was certainly never going to change his flirtatious habits. Further, she might be the favourite for a time; but what if Jai tired of her and took a fourth wife?

Not surprisingly, the barrage of objections caused Ayesha to write for reassurance. The family, in fact, underestimated the depth of feeling they had for each other. Everything was soon smoothed over:

5 March 1939

> Beloved Pat
>   The Viceroy's visit kept us all very busy so I hope darling you will forgive my not writing to you but what has kept you busy!! Are you up to any good or not darling?! Thank God the Viceroy's visit went off quite well . . . I had an awful time on the banquet night having to make that long speech and I was pissing in my pants till I had a few drinks before facing the ordeal. Then all went well.
>   . . . all my love beautiful and I think of you every second of my life.
> Yours forever Jai.

The objections to the marriage did not come only from Ayesha's side. Jai's family, the Jaipur nobles, and indeed the whole Rajput establishment, were bitterly opposed to it.

The first objection was that the Cooch Behars belonged, in Rajput eyes, to an inferior branch of the Kshatriya caste. (The Cooch Behars judged themselves purer.) The British were doubtful. Sir B.J. Glancy, now Political Adviser to the Viceroy, noted:

> The rulers of Cooch Behar . . . though they describe themselves as Kshatriyas, would have great difficulty in establishing their claim to this distinction . . . It is for the Rajputs themselves to maintain their prestige and traditions in such matters and all that we can do is to point out to them, as has been done in this case, the consequences of departing from their customs.

Non-interference, as the British thought of it, could seem pretty much like interference from the Indian point of view. Jai had a powerful argument in his favour which was that in 1596 (as we saw in Chapter 3) his ancestor Man Singh I had married Kshamadevi, the sister of Lakshmi Narayan, Raja of the then new kingdom of Cooch Behar. The Rajputs of neighbouring states dismissed this, on the grounds that a man whose sister was married to Akbar and his grand-daughter to Jehangir was hardly likely to observe the pro-prieties himself. The point did, nonetheless, carry some weight with his own people.

The next objection was more rational. Many of the Jaipur nobles either came from Jodhpur families – for example Amer Singh – or had wives from Jodhpur. They therefore felt that this marriage would be an affront to the two first wives, both of whom came from Jodhpur. This objection weighed heavily with Jai's fellow Rajput Princes. The Maha-rajas of Bikaner, Udaipur, Dungapur and Jamnagar were all related to one or other of Jai's wives. They made representa-tions to the Viceroy, Lord Linlithgow.

Linlithgow sent for Jai and, according to Major Parbat Singh, warned him that a marriage with Ayesha would have a serious effect on Jaipur's relations with the other Rajputana states. Jai, says Major Parbat, told the Viceroy that he could, if he wished, depose him, but that he could not interfere with his private life. No matter what the consequences, he

138

was going to marry Ayesha. 'The Viceroy, seeing his determination, shook his hand and wished him luck.'

It was the custom for a Rajput Prince to take with him to his wedding a large number of his nobles and it was usual for the other Rajput Princes to attend the weddings of their fellows. With his own nobles, there was little trouble. They were either too loyal or too obsequious to voice any objection to Jai himself and merely contented themselves with grumbling to each other. According to Amer Singh, the only two who actually told Jai what they thought were Jai's father – the Thakur of Isarda – and Amer Singh himself. In January 1940, the latter wrote in his diary that the Maharaja Sahib had asked him whether he would be coming to his marriage. He replied: 'Certainly not; if you marry a good Rajput family I will with pleasure but not when you marry into that family.' Amer Singh particularly disapproved of Ma's unconventional ways.

The Princes were a more important and trickier matter. Major Parbat Singh says that he was sent to Udaipur and Dungapur to persuade them to attend the wedding: 'Dungapur refused at first. I cursed him for refusing the request of a friend. In the end he came.' Parbat Singh is mistaken here – Dungapur did not attend the wedding. Udaipur was a cripple and in poor health. He said that he would come if he felt better.

The Maharana of Udaipur was the most senior of the Rajputana Princes and his lead was most important for Jai. He evidently went to Udaipur himself to reinforce the request, for in April 1940 he wrote the Maharana a letter which is interesting also as an example of the formality which the Princes maintained in their dealings with one another:

> . . . The relations existing between our Royal houses have always been of the most cordial nature and I am so glad that after this recent visit of mine they have been cemented still further . . .
>
> I have invariably looked up to Your Highness for advice. The guidance which I received from you and the assurance given by Your Highness have strengthened me considerably. I could not expect a greater practical proof of

139

Your Highness' goodwill towards my person and my
house . . .

With kindest regards

Man Singh.

In the event, the Maharana was not well enough to undertake
the long journey to Cooch Behar for the wedding. He did,
however, send two representatives – a gesture which put the
formal Rajput seal of approval on the marriage, although of
course it did not stop the endless rattle of tongues in Jaipur.
Nor did it satisfy the British.

Major Parbat's memory of the Viceroy's reaction may be a
little optimistic. The British were busily poking their noses
into the matter right up until the last minute. Colonel
Barton, Resident in the Eastern States, went to see Bhaiya
and reported, on 1 April 1940, that he had learned to his
surprise that the marriage was going ahead. He had imagined
that it must be cancelled after the 'unofficial warning' given
to Jai. He portrayed Bhaiya's natural concern for Ayesha's
future in purdah and as a third wife as disapproval of the
match.

The British believed that when Udaipur gave his 'reluctant
agreement' to the marriage he had done so on the condition
that no child of the marriage should succeed to the Jaipur
gaddi. As was so often the case, the British were wrong – no
such restriction was imposed.

There was certainly no echo of good-luck wishes in the
pettily expedient edict issued by the Viceroy about invitations
to the wedding:

> No officer of my Government should attend, whether
> from Cooch Behar or from Jaipur, or anywhere else, and
> no congratulations or good wishes should be offered
> unless with the preface that the offerer stands in his
> private capacity only.

Even after the wedding, they were filing reports from a
spy in 3rd Battalion 6th Rajputana Rifles saying that Rajputs
did not like the marriage and that Jai had 'greatly weakened
his position in the state'.

140

There were other delays. A month before the 'auspicious' day chosen by the Pandits, Ayesha got diphtheria. Even nearer the date, her Baroda uncle fell down stairs and died. Eventually, the wedding took place on 9 May 1940. Despite the war, the occasion was quite as splendid as either of Jai's two previous weddings. He arrived with a retinue of forty nobles and the celebrations lasted for a week. Ayesha maintains that the Cooch Behar Resident did attend and that the Viceroy's daughter sent her congratulations.

When Ayesha arrived in Jaipur, she, in her turn, was to transform many of the medieval aspects of life, which had to a large extent lingered on from the days of Madho Singh. She was still only twenty-one and regarded with much suspicion. She could not rush in and start trying to overturn old customs and manners.

In July, two months after their marriage, Arthur Lothian, the Agent General for Rajputana, visited Jaipur and wrote:

> The new Maharani, although she had tea with my wife and myself, has not appeared so far at any public function . . . I gather that the Maharaja is hesitant about the degree of freedom which it is polite to give her in Rajputana . . .

Ayesha was not in purdah, but was subject to many of the restrictions it imposed. She was allotted a house in the zenana in the City Palace, but she, like Second Her Highness, lived entirely in the Rambagh Palace. Unlike Second Her Highness, her apartments were not in the women's section. Jai had done up his own rooms for her and now moved to another suite next door.

In her memoirs, Ayesha makes light of the awkwardness of her position and in particular of her relationship with Second Her Highness. The older, senior Maharani would not have been much affected by the third marriage. Her disappointments had come earlier when, according to her adherents, Jai had neglected her. She had never got on with her niece, the second wife, but she retained her dignity,

141

despite consoling herself with a moderate amount of drink, and lived her own life in circumstances which, by upbringing, she could easily accept. Ayesha's good manners were even a welcome change for her.

In the case of Second Her Highness, it is harder to give complete credence to Ayesha's account of how they formed a close friendship unmarred by jealousy. Jai's second wife was fairly pretty, but spoilt and something of an intriguer. She had never gone back to Jodhpur since her marriage, because they would not give her a gun salute equal to that fired for her aunt, the senior Maharani. She was not very popular, partly because she lacked First Her Highness' generosity. Against all that, she really loved Jai. After his aeroplane crash, seven months before his third marriage, she presented a pair of legs made of silver to the goddess Shila Devi, by way of thanksgiving for his survival.

She was undoubtedly much saddened by Jai's marrying again, and not much placated, one would have thought, by his giving her a party to cheer her up on the night he told her of his engagement. She was only twenty-four and, apart from her pleasure in her two sons, she had little to look forward to. It was she, rather than the first wife, who took refuge in drink. Nonetheless, we must accept that, given the inevitability of the situation and the traditions of princely families, the two younger wives did gradually, over the years, become friends.

The constant problem of deciding whom to believe in Jaipur makes it difficult to be certain about Second Her Highness' character. One cannot be sure that those who speak ill of her do not do so out of some obscure loyalty to Jodhpur, or because she may have reprimanded them – and these things are long remembered.

Other accounts say that she was lively and mischievous, with a great sense of humour. She was fond of music and used to sing for Jai. Ayesha maintains that Jai and his second wife were very close, moreover that until she died she was in charge of the zenani deodhi and had a lot of power. Certainly she held the keys to his private treasure vaults in Moti Doongri. She also looked after Jagat, Ayesha's son, when they were away. Jai obviously trusted her and,

142

while she may have been autocratic, her drinking, although damaging to her health, was clearly not gross.

That Jai understood that life in Jaipur was difficult for Ayesha is shown by the letter he wrote to her shortly before New Year 1941, when he was away on military duty:

> . . . you go and stay with Ma in Calcutta . . . as I'm sure Ma will be upset if you don't. Also it must be pretty awful for you at home shut up and surrounded by evil thoughts all the time. Please darling go and enjoy yourself and remember I just live for you and you alone . . .

The rest of the letter reveals that now she was married to him she must be circumspect, even in British India:

> . . . you will take Prithi [an ADC] with you or . . . take Achrol our home minister and when you get to C.B. you can send them back. In Calcutta they better remain with you just for show . . . Darling one thing when you are in Calcutta don't go to big or official parties at the Viceroy's house or Government house but you can go to both the places with Ma to private parties. Don't go to any ruling Prince's house. Anyhow use your discretion and don't let Ma mislead you!!

It took a long time. Almost a year after their marriage, when Jai was trying to ease the rigours of purdah, Amer Singh, when out pig-sticking with them, pretended not to see her. Later in the day, he asked her permission to smoke and enquired whether she could understand the local language. Even he was beginning to melt.

Ayesha was too energetic a person to contain herself for long. Sometime after her arrival, one of the ADCs complained that very severe restrictions were being put on the amount of food and, particularly, drink that was available at the Rambagh Palace. They all discussed whether this was due to wartime economy or a sudden decision on the part of the Maharaja that people should not drink and be so merry at his expense. They came to the conclusion that it was less

143

likely to be the war, but more likely to be the strict supervision of the new Maharani, who now controlled the household with its four hundred servants. She did manage to cut the household expenses by half.

The war effort gave her many opportunities to break down barriers which at any other time might have defeated her. Jai, at the outbreak of war, had given 300,000 rupees to the Viceroy's War Purposes Fund. He had also subscribed one million rupees to War Loans. (By the end of the war, the total of war investments amounted to ten million rupees.) He put his airport at the disposal of the RAF and his new, vast house in Delhi, and another in Agra, he offered to the Government. His state's three aeroplanes, including his own new Lockheed, were there for use by the British Government if needed.

He also tried to interest the people of Jaipur in the war effort, though there was an obvious divergence of interest here. Many Indians, their minds now set upon Independence, saw little reason to support the British in their European war, despite Gandhi's belief that it was a just one. When the Japanese crept closer, however, the task was easier. Jai addressed the grandees and the ministers in the Albert Hall (the huge edifice put up by Ram Singh II when Edward VII visited Jaipur as Prince of Wales). He asked them to economise and to cultivate. He intended to give cultivable waste land to people rent free for five years and suggested that the Sardars should make equivalent concessions.

Jai was away for much of the war and Ayesha took the chance to establish herself in her new role. Raising money for the war effort was an ideal method of getting to know people – and not just the purdah ladies in the zenana. She started a silver trinket fund for the Vicereine, Lady Linlithgow, and raised 10,000 rupees. She held work parties at the Rambagh Palace and at the Ladies Club. She organised tournaments and raffles, collected clothes, food, books and magazines for Indian soldiers overseas and for wounded British soldiers in Delhi and Poona. She had her own fund for the welfare of soldiers from Jaipur state. This fund managed to buy two electro-therapeutic machines, one of which was sent to the Indian military hospital in Palestine.

All these activities brought women out of their age-old seclusion and paved the way for the breakdown of the purdah system. There are old ladies in Jaipur today who say that Ayesha was their liberator, that she opened up for them a world which they might otherwise never have seen. While some were grateful, others were horrified.

By 1942, Ayesha felt bold enough to start a school for girls, for she believed that it was only through education that emancipation for women would come. At that time, miserably few girls had any real education, beyond instruction in what were thought of as wifely accomplishments. The most restricted were the upper classes, so it was for them that she opened the Maharani Gayatri Devi School. At first, few of the nobles were enthusiastic and many of them were positively opposed to the scheme. Gradually, the forty hesitant students increased in numbers to several hundred and eventually the school became a national institution.

CHAPTER 9

The war brought out in Jai all his Rajput warrior inheritance. Far from having any of the feelings attributed to him by the meddlesome Miss von Pott, he was passionately, almost obsessively eager to serve the King Emperor in the way that his ancestors had served the Moghul emperors.

On 3 September 1939, the day that war was declared, Jai sent a cable to the Viceroy, asking him to beg the King to let him go with the Life Guards to the front. The Viceroy replied that he would do better to stay in India and attend to his duties in his state. On 12 September, he cabled to Buckingham Palace, 'placing my personal services at the disposal of my beloved Sovereign'. Buckingham Palace answered in the same vein as the Viceroy, having doubtless consulted with him through the India Office.

Throughout 1940, he made repeated attempts in all sorts of directions, including showing a desire to go to train with Probyn's Horse. The only thing, most surprisingly, that he did not seem to want was to go to battle with his own army. The Sawai Man Guards were serving in Baluchistan. Later, they went to the Red Sea, to Asmara and Massawa, Egypt and Italy. The Jaipur Infantry also went to the Middle East and Italy. Rabbit went with them to the Middle East, but came back under a cloud.

Jai did manage, in September 1940, to get attached to the Indian Army. He was posted to Risalpur to join the 13th Lancers. He was allowed to take Ayesha with him and there, for a few months, they lived a simpler life, as a young

Captain and his wife. Shortly before Christmas of that year, the Afghans threatened to attack and Jai's regiment was sent to put them down. Ayesha went back to Jaipur and her more restricted life as a Maharani.

Jai hugely enjoyed his first experience of action. He wrote to Rabbit from Bannu in the North West Frontier Province:

> I have just been in a Frontier show and damn good fun it was. We were in the thick of trouble and I had a chance of opening fire with M.C. and shot some of those fucking tribesmen and wild M... [illegible]! We lived in tents & used to be sniped most nights.
>
> I am now taking a convoy back to Kohat tomorrow & then go back to Risalpur wish you were up in this party we would have some fun.

None of this meant that he had given up hope of joining the Life Guards. He continued to pester the Viceroy with requests to be allowed to do so. The Viceroy tried telling him that the Household Cavalry were now mechanised, hoping that this might put him off. It didn't. Finally, his persistence paid off. In April 1941, he was granted an emergency commission and posted to the Household Cavalry Overseas Composite Battalion. The Political Department melted slightly and Sir Francis Wylie wrote to him: 'Take care of yourself on active service . . . you were far from careful when you went to the North West Frontier.'

Jai cabled ecstatically to George VI, thanking him and assuring him, 'of the unflinching loyalty and everlasting devotion of myself and my house to your Imperial Majesty's person and throne'.

Jai was the first Indian ever to get a commission in the Household Cavalry. It was obviously a matter of immense importance to him. He kept every scrap of paper about his orders and the amount of luggage he was allowed to take – 'the Field Services scale of baggage in accordance with paragraph 364 of the Passage regulations, India, plus one maund'.

He even scribbled much later, and preserved, an innocent account of his excitement:

On 2nd April Maj Russell the resident gave me good news of commission of 2nd Lt in Household Cavalry & ready to proceed by 12 April embarkation active service. We had wonderful celebration in Jaipur & altho' everybody & mostly the family were depressed I was full of happiness & thrilled at idea of going on active service. My only supporter in this venture was my loving wife Ayesha. Whatever her inner feelings may have been she supported me & shared my feelings of happiness. A wonderful girl & the best companion one could ever wish for . . .

On reaching Bombay, Jai had to wait, as there was no room on any ship:

> . . . I settled down to a round of good parties in Bombay & had lots of fun, thank goodness we had no prohibition in those days. My grandmother Baroda [actually Ayesha's grandmother] was there also & gave me a long lecture how stupid I was going to the war serving in the British army. I should remain at home where there was a lot of work to be done & even more ruling with my position as a ruler. Finally I received orders to report Ballard Pier 9th May . . . I was thrilled and considered a good omen that I should sail off on 9th May which was my wedding day . . . 9th May morning will remain an historical day in my life. I was at last going to war in Middle East joining my regiment the Household Cavalry. On the other side I was bidding farewell to the family & my beloved wife whom I'd had only one year of happiness. A sight I shall never forget was her standing on the pier . . . two gifts I will remember on parting a lovely ginger cake from Mother which was a blessing as we got nothing but ration food & dry biscuits & a bottle of champagne & Napoleon brandy from George Dissan. The bottle of champagne made friends on the boat first day & the brandy my companion through many campaigns.

The scrap ends there, but it reveals the absolute determination to ignore all opposition. The British Army, above all the Household Cavalry, meant more to him than his own army, which he had gone to such trouble to create ten years before. For most people, to lead their own private army into war, wearing their uniform and shouting their name as a battle cry, would be infinitely more satisfying than a humble lieutenancy in someone else's guards. Perhaps that was the trouble – Jai's Sawai Man Guards were the imitation. Again, his loyalties were split. This time, Britain won.

It had been a contest. The Rajput Sabha had called a special meeting in order to put a plea to Jai not to go to the war – with the rider that if he insisted he should go where the Jaipur troops were fighting, in order to cheer them up by his appearance. There were objections from all quarters, but the gentle determination which now informed his character won for him what he wanted.

There were setbacks to his dream. When he arrived, he found he had missed his regiment and he was sent to Gaza to be attached to the Royal Scots Greys. Soon, he was sent back to Cairo and in June was appointed liaison officer with the Indian State Forces. Within the Indian Army, Jai became a Major-General, which led to the usual confusions as to how he should be treated. Whenever possible, he wore his Life Guards uniform and as a temporary Captain would be obliged to salute all senior officers. When on duty with the Indian Army, he would wear his Major-General's uniform and those officers whom he had saluted the day before were now obliged to salute him.

He wrote to Ayesha from Shepherd's Hotel in Cairo on 14 July:

> . . . I am now liaisoning with the State troops at H.Q. It is nice and I see lots of our people and of the same colour as your beautiful self . . . enjoy yourself darling and I only wish I was with you. Some of us have to do a bit of a job and some are bloody lucky and have all the good time . . . I had lots of Indian food & have gone up enormously in weight. All my good efforts have been wasted . . .

Unfortunately, the series of accidents which he had had on

the polo fields and when flying had left their mark on Jai. In August, he was pronounced unfit and, after only four months, flown back to India to recover.

Elements of comedy arose in Jai's dealings with the British Army bureaucracy. When he got back to India, he got a request from the Paymaster's office in Jerusalem, asking for his marriage certificate and the birth certificates of his children so that they could calculate his allowances. He wrote explaining that there were no such certificates in India. He gave the date of his marriage to Ayesha, but made no mention of his other wives. He also listed the birth dates of his four children, which all preceded the date of his wedding. One can only imagine the effect of these details on the orderly minds of the British clerks – but they paid up.

Jai was not altogether sorry to go back to India. In the first place, there was a famine and he felt his new Prime Minister was dealing with the problem ineffectively. Almost as soon as he arrived, Gyan Nath managed to antagonise many elements of the population. In particular, he provoked the Praja Mandal. Jamnalal Bajaj, with whom Jai had, as the British suspected, kept in touch until his departure for the Middle East, made constant representations about Gyan Nath's behaviour.

On 10 November 1940, Bajaj wrote to Jai: '. . . Gyan Nath has become all the more reactionary in his attitude. He seems determined to crush the P[raja] M[andal] if he can.'

He went on to complain that the Jaipur police had raided his house in Sikar. He maintained that the search should not have taken place after he had admitted making a statement to which the state had objected. The search had been conducted 'with more than the usual show'. His personal diary had been removed. After challenging this repressive policy and complaining of false charges and the ill-treatment of a detainee, he ended:

> . . . am glad to tell you that Praja Mandal workers are using great restraint even in face of grave provocations, but I'm not sure if Raja Gyan Nath will not force them to lose patience by his present policy.

Jai was well able to sift the truth from the propaganda in Jamnalal's constant stream of requests, advice and polite threats, but he was impressed by a resolution passed by the Praja Mandal meeting, attended by several thousand people, requesting him to replace Gyan Nath by another Indian Prime Minister of greater eminence.

The dissatisfaction came not only from the populace. Rather reluctantly, Jai had lent his Finance Minister, Raja Amarnath Atal, to the Maharaja of Kashmir. Kashmir had written 'One good turn deserves another . . .' and reminded Jai that he had begged a dagger from him, and had also borrowed a Minister-in-Waiting. Jai replied: 'I never realised you will drive such a hard bargain . . .' but princely honour meant that he could not refuse, though he put a time limit and asked Kashmir to pay one sixth of Atal's salary. When he went abroad, he asked for him back, as he was the only person who knew anything about Jai's private finances.

Gyan Nath and Atal soon fell out. Gyan Nath described Atal as a 'sinister influence' and put it about that he did not 'have the interests of the state at heart'. This did not endear Gyan Nath to Jai. Atal had been Finance Minister for all of his reign. He was scrupulously honest and loyal.

There is an undated, unsigned report on aspects of Gyan Nath's Prime Ministership. It states that immediately after his arrival, the policy of personal contact with the people was completely reversed. Famine relief work was much reduced. State officers were soon hesitant about meeting any representative of the people. In spite of the new laws about public societies, he openly denounced the Praja Mandal. Moreover, he sent a circular to the police instructing them that the legalisation of the Praja Mandal should mean no change in policy towards the organisation and its members. Praja Mandal workers should be kept under watch. He spent more money on propaganda than on real famine relief.

The lack of a personal touch was particularly repugnant to Jai. He believed very strongly that a ruler should be available to his people. A few days after his return, according to one of his admirers, Jai saw a procession of people carrying banners saying, 'We are hungry'. Jai went up to them, saluted and asked, 'What service can I do for you?' They explained that there was no wheat. Jai asked that they should allow him one week to put the matter right. If he failed, he would eat barley like them. Price-controlled shops were instantly opened. Like so many stories told in Jaipur, this one had a mythical ring to it, but it does illustrate Jai's belief in his duty to be accessible.

Within a month of his return, he gave Gyan Nath notice to leave. The way in which he did this also happens to illustrate Jai's habit of teasing those he thought were silly. One of his ADCs had, in Jai's view, made a fool of himself by endeavouring to flatter Gyan Nath. Jai called in the ADC and gave him the letter of dismissal to deliver to the Prime Minister.

In June 1942, Jai appointed Sir Mirza Ismail as his next Prime Minister. Sir Mirza was a Muslim, a first indication that talk of Jai being anti-Mohammedan is nonsense. He was also an extremely progressive, although circumspect person. In many of his photographs, he bears a remarkable likeness to Groucho Marx.

Jai was not pronounced fit again until August 1942, when he was posted to Dehra Dun Staff College at Quetta. Once again, he started a barrage of requests to the Viceroy to be allowed to go back to the front.

At this point, the British decided to use his enthusiasm to try to check the activities of Sir Mirza, who was already stirring things up as Prime Minister. The Viceroy wrote to say that only when 'certain matters' within the state had been safely decided would it be possible for him to go abroad for a time on military duty.

Jai replied with firmness. He assured the Viceroy that he himself had attended to all these questions. He was confident that there was no cause for concern about anything within his state, except the matter of food supplies, which was a problem all over India. He agreed to abstain from unnecessary public expenditure.

He went on not just to defend his policies but, in effect, to challenge the British attitude. He pointed out that various beneficial acts had been passed and were now being implemented. He was referring to the Village Panchayat Act, which gave administrative functions to local bodies and protection to farmers; and to the Municipality Act, which

Sir Mirza Ismail (*Topham Picture Library*).

Jai and Ayesha with a hunting party at Sawai Madhopur in February 1946. Among the guests are Lord and Lady Mountbatten and Pamela Mountbatten.

Jai at the front during the Second World War.

Army officers greet Jai at Bikaner airport during his official tour as Commander-in-Chief of the Rajasthan Forces. Touching the feet is a traditional sign of deference.

(*left to right*) Pat, Joey, Bubbles, the Maharaj Kumar of Jamnagar and the Princess of Jamnagar.

Jai with Ayesha and Jagat at Saint Hill in Sussex in the late 1950s (*Popperfoto*).

ordered that half the seats of the Jaipur Municipal Board should be filled by election.

Jai said he was expecting a great and welcome change in the outlook of the people generally, whether Thakurs or others. There would be a healthy diversion of energy from petty personal considerations to activity for the public good. He said he was pleased with the daily improvement in the administration. Much still needed to be done, but they were doing their best. He wrote:

> I would add that while I have the keenest personal desire to get to the front again, and play a more active part than is possible here, I well realise how important is the effort towards victory that can be made at home. Neither in men nor in any sort of contribution shall we be found to fall short. No State understands better than Jaipur that the single duty of working, in all ways, for speedy victory requires all our energies and resources. While, like the Government of India and the Army itself, we have also been looking beyond victory and endeavouring to prepare for the future, we well know that the immediate demands of war are paramount and shall allow no others to compete with them. Nor is this a mere matter of duty to us.

This was a very different Jai from the one who appeared to think of little but his commission in the Household Cavalry. It was the voice of a ruler, determined to run his state on the lines which he thought best for his people – lines which might well conflict with the views of those who represented his beloved King Emperor.

The arrival of Sir Mirza Ismail in Jaipur must have seemed like a hurricane. There was almost no aspect of the administration, indeed of the whole life of the state, which he and Jai did not reform in one way or another. Having chosen his man, Jai not only gave him full support, but also joined in the running of affairs with an enthusiasm he had never exhibited before.

The first thing they tackled was the city itself. The population of the city, which had fallen in the first twenty years of the century, had started to rise quite rapidly. In 1921, it was 120,000; by 1941, it was nearly 180,000. The city was dirty and overcrowded. Shopkeepers had built extensions out onto the pavements; many buildings were in a poor state of repair, and most of them had not been painted for at least a quarter of a century.

With a measure of ruthlessness, Sir Mirza tore down all encroachments and restored the original building lines laid down by Jai Singh II, the founder of the city. All the houses were repainted in the rich, pink colour which Ram Singh II had chosen, perhaps in imitation of the red sandstone used in so many Moghul buildings. Sir Mirza removed many Hindu temples from the middle of the streets. This was a notable achievement for a Muslim, for no Hindu or Englishman had attempted it. His simple expedient was to undertake to build a brand new temple in a more suitable place to house the deities from the tumble-down shrine he wished to remove.

At the suggestion of Cecil Beaton, who happened to be visiting Jai, they restored many of the old monuments and garden-houses on the road to the ancient capital of Amber. Beaton wrote in *Vogue*, when he got home:

> Sir Mirza is the arch-enemy of corrugated iron sheets, brass bands (Indian) and of almost everything else that is crude and vulgar . . . Already the metamorphoses he has achieved in a short time are incredible, but his plans are as countless as his inspirations.
>
> The legacy of this wonderful city has fallen into safe hands. The Maharaja of Jaipur is a young man with a proud appreciation of the beauties of his State and a keen interest in building anew.

Sir Humphrey Trevelyan, retired from the Indian political service, was not quite so complimentary about Sir Mirza's taste and wrote of his unfortunate fondness for coloured fountains. He had installed many of these in Mysore, where he had worked for the extremely enlightened Maharaja.

Schemes and plans, however, there were in abundance

and an interest in building anew. Jai used to fly round and round the city in his Gipsy Moth, getting ideas for the new developments outside the city walls. One day, the propellor fell off, but he landed safely for once. They planned five suburbs and Jai sold the land for 25 paise (2p) a square yard, to encourage people to build in areas which, only ten years before, he had been guarding jealously as land for the royal shoot.

One of the engineers who worked on the projects describes Jai's enthusiasm for any development as being so great, 'that you could take him out at midday' – the implication being that it was so hot that no ordinary person would have ventured out at all. He adds that any ceremonial attached to building gave the Maharaja particular delight. There was nothing he liked better than laying a foundation stone or declaring a building open, with much cutting of ribbons and unveiling of plaques.

Of course, a certain amount of the building was done purely for the benefit or the glory of the royal family. There was often talk of the possibility of building a grand new palace, to be called the Man Palace. The idea may have been to compete with the enormous, domed Umaid Palace being built by the Maharaja of Jodhpur, whose status, in Rajput eyes, should not have entitled him to a larger palace than that of the Maharaja of Jaipur. Jai had the sense to regard this plan, which would have cost at least a million rupees, as an unnecessary extravagance. He had already spent 300,000–350,000 rupees on the Rambagh, many of the alterations being designed in England and the Lalique fountains being imported from France.

He had also employed a rather indifferent architect, called Blomfield, to build Jaipur House in Delhi, one shooting lodge at Ramgarh, another at Sawai Madhopur designed, for some obscure reason, like the superstructure of a liner, and a large house in one of the new suburbs for Rabbit.

The City Palace remained the centre for all important royal functions. Jai wanted to create a major highway running directly southwards from the city. The main gate of the Palace, used for all 'auspicious' occasions, was on the east side. Hindu custom dictates that the main entrance shall not face to the south. It is one of those practical things which has become doctrine. Nonetheless, Jai decided, for convenience and ease of getting to and from Rambagh, which lies to the south, to build a new gate in the city walls to line up with his highway. It would also lead to a new main entrance to the Palace. Sir Edward Lutyens' son, Albert, was commissioned to design it. Once again, his scheme proved too grandiose and expensive. Jai built instead a perfectly adequate gate which still stands today.

It was by no means merely building which concerned Jai and his Prime Minister. Sir Mirza was decidedly progressive although, curiously enough, he did not want the British to leave India altogether. At the time when he was in Jaipur, he favoured an Indian government composed of all religions, responsible to the Viceroy. The British would be in charge of defence. As far as the Princes were concerned, he envisaged their role as being that of constitutional monarchs, although in any state that he administered he made full use of the autocratic power of the Maharajas to push through his reforms.

The British had left the general principles of administration in Jaipur undisturbed – a Council of ministers presided over by the Maharaja. Jai had complete power to appoint or to dismiss his ministers, through whom he ruled absolutely. Sir Mirza suggested that it might be better for him to distance himself somewhat from the administration, so as to be above public controversy. Jai agreed with this and ceased to preside over Council meetings.

In order to placate the growing demand for representative government, they established two bodies. In Sir Mirza's words:

> The larger house was to represent the masses of the people, particularly of the rural areas, whose members could freely convey to the Government their wants and grievances, and also express views on matters on which the Government might choose to consult the house. The members could ask questions and influence the administration, but had no other powers. The smaller house, elected on a more restricted franchise and

156

modelled on the British Indian Legislative Councils, had a non-official majority but was invested with real power. Subject to the Maharaja's assent, it could pass laws, discuss and vote on the budget, and ask questions and pass resolutions on matters of public interest. Sufficient powers were reserved to the Maharaja for use in an emergency.

The composition of the Council was to be broadened gradually to include people other than the Sardars and traditional official classes. These reforms, instituted by proclamation on 1 January 1944, only eighteen months after Sir Mirza's arrival, were among the first moves towards democratic government in any princely state. They came, of course, too late to avert the ultimate, total erosion of princely power.

As a result of these policies, the general unrest in India as Independence approached affected Jaipur less than other areas. When Sir Mirza had been in Jaipur for only six months, a *New York Times* correspondent, Herbert L. Matthews, wrote from Jaipur:

> . . . there is powerful sympathy with the Congress party's general program, even though it does not take violent form . . . Sir Mirza says to students, workers and agitators:
> 'Go ahead and demonstrate, strike and parade to your heart's content. I shall not stop you as long as you really remain non-violent according to the Congress program. There will be no repression and no terrorism in Jaipur.' As a result there has been no rioting or sabotage here. The police and troops have made no lathi charges, nor have they fired into crowds. There is no bitterness on the part of the people towards the authorities.

The British disliked all this on several counts. They deplored what they thought of as a waste of money – which should have been devoted to the war effort by being invested in Government of India securities. Even more, they disliked any rapprochement with Congress in the shape of the Praja

157

Mandal. The Viceroy wrote to Jai advising him to go slowly. The Political Department advised him to postpone all public works expenditure except the absolutely essential items. Jai replied, perhaps tongue in cheek, that he would undertake no new work that was not vital. Then he and Sir Mirza went blithely on with their plans.

Although many of the British respected Sir Mirza, there were attempts by pettier officials to discredit him. One Political Agent was attacked and lightly wounded by a teacher when he was going round the School of Art. The teacher, a Muslim, had evidently mistaken him for the head of the Education Department, against whom he bore some grudge. Backed by two other British officials, the Political Agent suggested that Sir Mirza, who was also a Muslim, had somehow perverted the course of justice in order to get the teacher a light sentence. The man had been sentenced to seven years hard labour. The question was referred to Delhi, where wiser councils prevailed.

Petty harrassment took many forms. In 1943, the Viceroy, through the Political Department, objected to the use of the words 'Royal Salute' when applied to Jai in commands during Jaipur ceremonials. This was regarded as an insult to the King Emperor, the only person to whom such a phrase could apply, though there seems no reason why his should not have been termed 'Imperial Salute'. Sir Mirza replied to the Political Agent that, 'His Highness had been deeply wounded by that communication.' The Indian Government, he said, was asking that Jai should give up a custom that had been followed by the state for generations and that 'possibly it had not been quite realised how his position in the eyes of his people, and, in particular, of his troops, would be affected'.

This protest was rejected. Jai agreed to accept the ruling, adding mildly that he presumed that it was equally applicable to all states. The question came up again later. It is hard to see how the war effort was served by such matters as these. Indeed, the British might have done better to pay more attention to the accommodation which Jai and his Prime Minister had come to with the Praja Mandal.

When the Viceroy, Lord Wavell, came to Jaipur in 1946, he was able, much to the alarm of the Inspector General of

158

Police, to go through the heart of the city in procession, unlike his predecessor who had been taken through deserted streets a few years before. Sir Mirza had talked to the Praja Mandal and other leaders and agreed with them on a peaceful tour. The crowds cheered the Viceroy and his wife, showering their car with flowers.

An unnamed Congress leader wrote to Sir Mirza: 'I do not think that in the year 1946 such a grand reception can be given to a British Viceroy in any other part of India . . . in these turbulent days, when the anti-British feeling is running so high.' As Sir Mirza was to point out, the British, when they talked of the princely states, really talked of the rulers, never of the people. The Political Department upheld and even encouraged autocratic rule. It discouraged, 'any attempt to associate the people in the administration and to make it responsive, if not responsible to their wishes. This was my experience in Mysore, and even more so in Jaipur . . . Had it not been for the strong support of the Maharaja, I should have left Jaipur.'

In all the difficulties, Jai supported Sir Mirza with what his Prime Minister called 'considerable courage'. He referred in his memoirs to Jai as 'an enlightened ruler who, true to his promise, gave me his full support'.

That full support must, as often as not, have been needed in face of opposition from his own people, quite as much as from the British. The Rajputs, disdaining the plough and books, disdained industry even more. There were, in 1940, virtually no factories in the whole state of Jaipur. Apart from the copper mines in Khetri, there were some flour mills and oil mills, an ice-making plant or two and one cotton-ginning mill – small enterprises, catering only for domestic demands. Although Jaipur had produced several businessmen, they all operated in Bombay or Calcutta – the Birlas, Goenkas, Podars, Sakserias and several other families from Jaipur were all famous names in the Indian business world.

The Birlas, who came from Pilani, were especially prominent and outstandingly generous as public benefactors. They had established an Intermediate College at Pilani, opened by Jai in 1932. They had repeatedly been refused permission by the Jaipur Government to raise the status of this school to that of a degree college, although they intended to bear all the costs of running the establishment. When the Chief Justice of India and the education adviser to the Indian Government went to Pilani on a private visit as guests of Mr G.D. Birla, they were afterwards asked by the Jaipur Council why they had not asked for permission to go there. Sir Mirza persuaded Jai to let him ask Mr Birla and Sir Badridas Goenka to Jaipur for a meeting with the Maharaja. Pilani college was given degree status and the first industries came to Jaipur – a ball-bearing factory, a steel-rolling mill, a spinning and weaving mill, and a metal and electrical works. It was a start.

Towards the end of his four years in Jaipur, Sir Mirza persuaded such Rajputana States as had degree colleges to combine together to found a University of Rajputana, which was to be situated in Jaipur.

Those four years had transformed Jaipur. They had also changed its Maharaja from a charming, autocratic ruler, somewhat lacking in any specific purpose, into a serious (although still charming) semi-constitutional head of state, with a definite sense of the way in which he wanted things to go – a sense, also, of which way they were going to have to go in the post-war world.

For the rest of the war, Jai's time was divided almost equally between military duties and the administration of his state. He did not much enjoy his time at Dehra Dun Staff College at Quetta. In May 1943, he wrote from an exercise to Ayesha at Quetta itself:

> After two days of bloody hard work and walking about on these beastly hills my legs have given way . . . the food is bloody but the bar is good saving grace . . . It's been raining here since we arrived and bloody cold. I wish you were here darling to warm me up. No rugs can keep the cold out but your arms.

Two months later he went to see the Viceroy and wrote again:

> My work with the Viceroy has gone off well and it was

all advice and no ticking off which pleasantly surprised me, but wants me to remain in the State, I suppose you are delighted. Look after yourself angel . . .

He was still in India in January 1944, writing to Ayesha, who had gone to Bombay for a visit:

Darling beautiful,
. . . anyhow your good wish brought me luck and had a long talk with all the Sardars and all is well and now they have taken up the constitutional reins and agreed to an appointment of committee and thrashing all the things out . . . I have had a pretty rotten time since I have been here apart from the day I arrived and have been in bed with cold & fever and only got up today . . . How I have longed for you all these days to hold my hand but one thing made me laugh that if you had been here I would have had nothing but medicine and thermometer down my throat all the time but took things my own way and told [his valet] to go to hell . . . and don't you go gallivanting with all the worst people just because I'm not there . . . always Jai

Soon after that he was at last allowed to go abroad again, doing liaison work with the Indian State Forces. This meant that he was away a great deal, but managed to pay many visits to India – much to the delight of Ma who, every time he left for the Middle East, Italy or wherever, gave him a long shopping list as if Rome and Florence were as she had always known them.

British Embassy
Cairo 23.5.44
. . . I am having a grand time and seeing lots of new places and found old friends which I hadn't seen since before the war in England. Now don't get excited they are all my boyfriends and most of the time we celebrate in the bar which I hope you approve . . . Old Masood [an Indian friend] has given me some ponies and I'm playing polo regularly twice a week. I suppose now you

161

will say that I come overseas for fun and not work. But
don't forget the pictures you have seen of me in
England 'Maharaja who puts duty before pleasure'
which is true . . .
                    yours forever Jai.

He did enjoy finding his old friends, such as Lord Roderick
Pratt and the Duke of Wellington, and he managed on one
occasion in Italy to visit the Household Cavalry. But he also
enjoyed encouraging the Indian troops and sorting out any
difficulties they might have with British commanders who
had not served in India. His only embarrassment was that
when he might be escorting some grand General on an
inspection of Indian troops, the men would give him a
rapturous welcome and ignore the brass hat who had come
to see them.

Jai had a huge capacity for enjoyment. Despite the war,
which was after all fairly easy to forget in Jaipur, life went on
in a grandiose style. Somehow there were always guests at
the Rambagh, some of them the wives of British officers
serving in the Middle East who could not get back to
England, such as the Duchess of Roxburghe. Another visitor
was Jai's soldier-servant from his days at Knightsbridge
Barracks. Rout, as he was called, was now a Captain in the
Gurkhas. He wrote to Jai, who characteristically invited him
for the weekend.

Other princes came on visits, bringing with them the
usual retinue of forty or fifty people, ranging from their
attendant noblemen down to their servants' servants. There
were picnics and shoots and all the grand receptions associated with the religious festivals.

It is interesting to look at the records of the Shikar Khana,
which one could translate as the Ministry of the Hunt. The
number of tigers shot by the Maharaja and his guests varied
over the years from as few as two to a maximum of seventeen
in 1938. When now the rarity of tigers is blamed upon the
excesses of the Maharajas, it is worth noting that one of
Jamnalal Bajaj's often reiterated complaints was about
tigers. In 1940, he complained that the year before fifteen
people had been killed and forty injured by tigers. Already

in the first three months of 1940, seven people had been killed. He estimated that tigers destroyed half a million rupees' worth of cattle every year.

Jai's shoots became more and more modest in the number of creatures killed, although Ayesha enjoyed tiger shooting more than he did. Lord Mountbatten came to the Rambagh early in 1945, when he was commander in south-east Asia. In his letter of thanks for the visit he wrote:

> I am glad you were so understanding about my not wishing to shoot the magnificent tiger which Ayesha finally shot, but, much as I would have liked to in peacetime, I feel it would have been most wrong for me to have done so with the battle raging in Burma.

There were sadnesses as well as 'fun' and progress during the war. First Her Highness died at Christmas time in 1944. She was forty-five. Jai was away and their son, Bubbles, who was only thirteen, dressed all in white with a white turban, had to light the funeral pyre. Perhaps more distressing, Jai's mother died in 1945. His memories of Isarda had always been important to him. The old doctor there recalls that he used to return 'to honour his birthplace by bathing in the river Banas and covering his body with sand.' When he was at Woolwich, Jai wrote touching letters to his mother asking her to have special achar and puri ready for when he came back. His home life had come to an abrupt end at the age of ten, so that his few years at Isarda as a child held especially emotive memories. The loss of his mother was a great sorrow. His relationship with her was able to be more natural than with his father. The Thakur of Isarda was one of his nobles and, under the strict Rajput rules, owed him allegiance and feudal duty. However great his respect for his father, it could never be the ordinary relationship of a father and son.

The end of the war was a great excitement. Jai sent £1,000 to the Life Guards for the benefit of the other ranks and their families. He had already contributed £200 for the restoration of the Guards Chapel. Then he wrote to apply for the medals of every theatre of war which he had visited, and was therefore rewarded with a large number of ribbons. The Army also offered him the standard demobilisation suit, offered to every soldier on leaving the Army. The style was hardly what he was accustomed to, so he asked if he might have clothing coupons instead, for clothes were rationed in England. The Army refused.

Jai was now thirty-five. He had been on the throne for twenty-four years.

CHAPTER 10

Once the war was over, there was a short-lived return to the full glory of princely India. The splendour of the great festivals of Dasehra, Dewali, the Maharaja's birthday and Holi, when everyone throws coloured water and powder at one another, continued. The nobles, dressed in the appropriate, auspicious colours for each occasion, came and paid homage to their ruler. The regiments paraded and the new, mounted Rajendra Hazari Guards (formed in 1942 in imitation of the Life Guards) in their white uniforms with pale blue and silver facings, riding on long-maned black chargers, added to the glamour of state events. In many ways, the life of the court was even more enjoyable now that the third Maharani was encouraging women to play a greater part in social life.

There was a new club, the Ashok Club, not far from the Rambagh Palace, where everyone went in the evenings and where any new arrival or returning traveller went at once to hear the latest news and gossip.

The city of Jaipur looked better than it had done for a century or more. The buildings were all freshly painted in their rich terracotta pink. Young trees lined the wide, uncluttered streets. Outside the walls, building was going on apace in the new suburbs. There was an air of general prosperity and optimism. New hospitals, new colleges, new temples. The twentieth century was arriving; a little tardily perhaps, but nonetheless exciting for that.

The progress marked something far more fundamental

than the chance benevolence and the good government of an enlightened ruler. Progress had never been a noticeable aim of the British in the princely states. What they sought was stability, preferably without modernisation. What had set off the move to progress was the realisation that the British were not going to be there much longer to ensure stability. The Constitutional Reforms Committee, which was responsible for the setting up in Jaipur of the Legislative Council and the Representative Committee, was a response to the new understanding that, with no paramount power to control unruly elements within the state, something must be done to satisfy the aspirations and expectations of the people, as represented by the movements which had seized upon the Sikar Revolt as a vehicle through which to demonstrate their grievances and express their hopes. Independence was coming. The Princes had to find a way to adjust themselves to the disappearance of a bulwark which had, at some expense of real power, protected them for, in the case of Jaipur, some one hundred and thirty years.

Jai's own thinking in the matter had changed gradually over the years. As far as the Princes were concerned, their first real awareness of the problem came with a series of Round Table Conferences convened in London in the early 1930s, to discuss the future of India. In 1932, Jai had gone to Udaipur to discuss with his fellow Rajput Princes the question of the proposed Indian Federation, which he believed was the proper solution. When the Viceroy, Lord Willingdon, visited Jaipur in December of that year, Jai thanked him for having allowed Udaipur, Jaipur and Jodhpur to send a joint delegate to the Round Table Conferences. He added: 'I also consider it essential that the relationship that now exists between the Crown in England and my state should remain unaltered and this should definitely be provided for in the constitution . . .' At that point, he had never imagined a severance of that relationship.

It would be impossible to say exactly when he changed his mind. We have seen how his resistance to British interference developed as he began to realise that the interests of his own people and those of the British did not necessarily coincide. So, he came to welcome the idea of Independence

166

and to prepare for it. In consequence, the authorities did not like him very much. Lord Wavell, the Viceroy, was especially antagonistic in his reports.

After his visit to Jaipur in March 1946, Wavell wrote to the King (George VI).

'HH of Jaipur is probably known to your Majesty, as he was often in London before the war, playing polo. He has great personal charm and is an attractive character but takes very little interest in the affairs of his State. The only subjects on which he asked my support during my visit were to obtain vacancies for his sons at Eton and to retain on the Reserve the commission in the Life Guards which he was given during the war, by which he sets much greater store than the honorary rank of Major General which he holds. On all State matters he referred me to his Prime Minister, Sir Mirza Ismail, who is able, very ambitious and to my mind untrustworthy. Jaipur's present Maharani (his third) is a sister of Cooch Behar, pretty, attractive and sophisticated.

It did not seem to occur to Wavell that perhaps Jai thought that those were the only two subjects on which he could hope for any real support from the British. Nor did it strike him that Jai might have referred him to Sir Mirza not only because the Prime Minister might have more details at his fingertips, but also because, in his endeavours to become a more constitutional monarch, he thought it proper to refer the Viceroy to his Prime Minister.

Wavell went on to say that:

Jaipur is a most interesting and attractive place, and the old palace of Amber is about the most beautiful place I have seen in India. The State is run very much with an eye to impressing the visitor to the city itself; and some of the nobles in the outlying districts do pretty much what they like, I should say, but the villages I passed through . . . seemed prosperous.

To the Political Adviser Wavell wrote:

> Has the question of his commission in the Life Guards
> been raised before, I know nothing of its history, except
> that he came out to Cairo early in the war to join the
> Life Guards, who were then in the Iraq desert, and
> preferred to remain in Cairo, nominally attached to the
> Scots Greys but really doing little except amuse
> himself . . .

This was both untrue and unfair. It was always Jai's mis-
fortune that, because of his great capacity for enjoyment and
because he was always smiling, people were inclined to
think that he was not a serious person. The puritans, and
Wavell was a puritan, having no idea of fun, despise the
cavaliers, believing them incapable of real purpose.

In June 1946, by which time the Labour Government in
England was becoming impatient for progress to be made in
the negotiations for Indian Independence, the Chamber of
Princes set up a States Negotiation Committee, who were to
act for the Princes in working out what part the states
should play in the interim government – the Constituent
Assembly. The Princes, as was to be the case in all their
dealings until the day when everything would be taken
from them, failed utterly to agree on a united policy. The
Nawab of Bhopal, the Chancellor of the Chamber, and his
supporters believed that they should wait until the Constitution of Independent India was being framed before joining
in the deliberations of the Constituent Assembly.

Bhopal and his followers, who constituted the majority,
were really hedging, being uncertain whether they wanted
to join India until they saw what sort of India it was to be.
They were still toying with the possibility of not joining a
Union of India, but of forming instead an entirely separate
federation composed only of the princely states.

The Maharaja of Bikaner, together with Jaipur, Jodhpur,
Patiala and Gwalior, was for plunging in at the earliest
opportunity in order to have a real share in the creation of
the new India. It was logical for Jai to join with this group.
He had always believed in an Indian Federation. Tradition-
ally, the Maharajas of Jaipur had always backed the central

government, whether Moghul or British. Now that his allegiance to the King Emperor was about to become meaningless (even though he still wanted, for sentimental reasons, his Life Guards commission), he would wish to give his ultimate loyalty to India. Naturally, he would want a say in the kind of India it was to be.

Jai never, at any time, believed in the possibility of a third country composed of the princely states. Lord Mountbatten, long afterwards discussing the possibility with the authors of *Freedom at Midnight*, said that if they had all got together and banded their armies together they might have had a chance but they 'never worked together in any shape or form . . . now if you ask the Maharani of Jaipur she will tell you . . . that she and her very sensible and clued-up husband were under no illusion whatsoever that this could continue . . .'

The negotiations on all sides were bogged down. Wavell was not in any way able to cope with the complexities of the Muslim and Hindu divisions, quite apart from the question of the states. He was inclined, for want of any real solution, to divide India into fragments. In February 1947, the British Prime Minister, Clement Attlee, announced that India would be given Independence in June 1948. Wavell resigned. Mountbatten took over on 24 March.

In April, the Maharaja of Bikaner, with dramatic effect, walked out of the States Negotiation Committee and appealed to the Princes to work towards a united India. This gesture ended the possibility of a separate princely India.

With the arrival of Mountbatten, Jai felt much happier. Mountbatten was an old friend. Jaipur and Bikaner were the only two Maharajas who were on Christian name terms with the new Viceroy. Jai and Mountbatten had a great deal in common: they were both keen polo players; they were both extravagant admirers of the British Royal Family; both loved ceremonial and medals and all the panoply of power. They were both politically shrewd, impatient of inefficiency and extremely good at whatever they set their hands to. Neither of them was an intellectual, but both had logical minds which saw to the heart of a problem. They shared also a love of parties, social occasions and frivolity. The great difference in their characters was that Jai was essentially modest.

In any event, Jai felt safe enough to go to England, in May

1947, despite an urgent plea from his brother-in-law, Yad-havendra Singh, the Maharaja of Panna:

> My dear Jai,
>   . . . I hope you are not unmindful of the talk we had here about the utter need for some sort of cohesion and unity in Rajputana and the neighbouring region. The political situation is nearing its climax and the next few months will witness hectic developments . . . we may find we are faced with a formula not to our liking . . . At that stage it may be truly difficult – well nigh impossible to upset the apple cart . . .
>   As I said then I repeat again that you are in that enviable position to give an inspiring lead in regenerating that constructive spirit of mutual understanding and cohesion which would bring about the desired solidarity of Rajputana and its neighbours . . .

He begged Jai 'with folded hands' to act. He asked him not to be angry and to enjoy his holiday, but to give the matter 'serious thought' all the time.

Perhaps Jai had not, at this stage, given much thought to what the position of the smaller states would be in the Union. His own state was a large, viable unit, which would continue autonomously within the new framework of an independent India. Above all, Mountbatten would see to it that the princes got a fair deal.

By the time Jai returned in July, the new Government had set up a States Department under Sardar Vallabhbhai Patel, with V.P. Menon as his secretary, to conduct relations with the states. It was a matter of great urgency, given the new timetable Mountbatten had set for Independence by 15 August, that the states should accede to the Union. If they did not accede, they would be in a position to disrupt the whole country. The railways to Calcutta, Bombay and Madras all ran through princely states. They could have been brought to a standstill. So could the postal and telegraph systems and the airways.

Menon, therefore, proposed that the states should be asked to accede only in three respects – defence, foreign affairs and communications. Patel, in asking the Princes to agree to this, assured them that their autonomy would be scrupulously respected. He told them that Congress did not want to interfere in any way with their domestic affairs, nor had they any thought of dominating the states. They wished the Princes well and were not their enemies. Sir Conrad Corfield, who had once been Resident in Jaipur, was now on Mountbatten's staff. He was thought, out of fondness for the Princes, to be encouraging them not to accede so that, when Independence came and British paramountcy ceased, they would be in a stronger negotiating position. Some Princes interpreted his advice as meaning that they should still consider the possibility of remaining outside the Union. Mountbatten sacked Corfield. The Viceroy then undertook to negotiate with the Princes himself.

As well as having private meetings with individual Princes, he summoned a full meeting of the Chamber of Princes on 25 July 1947. It was one of those occasions at which Mountbatten was so skilled. Even Dr Karni Singh, the son of the then Maharaja of Bikaner, who is not given to flowery prose, in writing his account of the occasion could not resist saying of the Viceroy that he 'was looking handsome in his naval uniform'. (It is almost the only physical description of anyone in a 400-page book of history.)

Mountbatten was wonderfully persuasive. He, too, gave them assurances – that there would be no financial liability put upon them and that there would be no further reduction of their internal sovereign powers.

Jai happily signed the instrument of accession. One clause read:

> Nothing in this instrument affects the continuance of sovereignty in and over this State, or save as provided by or under this instrument, the exercise of any powers authority and rights now enjoyed by me as Ruler of this State.

In one sense, nothing had changed. As a ruler, he had never had control over the three areas which he now agreed to leave in the hands of the new central power in Delhi. In all other respects, he was in some ways freer, for there was no Resident looking over his shoulder, no Viceroy to give him a ticking off. He was the Maharaja of Jaipur, at liberty to negotiate as an equal with the new Government, of whose goodwill he had so recently been assured. His friend Mountbatten was still there, as Governor-General of the new country. Even before Independence Day, Jai flew off to take his two elder sons, Bubbles and Joey, to school in England.

He was soon back, however, alarmed lest the communal violence which had broken out as the result of partition should spread to Jaipur.

There were about 20,000 Muslims in Jaipur, about one tenth of the total population. Once again, Jai proved the falsity of the British accusation that he was anti-Mohammedan. While several Hindu Maharajas did nothing to stop their Hindu subjects from killing their Muslim subjects, Jai regarded himself as responsible for all his people. Every night after dinner, he toured the city in an open Jeep. He took with him a Muslim colonel from one of his regiments. Jai would talk to the people, assuring the Muslims that in his eyes there was no difference between them and his Hindu subjects; and he threatened the Hindus with grave punishments if any Muslim was hurt. None was.

In October, Jai became aware that the Pakistani Army was trying to seduce Muslims from military families to leave Jaipur and move to Pakistan. Two drafts of a letter from Jaipur on this subject survive. The first is a diplomatic and tentative appeal to the recipient's goodness, with no mention of any malice on the part of the Pakistani Army. This draft was written by Jai's new Prime Minister, Sir V.T. Krishnamachari. The other was plainly Jai's own draft, and was, we may hope, the one which was sent. It was addressed to Colonel Iskander Mirza, the Secretary at the Defence Department. It read:

> I wish to take this opportunity of addressing you in
> connection with our Qaimkhanis. I have been informed
> very reliably that a Mohommedan Army officer,
> formerly of the 18th Cavalry and now reported to be a
> member of the Pakistan Army, has been actively trying

172

to induce our Qaimkhanis, who have lived peacefully for hundreds of years in this State, to migrate to Pakistan and is dissuading them from joining or supporting the Jaipur State Forces. Knowing you so well as I do, I feel I should request you as a friend to see that such action is definitely discouraged. Should our Qaimkhanis have any cause to feel dissatisfied I would be very glad indeed to look into and redress their complaints but it pains me considerably to learn that a section of my subjects – who have a record of loyalty second to none and for whom I have the greatest esteem – are being misled and induced to act in a manner prejudicial to the State. I would appreciate it very much if you could very kindly make necessary enquiries and drop me a line to put my mind at rest on this score.

Some months later, during some troubles in one part of the state, one of his officers asked Jai whether he should kill some agitating Muslims. 'Certainly not. They are my subjects. Protect them.'

It was axiomatic in Jai's mind that all his subjects were entitled to equal protection and security. And no communal violence was ever known in Jaipur. (It may not be too fanciful to suppose that something of this spirit survives today. After Mrs Gandhi's assassination, no one was seriously hurt. In a neighbouring state, a train on its way to Jaipur was stopped. More than twenty Sikhs, including a child of six, were dragged off the train and murdered.) Compared with other regions, few of Jaipur's Muslims elected to move to Pakistan. On the other hand, thousands of Hindus poured into Jaipur from the Sind and Pakistani part of the Punjab.

Four months after Independence, there was a triumphant demonstration that Jai was still the Maharaja of Jaipur. In December, he held his Silver Jubilee. It was a spectacular affair, with plenty of the grand functions and parades which he so much enjoyed. Fourteen ruling Princes came for the celebrations, many of whom were surprised at the free-and-easy attitude which now prevailed in Jaipur over purdah. The ladies from Bikaner were scandalised at the idea that men would serve them their food and quite threw out the catering arrangements by their refusal to accept such a thing.

Jai was weighed against silver and the money given to the poor. It being the polo season, he was in good training and so weighed less than he might have done at another time of year. Both his wives were weighed, too, in the privacy of the zenana. The culmination of the festivities was a huge darbar, conducted in full ceremonial dress, to which Lord and Lady Mountbatten came. Mountbatten invested Jai as a Grand Commander of the Star of India. All the other orders of the Indian Empire had been suspended with Independence. For some reason, the Star had not. Mountbatten asked the King if he might give it to two Maharajas who had been most co-operative and helpful in the difficulties over the accession. They were Bikaner and Jaipur – the two who called him by his Christian name.

Jai presented Mountbatten with a jade-handled dagger, bejewelled with rubies and emeralds. It had been captured by Man Singh I in 1585 from an Afghan warrior.

Naturally, the darbar was followed by a polo match. Mountbatten protested that he had not played since before the war and, in any case, had no clothes. Jai had anticipated this excuse and had arranged for some clothes to be made for him. One hundred and thirty six ponies were paraded, from which Mountbatten was to choose six. (Mountbatten, it goes without saying, recorded that he played pretty well.)

In the evening, they went to the opening of a new cinema called The Polo Victory. Jai had given the polo-stick maker who had accompanied him on his famous polo tour of 1933 a plot of land. On it he had built this cinema, named in honour of the tour. They all watched an old film of the victorious team in action. Unfortunately, it was run backwards, but everyone was too polite to mention this.

Soon there was to be an even greater display of princely grandeur. Jai's eldest child, his daughter by First Her Highness, known as Mickey, was now nineteen. She was to be married to the Maharaja of Baria's eldest son, the nephew of the Prithi Singh of Baria who had been one of the members of Jai's polo team in England in 1933.

Mickey was the first Princess of Jaipur to be married in

more than a hundred years and the splendour of her wedding made up for the dearth of predecessors. Princes came from all over India. The festivities, which lasted two weeks, were planned like a military operation. The list of parties and ceremonies, with all the seating plans and menus and time-tables, filled a thick book.

Ayesha wrote in her memoirs:

> It was the only time I saw the City Palace fully alive, bustling with people and parties, all the apartments of the zenana in use, and everywhere the vivid colours of the flowers and the women's Rajputani costumes, the sound of laughter and music and the jingling of the ladies' anklets. From the terraces we could see out across the city to the hills beyond, where each of the forts encircling Jaipur was picked out in lights.
>
> For the wedding banquet itself, long tables were decorated with more flowers and, since the meal was entirely Indian, loaded with rich meat curries, several kinds of pilau, and sweets covered with gold leaf. All down the tables there was the bright gleam of gold and silver thals, bowls and goblets . . . the palace musicians played.

The poor and the Brahmins were fed. Prisoners were let out of jail. The wedding reached the *Guinness Book of Records* as the most expensive in the world. The extravagance was traditional. Even today, quite humble Indian families, earning less than £30 a week, mysteriously manage to spend £2,000 on a wedding. But nothing quite so splendid ever happened again.

Soon after the wedding, Jai and Ayesha went off to England. While they were there, they bought a house near East Grinstead called Saint Hill. It was a late Georgian house built in about 1820. It was a substantial building with a panelled drawing-room, where they hung a large portrait of Jai over the fireplace and another portrait of Ma. There was also a billiard room, a cosy library and a dining-room, hung with a portrait of Ayesha by James Gunn and some Indian minia-tures. In the usual Indian style, they had, in the conservatory, a bar on which stood a Coca-Cola dispenser. It was very much a family house. A 400-acre farm went with it – Ayesha maintains that they bought Saint Hill so that the children, who were now at school in England, could be assured of milk and butter, which were still strictly rationed.

It seems probable that, despite the splendours they had just left, there were already doubts in Jai's mind about what was going to happen in India and that he thought a refuge in England might not be a bad thing to establish. That he had such doubts is confirmed by an interview which he gave in New York in September 1948. When he was asked why he was sending his children to school in England, he replied: 'What more can an Indian ruler do for his children today than give them a cosmopolitan education? It is unlikely they will be rich when they grow up. At least they can become good diplomats.'

It was the first time that either Jai or Ayesha had been to America. They were still young and Ayesha almost at her most beautiful. They appeared to the Americans, especially in Hollywood, like a fairy-tale prince and princess.

They returned to India to face the most difficult period of Jai's life, in which the fairy-tale was destroyed.

Even before the accession agreements had been made, it was plain that the smaller states, many of them only a few square miles in area and often entirely surrounded by the new India, were not practical units for any form of autonomy. Many of the rulers of these states, having little option, agreed to merge their states with the main body of India, surrendering their position as rulers in return for a guaranteed Privy Purse. They were also allowed to retain the dignity of their titles and all their existing privileges.

There were eighteen states which had been declared by the Dominion Government to be viable units. Jaipur was one of these. There was every reason to believe, for repeated assurances were given by Nehru and by Sardar Patel, that these states would be left alone – the more so because states such as Jaipur and Bikaner had already gone a long way down the road towards democratisation. The argument that

176

Jai performs Puja in the City Palace at the start of the celebrations for his Silver Jubilee in 1947.

(*above*) Jaipur during the celebrations for Mickey's wedding (Henri Cartier-Bresson – *John Hillelson Agency*).

(*overleaf*) The wedding of Princess Prem Kumari (Mickey) to the Maharaja of
Baria's eldest son at Jaipur in 1948 (Henri Cartier-Bresson – *John Hillelson
Agency*).

the people of the states must have the same measure of freedom as those in the main body of India was invalid. Negotiation with the reasonable Princes could have ensured that the people were given parallel rights under a constitutional monarchy.

The Congress movement in Jaipur had always affirmed its loyalty to the Maharaja and, had a referendum been taken, there is no doubt that the people of Jaipur would have voted to keep their traditional ruler, probably as an autocratic monarch, but certainly as a figurehead.

Sardar Patel and V.P. Menon planned otherwise. In January 1948, after the complete merger of the states of Orissa and Chhatisgarh, several of the rulers requested a meeting with Mountbatten. Once again, V.P. Menon assured them that the principle of merger would not apply to the viable states.

The net was soon closing round Jai. The important states of Rajputana were among the oldest in India. They had existed long before the British came, indeed before the coming of the Moghuls. Now, in the south-east of Rajputana, nine of the smaller states, headed by Kota, where he had been educated in his early childhood and where his first cousin ruled, agreed to merge with the Dominion and lose their identity.

Barely a month later, the Maharana of Udaipur, the man to whom Jai had deferred so respectfully as the head of the senior Rajput family, gave in and joined Kota. Together they formed Rajasthan. This was a particularly bitter blow, not only because Udaipur historically represented defiance and Rajput honour, but also because it was one of the 'viable states'. If any of them gave in, what chance did the remainder have?

At much the same time, states to the north and west merged – Alwar (which had once been part of Jaipur), Bharatpur, Dholpur and Karauli forming the Matsya union. Much pressure had been brought to bear on these states. Alwar had been kept under house arrest in a Delhi hotel because there was communal violence in his state, some thought encouraged by him. Bharatpur was threatened by the Army on the pretext of maintaining civil order.

Jai's reaction to these mergers may be judged by an undated note found among his papers:

177

On Aug 15th 1947 the most memorable day in the history of India ever since we became a subject nation 'or race was the day of our independence & India once again threw [off] the yoke of foreign rule . . . This memorable time in the history of India, there was not a genius to be found among the Princes of India so the fate of the Indian States drifted with the rest of India & its leaders.

Were there no men of cool common sense, who considered the main duty of state leadership to be the preservation of the states entrusted to their care.

Many of the rulers who talked big & of fighting to the last ditch did what weak characters always do when they should be acting up to it. Decamped from their thrones. Most of these rulers had seen themselves as suns round which the whole of Hindustan revolved wrote to the states ministry & said . . .? [sic] It was a bit late on their part to [put] the ideal of the country above all things.

It did not occur to them for a moment that lakhs of their subjects had spent their whole lives without any guarantee of safety from them & that they [the people] had taken this [safety] for granted as the main fulfilment owed to them. However they [the rulers] left reality behind, the reality of countless lives wrecked and unprotected, [despite the people's] unswerving loyalty to the ruler & unremitting toil in his service . . .

Jai's evident, if uncharacteristic, anger when scribbling this note garbled still further his haphazard grammatical style. What emerges clearly is his belief that he held his state as a trust, that his duty was to protect his subjects – subjects not really of his, even, but of the god Govind Devji. It is also clear that he held this belief very strongly: to give up his throne would be to betray a sacred trust.

There still remained four important states of Rajputana – Bikaner, Jaipur, Jodhpur and Jaisalmer. Their loyalty to India was unquestioned. Jinnah, the founder of Pakistan, had invited them all to join him, offering Jai *carte blanche* to write his own terms. All had refused, feeling safe in the assurances given them by Mountbatten, Nehru, Patel and Menon that their sovereignty in all matters, save the three points of the accession, would remain undisturbed. The first three of these states were classed as viable.

It is questionable whether Mountbatten's role was strictly honourable. He had traded on his friendship with the Princes, in particular with Jaipur and Bikaner. By agreeing to become Governor-General of the new Dominion of India, he abandoned them. He might hand out Stars of India, but he could no longer help them, because he was now a servant of the Dominion and necessarily obedient to its leaders.

Sardar Patel and Menon began to play a cat and mouse game with the remaining, unmerged states. Bikaner, Jaipur and Jodhpur held many meetings and consulted over the telephone but, as is the way with Rajputs, they could never really agree. Bikaner and Jaipur felt certain restraints, in as much as Bikaner was much older than Jai, but Jaipur was dynastically more important. Jodhpur was wilder and far less politically sophisticated than the other two. According to Dr Karni Singh, the next Maharaja of Bikaner, who was present at many of the meetings, Jai was if anything more flexible than the others. But he agreed that whatever decision they finally took would be jointly agreed by all three of them. In the end, this did not happen. Dr Karni Singh says that, 'it would be indelicate to say why it did not happen'.

Part of the reason was Sardar Patel's devious skill as a negotiator. According to one of Jai's nobles, Devi Singh Mandawa, he managed to tap the rulers' telephones, so that he knew precisely what tactics they were planning. He would talk to their ministers and try to enlist their help against the Princes.

Something of the atmosphere which he managed to engender can be seen in a letter of resignation from one of Jai's long-serving ministers, written in September 1948:

> . . . I was hoping that never in the few remaining years of my life I would have to leave Jaipur . . . But little did I know that there would be a day when I would be told by my master . . . that unless I joined hands with a group which according to me was not acting in the best

179

interest of the state (and this now, is not only my opinion but the opinion of thousands both in and outside the state) I must prepare myself for the 'High Jump'; in other words I must go . . . There is no doubt that while Sir V.T. [Krishnamachari] remains here he will endeavour to avert a collapse of administration but there are indications that even he is getting fed up with the under hand tactics that seem to dominate the administration of the day.

Sir V.T. Krishnamachari, Jaipur's Prime Minister, was a good administrator. Jai was a good judge of men. Nevertheless, he was a cautious man. Although a perfectly loyal servant of the state, his instinctive sympathies lay with the central Government. He was in favour of merging.

Patel never let up. There were comical moments. Jodhpur heard that Patel insulted people. He declared, when Patel was due to visit him, that if he insulted him he would shoot him and then commit suicide. Patel, of course, heard of this threat. He arrived, smiling and courteous, addressing the Maharaja as 'my dear nephew', thus disarming him in every sense.

It is hard to say which of the three surrendered first, for each would naturally charge the others with frailty. It seems probable that it was Jodhpur, who sent his Prime Minister to see Patel with instructions to get the best possible deal. Jai, seeing that there was no hope, was next. Devi Singh Mandawa maintains that Jai toyed for a while with the idea of standing out alone, but was afraid of bloodshed.

That this was so is confirmed by a formal letter which Jai wrote to his eldest son, Bubbles, when he was making his final decision. The letter also suggests a different explanation of the breaking of the agreement on unified action by the three states.

This letter is so different from the ones that I usually write and I know I have no business to worry you with these problems. I should leave you to your studies but all the decisions I take today will affect you and bind you down in the future and so I consider it my duty, not only as your father, but as the Ruler of this historic State, a heritage handed down from our renowned ancestors to which in turn we all dedicate our lives, to paint you a true picture of our position today.

Our country is going through a revolutionary change and those of us who are going to be of any service to her must adapt ourselves to the changing circumstances. If we still persist in living on our laurels and in the way of life that existed fifty years ago we shall be asking for trouble and be wiped off the map.

I shall now try and give you a clear picture of Rajputana as it is today. It breaks my heart to say so but I am afraid Rajputana is in the melting pot, and I see no bright future for her unless one of the Rulers is prepared to make a sacrifice and take the lead. The picture of the States today is as follows:

Udaipur voluntarily gave in and is today part of the Union of Rajasthan. The poor Maharana is a cripple and his advisers have been far from loyal, and have taken advantage of him and guided him on the wrong lines. The premier Rajput State of Rajputana is no more that now.

Jodhpur thanks to its young Ruler, your cousin is not only financially broke, but the Ruler has made history by marrying a common Eurasian girl and has lowered himself and his State in the eyes of the public.

His Highness of Bikaner, who has a good opinion of himself, has brought ruin on his State and himself by smuggling stuff into Pakistan. He and his ministers were personally involved in the smuggling. The result was the whole Administration broke down and now the State is run by an Administrator appointed by the Government of India.

Jaipur, the State to which we all have the honour of belonging, stands out by itself. There is not a person today in India, who can find a fault or point an accusing finger towards its Ruler, administration or people.

This is the picture of Rajputana today, and now I come to the great decision I have to take, and that is whether to stand out and remain as we live today or whether to go to the help of Rajputana and form another Rajasthan and be their leader. If I become the leader of Rajputana it will mean sacrificing the independence of Jaipur. On the other hand no one can forecast how long we or any other State can remain independent because all the forces in the country are moving towards democratic ideals. So my dear boy, the sacrifice which seems so great today may prove in the end to be no sacrifice at all. Time and history will alone prove that.

I personally feel that every sacrifice is worth making if you can serve your country better and for a greater cause, when I say SERVE I mean it in the real sense of the word and I do not mean just being a mere figurehead. If I cannot guide the destiny of my people as their Ruler at least I will be in the new set up serving them and looking after their interests, which in itself is more service than giving up completely.

However, before coming to a final decision of whether to remain as we are or join and lead the others, I shall ascertain the wishes of my people and possibly of the rest of Rajputana, and will be guided by their wishes . . .

Jai went on to say that he had consulted Mountbatten and was attaching his letter and Mountbatten's reply. These are lost, but we may guess that Mountbatten advised him to merge his state with Rajasthan.

What shines through the letter is the powerful tug of history upon his emotions, along with echoes of ancient rivalries, which then yields to his common sense and his political awareness. To stand out would never have been a real possibility. Menon admitted at a meeting in Bikaner, held ostensibly to discuss with the leading citizens the whole question of the merger, that the matter had already been decided – this only nine months after he had specifically said that it was 'not the Government's intention to touch any of the major states'.

Discussions went on between Jai and representatives of the Indian Government throughout November and December

1948. In November, he had another crash. Some Americans wanted to demonstrate a two-engined plane to him. The plane had the signal advantage of being able to land and even take off on only one engine. Jai was supposed merely to watch from the ground. He decided to go up with the demonstrators. The claims for it may have been excessive. It fell to the ground. Jai was badly hurt.

His dealings with the Government were conducted in some physical pain, to add to the mental distress.

Menon continued to play games. On 11 January 1949, Menon came to Jaipur. It was agreed that Jaipur would be integrated into the new Union of Greater Rajasthan, which would merge with the Dominion of India. The Union would include the whole of Rajputana. Jai would be made the hereditary Governor, or Rajpramukh, of the Union.

The formal record of the meeting says:

> The following guarantees and assurances having been given by the Government of India . . . to the rulers of Jaipur, I, on behalf of my successors and my State, agree to the integration of Jaipur State to the Union of Greater Rajasthan.
> A. The rulers of Jaipur will be the hereditary Rajpramukhs of Greater Rajasthan.
> B. Jaipur will be the capital of Greater Rajasthan.
> C. The ruler of Jaipur will have a Privy Purse of 25 lakhs.
> D. No Uprajpramukh [deputy governor] will be appointed.
> E. There will be an efficient administration set up.

The last clause reveals a mistrust on Jai's part of the likely quality of government.

Three days later, in Udaipur, Patel announced that the last four states had agreed in principle to integrate with Greater Rajasthan. The next two months were taken up with feverish negotiations about the details of the changeover. The first thing that happened was that the Government immediately went back on their undertaking about the hereditary governorship. It was reduced to Jai's being Rajpramukh only for life.

183

His privy purse was fixed at the agreed figure and included an allowance of 550,000 rupees as Rajpramukh. It all amounted to 2,350,000 rupees, less than £200,000. This may sound an enormous amount, but it should be remembered that in handing over his state he gave all the money in the Treasury to the Government. In cash, this came to 45,800,000 rupees or three and a half million pounds. As well as money, the Dominion got the whole railway system, including rolling stock. (In Bikaner's case, this was worth six million pounds.)

Besides this, an immense amount of property was transferred. All the official buildings, many of them built by Jai, were surrendered. The fine barracks built for the Sawai Man Guards is today the Secretariat of the Rajasthan Government. Many historic monuments were handed over. The Amber Palace, except for the temple of Shila Deviji, many of the buildings of the City Palace, The Palace of the Winds, Jai Singh's observatories in Jaipur and Delhi, the Royal Cenotaphs, Nahargarh Fort, Ramthambhor Fort – all these were given to the Government. One estimate put a total value of fifteen million pounds on what was handed over.

Jai also undertook to set up a trust which would preserve, in a museum in City Palace, many of the family treasures – carpets, paintings, arms, furniture and other items of historical interest.

It should also be remembered that any Maharaja had a prodigious number of dependants. There were still several hundred people living in the zenana. There was a myriad of servants who could not be abandoned. There were at least seven temples with their staff to be maintained. While the pleasures of the Princes had been great, their obligations were extensive.

All these details were enshrined in a covenant. There were many clauses dealing with the privileges and titles, even down to the flying of flags on motor cars. There were also lists of what was agreed to be private property, even listing camping equipment. It is worth noting two of these points. First, 'that a public holiday will be observed within the Jaipur Division of the United State of Rajasthan on His Highness' birthday'. Second, Jai provided a most precise list of the gold and gold coins in his private treasury.

One of the great personal sadnesses for Jai was having to

give up his army, all the regiments of which were merged with the Indian Army. Only the Sawai Man Guards retained any identity, being known henceforward as the 17th Battalion of the Rajputana Rifles – Sawai Man. The cavalry were incorporated into the 61st Cavalry.

Jai addressed the senior officers on 27 March 1949, and, from his notes for the speech he made, we can again see something of how his decision had been reached.

> First move made [by Government] early November . . .
> First reactions bad . . . after hearing all party's views
> my appreciation was:
>   (a) that the independence of Jaipur State could be
>   held at great sacrifice – and possibly bloodshed –
>   and then too only for a temporary period
>   (b) advantageous position in which Jaipur was
>   placed . . . personal vanity would suffer . . .
>   great things could be done for the State by joining
>   the new set up. This will give me an opportunity
>   to serve the people . . .

Three days later, on 30 March 1949, Patel and Menon came to Jaipur to inaugurate the new state of Greater Rajasthan. Menon arrived first. Sardar Patel's plane did not come. It was known to have left Delhi. Menon flew back to Delhi in a panic. It turned out that Patel's plane, also carrying the Maharaja of Jodhpur, had had to land in a river bed in Alwar. He came on by car; Menon flew back. The inauguration took place with due solemnity in the City Palace. Jai was no longer ruler of Jaipur.

It is easy to see now that the Maharajas could never have survived. Once they had agreed to the accession, they were doomed. It would have been impossible, within a democracy, to have had a patchwork of monarchies, even constitutional monarchies. It would have been as if in the United States of America, mingled within the ordinary states, there had been some eighteen kingdoms of say Texas, Nebraska, Vermont, Oregon and so forth.

What was unattractive and disillusioning was the patent duplicity of the Congress leaders. There can be little doubt that, with the probable exception of Nehru, they never had any intention of honouring the guarantees which they repeatedly used to soothe the fears of the Princes.

It was a cast of cynicism which informed all their dealings with the Princes until the very end.

There was a legend that the state of Jaipur would last as long as an image of Narsingh stood in its place in a temple at Galta in the hills near Jaipur. A few days after Jai signed the merger documents, it vanished.

CHAPTER II

Jai had a notable ability, once something was done, not to brood about it. If there was no question of being able to reverse something unpleasant, he always decided to make the best of the situation. Having convinced himself that he had made the best choice for his people, he threw himself into his new role as Rajpramukh with enthusiasm.

He was hesitant and shy about some of the old traditions and he cut down drastically on the celebration of festivals, eliminating some of the rituals and pageantry. He was far from shy in his eagerness to perform the duties expected of a Governor, although he was careful to remain well within the constitutional role allotted to him.

Many of his duties were purely ceremonial, such as the opening of the State Legislature sessions, the swearing-in of ministers and the laying of foundation stones. At the beginning, he had a limited power of veto. Such papers as survive show him involved in milder matters – for instance, going to see the Maharaja of Alwar, who wanted help with the creating of Sariska Game Park in his former state, dealing with Army affairs, attending visits by the President of India whenever he came to any part of Rajasthan.

Some of the problems brought to him were hardly governmental. Jai noted: 'The Nawab of Tonk saw me on Aug 31st 1949 and complained to me about the difficulties he has been having with ladies of the late ruler. One begum in particular . . . is living in a manner not becoming to the member of a ruling family.' Jai explained patiently that he would have to sort the matter out himself. He pointed out that if the Rajpramukh took anything up, it became a public matter, which would hardly help the Nawab, whose whole object was to keep the lady's behaviour private.

This kind of misconception was by no means confined to old-fashioned grandees. A large section of the general populace had not begun to understand the change that had taken place. People in the streets, seeing Jai, would come up to ask for his help – for the favour of some land, to enlist his interest in a family dispute – exactly as they had always done when he was their ruler. His continuing popularity was a source of some irritation to the politicians. It was galling for Congress leaders from Delhi, who came grandiosely to perform the opening of a new electricity works, or whatever, to find that the Rajpramukh, supposedly dancing attendance on them, was greeted by the crowds with louder acclaim than they were.

Jai's apprehension and its gradual resolution is shown very clearly in an innocent and touching record that he scribbled after his thirty-eighth birthday celebrations in 1949. He had much reduced the pageantry, fearing that no one would now care for such displays:

22nd Aug Self Birthday

I am writing an account of my birthday under the new changes. As this was the first occasion after the formation of Greater Rajasthan. I feel happy and proud that I find no change in my people's love, affection and loyalty towards me and I had a rousing reception from all sects of my people wherever I went and met them at most functions.

I was greeted at sunrise with booming of the guns from Nargarh and a kiss from my beautiful wife which made a perfect beginning. I then had a swim after which all the personal servants came and did their nazars to me which I touched and did not take. Then I changed into 'Achkan and Safa' to go to the City Palace for puja and other ceremonies.

The route most of the way was thronged by the people and as I passed them I was greeted with shouts

188

of 'Maharaja Man Singhji Ki Jai' which I responded by a waving to the people.

At 11am I did puja at . . . and the haveli and then went and did the walbati[?] at Shri Gobindevji's temple. The gardens were thronged with townspeople who gave the greater welcome than ever till I came back to Chandra mahal.

Then I went and did 'Baras pojan' in Shereth Newas doing bhati to Gurji on the way.

Then I held a darbar in Sarbata of rather an unusual type from the ones we use to have on birthday occasion. I only invited 'Tazimi & Khas Chofti' Sardars and their eldest sons. This was well attended and all the Sardars turned out in red and gold and we had a collection of about 90 Sardars & sons. After the nazars were over I sat down and called the Sardars close to me so that [I] could talk to them.

In few chose words that came from my happy heart I told them that –

I have never been more happier than having so many of them in the darbar and that with all the changes in Rajputana States. I was proud that Jaipur was like before and this was owing to their loyalty and affection for me. I wanted to adopt some changes but not without their wishes for which I proposed a Council under Maharawal of Samode to make suggestion what customs we might keep and what we could do away. I also told them that we are one family and that it rest on one another to hold our prestige and honour in the new changes. I assured them on my side that I shall always look after their interest and prayed to Mataji that she will always guide us all and save us from doing any deed or action which would disgrace or shame on the 'Kachhawa family or the Jaipur State.'

We then dispersed from the darbar and they all came and had drinks with me in Chandra Mahal.

I then freely mixed with them and talked to them and was greatly touched with their expressions & sentiments of loyalty and devotion to me and my family.

We then dispersed for lunch. I had quite a lunch with the family which was attended by both my wives . . . and Isarda Bhabi.

I then had some rest till I went to the garden party to which all those who usually come to the darbar were invited.

Before going to the garden party I had a request from the old officials of the Jaipur State that they would like to present nazars to me so I asked them to come before the garden party. I received them in Sarbata. They all came and presented their nazar in the usual manner but in their case I only touched it and did not take it which created quite a surprise to some of the officials. I then gave them a short talk and said:

'Gentlemen I am greatly touched by the display of loyalty and affection shown by you all on this occasion and assure you that whatever change may take place my love and care of you all in no way will be affected as Jaipurians.' (All the officials were greatly moved by my words.)

I then went to the garden party held in the City Palace garden and was well attended by all people officials and politicians. I spent about half an hour going round the people and talking to them and then left the party after the band had played the Jaipur Anthem.

I then changed and bathed and then went to the Zanana Majils in 'Bada Rawala' which was as usual full of screaming women and children, but they all gave me a happy smile and after taking nazar of the ladies I came away.

The Army officers had also requested that they all wanted to present nazar so I had arranged to see them all at a special party 'cocktails' after the Zanana Majils. So now I went to see all the officers of the Rajasthan Army who had collected in the City Palace garden. They were all lined up and after I had taken my place on the Silver Chair they all came one by one and presented their nazars which [I] took standing up and kept it . . . Then all the retired officers also did the nazar but my surprise had no limit when the Indian Army officers . . . came forward and did nazar. I took their nazar and kept it as I did not want to make a difference between the two by which their feeling might be affected.

I then asked all the officers to come round me and in few chosen words said:

'Brother officers you have greatly touched my heart by the display of love and loyalty shown to me by this gesture of yours this evening and presenting nazars and that happiness is still greater that today the feelings of State and Indian officers is equal for me. There is no reason for the two forces to feel different in any way for today we all stand for one cause and that is to serve our country to the best of our ability. I want to assure all those under my command that I consider my first and foremost duty to serve them and watch their and their family interest at all times. Words fail me to express my feeling adequately this evening but you will understand my feeling better than I can ever put them in words. I hope you will all join me in having a glass of champagne and asha.'

We had a happy party in fact one of the best I have ever had with the Army boys. We were all in happy mood and proposed each other's toasts. The party was so good that it lasted from 8pm to 11pm and they all carried me away by feelings difficult to express that I forgot my dinner engagement. I left the party at 11pm with fond farewells. I am proud to have this fine lot of men under my command and am confident that the spirit that was displayed on this occasion make me believe that no task is insurmountable for us.

I came back to Rambagh for dinner where we were having a family party composed of relations & members of staff and their families. After good drink and good food in a hilarious mood I said good night to all and went to bed.

This was my first birthday as Rajpramukh of Greater Rajasthan and can confidently say that it was just as happy and gay as the ones I had as Ruler of Jaipur and the display of love, loyalty and devotion shown by all the people greatly touched my heart.

I pray to Mataji that she will always guide me and bless me so that I will serve the people well and that the whole of Rajasthan will love me and trust me. I could not have wished for a happier birthday.

This long account tells us much both about Jai himself and about the people of Jaipur. There was, in reality, no need for anyone, except for the ladies in the zenana, most of whom were still dependent on him, to present their nazars to him. The land tenure system was about to be abolished and the Sardars, strictly speaking, had no more need of him. The officials and the Army officers made their obeisance at their own request, not because it was either asked or expected of them. The people, too, quite spontaneously gave their acclaim as their former ruler when through the streets.

Jai's reaction to all this may seem a little naive, but what yardstick do royalty have to measure their success or failure other than their popularity with the people? A spurious popularity may be bought with bread and circuses, but real popularity can only be achieved by the proper exercise of power. Allowance must be made, especially in India, for the mysterious aura of royalty and the apparently instinctive desire of human beings to admire kingship; but Jai inspired much more than that. It may be that, quite apart from his personal charm, he really did manage to convince his people of his desire to serve them and, again of great importance in India, of his belief that his responsibility to them was God-given. There are, in the account of his birthday, little touches of thoughtfulness, a sense that he was always aware of the effect of his actions.

In all of this, there is an echo of the parting letter which Jai's first tutor, Mr Mayne, wrote to him twenty-two years before: 'If you really understand "Noblesse oblige" I have no fears for you – this and "Ich dien" ('I serve') . . . a Maharaja who has not the love of his subjects is like an egg without a yolk . . . Don't forget your prayers . . . I have always told you that Parameshwar has made you Maharaja of Jaipur: it was not just chance . . .'

Jai was now trying to carry these precepts over into the new order and was willing to be happy. That year, there was another great happiness for him and Ayesha. In October, she gave birth to a son. It was still early days under the new system and the birth of a Prince was an occasion. Gun salutes boomed again. There was an official holiday in Jaipur City and the ministers came to the Rambagh Palace to congratulate Jai. The customary release of prisoners, which had been done at the births of the first three Princes, did not happen. Jai could, when he was a Maharaja, release people imprisoned under his laws, but he could hardly let out people imprisoned under the laws of India.

In many ways, life resumed much of its old pattern. During his first year as Rajpramukh, he did not go to England for the summer, but he did resume his polo playing. Before the war his handicap had been nine, putting him among the top fifteen players in the world. After his series of accidents, he could not hope to achieve quite such a high standard. His handicap in the fifties was five, but this rather underestimated his steadiness as a player and his consistency as a striker.

The Argentinians came to India in 1950 to play in Delhi, Bombay and Jaipur. Before the war, Jai's team had won the Indian Championship Cup there seven years in succession. Crowds of 25,000 people would besiege the ground. Jai was their hero and they would even physically pick up his car and carry it. Polo did eventually return to Calcutta and, as the game became more popular again all over the world, Jai, who became President of the Indian Polo Association, retained in Indian eyes much of his hero quality.

As Jai's three eldest sons now went, one after the other, to Harrow, it was natural that Saint Hill, their Sussex farm, should become a second home. Jai, with his love of the English and his need to get away from the always slightly cloying atmosphere of Jaipur, now just as riddled with party intrigues as it used to be with the wrangles of the nobility, found the farm a comforting refuge. Polo again played a part in this. Since the arrival on the scene of Prince Philip, polo had once more become a popular sport in Britain.

*   *   *

193

Almost from the very beginning, the Indian Government began chipping away at Jai's position, and at the Princes in general.

In August 1949, there came a sharp letter from the Army in Delhi questioning promotions he had made and suggesting that he was showing an undue preference for Jaipur officers. Not long after that, a fierce 'personal' note from V.P. Menon arrived, reminding him that the new rule was that the Rajpramukh should not 'designate himself as Commander-in-Chief. I hope you have discontinued using this designation. Please let me know.' It did not matter that the original agreement had included the arrangement that the Rajpramukh should be Commander-in-Chief.

India's first elections took place in 1952. It is amusing to see that the old Congress 'agitators', who had so alarmed the British, came to consult Jai about their problems – the Congress in Rajasthan was full of factions, many based on old inter-state rivalries. Jai had to explain to his old friend Hiralal Shastri that he was a constitutional head of state and could not, therefore, take an interest in the internal affairs of one party.

The Congress could certainly congratulate itself that this was so. The appointments of Maharajas to Rajpramukhship had a double purpose. First, it had flattered them – in some cases sufficiently to get them to agree to merge their states. In the longer term, it paralysed the Maharajas politically. Had Jai been free to stand for parliament, the history of Rajasthan might have been very different. In the 1952 elections, the Maharaja of Jodhpur stood as an independent. He died in an air crash two days before the results of the voting were announced. He had, in fact, won the seat with a majority of 10,000. His Congress opponent, Jai Narain Vyas, had forfeited his deposit. In the subsequent by-election, Vyas was elected and became the Chief Minister of Rajasthan. It was as well for Congress that Jai was, perforce, above politics.

The first salvo in an eighteen-year battle came in the form of a long, diffuse letter from the Prime Minister, Jahawarlal Nehru, starting, 'Dear Friend'. He began by recalling the creditable role played by the Princes in the creation of a united India. He did not give them all the credit, but just enough to satisfy the demands of courtesy. He then generalised about world economic problems, the land tenure question, agrarian reform, the history of the abolition of slavery and the nature of property. Half way down the fifth closely-typed page comes a hint that the letter has something to do with the Princes' covenants, and how the Congress Party is worried about them.

Then, in the seventeenth long paragraph, comes the nub:

> 17. The fixation of very large sums of money as privy purses is totally out of keeping with the Directive Principles of our Constitution and the temper of the age. So also is the provision to have Rajpramukhs for life . . .
> 18. How long can we continue these anachronisms? How long can we justify to our people the payment of large sums of money from public funds to the Princes, many of whom discharge no function at all?

It was less than six years since the rights of the Princes had been inscribed within that Constitution with which they were now said to be out of keeping. They had been written into the Constitution just so that they could not be reneged upon, unless by a change in the Constitution, requiring a two-thirds majority in both houses.

That provision had been thought of by V.P. Menon, who also wrote in his *Integration of the Indian States*:

> There has been a tendency recently to regard the price paid for integration in the shape of privy purses as too high . . . we may ignore the consummation of the great ideal of a united and integrated India . . . the federal sources of income including the railway system of about 12000 miles which the States surrendered to the Centre without any compensation; and the abolition of internal customs . . . which has greatly benefited trade and commerce . . . But we should certainly take into account the assets we have received . . . in the shape of immense cash balances and investments amounting to

Rs. 77 crores, as well as buildings and palaces. If these
are weighed against the total amount of the privy
purses, the latter would seem insignificant.

The cash balances alone, then, were more than sixty million
pounds. The total amount of the privy purses, always dim-
inishing with each prince's death, started at four and a half
million pounds. It was already much reduced. Before integration, the Princes' privy purses had totalled at least fifteen
million pounds.

The Princes' bargain began to take on a shaky appearance.
What they had given could never be reclaimed. The unequal
amount they had received in return was evidently in danger.
Nehru had ended his letter with a veiled threat, but said he
was asking the Princes for suggestions as to 'how best we
can deal with this situation'.

Jai wrote several draft replies to Nehru, the final one being
the most temperate. He pointed out that, 'the rulers had
thrown in their lot with their countrymen' and:

> . . . with one bold stroke of the pen made over their
> ancient heritage . . . The hope that these agreements
> would be a precursor of mutual cooperation and
> understanding has been amply fulfilled. And this
> sacrifice and good-will gesture . . . unparalleled in
> history evoked universal admiration.

He said that the Government of India had guaranteed the
agreements and that it was 'specifically provided that the
privy purses would neither be increased nor reduced for any
reason whatever'. He went on:

> It is a primary duty of everyone to safeguard the
> sanctity of the Constitution . . . we must emulate the
> advanced democracies like England and the U.S.A.
> where even minor amendments . . . are made with
> meticulous care and serious thought so that it may not
> be interpreted as if the party in power altered the
> Constitution to consolidate its position or to suit its
> own administrative convenience.

Many of the Princes did not even trouble to reply, but those who did were extremely indignant at what they regarded as a total breach of faith. Nehru did not return to the attack until June 1954. Then he wrote another long letter, the first two pages of which mysteriously embraced the peace talks in Geneva and, rather more relevantly, the progress of India's Five Year Plans, as reasons for raising again the question of the privy purses.

This time he made positive proposals, which, in Jai's case, would have meant giving back fifteen per cent of the privy purse and investing a further fifteen per cent in a National Plan Loan.

Jai was in no particular hurry to reply, but when he did, about ten weeks later, he wrote a helpfully polite answer, addressing Nehru as, 'My esteemed and valued Panditji'. He gently rejected any idea of the nominally voluntary surrender of any part of the privy purses, rather artfully mentioning how much, 'The Princes appreciate and are grateful for the guarantee of all [the Covenant's] provisions given by the Government of India'.

On the other hand, Jai did encourage the idea of the Princes investing in the National Plan Loan. He even suggested that in cases such as his, the investment might be as much as twenty-five per cent, with the interest on three-fifths of the amount waived until the end of the second five-year plan.

He did also point out that, as far as he knew, nobody else was being asked to make a comparable contribution to public funds. 'The Princes are not the only people who have a large stake in India; there are others who could be asked to contribute, such as Zamindars and Landowners who receive compensation, and also business magnates.'

The Congress cannot have had much faith in their contentions, for nothing more was said for another year. Then, in August 1955, the Home Minister, Govind Ballabh Pant, wrote referring to Nehru's last letter and Jai's reply. After saying that the fullest consideration had been given to Jai's alternative suggestions, he ignored them. He said vaguely that:

People are all astir and have been responding to the

calls made on them and are eager to do their fullest bit and are ready to help the country march towards better economic and social conditions. I trust that this eagerness is shared by you. I earnestly hope that you will . . . be so good as to fall in line with the suggestion made by the Prime Minister and contribute 15 per cent in Government loans.

The underlying suggestion in all these letters was that the Princes were somehow lacking patriotism. From the Congress point of view, to be richer than others could be seen as a denial of the principles on which India was now founded. From the Princes' point of view, their sacrifice was already more than could have been reasonably expected and was, in itself, abundant proof of their patriotism. Six years might seem a long time to the Congress, long enough for them to forget how desperately they had needed the co-operation of the Princes; the Princes, however, many of whom realised that their privileges would not last forever, regarded six years as an indecently short time in which to start questioning solemn agreements.

Jai replied to the Home Minister that he had said all he had to say in his letter to Nehru. He advised against any hasty action over the privy purses, which might damage India's reputation internationally. He added that he had already invested more than fifteen per cent of his privy purse in the National Plan Loan. He also gave 150,000 rupees (about eight and a half per cent) annually to the Maharaja Sawai Jaisinghji Fund, 'which has been created for the welfare and benefit of the people of the erstwhile Jaipur State'.

There the matter ended for quite some time. It is interesting that, despite all this, Jai's personal relations with Nehru remained, as is so often the case in India, perfectly cordial. In February 1955, for instance, he had written to Nehru about the inactivity of many of his fellow Princes. This had been a concern of his ever since Ma had written to him about his brother-in-law, Bhaiya, the Maharaja of Cooch Behar, late in 1951:

Take my poor Bhaiya's case, he will be 36 this

December and yet no wisdom, it breaks one's heart to
see this deterioration. These two years of sitting idle
since the merger have done their damage . . . I could
not be more disheartened and without hope! I will now
try some religious vow . . .

To Nehru, Jai wrote that the ex-rulers were deeply frustrated.

. . . they seem to have no present and the future shows
no silver lining. Naturally, the tendency is, to say the
least of it, disinterestedness in some cases probably
amounting to dissatisfaction with the policies and little
interest in the continuation of the present Government.

He suggested that the unhappy rulers thought that the worst
had already happened to them and warned that they might
be tempted to change the existing system of government or
to create disturbances in the country.

'I therefore feel bold to suggest that the services of most of
them (after all there are hardly 50 or 60 ex-rulers worth the
name) excepting those who are minors or definitely without
brains, might be usefully employed by associating them in
some form or other with the local, or under the Central,
Government . . . where they can feel that their existence is of
some use to the country.' He had in mind various possible
roles for them – on local committees, involved in the five-
year plans or, for the dimmer ones, as ADCs.

Nehru also came to stay with Jai at the Rambagh, bringing
with him his daughter, Indira.

If the Congress felt itself on unsure ground in the matter
of the privy purses, they were confident of their case over
the Rajpramukhships. These appointments had been made
at the same time as the Covenants were agreed and had
often been used as an inducement to sign, but they were not
enshrined in the Constitution. Moreover, while the objections
to the privy purses were founded in spurious notions of
equality (this not being one of the readily observable facets
of Indian society), the argument against hereditary Rajpramukhships was soundly based. The Governors of the main
ex-British states of the Dominion were appointed for five-

year periods. Even the President of India was elected for only five years. In such circumstances it was, logically, wholly unreasonable to have the Rajpramukhs entrenched for life. The mistake was ever to have appointed them.

Early in October 1956, Jai received three letters. One was from the President of India, Rajendra Prasad, the next was from Nehru, the third from the Home Minister, Pant. They all said the same thing. From 31 October, he would no longer be Rajpramukh.

The occasion for this abrupt and unheralded dismissal was a reorganisation of the states. The old princely states, even when several were gathered together as in the case of Rajasthan, had had a different status from the old British states. Now they were all to be made uniform. Among other changes, the Rajpramukhships would go. Instead, they would have Governors appointed for a fixed period. All the letters praised Jai's work as Rajpramukh. Nehru was at his most humourless and sanctimonious:

> It is fitting that, as India advances towards her goal of a Socialist State, a greater degree of uniformity and equality should prevail in the country. The highest privilege that any of us in this country can have is that of a citizen of India with equal rights and obligations with others.
>
> Whatever office we may hold or whether we hold an office or not, those privileges and obligations continue. I have no doubt that you will continue to take deep interest in the progress of the country and, more especially, in the welfare of the people of the State . . . I feel sure we will have the benefit of your guidance and cooperation.

They could, of course, have had that guidance, as well as his experience and counsel which the President had so much valued, by the simple expedient of appointing him Governor of the newly-arranged state. That was very far from their intentions. They were more interested in playing to the gallery, in bashing the Princes.

Jai had, in fact, served them very well. He had tackled his

200

Jai and Lord Mountbatten after the Silver Jubilee polo match played on the inauguration day of The Polo Victory Cinema.

Jai with Ronald and Nancy Reagan during his visit to the USA in 1948.

Jai with Nehru and Indira Gandhi at the Rambagh Palace in 1951.

Jai with Krushchev and Bulganin after a polo game at Rambagh in 1955.

Jai and Ayesha with Jacqueline Kennedy and Princess Lee Radziwill during the First Lady's visit to Jaipur in 1962.

Jai and Ayesha with the Queen and Duke of Edinburgh.

Jai, as Indian Ambassador to Spain, with General Franco.

Sardars with great severity when they were recalcitrant about the abolition of the Jagirdar system. He had been a stabilising influence when the internal party dissensions and the struggles for local leadership had threatened the administration. He had nursed the assembly through frequent changes in ministries. He had endeavoured to persuade ministers to take the broader interests of the whole of Rajasthan into consideration, rather than pursue local, regional interests which might please the electors in their constituencies.

It was churlish, therefore, of Delhi to dismiss him without warning or consultation. Not surprisingly, he was hurt. For once, the reply which he sent to Nehru was more strongly-worded than the first, more carefully-reasoned draft of his letter. He wrote on 18 October 1956:

> My dear Prime Minister,
>
> I am writing to express my deep sense of gratitude to you for the kind terms you referred to me in your letter of the 4th October and for the appreciation of my services as Rajpramukh by the Government of India.
>
> I hope I shall not be misunderstood when I say that I feel hurt at the manner in which my services are being terminated after all the assurances which had been given to me by persons in authority on behalf of the Government of India and provision made in the Constitution of our country, all of which I regarded fondly as sacrosanct and which had given me a sense of security. I now find it most distressing that in spite of sincere co-operation and unflinching loyalty on my part throughout the last 7 years my official connections with the administration should cease so abruptly.
>
> I would, however, like to take this opportunity of assuring you that wherever I may be placed I shall, in future as in the past, continue to devote myself to the service of our country, and in particular to take deep interest in my home state of Rajasthan with which I and my family have had the closest ties for hundreds of years
>
> With kind regards, yours sincerely
>
> Man Singh.

This elicited a tart response from Nehru:

> . . . You have written to me on a subject which raises
> interesting and important issues. What you have
> suggested means that our Constitution should be
> petrified and no changes take place in it.

He went on about the need for revolutionary changes, 'not
only on the political domain but on the economic domain . . .
The major fact of India is the poverty of our people and the
major problem is how to raise them.' Was this a hint about
the privy purses? If so, the opening of the next paragraph
was marvellously disingenuous: 'I am not aware of any
changes being made except in so far as the Rajpramukhship
is concerned. I do not know how this particular change
indicates lack of security . . .'

The particular change might not itself threaten security,
but the attitude behind it certainly did. It was another notch
on the irreversible ratchet system. It reduced Jai's importance.
It also left him with nothing official to do. The British
Government, with little justice, had so often accused him of
doing too little for his people; the Indian Government, in
the name of justice for all, made it impossible for him to do
anything. The Government did offer him an ambassadorship
to the Argentine, but Jai refused this, as his property arrangements as a result of the merger were still largely unresolved.

The next few years were confusing and frustrating, not that
Jai outwardly betrayed anything of his inner feelings. He
continued to enchant people, to give parties at the Rambagh, to have 'fun'. Once more, he was hesitant about
celebrating the great festivals, but they continued in their
modified form.

His first reaction to his dismissal was to concentrate on
collecting together a polo team to represent India in a series
of international matches in England in the summer of 1957.
But 1957 was also election year in India. Jai's own views on
politics were to some extent somewhat contradictory. First,
he was inclined to believe that a Maharaja should be above

politics, for he was the ruler of all his people and should not favour one group rather than another. Secondly, by tradition and the fruitful example of his ancestors, he was persuaded that Jaipur should always align itself with the central power in Delhi, which was now the Congress Party.

Against these points, he felt betrayed by the Congress Party. Moreover, being a Maharaja – in terms of real power – had been made meaningless. If he was to be in a position to do anything positive for the benefit of his people, perhaps the only way was to stand for parliament, as many people had asked him to do. With this in mind, he tried to see Nehru. Failing to get an interview, he wrote to him on 24 January 1957:

> My dear Panditji,
>   I had so much hoped to see you and ask your guidance about my standing for Parliament at the request of Jaipur people. Ever since my return from Calcutta and your constant absence from Delhi this month I could not get an opportunity of contacting you.
>   Things have moved so fast that I have been swept off my feet and I had to inadvertently commit myself to a certain extent to the people.
>   What ever responsibilities that are thrust upon me by the public I shall hope I shall have your blessings.
>   With love and respects,
>   Yours very sincerely,
>   Jai

This letter must have puzzled Nehru. Plainly, if Jai was thinking of joining the Congress, he would be a great catch for the party. So Nehru wrote back promptly, saying that he had not been connected at all with the choosing of candidates, but '. . . I sent on your letter to my colleagues of the Central Election Committee. I do not quite know what they have done about it.' (He had blithely ignored that it was marked, in capital letters, 'PERSONAL'.)

Of course, if Jai was not thinking of joining Congress, it would be a sorry nuisance to have him standing for parliament, for he would surely win. Nehru continued in his lofty style:

But quite apart from this, I do not quite understand what you would like me to do about it. I am connected, as you know, with an organisation, namely the Congress, which is putting up candidates all over the country for the general elections. As a member of the Congress, necessarily I have to support Congress candidates. It would be not only odd but an act of indiscipline on my part to oppose a Congress candidate or to support a person who is opposing a Congress candidate. I take it that you intend to stand for election as an independent.

If Jai had hoped to have it both ways – to stand as an independent champion of his people and to keep on good terms with Delhi – this letter showed that he could not.

Then came another idea. Either Mohanlal Sukhadia, who had been Chief Minister of Rajasthan since 1954, or Jai himself considered the possibility of Ayesha's standing for parliament as a Congress Party candidate. From Jai's point of view, this was an ingenious solution. He could remain aloof, joining no party. Delhi would not be offended. His people's interests could be equally well served by Ayesha as by himself.

Partly from his everlasting sense of fun and partly from a certain wisdom, he did not mention the idea to Ayesha, but let the Chief Minister approach her, so that it came as a complete surprise. The result was that she came rushing to her husband bubbling over with amazement and pouring out her instinctive reactions. Had Jai suggested to her that she join the Congress, she might well have done so as an obedient wife. As it was, she told Jai that she could not, with any measure of self-respect, join the party which was, particularly in Rajasthan, steeped in corruption, which was administering the state so badly and which had forsaken all the fine Gandhian ideals.

Jai put to her the point that she might, from within the Party, be able to correct some of these things, but he respected her opinions and he had no wish to persuade her against her will. The deciding factor, from Ayesha's point of view, was the earnest plea from one of the young Jaipur nobles not to support Congress. (There was still no such thing as a secret in Jaipur and news of her possible candidature was soon public knowledge.) He was a member of a new opposition party in Rajasthan. All its hopes would crumble if the Maharani joined the Congress. She refused the Chief Minister's offer.

In the event, Jai could not have stood. It was found that he was not on the electoral roll. Perhaps it had been drawn up when he was still Rajpramukh and therefore ineligible to vote; or perhaps it was an early example of the cooking of the roll which later became commonplace.

For the time being, he gave up all thought of politics and went off to England with his polo team. The English part of the trip was not a great success, but at Deauville Jai – with his old team mate Rao Raja Hanut Singh, the Maharaja of Ida and Hanut's son Bijay – won the Gold Cup for India.

During that summer, he reflected upon his situation. It was clear to him that nothing was going to get better. The likelihood was that most things would get worse. Two things had priority. Firstly, he must make arrangements for the protection of his family, in case things got very serious. It was about now that he set up various trusts to provide for his children. Secondly, he wanted somehow to protect what he could of the history of Jaipur and his family from the vandalism which was being wrought in the city.

When he got back to Jaipur, he began energetically to build up the museum which he had agreed in the Covenant to create in the City Palace to house and exhibit those treasures, which, although they belonged to him, it was intended should never be sold. The trust had been formed. The work began.

The story of the City Palace Museum is, in part, a sad one. In his public life Jai was a good judge of men. He chose the best man for a job and, largely, let him get on with it. In his more private life, he allowed other considerations to influence him. He would take on people, usually cousins of some sort, or at any rate Kachhawas, who would have little hope of other employment. He expected in return loyalty and a sense of family feeling. He would forget his own adage: 'Never trust a Rajput.'

The Museum he regarded as a family affair. He entrusted its organisation, in many cases, to not very talented people whom he felt obliged to support. Many were simply inefficient; others were downright dishonest. In the general clearing up, a large number of objects were sold for nothing, still more were stolen or lost. The curator was eventually prosecuted for theft and it was not until after Jai's death that a trained, distinguished curator from outside Jaipur took over, having as his deputy one of the few honest members of the old regime. Nonetheless, the Museum is one of the finest treasure houses in India.

Jai was ahead of his fellow Princes in recognising the reality of his situation. In 1958, he decided to turn the Rambagh Palace into a hotel – at least it could be properly maintained. It would provide an income and serve a useful purpose. Jaipur had at that time no hotel worth the name. He and Ayesha moved into a house which had originally been the British Residency, now renamed Rajmahal.

In that year, Second Her Highness died at the age of forty-two. When Jai and Ayesha moved to Rajmahal, they were just themselves and their son Jagat.

The reader may wonder that so little mention has been made of the other children by Jai's first two marriages. The fact is that they impinged very much less than might be expected on their father's life. This was partly due to the pattern of Indian and more particularly a Maharaja's life. The children were brought up in the zenana. It was there that their father would see them. They would not come much to his part of the Palace. This situation, although it relaxed somewhat after Ayesha's arrival, was not conducive to an intimate relationship.

The children remember their childhood as being much more connected with their mothers.

> It was jolly good fun having three mothers. They
> treated all the kids equally. We were very happy doing
> the rounds between them, getting presents from all of
> them, feeling they were all the same, making no
> difference between us.

But they were awed by their father.

Beyond the cultural restrictions, for some reason Jai was never able to form an easy relationship with his children. It may be that, having had so peculiar an upbringing himself and having been snatched away from his own family, he had no idea how such a relationship is formed. He may also have had some inhibitions based on dignity. Whatever the cause, there was always a great distance between him and his three elder sons. (He was more relaxed with Jagat, and later indulged him more than the other children.)

The universal bonhomie, which charmed everyone else, was often absent with his children. In the evening, when they ate together, there was little conversation; and when it was over, the children got up and went straight to bed.

There was certainly no intentional unkindness. An English friend says, 'He never criticised his children, not even when Joey emptied his pudding over one of the servants.' Even at a later age, he was apparently reluctant to criticise. When one of them persistently drank too much, he said nothing. But the son, when the same English friend remonstrated with him, said: 'If my father told me to stop drinking, I would.'

Even with his daughter Mickey, Jai was equally inhibited. She was always a mildly rebellious child, but she was clever and became head girl of Ayesha's school. Her marriage was an unhappy one. Like so many of the family, she took to drinking. Jai knew her problems, sympathised with them, but again felt unable to help. It was as if he thought that her life was her affair and that she must deal with it herself.

His sons were sent away to school and Jai himself was often away from home, so that the boys did not really have much opportunity to get to know him, although later, when he had more time and they were older, he became more companionable, particularly with Pat, the third son. As soon as they left Harrow, he sent them out to work. This was another field in which he was ahead of his fellow Princes. Other Maharajas were inclined to mock. Was he so poor that his children had to work? Rajput dignity was much affronted.

By 1958, Bubbles was in the Army – the Adjutant in the President's Bodyguard. Joey, after a spell in Rothschild's

Bank in London, was working in Calcutta. Pat was also in Calcutta, in the tea business.

Jai's life over the next few years was divided, then, between his endeavours in a private capacity to maintain some of the prestige of his position, while making provision for its inevitable erosion, and at the same time enjoying the privileges which remained to him and having fun in Europe.

Early in 1961, the Queen of England made her first visit to India since Independence. Her tour included a private visit to Jaipur to stay with Jai and Ayesha. This, as might be expected, did not much please the Congress, who preferred to keep Jai as much as possible in the background, disliking his popularity.

Not all the trouble came from Delhi. The Anti-Blood Sports League in Britain heard that Jai was to arrange a tiger shoot for the Queen. They protested and the Indian newspapers made much of this. Nehru wrote to Jai asking for an assurance that no live bait would be used in the shoot. As it was never Jai's practice to use live bait, but rather to drive the tigers towards a high hide, he was able to satisfy Nehru. Then came another letter from the Prime Minister.

> I see in the Statesman today something about a Durbar being held in Jaipur. I do not know what this is, and perhaps the description is exaggerated. Anyhow, it will not be proper to hold anything in the nature of a Durbar or to call it as such. I have already received objections to it. We must always remember that India is a republic. We treat Queen Elizabeth as an honoured guest and show her all courtesy, but anything even indirectly suggesting that she holds any other position in regard to India would not be right.

Jai obviously had no intention of suggesting any such thing and he replied accordingly, adding that he was put out that the Prime Minsiter could possibly think him so irresponsible. Nonetheless, his extravagant admiration for the British Royal Family and his love of pageantry did make him a little over-excited and perhaps carried him beyond the bounds of what was proper. He was still a Maharaja and he was determined to receive the Queen in princely style.

The leading occulist of the day recalls that, three days before the Queen was due to arrive, Jai went to a military parade at which a horse lashed its tail across his face, cutting his eye deeply. He rushed to the hospital. 'I never saw him look so pitiable,' says the occulist. 'He said to me "I don't mind if you have to remove my eye after her visit, but I must be all right for the Queen."' The doctor told him he might have to wear an eyepatch, but in fact he recovered in time. As a reward, Jai managed to have sent from England a large supply of corneal grafts.

The reception for the Queen, whether it was called a darbar or not, was superbly beautiful. She drove in a car with Jai through the streets. Prince Philip followed in another car with Bubbles. At the gates of the City Palace, they got out of the cars and were mounted on elephants. In the audience pavilion all the nobles were assembled, wearing turbans, brocaded achkans and swords.

All this had caused a tremendous fuss. According to a report of the Governor, Jai had at first only invited the Chief Minister and the Public Works Minister, who happened to be the Maharaja of what had been a small Rajput state. He had specified that turbans should be worn, which was customary at that time. The Chief Minister had, in pique, threatened to come in a topee. After official complaints were lodged, Jai invited all the ministers and he abandoned the insistence on turbans. They all came and, of course, wore turbans. The Governor was still much agitated. His report, which was little, if at all, founded on fact, said that although it was not called a darbar, the event followed all the old procedures of a darbar. Furthermore, tickets were sold for people to watch the reception, but the state Government intervened and all the money was refunded. He reported also that the Ministers were not introduced to the Queen and that she and Prince Philip were kept in a separate box.

The Congress leaders really wanted it both ways. It was to be a private party, but they had to be invited and presented. Their real fear, expressed by the Governor, was that the visit might rekindle the feudal, pro-monarchical sentiment which

209

was already influencing politics in Rajasthan, and might affect the forthcoming elections.

The Queen did not spend a night in Jaipur City. After the reception, Jai, Ayesha and the four sons took the royal couple to the shooting lodge at Sawai Madhopur, so strangely built to look like a ship. Prince Philip duly shot a tiger, nine feet eight inches long. The Queen contented herself with merely watching the game.

That part of the visit passed off agreeably and quietly. The Queen left to continue her tour. But the Governor had been more right than he realised, not about any dark intentions to do with the royal visit, but about the dangers to the Congress of feudal sentiment.

Ayesha, without much thought to the question of tactful timing, had, a few days before the Queen's visit, joined an opposition party founded by Chakravarti Rajagopalichari, a former Congress leader and Mountbatten's successor as Governor-General of India. He had come to dislike Nehru's lofty and unrealistic socialism and his inappropriate attempts to impose collective farming on a people whose every instinct was opposed to such notions. He started a new party, called the Swatantra Party.

The rage induced by Ayesha's action was quite startling. The Chief Minister of Rajasthan propounded in the State Assembly the principle that princely families which indulged in party politics should automatically forfeit their privy purses. He was evidently forgetful of his invitation to Ayesha a few years before to stand in the Congress' interest.

Sir V.T. Krishnamachari, Jai's former Prime Minister, now a civil servant in Delhi, wrote to Jai in April 1961: 'I hope Her Highness has received my letter about her joining the Swatantra Party. I think this is not desirable ... The best thing for her is not to take any further steps in regard to her membership.' He was anxious that Ayesha should not address a meeting planned for four days ahead. Sir V.T. had always been an establishment-minded figure. His fears were based on the possibility of the Government taxing the privy purses if Princes or their families entered party politics. By this, he too meant in opposition to the Congress.

Among the nobility of Jaipur, there were also grave doubts

210

about the wisdom of Ayesha's action. It was breaking with tradition to oppose Delhi. Opinions as to Jai's own attitude vary. Many old people, with the benefit of hindsight, say that he was opposed to the idea. Others say that he was so much in love with her that she could persuade him to do anything.

Neither proposition can be the truth. Had he been strongly opposed to the idea, he would have stopped it, whereas he gave his permission which, in her eyes as an Indian wife, was essential. As for her ability to make Jai do what she wanted, it simply was not so. At this very time, they were conducting an argument about Jagat's education. He wanted the boy to be educated in England. She wanted him to continue at Mayo College, where he had started. He was soon installed at a preparatory school in England.

Love for Ayesha may, in a different way, have had much to do with his views. He had married her because of her strong, independent spirit. It would not have occurred to him to trample on her principles. It was her sense of justice and that of her Baroda family that he admired and, despite the ties of tradition, came fully to share. The platform of the Swatantra Party appealed to Jai quite as much as to Ayesha.

The fuss died down and they went off for the summer to England, to settle into the smaller house which they had bought near Ascot, instead of Saint Hill (which later became the centre of the Scientology movement). Jagat was installed in his school nearby and, as always, Jai played polo.

When they came back, Ayesha plunged, for better or worse, into the centre of politics. The Swatantra Party wanted her to stand in the 1962 elections for one of the five Jaipur parliamentary seats. Jai once more agreed, wryly pointing out to her that while the invitation to stand might be a surprise to her, he had always realised that this was the logical outcome of her joining the party.

He must himself have been toying once more with the idea of standing, for in December 1961, Sir V.T. Krishna-machari wrote another of his fussy letters:

As regards the question you put to me, I am strongly against your standing for election either to Parliament

211

or to the local Legislature. I am on principle opposed to persons in your position getting mixed up in political life at present in India . . . After watching the reactions to Her Highness standing as a candidate, I am confirmed in the correctness of the advice I gave.

Jai did not stand. Ayesha became the leader of the Swatantra Party throughout the whole of the old state of Jaipur. Although many people wished to support her, not a few leading figures were reluctant to do so for fear of reprisals by the Congress. Businessmen feared the loss of contracts or permits, the Sardars and Jagirdars feared a reduction in the compensation for the loss of their feudal dues. It was difficult to find candidates for all the seats in her district. Eventually, Joey stood for a seat in the local assembly and Pat for one of the parliamentary seats.

Overcoming any hesitation he may have had about offending Delhi, Jai backed his wife's campaign in many ways. Devi Singh Mandawa, who was one of the more energetic nobles and is now the president of the official Rajput organisation, the Kshatriya Mahasabha, maintains that because Ayesha had no experience in politics, Jai told him to join the Swatantra Party and help her. 'Thus commanded I did so.' Another noble remembers a meeting at Rajmahal where, 'one way and another by His Highness and Devi Singh, the big wigs were told to join, so they did.'

Until she gained enough confidence to go on her own, Jai went with her on a few canvassing tours. He made two major speeches in her support. The points which he made in the first speech illustrate well his frustrations:

> Loving subjects of Shri Govind Devji,
>
> You all know that this is the realm of Shri Govind Devji Maharaj and we are his devotees and dewans. When we are protected by Shri Govind Devji and you all love us we need not be afraid of anything.
>
> The only change that has occurred is that our Chief Minister and other ministers are not as competent as Sir Mirza Ismail and Sir V.T. Krishnamachari were. So it is that your difficulties cannot be so readily removed

212

as before, because these people are not of that calibre. It is difficult to make them understand anything.

The Ministers of today feel no responsibility to Rajasthan as a whole. Their vision is limited to their region, city or even their home.

You have seen that with the help of Sukhadiaji [the Chief Minister who came from Udaipur] Udaipur has become a fine city, while Bikaner and Alwar are neglected. The beautiful and world-famous City of Jaipur is being disfigured by unnecessary demolitions and alterations. [Ayesha had managed to persuade Nehru to intervene to stop the tearing down of the ancient and beautiful city walls.] Our famous Johri Bazaar has been reduced to the condition of an ordinary Bombay street.

Our Sindhi and Punjabi brothers who have come here [as refugees] after experiencing great difficulties, are still lying on the footpaths . . .

The Congress has started strange propaganda since the opening of the election campaign. One of the leaders has objected to the candidature of the Maharani of Jaipur . . . but what about the Maharani of Gwalior? [She was at that time still allied to the Congress.]

. . . We can understand to some extent that they make propaganda against us, but they also make propaganda against the important and honest leaders of their own party, out of pure self-interest. You may consider the honesty of this. Many big leaders who worked . . . for the formation of Rajasthan now sit silent or even oppose those in power . . .

Hiralal Shastri, the great confidant of Sardar Patel, is silent. The fearless Jai Narain Vyas and Aditendra, one of the organisers of the Congress, are opposing those in the saddle. Why? Because they do not want to become a party to the corruption and other evils . . .

It is no wonder that Rajasthan is suffering. But you are responsible for electing them.

Now the power is in your hands . . . By now you have the experience to judge who is sincere and honest and who is a cheat.

He went on to speak of the good relations between Hindu and Muslim in Jaipur and to remind the people of their religious duties. He also gave a pledge to the Government, 'on my own behalf and on behalf of all the royalists of Rajasthan that we shall not claim or endeavour to retake what we have relinquished'.

He ended:

> 'I and my family will continue to serve your cause with the same love and sincerity as we have done hitherto. The Maharani of Jaipur has pledged herself to work for you. Her honour rests on you.

On the final night of the campaign, Jai addressed a huge meeting of at least two hundred thousand people. This time his speech was less measured, more of an emotional appeal. It was the speech of a real politician. He spoke to the crowd in the local dialect, using the familiar forms of address rather than the formal:

> For generations my family have ruled you and we have built up many generations of affection. The new Government has taken my state from me, but for all I care they can take the shirt off my back as long as I can keep that bond of trust and affection.
>
> They accuse me of putting up my wife and two of my sons for election. They say that if I had a hundred and seventy-six sons [the number of seats in the Rajasthan Assembly] that I would put them all up too.
>
> But they do not know, do they, [and here he made a gesture embracing the whole of the huge crowd] they do not know that I have far, far more than one hundred and seventy-six sons.'

Ayesha, Pat and Joey all won. Ayesha's majority was 175,000 – the largest majority ever won in a democratic election anywhere in the world. The Jaipur family achieved a second entry in the *Guinness Book of Records*. At least, Sir V.T. had the grace to send 'my warmest felicitations to Her Highness and the two Maharaj Kumars on their election with such

214

large majorities.' There was a large victory parade in which the whole city joined. Jai stood at the top of one of the Palace gateways, throwing gold and silver coins to the crowd in old-fashioned princely style.

The Congress Party and the Government were less than pleased with the family and kept up their petty harrassment. Mrs Jacqueline Kennedy, the wife of the President of the United States, came on a visit to India. In exactly the same way that he had invited the Queen, Jai asked Mrs Kennedy whether she would like to come and stay. Her visit to India was semi-official, but Jai's invitation was personal.

The authorities were taking no chances of a repetition of the Queen's visit. The officials wanted to take her round the City Palace, which would have been a snub to Jai. In the end, it was agreed that the Maharaja might show his visitor round his Palace, provided that the visit attracted no attention. Jai and Ayesha took her round by themselves at night, so that no one should see them driving through the streets together.

Jai soon went off to England, but Ayesha had to remain behind because of her party and parliamentary obligations. It was the first of many such separations. She joined him later in the summer and they were still in America when war broke out between China and India. Curiously enough, Jai seemed in no particular hurry to get back, while Ayesha was feverishly impatient. After a few days in England, they returned home.

Both plunged into activity and controversy. Jai had, by this time, been elected to the Rajya Sabha, or upper house. He did not often speak, but he was perfectly well aware of the shortcomings of Nehru which had led to this war. He had spoken to him privately about the poor equipment of the Indian Army, about the lack of generals of any standing, about the great superiority of Chinese intelligence and the paucity of officials near the border who had any knowledge of Chinese customs or their language.

Typically, he made no direct attack upon Nehru in his Rajya Sabha speech on the subject: rather, he made concrete suggestions, according to his philosophy of accommodation and compromise. The Prime Minister, he said, must have a

215

deputy. Jai had always favoured the idea of two Prime Ministers, each with equal power. He then proposed that General Timaya (one of India's many brilliant soldiers from Coorg) be given overall command and be made a Field Marshal. Next, he wanted India to regard Pakistan as a friendly neighbour. He went on to say that, given the new circumstances, Gandhian ideals of pacificism were unrealistic. Finally, he begged the Government to form an alliance with the United States and Great Britain. 'There is too much at stake to allow false pride and self-righteousness to sit back and not openly seek help from these two great friendly nations.' He went off, too, on a large recruiting campaign in Shekhawati.

Ayesha took a bolder line. She attacked the Government's concealment of the repeated incursions into India by China over the previous eight years. She criticised the use of the Defence of India Act to silence opposition to the Government policies. She even attacked Nehru personally, saying, 'If you knew anything about anything, we wouldn't be in this mess today.' To which Nehru replied, 'I will not bandy words with a lady.'

In an Indian context, however appealing Ayesha's attitude may seem to us, Jai's may well have been the wiser course. Nevertheless, his disillusionment grew over the years.

In 1963, he again went off to England, leaving Ayesha to her parliamentary duties. He wrote, rather tantalisingly, on 23 April:

> My Darling Love,
>   Darling what a party we had last night? Something one hears about but seldom sees. Most glamorous and colourful. The Queen looked wonderful and so did Princess Alexandra. There were about 20 other Royals . .. darling it is wonderful to be here but I am very worried about you and your stupid [illegible]s all over the place in this heat. Please darling look after yourself for someone who lives for you alone and come soon. You need a holiday badly. See you on the 9th our day!! . . .
>   Your only Jai.

A year later, Nehru died. Jai had always treated him with respect and he, for his part, was always courteous. But it is an inescapable fact that Nehru in some way always put Jai at a disadvantage. India is very much an 'establishment' country. Everyone of any importance, even today, knows everyone else. It is also a country of favours, even when there is not really any corruption or nepotism. It is for friends that one does favours. Nehru and Jai were never friends of that kind.

In March 1965, there was a more relaxed royal visit to Jaipur. Prince Philip came alone to stay with Jai and Ayesha for a week. This time, there were no political upheavals. It was, however, the time of the Holi festival. The origins of Holi are obscure, but it is a fertility festival marking the coming of spring. It has about it, as well, a kind of lord of misrule flavour, so that social distinctions and ordinary inhibitions are forgotten. Everybody throws coloured powder and sprays coloured water at everybody else. The Maharaja used to ride out on an elephant, which gave him considerable advantage over the populace, who nonetheless threw wax balls filled with red water at him. Jai, in the old days, had a mechanical spray with which he warded off attacks, but one of the nobles would usually get him in the end, even if it meant pushing him into a pool.

Prince Philip was treated with equal disrespect and in the family albums there are pictures of him soused and covered all over in pinks and greens and yellows.

He wrote to thank Ayesha from the President's House, Rawlpindi on 22 March 1965:

> . . . without the slightest shadow of doubt, I have never experienced anything like last week in my whole life. Every moment was sheer joy and it's only the bruises from polo and the pink stain on my fingers which remain to convince me that the whole thing wasn't some marvellous dream.

It was such fun that the following year, at the time of Holi, Prince Philip sent a telegram from an aeroplane in which he was flying over Texas:

217

From the Duke of Edinburgh a multi-coloured Holi to you all . . . Christopher, Joe, Sarah and I are green with envy and pink with nostalgia. Philip.

Soon, the new Prime Minister, Lal Bahadur Shastri, decided that Jai's skills and his connections were being wasted. He offered him an ambassadorship. When Jai had been offered the chance of being Ambassador to the Argentine, he had felt that this distant posting might be a way of keeping him out of the way during the 1957 elections, but this was different. Shastri offered him a choice of two or three countries. Jai chose Spain. The offer coincided with a peak of disgust with local politics, corruption and intrigue – and especially with the people he felt most obliged to help.

Before he left, in October 1965, he addressed the Rajput Leadership in scathing terms, explaining to them his decision to go to Spain even though, 'there can be no argument that one can serve the cause of our state better at home than abroad'.

Having said that, his wife and sons, with a few trusted friends and followers, had sweated blood for Rajasthan and Jaipur and had created the possibility of a new political awakening. No one had bothered to follow it up. Jai continued:

It is indeed heartbreaking and tragic to have to admit that perhaps no other community with such a glorious past has shown more lack of organisation, co-operation, unity and courage than the Rajputs.

He accused them of inherent instability, an utter lack of 'trustworthy loyalty' and 'mental, spiritual and political bankruptcy'. Before the elections, he said:

. . . a number of Jagirdars had voluntarily taken me to their thikanas, stood on the same platform and in public pledged us and our cause full support. Then after a few days they have come to say how terribly sorry they were as they now find they cannot associate themselves with us or our party as the Chief Minister called them . . . and told them that unless they

218

dissociate themselves from all activities of the Maharaja and the Maharani, their compensations will be affected. So those very people who with great enthusiasm took us to their homes, now asked to be pardoned and excused, but at the same time had the audacity to assure me of their continued loyalty and service like their forefathers.

What was stranger still, to continue the rout, others forgetting all age-old and honoured social ties and demands of normal hospitality conveniently left their houses so as to be conveniently absent when Her Highness addressed public meetings in their towns and villages. Where would a General have stood, what would have been his plight if his allies, his commanders, his troops and followers had thus deserted him on the eve of battle?

Nothing has shocked me more or shaken my faith in the Rajput community than this defeatist if not cowardly attitude . . . and I see little future in myself or, for that matter, of anyone else shouldering the dubious and uncertain responsibilities of Rajput leadership at a time when, alas . . Rajput chivalry, unity and courage appear at their lowest ebb.

He attacked them further for their squabbles and petty jealousies, for putting 'self before country or community' and their 'obstinate childlike attitude against giving up old outdated and outmoded ideas and ways of life'. It was, he said, the shortest road to self-destruction.

After weeks and months of careful thought . . . I am convinced that I can serve our country better in other ways than by remaining and vegetating in the senseless and useless morass of petty local politics of Rajasthan.

Of course, he was paradoxically appealing to the spirit of those outdated, outmoded ideas which he was condemning in them. Equally, he was doing so somewhat tongue in cheek. He had spent a lifetime dealing with their petty squabbles, their selfishness and their easy treachery. He knew just how to talk to them to shake them from their lethargy.

That he, for his part, was supremely loyal to them is apparent from the long letter which he wrote, before leaving, to Lal Bahadur Shastri, the new Prime Minister. He asked him to 'take a personal interest in the affairs of the state. Otherwise, I am afraid, I can only visualise things going from bad to worse and perhaps ending in a serious crisis.'

He listed the sources of trouble in Rajasthan. First, 'a corrupt and inefficient administration'. The ministers were feathering their own nests and indulging in nepotism on a vast scale. He said that, 'this now applies to many other parts of India, but Rajasthan seems to be more severely affected'.

The next problem was the 'permanent state of rivalry between the Rajputs and the Jats'. This rivalry was affecting agricultural progress. Jai proposed that the Revenue Minister be neither a Rajput nor a Jat. He went on to plead the cause of the Rajputs, who:

> . . . can, I am confident, play a great part in the shaping
> of the future of our state and the country as a whole.
> Unfortunately it appears to be the avowed policy of the
> authorities that they are neither given a fair
> opportunity nor trusted . . . This obvious partiality,
> injustice and step-motherly treatment greatly affects
> their morals and sense of responsibility.

Jai included himself as one of the victims of this campaign by the Rajasthan Government and asked Shastri to see to it that an end was brought 'to the long existing feud and state of political war that has been declared on me and mine . . . also in particular to stop the systematic victimisation of those . . . still in our service'.

He suggested that people were becoming restless under this oppression, feeling that:

> . . . justice cannot be obtained by any but the favoured
> few . . . Their forbearance might, now that I am away,

snap under the strain of such planned and persistent persecution . . . and perhaps eventually even take the form of a demand for a separate Rajput State as is now being voiced regarding the creation of a Punjabi Suba. The disastrous consequences of such a move . . . can well be imagined.

According to Devi Singh Mandawa, the other Princes were against Jai's going to Spain, because the privy purse question was looming again and they felt that he should stay to help in the fight. When Devi Singh put this to Jai, he smiled and said that he was doing the right thing.

He set off in high spirits and wrote to Ayesha on 29 October 1965 from Kings Beeches, their house near Ascot. She had had to stay for her parliamentary work.

> My darling Angel,
> It was wonderful leaving Delhi and I've never been happier mood but you little Pat upset the apple cart in Bombay! I never like seeing you upset, the most beautiful woman in the world. You may not realise it but darling all my success in life has been because of your support unreservingly with love & devotion.
> I can never forget the sight of you standing on the pier at Bombay waving at me as I sailed for the Middle East in 1941. You alone supported me as a brave Rajput wife should when rest of the family condemned me and my love I can never reward you enough for your courage and devotion. No words of mine can adequately express my feelings but I know you will understand what I mean? Just remember I will always stand by you and never never let you down. What ever sacrifice it may entail my life long companion.
> Look after yourself little girl and come to Madrid soon where I will be waiting to greet you with loving arms.
> All my love darling from your devoted
> Jai

On 11 November, Jai wrote from Madrid:

My darling love,

Here I am at last with flashes of bulbs and cameras and gay parties. I had a wonderful reception . . . Am keeping all the papers with my photo for you or shall I send them so you can practise your Spanish!! Darling it's wonderful here but please come soon as need your help and charm in my duties . . .

Hope you are not working too hard and making too many speeches. Please see the P.M. helps your career.

All my love darling and miss you more than I can say.

Your only Jai

P.S. Love to the darling dogs and my polo ponies?

Jai was the first Indian Ambassador to Spain and the Spaniards were a little puzzled as to what to make of him at first, particularly as he used to go jogging, which was certainly not the habit of the Spanish grandees. At a party, someone seeing Jai asked, 'Who can that strange gipsy be? I see him running through the streets every morning.'

Inevitably, the new Ambassador soon charmed the Spaniards. Although they might not be accustomed to jogging, Jai's other pleasures they understood and shared. The Spaniards like a show and no one was better than Jai at putting on a fine display. They are great horsemen and love shooting. Soon, Jai was a familiar figure at the polo club in Madrid and a regular guest at the huge shooting parties on the big estates of the aristocrats.

He did not play so much polo as one might have expected, but he did a great deal of umpiring and is remembered as an extremely fair and calm umpire. There are records of slaughterous shoots, with such people as the Marquess of Blandford and Stavros Niarchos, when fourteen guns shot 1,327 partridges one day and 2,272 the next.

Jai was a natural diplomat, though there was not really a great deal of work to do. There were virtually no Indians for him to look after, except in the Balearic and Canary Islands, which he visited regularly. There was one old Indian tailor living in the south of Spain, who appeared one day in Madrid and asked to see the Ambassador. He told Jai that he had lived in Spain for fifty years and that soon he would die. Before dying he wanted one last, real Indian meal to remind him of his youth. Where could he get it? 'You shall have it here,' said Jai. The next day, Jai told his guests that lunch would be an hour later than usual. The tailor was given a huge feast in the Ambassador's dining-room. When he came out, he touched Jai's feet and went away and was never heard of again.

There is no doubt that Jai did a good job for India. His country meant nothing to most Spanish people when he came. Lord Roderick Pratt, who went to stay with Jai in Madrid, remembers that everybody seemed to know him, not least the police who chased their car as he was showing Lord and Lady Roderick round Madrid on their first evening. When they caught him, the police saluted and laughed. It was like the days when Jai was chased into Knightsbridge Barracks. He had not changed.

By the time he left, Jai had opened a Hispano-Indian Chamber of Commerce in Barcelona. He had presided over performances by Ravi Shankar and introduced the Spanish to Indian culture. Both trade and tourism benefited.

He was very happy, liking the work and glad to be away from the unpleasantness of Indian politics. His letters to Ayesha over the years, at the times she was not with him in Madrid, were, apart from the fact that he missed her, some of the happiest he ever wrote. In November 1966:

> . . . things must have been pretty bad in Delhi and am
> surprised that the mob was allowed to get away with all
> that violence . . . Please love look after yourself and
> keep away from all the trouble spots. You can imagine
> how worrying it is when one is so far away? Come soon
> in this happy atmosphere as I long to have you with me!!

January 1967:

> How is the busy Queen doing? Hope not over working
> with the problems of Rajasthan . . . life is gay as we are
> having many farewell parties for the Pakistani
> Ambassador . . . have had some good shoots . . .

Vulchis asked me to go . . . this weekend but duty does not permit?! Don't laugh!

April 1967:

> I had a very gay time in Barcelona and won two
> prizes . . . I hope you will arrange for good Indian
> dancers to come as I am sure they will be very popular.
>   All my love darling and come soon the house is so
> empty without you my love and my success at
> entertaining not so good!!
>   So happy the boys have been good. Please look after
> them and keep them on the right path.

The situation in India had been getting worse in so many directions. In the 1967 elections, Ayesha had again won her parliamentary seat. In the local elections, an ugly dispute arose: the Congress Party had won by far the largest number of seats; the opposition parties, on the other hand, if they grouped together in a coalition, would have a majority of six seats. They agreed on this and expected to be asked to form a government. Nothing happened, the Governor, Dr Sampuranand, naturally a Congress Party man, delayed in order to give the Congress a chance to bribe some opposition members to change sides.

Ayesha was prepared for this. After keeping all the opposition MPs in the City Palace for a night, she had them taken to Kanota fort some twelve miles outside Jaipur. The Governor then imposed an anti-riot regulation covering the section of Jaipur where he and most of the ministers lived. Next, he asked the leader of the Congress Party to form a government.

In protest, a huge body of people marched on the Governor's residence. Ayesha endeavoured to stop them. When they entered the section covered by the ban, the police drove them back with batons and tear gas. Many of the marchers were arrested and a curfew was imposed on the whole city.

By this time, Jai had arrived on leave. He and Ayesha flew to Delhi to talk to the President, Dr Radakrishnan, and the Home Minister, Chavan. Jai and Ayesha guaranteed calm in

(*left and below*) Ayesha campaigning for a seat in parliament in the 1962 elections. The symbol she is holding up would appear beside her name on ballot papers, enabling the illiterate to recognise their candidate (*Popperfoto*).

(*overleaf*) The people of Jaipur travelled from all over the state to witness the funeral of their Maharaja.

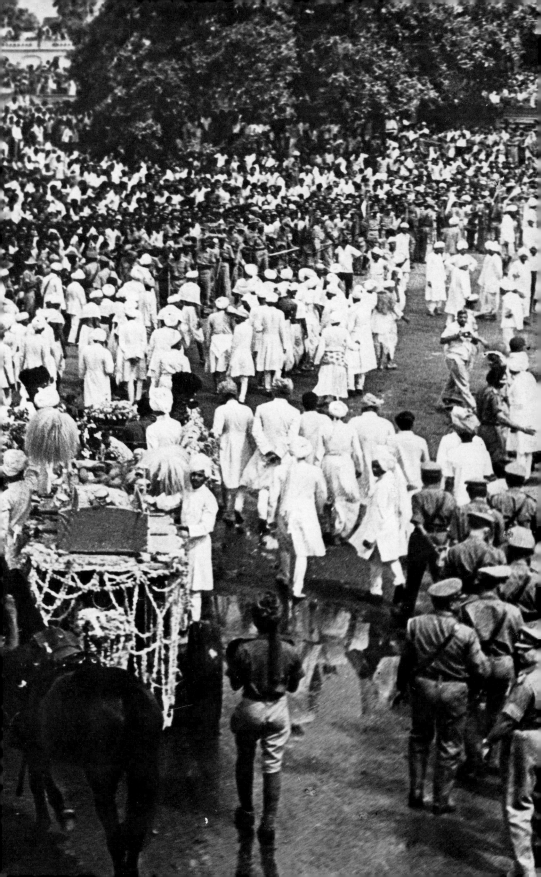

Jai's four sons in the traditional white robes of mourning stand by their father's body at his lying in state in 1970.

Jaipur if both the curfew and the anti-riot regulation were lifted. This was agreed. The lifting of the restrictions was announced on the national radio.

The people ventured out, they gathered in groups. The police fired on them. Nine people died. Forty-nine were injured. The police claimed that they had not been told of the lifting of the ban and had not happened to hear of it on the radio. There was an irony in the fact that Jai, in his letter to Shastri eighteen months before, had been urging a review of the police force.

The coalition was still intact. They still waited. Then President's rule was imposed upon Rajasthan. This is direct rule from Delhi, imposed when no party can form a government. It was not lifted for one and a half months, by which time the Congress had managed to lure away sufficient members with promises of jobs and money to gain a majority for themselves.

Jai, by this time back in Spain, became more disillusioned than ever with life at home. Lal Bahadur Shastri, the Prime Minister, had died in 1966. Now Indira Gandhi, the daughter of Nehru, took over. With her came a new wave of ambitious young men, of which Chavan was one. With the elections over, they thought it was time to raise again the question of the privy purses. It was the success of the Princes at the polls, as much in Rajasthan as anywhere, which spurred the Congress to abolish the privy purses.

During the elections in January, Mrs Gandhi had gone to Jaipur and attacked the Princes.

> Go and ask the Maharajas how many wells they had dug for the people in their states when they ruled them? How many roads they constructed? What did they do to fight the slavery of the British? If you look at the account of their achievements you will find a big zero there.

In Jai's time a huge reservoir had been created. The amount of metalled roads had doubled in his personal reign. The railways had been increased by fifty per cent.

At the end of July 1967, the All India Congress Committee

adopted a resolution to abolish the privy purses and all privileges held by the Princes as 'incongruous to the concept and practice of democracy'.

Possibly the last straw was when Delhi took to carping at Jai in Spain. They complained of his absences from his post. He was able to point out that when appointed he had been ordered to exploit his contacts all over Europe especially for the purpose of buying arms. In any case, in three years he had been away from Madrid for a total of one hundred and fifty-two days. That is to say, seven weeks a year, by no means all of them holiday.

Jai decided that it was time he went back to India.

CHAPTER 12

On his return, Jai recognised that the Privy Purses were a
lost cause. He joined in the meetings of the Concord of
Princes, but found their proceedings largely comical rather
than practical. As usual, the Princes were divided as to how
they should deal with the Government. There was a certain
amount of talk about secession, but everyone knew that this
was unrealistic. The Princes' case, while morally correct,
was hopeless. They had nothing to bargain with, as they
had given away everything in exchange for promises. The
Government's case was indefensible by honourable standards, but had a cold logic behind it. Backed by vindictive-
ness and reinforced by power, the Government could not
fail to win in the end.

The hardliners took the view that if they were going to
lose anyway, why should they help the Government by
agreeing terms? Jai, as was his wont, preferred the idea of
negotiating a settlement, partly because something might be
salvaged, partly because they would have to live with the
Government in the future and partly because he thought
that a unilateral imposition of terms by the Government
would damage India's reputation. His judgement was proved
right on all three counts.

In the Concord of Princes, he allied himself with the
moderates. He spoke rarely at meetings, usually voting with
the majority, accepting the decisions reached and being
always obedient to agreed common policy. He was also
always in arrears with his contributions.

Much of what was under discussion had very little to do

with money. The Government intended to abolish the Princes' titles, their exemption from the Arms Act, their exemption from customs duty, their gun salutes, their right to fly flags on their houses and cars, their red number plates, the tradition of a holiday in the old states on their birthdays, the military honours they were entitled to at their funerals, their shooting preserves and sundry other privileges.

Many of these were absurdly trivial, but in their sum they were as important, if not more important, to many of the ex-rulers than their privy purses. The Maharana of Udaipur had summed up this attitude earlier in the debate:

> Whether it would be worthwhile for me to live,
> whether I would deserve to live, whether those who
> value history and tradition would own me as an Indian,
> if I were to acquiesce in the derogation of this
> institution. It is not my private possession. I am a
> trustee and a servant.
> Hardships are to be endured, but not dishonour.

Even Jai, who did not bother much with red number plates, felt that he would be diminished. It is demeaning to have your name taken away from you. He was certainly prepared to negotiate over the purses, but felt that concessions might be won in other matters by being amenable. At the same time, there is a possibility that Jai had other plans in mind. At each rebuff, he came to wonder whether he should not enter politics.

Now he gave the possibility renewed consideration. In January 1969, *Current*, a Bombay weekly, said that the Maharaja of Jaipur had refused to represent India any more and that he was 'widely believed' to be about to 'plunge into politics'. The paper said that there had been much pressure on the Maharaja to join and to lead the Swatantra Party before he left for Spain. After the behaviour of the Sukhadia regime in Rajasthan, it would not be surprising if the Maharaja joined up with his wife who had vowed to overthrow Sukhadia at whatever cost. If he did, it would be a shattering blow for the Congress.

Devi Singh Mandawa says that Jai quite definitely wanted

to fight in the elections which were due in 1972. He held a meeting with Devi Singh and with his son Pat to plan a strategy by which the Rajput Princes could, with the help of Jat leaders, oust the Congress from the Rajasthan Assembly. The plan they devised was for each Prince of the old states either to stand or to put up a candidate quite independently. Only when they were elected would they band together. Devi Singh says that two leading Jats were approached and that a circular was sent to all the Princes. Devi Singh recalls a favourable reply from the Maharaja of Bikaner. (The one who distinguished himself at the time of the merger had died, to be succeeded by his young son.)

Pat does not remember this meeting and Dr Karni Singh, the Maharaja of Bikaner, has no immediate recollection of any such approach. Dr Karni Singh was an MP at the time and had been ever since 1952. He, also, was possibly less indignant about the removal of the privy purses than most of the other Princes. He held the view that once they had gone and the privileges with them, then the former rulers would cease to be the Government's whipping boys.

Ayesha does not believe Jai would have gone into politics at that stage. His disillusion was such at the time that she says he was toying with the idea of handing everything over to his sons and retiring to England.

Almost everything was ill-fated. In 1968, Ma had died. Little over a year later, Ayesha had a serious operation. The only cheerful thing that happened was that Jai, playing with the 61st Cavalry, once more won the India Polo Association Cup in Calcutta. Then, in April 1970, Ayesha's brother Bhaiya died. He had been, in many ways, Jai's closest friend.

As a result of Bhaiya's death, Jai had to cancel a meeting with the Home Minister, Chavan, about the privy purses and privileges. Instead he wrote to him:

> . . . I have read the letters . . . addressed by the Rulers of Baroda and Dhrangadhra to the President of India and I wholly associate myself with them. It is now for the consideration of the President and the Government to refer the question to the Supreme Court for its advisory opinion . . .

I do not know what the strict interpretation of the law might be. But I must put it to you, with all the force at my command, that it is the intention of the Constitution and the spirit of the law that must count . . . If the Rulers, or for that matter anyone else, are denied even a judicial hearing it will not redound to our national credit or to the prestige of the Government.

It was no use. The Government finally gave up negotiating and, on 18 May 1970, brought in a bill to abolish the princely order, its privileges and its privy purses. In what must have felt a fruitless task, Jai had, before this, spent a long time pressing the Home Minister to recognise Bhaiya's nephew as the next Maharaja of Cooch Behar. This agreed, Jai left for England on 7 May.

A few nights before he left Jaipur, according to Major Parbat Singh, he said to the Major's wife, 'You know, I won't be coming back.' Ayesha asked him what on earth he was talking about. Jai laughed and said, 'Oh, you can come and see me.' Ayesha says this story is pure fantasy.

Ayesha followed Jai to England in time for her birthday on 23 May. Their life once again became a welcome round of fun – parties, dances and, as always, polo. This year, Jai played rather less than usual. His handicap was now three and he was more inclined to umpire. He had a disagreeable fall at Windsor, but he recovered quickly and they gave the cocktail party at Kings Beeches, after the Queen's Cup, which they had given every year for five years and to which the Queen and Prince Philip always came.

Jai decided he would play on 24 June, when polo began at Cirencester. It was a poor sort of English day, grey and drizzling; and it was an everyday sort of game. Ayesha and Bubbles were both watching. Without warning, Jai fell from his pony. By the time he reached the hospital, he was dead.

His body was taken that night to Kings Beeches. On the next day, many of Jai's friends came to the house, where the body had been laid out in the drawing-room in a sandalwood coffin. Several of them, who had known Jai for years, were suddenly struck by how very Indian this solemn moment was.

230

The following day, Jai's body was flown to Jaipur in a chartered plane. The aeroplane arrived late in the afternoon; the twelve-mile road from the airport to the City Palace was lined with people. That night, his body, dressed in traditional Jaipur style and watched over by his four sons, lay in state in the Chandra Mahal. All through the night, the people of Jaipur filed past their dead Maharaja. Some fifty thousand people passed through the Palace and, when the time came for the coffin to be moved, the queue of people waiting was still half a mile long.

At nine in the morning, the funeral procession started on the traditional three-mile route from the Palace to the cremation ground of the Maharajas at Gaitor. First came three caparisoned elephants, the leading mahout carrying the gold rod given to the ruler of Amber by the Moghuls. The other mahouts scattered coins among the crowds. After the elephants came camels, then another row of elephants, followed by three ancient gun carriages, then horses, chariots, drummers, a police band – their instruments wrapped in black – and six hundred soldiers from various regiments. Next came the Palace officials, dressed in white, their swords in white sheaths, and after them some twenty royal priests with shaven heads and a huge truck filled with flowers and garlands and wreaths. At last came the Maharaja on a gun carriage, his head a little raised from the coffin so that all might see him. Jai's four sons, all in white, walked behind the gun carriage, followed by the nobles of Jaipur and the Ministers of State of Rajasthan. But this day had nothing really to do with Rajasthan.

The mile-long procession took two hours to reach Gaitor. All the day before and all through the night, people had poured into the city from every part of the old state of Jaipur – by bus, by bullock-cart or on foot. The whole route was jammed with people; every rooftop was crowded. At least half a million people watched the last procession of the man who had ceased to rule over them twenty-one years before. As the gun carriage went through the streets, they shouted 'Maharaja-ki-Jai' and 'Maharaja-amar Rahe', as they had done for nearly fifty years.

The whole hillside above the cremation ground was filled

231

with people looking down as the Maharaja's eldest son lit the funeral pyre and Jai's last nineteen-gun salute boomed from the fort at the top of the hill.

This amazing demonstration of affection was proof enough that nothing the Government had done had dented the real bond between Jai and his people. It was little wonder that the Chief Minister said with relief, 'the tiger has gone'. Had Jai come back from England and entered politics, he could have swept the Congress out of power in Rajasthan.

It was not only in Jaipur that he was remembered with affection. A month after his death, there was a memorial service to him in the Guards' Chapel in London. Lord Mountbatten had offered to give the address. He ended with the words that had echoed around Jaipur: 'Maharaja-ki-Jai'.

Lord Mountbatten had written to Ayesha two days after Jai's death. He explained that, at their regular cocktail party, Jai had said that he wanted to talk to him about the situation in India. Later that evening, after dinner with some friends, Mountbatten proposed that they 'retire into a corner and have our talk right away'.

> ... Then we talked about the present situation ... ending up with the appalling thing the Government is doing in trying to amend the Constitution to go back on their promise to the Princes about their privileges and their Privy Purses.
>
> I told him all the various steps I had taken in every possible direction to try and stop this and how deeply distressed I was at the disgraceful behaviour of the Government on this matter.
>
> Jai was extraordinarily understanding about the whole terrible situation. He remarked that it wasn't quite so bad for the heirs who had succeeded their fathers but for those who had been actual rulers on the Gaddi up to 1947 it really was an unacceptable insult and he doubted whether he would ever wish to live in humiliating circumstances in India.

Mountbatten had tried to persuade him that no one could humiliate him:

I was quite certain that there would never be any
humiliation for him anywhere in the world.

He appeared to be rather encouraged by my
conversation and I only hope so as I would like to feel
he died a happy man.

From this it would seem that it was unlikely that Jai had
intended to go back to fight in the next elections. It is true
that he was only fifty-nine at the time of his death, but he
had for some time been feeling tired. The gradual erosion of
his power had exhausted him. It is doubtful that so amiable
a man would have had sufficient pugnacity left to take on
the forces ranged against him, especially those fortified by
gratuitous malice or envy.

The question was now immaterial, but the Congress was not
finished yet with the Princes and least of all with the Jaipur
family.

Three months after Jai died, the bill to abolish the privy
purses was passed, with the necessary two-thirds majority,
by the Lok Sabha, the lower house. It was, however, defeated
in the Rajya Sabha.

In the original accession provisions, Mountbatten had
included a clause which allowed the President to derecognise
a Prince who grossly misbehaved or committed a serious
crime. Mrs Gandhi, in her pique, decided to use this clause
in a manner which had never been imagined, let alone
intended. She made the President write to the Princes de-
recognising each and every one of them.

The Princes appealed to the Supreme Court. Ignoring the
question of whether the President could, as it were, whim-
sically derecognise the Princes, the Supreme Court went to
the heart of the matter.

What is of the utmost importance for the future of our
democracy is whether the executive in this country can
flout the mandates of the Constitution and set at
naught legislative enactments at its discretion. If it is
held that it can then our hitherto assumption that in

233

this country we are ruled by laws and not by men and women must be given up as erroneous.

It was a lesson that Mrs Gandhi had to learn more than once. The Princes were restored. It was a brief remission. Mrs Gandhi called the elections a year early, in February 1971.

Ayesha, bereft and lonely, did not feel like standing, but was persuaded that she must. Once again, having done almost no electioneering, she was returned to Parliament with a majority of more than 50,000. By the end of that year Mrs Gandhi had her Twenty-Sixth Amendment to the Constitution passed by both houses of parliament. On 28 December, the President gave his assent to the bill. The Princes of India were no more.

Everything was not yet over. Throughout the history of Jaipur, there has always been a legend of a fabulous treasure. The story is one to appeal to anyone of a romantic nature and, like all legends, has many versions. In its simplest form, the story is that, during their service with the Moghuls, the Rajas and Maharajas of Amber amassed a vast amount of loot on their campaigns. This they stored in a large fort above their Palace at Amber, called Jaigarh Fort.

This fort was guarded by special guards belonging to the Mina tribe, the people from whom the Kachhawas originally won the land round Amber. They, and they alone, knew exactly where in the large fort the treasure was kept. Not even the Maharaja knew its precise location. Once in his lifetime, when he was judged to be of suitable age, he would be taken to the treasure store. The Mina guards would blindfold him and lead him through tortuous passages, with much clanking of keys and creaking of ancient hinges. At last, they would remove the blindfold and the Maharaja would find himself standing in an Aladdin's cave, filled with chests of gold coins, gold statues, jewelled swords, boxes of precious stones, goblets of silver and all the riches of legend.

The rule was that he might take out one object that took his fancy. According to some versions, he was also obliged to put some new treasure there in its place. That done, he would be blindfolded again and led out by the guards.

234

Early in 1975, the Income Tax Department acquired from some discontented person a document purporting to be 250 years old. It was a cryptic key to the secret hiding-place of the treasure in Jaigarh Fort. The authorities decided to use the possibility that the family was still hiding the treasure somewhere as an excuse to harrass them.

Ayesha was then living in Moti Doongri, the little fort on a hill not far from the Rambagh where, long before, one of Madho Singh's sons had been imprisoned for murdering his catamite. Jai had done the fort up and given it to Ayesha. It is an enchanting house with beautiful views over the city, although it is plagued by mosquitoes at night and monkeys by day.

On 11 February, a number of men appeared. At first they pretended to be tourists; then they demanded to inspect the place. Ayesha was at her prayers and sent a message for them to wait. When she came, they told her they were from the Income Tax Department and had a search warrant. The warrant authorised four officers. Ayesha counted twelve and sent eight of them away.

They would not allow her to telephone her accountant or her lawyer. Ayesha felt quite calm, as she thought the search would reveal nothing. The raiders asked her to sign a paper agreeing to the search. She said she would not sign until she had had legal advice. They insisted, but a witness was needed. Her staff were not admissible as witnesses. Ayesha had a passing boy brought in from the road. 'He will be my witness,' she announced, 'a person from Jaipur.'

The comedy went on through the morning. They searched through her papers and diaries. Finding among her correspondence some letters from a cricketer about fund-raising, they suggested that this must be a source of income. 'What nonsense,' said Ayesha and tore up the letters. The raiders wailed. She told them to keep the bits.

In her bedroom, a woman inspector was searching. Ayesha says: 'This lady had apparently never seen clothes or cosmetics before, she spent ages examining every sari and opening every bottle, powder box and lipstick.' The woman did, however, find nineteen pounds in English money in the dressing table and various oddments of foreign coins.

Later in the morning, Pat came. He told Ayesha that the
Income Tax Department had simultaneously raided the City
Palace, the Rambagh Hotel, Rajmahal, Joey's house, Pat's
farm and even the new house Ayesha was preparing for
herself in Jaipur. In Delhi, too, they had raided Ayesha's
house and two places belonging to Bubbles. The inspectors
asked if they might picnic on the lawn. Ayesha refused.

The search went on for two or three days. On the second
day, they came to Ayesha and said, 'We have found gold.'

'Of course,' she said. 'Why not? But mind you count it
properly.' There were two strong rooms at Moti Doongri –
one by the portico, the other in one of the towers. In the first,
there was a great deal of gold, worth between three and four
million pounds. The other contained jewellery and
ornaments.

The discovery caused great excitement. Here was the great
treasure of Jaipur, illegally hoarded and hidden. The villainy
of the Princes was gloriously revealed. Alas for Mrs Gandhi,
the truth was rather different. The gold had nothing whatever
to do with the legendary treasure. It was gold from Jai's
personal treasury. It used to be kept in quite another fort
called Nahargarh. In Amer Singh's diary, there is a reference
to a big upheaval in July 1942, when a lot of treasure was
moved from Nahargarh to Jaigarh, as part of a complete
reorganisation of both the public and private treasuries.
Something had evidently gone wrong at Jaigarh, which was
the main Treasury of Jaipur. All the men there had been
dismissed. The Mina guards had been arrested. The seal of
one part of the treasury at Jaigarh had been broken. Amer
Singh wrote: 'My brother told me that . . . the Maharaja
Sahib had told off Hari Singh very badly. He used such
awful language that Raja Gyan Nath . . . moved out of the
room.'

Three weeks later, he recorded that Jai and Ayesha had
spent about four hours in the chief treasury room looking at
ornaments. The room had been broken into and there were
lumps of earth dug out of the floor and uncut stones lying
about.

Eventually, Jai had his personal treasure brought to the
City Palace and stored half of it in the Kapadwara. The other

half of the gold, Jai sent to Bombay to sell so as to buy some shares. On this occasion, he sent the gold in the care of his Finance Minister, Raja Atal. Every time the train started up again after stopping at a station, the apprehensive Raja would draw his sword and poke under the seats in case some thief had managed to creep into the compartment unobserved. The roof of the Kapadwara was in poor condition, so that, in 1947, Jai moved his own gold and jewellery to the two strong rooms in Moti Doongri. Whenever Jai was away from Jaipur, Second Her Highness would move into the fort so that she could keep an eye on the strong rooms.

Jai had declared this gold at the time of the merger and every piece of it was recorded in the documents of the Covenant. What the tax raiders found corresponded exactly, to the very ounce, with the Covenant list. The only complaint that the inspectors could reasonably have was that wealth tax had not been paid on the gold. The responsibility for this lay not with Ayesha, but with the head of the family, who was now Jai's eldest son, Bubbles.

In any case, the Tax Department began to demand more and more papers and records. They returned for more searches, asking where anything and everything came from. The Foreign Exchange Directorate then joined in the harrassment, demanding details of all the trusts which Jai had set up abroad, although these had already been fully explained and declared.

Meanwhile, they started on a real treasure hunt. In May, the Income Tax Department, together with the National Geophysical Research Institute of Hyderabad and the Army Corps of Engineers from Jodhpur, began to dig and probe around Jaigarh Fort. They searched for a month or so. They found nothing.

Affairs then took a vicious turn. On 30 July 1975, Ayesha was in her house in Aurengzeb Road, Delhi. The police came with a warrant for her arrest. They told her that it was to do with contraventions of the foreign exchange regulations. She was not allowed to ring her lawyer. She went to pack. Bubbles was staying with her and she told him what was happening. He thought she was joking and went to find out who was there. The police arrested him too.

They were both taken to Tihar Jail. This is really a prison for men, but it is also used for women awaiting trial for fairly unimportant offences such as prostitution. Bubbles was given fairly reasonable quarters, with somewhere to wash and even a verandah. There was nowhere of that kind in the women's section. They gave Ayesha a little room which the doctor used to examine the female prisoners who fell ill. There were no washing facilities. They opened the so-called bathroom of the condemned cell for her to use. It had no running water.

Ayesha was never charged with anything. Her only offence under the Contravention of Foreign Exchange and Prevention of Smuggling Activities Act was not to have converted her nineteen pounds and ten Swiss Francs and some odd coins into rupees on returning to India.

Mrs Gandhi had, at this time, declared a State of Emergency, a situation which enabled her to ignore all the laws which might have protected Ayesha and Bubbles from this ignominious treatment. Mrs Gandhi imprisoned any powerful members of the opposition. She fostered informers and rewarded those who denounced others. It is reasonable to assume that she had, for a while, taken leave of her senses.

No appeals to her made any difference. Ayesha stayed in jail. A fellow MP, the Rajmata of Gwalior, who had been under house arrest in the north, was brought to Delhi. The authorities planned to cram her as well as Ayesha into the doctor's small examining room. On the grounds that their prayers and puja would conflict, the Rajmata of Gwalior being of a very orthodox and rigid Hindu persuasion, Ayesha managed to convince the authorities that they must have separate rooms. They gave the Rajmata the condemned cell.

Ayesha was allowed to exercise in the yard, walking and talking with the prostitutes. She was allowed two visits a week. Pat and Joey used to come, but most people were too afraid. It was not a time of courage in India and, indeed, courage had few rewards.

Bubbles was released after two and a half months, but no reason was given, any more than there had been any explanation as to why he had been arrested in the first place. Ayesha fell ill. She had pains in her chest. In September, she was found to have a lump in the region of her breast, but she was still kept in jail.

In November, Ayesha's lawyers filed a petition in the Delhi High Court. The petition contended that her detention had nothing to do with foreign exchange but that it was political. Secondly, the Customs Department had served notices on her about the gold, knowing that she could not answer when in prison. Thirdly, the petition pointed out that she was ill.

The counter-affidavit filed by the Government was a masterpiece of dishonesty. 'Smt. Gayatri Devi', as the document called her, was detained on the basis of 'extensive, recurring and continuing violation' of the regulations. Disclosure of these facts and materials was considered to be prejudicial to the public interest, so the information about her violations 'could not be disclosed to the detenue'. Further, 'the magnitude of the continued violations posed a serious threat to the economy and the security'. Again, it was against the public interest for anyone, and particularly the person who had committed them, to be told what these violations were. An opportunity for the guilty person to make any representation about the matter was obviously unthinkably perilous to the nation. Ayesha's detention was necessary 'for effectively dealing with the emergency, in view of the serious impact of violations by the detenue on the economy of the country'.

World opinion and protests from Lord Mountbatten may have brought about a change of heart, coupled with the fear of what might happen if Ayesha's illness became even more serious. After five and a half months, she was allowed to go to hospital. After some weeks of medical care, she was released on parole. She was allowed to return to Jaipur, provided she did not go by public transport. They feared a demonstration.

She was obliged to tell the police about all her movements and to apply every two months for her parole to be renewed. These conditions continued, still without any charge ever being brought, until Mrs Gandhi called an election in 1977. She lost. The new Government annulled all orders against Ayesha.

The difference between the two women's characters was

pointed up when Mrs Gandhi's son Sanjay died in an air crash. Ayesha telephoned to offer her condolences. Mrs Gandhi refused to take the call.

Some strange streak of vengeance drove Mrs Gandhi on to hound the Jaipurs. Perhaps she had felt neglected by them when, as a girl, she used to visit her aunt in Jaipur. Perhaps she thought Jai should have supported her father, Nehru. Whatever her motive, she did not give up about the treasure even after she had released Ayesha on parole.

At the end of February 1976, the Government served a notice claiming Jaigarh Fort under the Ancient Monuments and Archaeological Sites Act. No matter, of course, that it had been specifically listed in the Covenant as Jai's property. And they started to dig once more.

Three hundred men dug for six long months, making a great mess. The whole affair took on the quality of a farce. The officials in charge, inspired by the scientists who had tested the secret paper, decided that the treasure must be there. They exaggerated and fantasised to the press. The press, finding that their circulation rose as they reported the goings on published wilder and wilder tales. To justify what the authorities came to believe from what they read in the press, the diggers inflated their claims still further. It reached the point where the searchers were following a man who rode up to Jaigarh every day to exercise his horse. Horse-droppings are well known to be auspicious material for treasure seekers.

In December, when they had spent some £75,000, they gave up.

The question remains: was there or was there not any treasure? The family are contradictory on the point. Pat, who had most to do with the search, watching in case they did find something, believes that the paper probably was genuine. The treasure was Man Singh I's. It was discovered at the time of Jai Singh, the builder of Jaipur. Before his time, the state was poor. The likelihood was that he used the treasure to build the city.

There is another story, parallel with this, which is that the legend was deliberately spread abroad and that the map was a decoy. Invaders, being allowed to capture the paper, would rush to Jaigarh to get the treasure, giving the Jaipurians time to marshal their defences. This theory has a certain logic to it, as the only possible place to which the clues in the old document can lead the searcher is a chamber at the bottom of a water tank thirty-eight feet deep. There are three water tanks side by side at Jaigarh. Only one of these has extra space. It does not increase the water capacity much. It would only have been possible to reach the space by letting all the water out, so finding it would have delayed the invaders for a long time.

Against these theories, which conveniently melt away the treasure, there are other pieces of evidence. Jai used to tell his English friends the legend. Many of them today repeat the story, each with its own little twist. Similarly, in Jaipur three quite serious people told the author that they knew, but could not reveal, the truth about the treasure and what became of it.

Ayesha speaks of it. She says that Jai used to say that the treasure was a kind of banking system; something to be used only if Jaipur ever fell on hard times. She also says that the ancient rules stipulated that the ruler must leave 'a most secret note for the guidance of his successor'. This Jai had done.

And on the mantelpiece at Rambagh, says Ayesha, there used to stand a solid gold bird with ruby eyes and a huge emerald in its beak. This was the object which Madho Singh had chosen from the legendary treasure chamber.

'One day the emerald fell out of the beak and we put the bird away. I haven't seen it for a long time. I wonder what became of it?'

APPENDIX I

RULERS OF JAIPUR

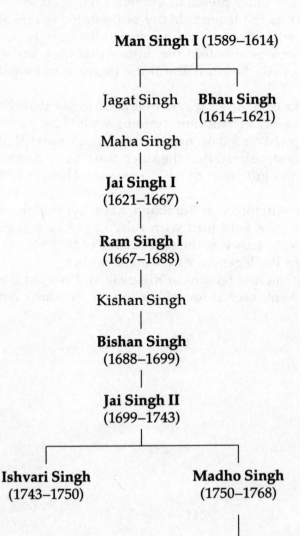

Man Singh I (1589–1614)

Jagat Singh

Bhau Singh (1614–1621)

Maha Singh

Jai Singh I (1621–1667)

Ram Singh I (1667–1688)

Kishan Singh

Bishan Singh (1688–1699)

Jai Singh II (1699–1743)

Ishvari Singh (1743–1750)

Madho Singh (1750–1768)

```
                    ┌─────┴─────┐
            Prithvi Singh    Pratap Singh
             (1768–1778)      (1778–1803)
                                  │
                             Jagat Singh
                             (1803–1819)
                                  │
                            Jai Singh III
                             (1820–1835)
                             (posthumous
                                child)
                                  │
                             Ram Singh II
                             (1835–1880)
                                  │
                            Madho Singh II
                             (1880–1922)
                                  │
                             Man Singh II
                             (1922–1949)
```

APPENDIX II

Jai's Family

Man Singh II (b. 1911, d. 1970)
|

(His Highness Saramad-I-Rajaha-I-Hindustan Raj Rajendra
Maharaja Dhiraj, Lieutenant-General Sir Sawai Man Singhji
Bahadur the Second, G.C.S.I., G.C.I.E., Maharaja of Jaipur)

married

(1924) Marudhar Kanwar
           (b. 1929) Princess Prem Kumari
           (b. 1931) Bhawani Singh (Bubbles)

(1932) Kishore Kanwar
           (b. 1933) Jai Singh (Joey)
           (b. 1935) Prithviraj Singh (Pat)

(1940) Gayatri Devi (Ayesha)
           (b. 1949) Jagat Singh

APPENDIX III

GLOSSARY

achar	pickle
achkan	high-buttoned, long tunic
ADC	the Maharaja had personal ADCs, who looked after the running of his household, the welfare of his guests, and also acted as secretaries
Agent to the Governor-General	British official responsible for a state or specified area of India
atar	essence of a flower, often rose or jasmine
bakaya	tax arrears owed by Jagirdars
begum	wife of a Nawab
bhati	loving devotion to God leading to Nirvana
chakri	cenotaph
crore	10,000,000
darbar/durbur	the court, sometimes the ruler himself, and often an assembly of the nobles and courtiers
deodhi	entrance or porchway leading to the zenana
dewan	prime minister
dhobi	man or woman responsible for washing clothes
gaddi	throne
hartal	strike
haveli	large room or hall used for entertaining
hawaldar	sergeant
howdah	a litter carried on the back of an elephant

245

jagir	a grant of land
Jagirdar	holder of a jagir
Jat	caste consisting mainly of agricultural peasants
Jharshahi	dialect spoken in Jaipur
Kachhawa	clan name of the Rajputs of Jaipur
kamdar	land agent
kapadwara	Maharaja's private treasury
khalsa	Crown lands
Kshatriya	military or warrior caste, the second of the four major Hindu castes
lakh	100,000
lallji	morganatic son of a Maharaja
Lok Sabha	lower house (House of Commons)
machan	raised platform used in hunting
mahal	palace
Maharaj Kumar	son of a Maharaja
Maharana	variation of Maharaja
Maharani	wife of a Maharaja
mahout	elephant handler/keeper
maji	senior lady of the zenana, or mother
maund	denomination of weight current in India, varying greatly in value locally
mohur	seventeenth-century gold coin worth fifteen rupees
Muklawa	The moment when a newly-wedded bride joins her husband. Immediately after the wedding, she will have returned with her parents.
naik	corporal
Nawab	Muslim ruler of a princely state
nazar	coin presented to a Maharaja on ceremonial occasions as a token of loyalty
niwas	garden
paan	bitter betel leaf chewed for its narcotic and cleansing effect
Pandit	Brahman learned in the Hindu religion
pojan	prayer, religious ceremony
Political Secretary	adviser to the Governor-General on the politics of the princely states

puja	prayer
punka	fan made of a palm leaf or leaves
purdah	the practice of keeping women in seclusion
puri	deep-fried, wholewheat, puffed bread
Qaimkhani	Muslim of military family
Raja	a ruler or landlord
Rajmata	Queen Mother
Rajpramukh	governor of a former princely state between Independence and 1956, when they were abolished
Rajput	branch of the Kshatriya caste, who gave their name to the area of India formerly known as Rajputana, now called Rajasthan
Rajput Sabha	council of Rajputs
Rajya Sabha	upper house (House of Lords)
Rana	variation of Raja
Resident	officer appointed by the British to each state
rupee	unit of Indian currency (during the Maharaja's lifetime, its average value was thirteen to the pound)
safa	flowing turban
sambha	deer with three-tined antlers
Sardar	senior noble
sati	the wife or concubine who climbs on the funeral pyre of her husband, hence also the practice of doing so
sepoy	private soldier
shikar	hunting and shooting
Shikar Khana	department responsible for hunting
sowar	trooper
syce	groom
Tazimi Sardar	most senior noble
Thakur	a noble
thal	small, individual dish, often silver
thikana	larger land grant, usually hereditary
tonga	bicycle rickshaw
vakil	secretary/agent
Zamindar	landholder
zenana	the women's quarters, where they lived in purdah

APPENDIX IV

BIBLIOGRAPHY

Collins, Larry &
Lapierre, Dominic
Freedom at Midnight (Collins, London, 1975)

Copland, Ian
The British Raj and the Indian Princes: Paramountcy in Western India, 1857–1930 (Sangam, London, 1982)

Gayatri Devi of Jaipur
& Rama Ran, Santha
A Princess Remembers – The Memoirs of the Maharani of Jaipur (Weidenfeld & Nicolson, London, 1976)

Gascoigne, Bamber
The Great Moghuls (Jonathan Cape, London, 1971)

Golish, Vitold de
Splendeur et Crépuscule des Maharajas (Hachette, Paris, 1963)

Griffiths, Sir Percival
The British Impact on India (Macdonald, London, 1952)

Ismail, Sir Mirza
My Public Life (George Allen & Unwin, London, 1954)

Kamal, K.L. &
Stern, Robert W.
Jaipur's Freedom Struggle and the Bourgeois Revolution (Journal of Commonwealth Political Studies, vol. II, no. 3, London, 1973)

Lothian, Sir Arthur
Kingdoms of Yesteryear (John Murray, London, 1951)

Menon, V.P.
The Story of the Integration of the Indian States (Orient Longman, Hyderabad, 1956)

Roy, Ashim Kumar
History of the Jaipur City (Manohar Publications, New Delhi, 1978)

Rubin, Barnett R.	*Feudal Revolt and State-Building – The 1938 Sikar Agitation in Jaipur* (South Asian Publishers, New Delhi, 1983)
Rudolph, Lloyd I. & Suzanne Hoeber	*The Political Modernization of an Indian Feudal Order; An Analysis of Rajput Adaptation in Rajasthan* (Journal of Social Issues, vol. XXIV, no. 4, Chicago, 1968)
Sarkar, Judanath (revised and edited by Raghubir Singh)	*A History of Jaipur – c. 1503–1938* (Orient Longman, Hyderabad, 1984)
Singh, Karni, Ph.D., M.P.	*The Relations of the House of Bikaner with the Central Powers, 1465–1949* (Manohar Publications, New Delhi, 1974)
Tod, J.	*Annals and Antiquities of Rajasthan, or the Central and Western States of India* (Routledge & Kegan Paul, London, 1950)
Various authors	*A Jaipur Album* (Jaipur, 1935)
Trevelyan, Sir Humphrey	*Public and Private* (Hamish Hamilton, London, 1980)

INDEX

251

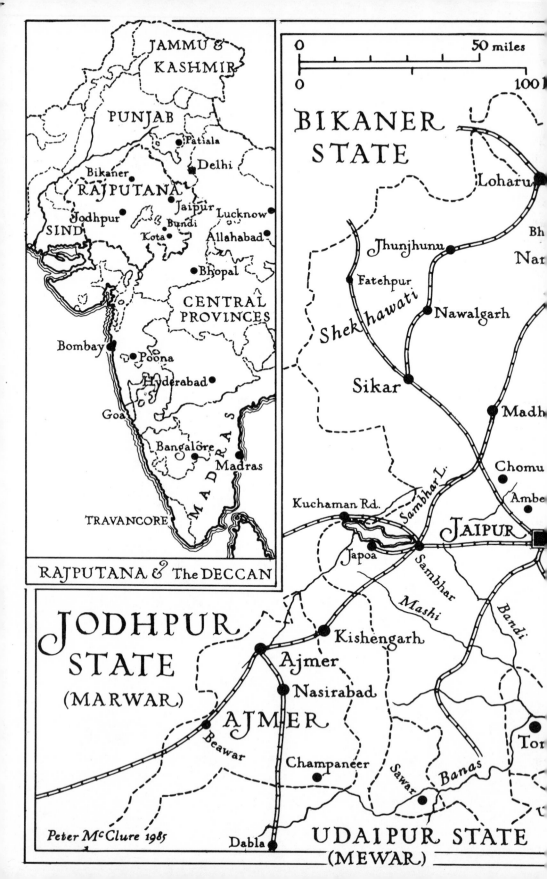

Inset map: RAJPUTANA & The DECCAN

JAMMU & KASHMIR

PUNJAB

- Patiala
- Delhi

Bikaner

RAJPUTANA

- Jaipur

Jodhpur
Bundi
Lucknow

SIND

Kota
Allahabad

Bhopal

CENTRAL PROVINCES

Bombay
Poona
Hyderabad

Goa

MADRAS

Bangalore
Madras

TRAVANCORE

RAJPUTANA & The DECCAN

Main map

0 ———— 50 miles

0 ———— 100

BIKANER STATE

Loharu

Jhunjhunu

Bh

Nar

Fatehpur

Shekhawati

Nawalgarh

Sikar

Madh

Kuchaman Rd.

Sambhar L.

Chomu

Ambe

JAIPUR

Japoa

Sambhar

Mashi

Bandi

JODHPUR STATE (MARWAR)

Kishengarh

Ajmer

Nasirabad

AJMER

Beawar

Champaneer

Sawar

Banas

Tor

Peter McClure 1985

Dabla

UDAIPUR STATE (MEWAR)